THE TURNED GODS SERIES | BOOK 1

ORIGINAL GRACE

JOYCE SERRANO

CHAPTER ONE

"You're not talking me out of this, Lukkas!" Grace shouted in exasperation after having made her intentions clear for the tenth time.

"Why do you have to do this now, and why do you think you have to do it alone? I don't want you out there on your own. It's too dangerous," Lukkas snapped back.

"Seriously? Too dangerous for me? Are you afraid if I find them, I won't come back?"

"Do you really think I don't want you to figure out who's looking for you? I am the only one who has helped you! Maybe when you finally know what happened, we can have a normal life!"

"Normal? How could you ever consider our life normal?" Grace sighed and walked across the large bright bedroom to Lukkas, placing her hand on his arm. The patio doors behind her were open, letting the breeze lift the sheer white curtains, creating an illusion of wings. She reached out her other hand to stroke his cheek with the back of her fingers and spoke softly.

"I know you're afraid and I'm scared too, but I have to do this, and you know I have to do it alone," she said. Her forehead wrinkled with worry.

Lukkas sighed, and Grace lowered her hand to pat his chest. "We'll talk more after I get cleaned up." She looked up at him before turning away. "The west field was tough today. I forgot how much work it is to prepare the vines for winter."

She grabbed a clean towel and headed for the shower. Stopping in the doorway, Grace turned back to Lukkas with an encouraging smile. "Can you have Mrs. B. send up dinner tonight? I'd like to set up on the patio and finish this conversation in private. No need to involve the family until we agree on how I'm going to handle this." Ever the peacemaker, it wasn't in her character to leave a conversation on poor terms. In her experience, fate didn't always allow one to make up for harsh words.

Lukkas raised his hands in a gesture of surrender and backed out of the room. "I doubt we'll agree on anything, but at least we can enjoy one last meal before you disappear again." Disappointment permeated his voice as he shook his head at her.

He continued his retreat, closing the massive wooden doors to Grace's room behind him. Lowering his head in defeat, he proceeded down the hallway toward the open balcony on the second floor. On the way, he passed another set of double doors to his own room on the left. There was something different about today that made the hallway feel longer than usual.

When he reached the last door of the wing containing his office, tension built in his neck. Lukkas let out another deep sigh before reaching the grand staircase on his right. The breathtaking view from the foyer balcony greeted him with the soothing warmth he needed. The entrance hall jutted out from the south side of the building in a semicircle, with windows covering the entire top of the curve. Lukkas could feel the sun on the right side of his face as he looked out over the fields to the south and west. A view like that made it impossible to be tense. His body sagged against the railing while he unwound his feelings.

The early autumn view of the land his brother persuaded him to purchase calmed him. This was becoming one of the best vineyards around the city of Kelowna. Rows of vines becoming dormant stretched over rolling hills to the mountain bases in the distance. The vineyard sat on the edge of the Okanagan Valley, with mountain views on every horizon. Lukkas would never have considered a vineyard in Canada. Italy or California would have been his preference, but this was better than either. More land, fewer people; it was ideal for their small clan.

He lost track of how long he had been standing there when his peaceful sunset was interrupted by his youngest niece, Asta, and her Uncle Vito—her mother's brother, not his. Vito was a great guy and all, fiercely loyal to his family, but too loud and conspicuous for Lukkas's taste. Vito was the guy you noticed in a room while Lukkas was the guy who hung in the back, observing everything.

The pair blew into the main hall, just under the staircase, engaging in an extremely lively debate, not noticing Lukkas on the upper balcony. They were both loud and animated speakers. The image of Vito, with his thick Italian accent, waving his hands with every word and Asta making surgically precise gestures to Vito's exaggerated ones was a comic experience. Vito was a towering man, standing tall and thick as a tree, with darkly tanned skin and coal-black hair. Asta was barely a slip, slender and gangly with bleached blonde hair and the bright blue eyes of youth, coming in at less than half her debate partner's weight. It was apparent they had just returned from thinning the west fields. Both still wore dusty shoes, and one of Asta's hands clutched an oversized sun hat and gloves. With her other hand, she was attempting to unravel a thick tangled tie from her unruly hair. They were both laughing and jabbering back and forth in a maddening mix of Italian and English, far too quickly for Lukkas to keep up.

"What the hell are you two arguing about?" Lukkas shouted at them.

"Hey, Uncle Luke. We're discussing medieval folklore and the differences with the way vampires, werewolves, and other creatures are depicted in movies and TV. It's outrageous that people think a cross or holy water will do anything to a vampire, isn't it? Does no one ever consider that they are anything other than Christian? Do they think there aren't any Buddhist or Hindu or even pagan vampires? Vito thinks that most of this stuff was made up because the religious leaders of the time were trying to instill fear, making people think they would be safer if they were Christians. They wanted people to believe that they were the only religion that could defeat what they said were monsters to be afraid of. What do you believe in?" Asta put her hand on her hip after finally taking a breath.

"I believe you finished your sentence with a preposition."

Vito chuckled at Lukkas's remark.

"I don't find that particularly funny. If you didn't want to give me your opinion, you could have just said so." Asta pouted childishly, cutting her eyes at him.

"Asta, stop listening to campfire stories and grossly misrepresented mythology. No one's skewed opinion should matter more than the facts, and you shouldn't rely on the romantic imaginings of unrealistic human beings who fantasize about being immortal. I will not let you draw me into this debate. Good luck to both of you, especially when Mrs. B. sees what you've done to her clean floor." Lukkas descended the stairs, chuckling to himself, turning right past the two verbal combatants and down the back hall to the kitchen. As he moved further away, he could hear Asta throwing a few Italian curses at his back along with some other non-lethal words mixed in that he couldn't quite make out. He smiled at the thought of working her up into a fervor that would surely last for several days. She was not the type to let things go once she dug into them. He was glad to be having dinner with Grace upstairs tonight rather than continue this never-ending conversation. He also didn't want anyone to see how worried he was.

As he made his way down the hall, he could hear soft rock music playing below the clatter of metal utensils. The commercial-grade kitchen took up most of the first floor in the north wing. It was the only room on the estate that was modern, and they had remodeled it to perfection. At least that's what Grace kept telling him. Personally, the sleekness of modern styles made him a little uncomfortable. The one thing he did appreciate in this design was that they kept the gas appliances. Cooking without an open flame wasn't really cooking at all, as far as he was concerned.

He carefully made his way between the huge gas cooktop in the center island, which held a six-burner grill and rotisserie, and the two large ovens on the wall perpendicular to the door.

The sun was slowly dipping below the horizon, casting a warm golden glow across the oversized marble island. The open folding wall allowed a cool breeze to waft into the room, carrying the green scent of freshly cut vines, mingling with the deep notes of roast pork Mrs. B. was braising on the rotisserie while swaying to the music.

Lukkas slid out the last barstool at the end of the counter, closest to the open wall, and reached for a large stemmed glass hanging in the rack above his head.

"Evening, Mrs. B. Beautiful sunset out there, isn't it?" Lukkas glanced back over his shoulder at the opening behind him.

"It certainly is, Lukkas. White or red?" she asked, pointing at his glass.

"Dealer's choice, my lady. What are you having?" Lukkas answered, giving an overly animated bow to the woman before he sat.

"I'm having last year's Pinot Grigio brought up from the cellars this morning. It's a little more citrus than I normally enjoy, so you should appreciate it."

"Sounds perfect." Lukkas accepted her recommendation.

Mrs. B. was an incredible find in a place like this. She had worked in local vineyards all her life, and she also ran a tight ship with the house staff. It had been more than a decade since she retired from the fields, but she knew her grapes and loved being able to stay around the vines. There was no one they could have trusted more to run the household for the family, and she was worth her weight in gold.

"Would you mind having one of the staff set up dinner for me and Grace on her terrace tonight? She's leaving on another trip tomorrow, and we need to discuss some things without the rest of the family around."

"That woman has given me most of these gray hairs," she said, pointing to the top of her head.

Lukkas could clearly see thin streaks of silvery gray intertwined with her natural deep red.

"What's the mission this time?" she asked, grimacing with a mixture of annoyance and concern.

"Something I don't like one bit," he replied with a dire glance.

"I'll be glad when she stops looking."

"I'm sure you'll be dead long before that."

"I'm sure you're right." Mrs. B. gave a hearty snort and turned back to the stove. "I'll send up a bottle of the Pinot with dinner. Maybe you can get her to say yes, this time."

"I've asked her a thousand times, and she's never said yes."

"Well, she's never left you, either. At least you know she's not in it for the money."

Lukkas chuckled, "You'd better send up two bottles then. It's going to be a long night."

He topped off his glass and headed for his room to shower before dinner. As he passed his office, he stopped for a moment to grab a folder from his desk. The atmosphere of the office was rich and dark, with a heavily carved wooden desk at the back of the room near thickly draped windows. It smelled of aged mahogany with a hint of lemon oil. Usually, the soothing, cave-like feel of the dim space comforted him. Tonight, with the file in his hand, the room was stifling. He needed to review the information before showing it to Grace. He had to make sure that everything was as it seemed. Glancing through the file satisfied him that nothing had changed since the last dozen times he had looked at it. With a decisive nod, he snapped the folder shut and headed down the hall.

His bedroom was just the way he left it. Housekeepers were a wonderful luxury, but he never felt right allowing someone else to clean up after him. He didn't work the land like the rest of the family and often felt he didn't contribute as much. Managing the money was where his expertise lay. He sold the wines, arranged the tours and tastings for prominent clients, and made sure the portfolio was always in the black.

By leveraging the family's extensive wealth, he was able to establish connections with individuals of questionable character, ultimately obtaining the information that would completely upend their lives. Looking back, he wished he had never told her what he had found, but it was too late for that.

He took a big gulp of wine and climbed into the shower, hoping to wash away an ominous feeling that had enveloped him.

~~~~

The evening was crisp and cool enough for a thick sweater. Grace enjoyed eating on the terrace under the stars. It was peaceful and could be romantic, although she didn't think this particular evening would end in romance. Lukkas hadn't arrived yet. The man was late for everything. Sometimes she thought he enjoyed making everyone wait for him. While she sat contemplating the possibility of life in a far-off universe, Grace poured herself a glass of wine. There was a knock at the door, jolting her out of her head. Before she could answer, Lukkas burst through with a huge smile on his face. He was physically attractive, but it was his confidence that made him irresistible. It permeated the room when he entered. His ash-blond hair was still damp, with strands clinging to the sides of his neck. He wore a thin deep-blue sweater that matched his eyes, and pulled slightly taut over his chest and arms. Maybe this night could have some romance after all, she thought. She couldn't resist matching his smile with her own.

Lukkas walked across the room, dropping a folder on her desk without breaking stride, continued onto the terrace, and ended with his arm around her
~~~~

waist. He took the glass from her hand and sipped it before giving her a playful kiss on the lips, letting her take in the inviting scent of his sandalwood soap. She snatched the glass back and gave him a quick kiss on the cheek before spinning out of his grasp with an impish smile grazing her lips. She set her glass down on the table and poured Lukkas one of his own. "Glad you could make it."

"Have I ever passed up a chance to spend time with you?" he asked as he grasped her hand and kissed the back of it. "You know there is only one thing I would ever want to change about us, but you keep telling me no."

"I already adopted your surname."

"That was convenience. You didn't have one."

Grace's entire demeanor collapsed. "I don't need a ceremony or any of that sentimental, archaic stuff. It's not my intention to change who we are. Your family accepts me without ceremony, and it's not like we don't already sleep together. If you move into my room, we will never have to be apart."

"You mean except for the times when you go on your missions?" Lukkas sounded playful, but Grace detected resentment.

"Or the times you go on your business trips?" Grace bit back, matching his tone. "I don't want to change you, so why do you feel the need to change me? No matter how long we're apart, we inevitably end up together."

"I guess I'm a traditionalist. I just want us to be happy."

"We are happy," she sighed and smiled.

He wrapped his arm around her shoulder, kissing the top of her head. "You're right, we are happy. When you get back, if you still want me to move in here, I'll think about it."

It seemed to be all the commitment she was going to get from him.

"Well, that only took seven hundred years of convincing," she said in a sarcastic tone.

"That doesn't say much for your powers of persuasion." He laughed and ducked from the napkin she threw at his head.

Dinner had finally arrived, and she was starving. The aroma rising from the plate was tantalizing. Lukkas turned to the young man who had brought up the food. "Thank your mother for us and tell her not to wait for the dishes; we'll make sure they get to the kitchen before breakfast. Have a good night."

"Yes, sir, Mr. Luke. You have a good night too. Is there anything else you need before we go down to the house?"

"No thanks, Billy," Grace added. "Make sure you take the blue golf cart tonight. The battery on the yellow one died earlier, and I don't think it will have charged yet."

"Yes, ma'am," Billy said, pulling the doors behind him as he spoke.

"Okay, Gracie, explain to me again why you feel compelled to find these people who dumped you in the middle of nowhere with no memory."

"Don't call me Gracie. You know I hate it," she growled at him as she sat back, taking a sip of her wine. "You know, it's a lot more complicated than that. They're looking for me, and we don't know if they're the same ones who dumped me or not. What we do know is that if they are looking for me, they know something about me. I have to go to them to keep you all out of it. I don't want them to track me here. I won't risk losing everything we've worked for or endanger the family."

"Won't you at least consider letting me come with you?"

"Absolutely not. You are recognizable, which means you are traceable. If they see you, they'll make their way back here, which is exactly what I want to prevent. They are looking for me for a reason; I don't think they want to hurt me. I think they need something from me."

"How can you know that? I should tie you up and lock you away in a safe place."

"As appealing as that sounds, you realize that I'm the one with the knife in my hand."

"You couldn't hurt me," he said, feigning injury.

"Couldn't and wouldn't are two different things," she scoffed, waving the knife in his direction with an evil little half smile.

"I surrender. Since you're so set on it, let's figure out how to get you in and out in the safest possible manner. Finish up; I have some things to show you."

Once they finished eating, they topped up their wine glasses and went to the desk inside the terrace doors. Lukkas opened the folder he had left earlier.

"Let's look at some of the major players first. This guy is in charge, Ben Olsen." Lukkas took the first photo from a stack and laid it on the desk in front of Grace. "We don't have much information on him. Until last year, he didn't appear to have existed. He's definitely military trained."

Grace looked at his picture. Ben was muscular and tall, though not as tall as Vito, with medium-length, wavy dark hair that touched his shoulders. There were several visible tattoos, but from the quality of the photo, it was not clear what they were. She couldn't see much of his face, but somehow, he looked familiar. He resembled a guy from one of those Viking/barbarian TV shows. How does someone like that not show up on anyone's radar before now?

Lukkas continued, "He speaks several languages and hasn't shown any violent tendencies. At least none that we've received reports of. The next three guys are former military, all with elite forces from different European countries. One of them always travels with Ben, but all three usually do. They are all the same age, born on the same day to different families in different countries, but they look identical, possibly altered by plastic surgery. Their names are Alex Johnson, Erik Johnson, and Michael Johnson."

Grace slowly collected the picture. She could discern differences between them, but she didn't want to give Lukkas any indication that they looked familiar. Her eyes fixated on the photo giving her a sense of déjà vu. She remained silent, unwilling to alarm him into shutting the whole thing down. Some indistinct feeling was telling her that these men were her sons. Names flashed in her mind as her stomach sank—Aleksander, Erik, and Mikkel. Her head was spinning as their names swirled around in the distance like a tornado that hadn't reached the ground. Dizziness clouded her thoughts, and she felt like she was going to pass out. Her stomach clenched tight. She had no idea how she knew they were her sons, but she felt it scratching somewhere deep in her memory, pushing to get out.

Even through the black and white of the photo, she knew in person they would have her distinct green eye color. The photo showed them to be in their twenties, although looks could be deceiving in her world. She turned her back on Lukkas and walked over to the chair on the other side of the desk, hoping to get there before her knees buckled. Grasping the photo, she traced her fingers over their faces and sat down as her legs gave way.

"Hmm, this is unusual," she managed to say in a manner that was surprisingly nonchalant. "Maybe they were adopted?" She phrased it as a question so that he would think she was looking for options to his plastic surgery theory. It took intense concentration to keep her breathing and heart rate under control. Fortunately, Lukkas was too preoccupied with his conspiracy theories to pay her any attention.

"Well, that would be a twist, placing them in different countries. Leading them to elite forces and managing to put them in the same task force/secret unit. Maybe they're clones. Could be more of them," Lukkas offered excitedly. Cloning had only recently become plausible, but since he was heavily invested in science fiction, in his mind, it was a practical answer.

"Or …" She looked up at him, raising an eyebrow. "They have fake papers?"

"Well, yeah … or that." Lukkas's words dripped with disappointment.

"Who's next?" Grace asked, placing the photo on the table, increasing the distance between it and the gnawing in her mind. She had to get away from the subject of the three young men, or Lukkas would start asking her questions she couldn't and didn't want to answer.

The two of them went through photos of people Lukkas's sources called sentinels. There were various people of all ages and backgrounds who observed without interfering. They were simple intelligence gatherers of little importance to her. Grace had seen a few of them over the years, but she didn't know if they were watching her specifically, or if they were monitoring some events she was involved with. Either way, she was sure their reporting was how she had gotten on Ben Olsen's radar.

Lukkas handed Grace the last piece of paper in the folder. "There's no picture of the last person on the list. They call her the Keeper. She is also known by the name Seshet and seems to be the organizer of the group. We don't know if she is the only Keeper, if there are others, or if her name is what they call all Keepers. We have found Seshet in texts dating back to ancient Egypt, so our informant tends to think it is more of a title than a name. As far as we know, she has never been seen or photographed."

"So, how do I contact them?"

"We don't know where their specific location is, only a general geographical area. What we do know is that most of them have been seen, often in small groups, at a coffee shop in Helena, Montana. They appear to be communicating with one particular barista." He fished out a picture from the stack they had already discarded.

"Maybe they just really like coffee. Doesn't mean he knows who they are or how to contact them. It's not unusual that if you want to order a coffee, you talk to the person behind the counter. All you can conclude is that it is an occasional gathering point, and he works a lot. Whenever I go to Tokyo, I visit the Skytree. Would you assume I live in Tokyo?"

Lukkas bristled at the dismissal of his theory. "Throughout the day he makes calls from a pay phone in the mall even though he has a cell phone."

"Sounds like he could have a gambling problem," Grace retorted.

Lukkas continued, undeterred. "What you need to do is order a coffee and tell him you're there to see Ben. If he doesn't know anything, you'll get a long trip and a cup of mediocre coffee. If he does know something, you'll find out pretty quickly."

"Sounds like a plan. Do you have open surveillance?" she asked. Not that she was endorsing his theory; she had simply become tired of challenging it. A lot of effort had gone into gathering this information and the least she could do was follow the lead until it went dry.

"Yes, we're tapped into local street cams, mall security, and the security cameras in the coffee shop itself. We'll be able to monitor you from anywhere."

"Whatever happens, promise me you won't interfere. If I have to, I can get out on my own," she said, not waiting for him to answer. "How do I get in and where is the exit?"

"I've set you up as a crew member on a plane to Helena, shipping in aircraft parts. You'll meet your contact at a restaurant in that mall on the other side of town," he said, pointing to an area on the city map. "Change clothes, exchange credentials, then she'll come back here, and you'll go to your destination."

"Who's my contact?"

"Violet."

"So, I'll wear platform boots and she'll stuff her bra."

"Yeah, sounds right," he chuckled. "She's happy to be home for a few days and she isn't due back at the Napa office for another week, so they won't even miss her."

"What time is the flight?" Grace asked. It was already after eleven. The drive would be about four hours and crew check-in was an hour earlier, so she didn't think she'd be sleeping tonight.

"Departure time is six in the morning, so you have two hours before we leave."

Grace grinned at Lukkas. "I've already packed a bag. What else can we do for the next two hours?"

CHAPTER TWO

At a quarter to five, the cargo terminal appeared over the hood of the Range Rover in the distance.

"You better drop me off here, so the security cameras don't pick up your car."

"Josh is meeting us at the gas station outside the terminal to drive you in. He's also bringing Violet back to me when they return."

"No cameras?"

"The station is clean. There's Josh," Lukkas said, pointing to an older-looking man with a well-groomed gray beard sitting in an even older pickup truck behind a gas pump.

Slick Josh, as he was called, had seen Grace off on many an adventure. The man was a junkyard dog. There was nothing he couldn't get his hands on; he was mean as a snake and she loved the old codger. Grace had helped him a lot when his wife developed dementia. There were some days she had been the only person Molly recognized. Grace had made Molly's last days happy, and Josh felt he could never repay her.

"Are you ready for this, Gracie girl?" He swept her up in a bear hug, pulling her feet off the ground. He was still a bear of a man, even if the years had made him a little paunchy. It made her feel like a ten-year-old, the way he could throw her around like a rag doll.

"Ready when you are, Pops."

"Oh, so he gets to call you Gracie?" Lukkas asked, sounding a little jealous.

"He can call me whatever the hell he wants." Grace gave Josh a big squeeze before he set her back on solid ground. She wrapped an arm around Lukkas's neck, kissed him on the mouth, and hopped into the passenger seat of the truck. "See you on the other side!"

Lukkas walked around to the driver's side of the truck and tucked a couple of hundred-dollar bills into Josh's shirt pocket. "Take care of my girl, Josh. Call me if you need anything."

"Absolutely. Meet you back here tomorrow, with Violet." Josh had known Lukkas long enough to see that he was worried. Of course, he would never embarrass him by saying anything like that out loud.

Lukkas waved and sat on the hood of his Rover until Josh's truck disappeared in the distance. He thought about following them and pulling her out, but she would never forgive him for that. Slowly, he slid off the hood, climbed into the driver's seat, and began the four-hour drive home. There wasn't time to explain what was going on before they left. Nor was he looking forward to explaining where she was going when he got back home either.

It didn't take long for Grace and Josh to get through airport security and onto the tarmac. The credentials Josh gave her worked flawlessly. Grace stared at the massive aircraft growing larger as they got closer. Flying on these big cargo liners wasn't her favorite way to travel; however, she got a kick out of flying with Josh, who was hands down one of the best pilots she'd ever seen. The manifest had her listed as his daughter, so it was sort of like what she thought a normal family would be. The crew, consisting of Josh's four sons, liked it when Grace flew with them. It always meant Josh was in a good mood.

The warehouse had packed the plane out heavy today, which meant Josh's boys needed an extra hand from a man Grace had never met and tried to stay away from. She didn't want him to ask questions when he saw Violet on the way back, so she stayed in the cockpit jump seat while Josh's oldest son, Jack, ran interference for her. The boys knew the guy, but he wasn't their regular spare. Better to be safe and stay low-profile than to cause Violet trouble later.

Josh had taught her how to take off and land in an emergency in a puddle jumper years ago. This one had a lot more complicated controls and Grace was unsure she would be any help in an urgent situation. Not that she was anticipating an issue, but she couldn't help but think of the worst scenarios. She took comfort knowing Jack was on this trip and could fly anything. Today was clear, but there was some wind shear that caused her apprehension. She wasn't looking forward to takeoff—it was sure to be rough, even with Josh at the controls.

The takeoff ended up being smooth, although it should not have been. After a few uneventful hours in the air, they were ready to land. First stop was SeaTac and Customs. This was a routine weekly shipment, so the process was mostly automated and took less time than if they had trucked in the parts. Instead of taking days like it used to, it was usually over in a few hours. Officials checked the manifest and inventory, did a couple of spot checks, and opened a few boxes. As long as there wasn't anything fishy, it was off to the final destination by the middle of the day. While the cargo was being inspected, the crew was taken to a holding area. Grace took advantage of the opportunity to sleep for a few hours. She slunk into a recliner at the far corner of the room and pulled her cap down to cover most of her face. Who knew when she'd get another chance to close her eyes?

It felt like she had just fallen asleep when Jack shook her. "I thought you died on us. I couldn't see you breathing."

"I can be a heavy sleeper when I'm wiped. How long was I out?" Grace stretched and rubbed her eyes. She hadn't slept like that in a long time.

"About three hours. We're getting ready to board. Grab your crap."

"All right, let me splash some water on my face."

"You better make it quick, or I'll come in and drag your ass out of there."

"Oh Jackie, are you getting excited to see Violet?" Grace teased.

"Damn right I am. She owes me money." Jack winked and sat back in the recliner Grace had vacated. "Hurry up!"

Back on the plane, ready to take off, Grace felt herself getting anxious. After a few more hours, she may have the answers to her questions. She hoped it would pan out. Lukkas had put in a lot of work to make sure they didn't know she was coming. If she knew what they wanted with her, she would have driven over the border like any other day tourist. The problem was, she didn't. It made her wonder how her sons were involved and how they were even her sons. So much of it made no sense at all.

Touchdown at Helena airport jolted her out of her thoughts. Time to get this show on the road. She walked through the security gates and into the terminal. All she had to do now was hail a cab and catch up with Violet. It was still an hour before they were supposed to meet. She had time to spare for some shopping and a drink.

Grace checked her reflection in the glass storefronts once she finished making a few purchases to ensure she wasn't being followed. Satisfied there were no suspicious lurkers, she headed to her destination. The restaurant was dark for this time of day. It looked like there was a possibility of rain. She found a table where she could see the entry door from the mall and the window outside. Violet was late as usual, and Grace took the opportunity to place their order while she waited. The server brought two loaded salads topped with medium-rare steak and two glasses of Malbec as Violet strolled through the door. She was a few inches taller than Grace, with dark auburn hair. Except for the hair color, she looked like a younger version of her mother. There was no resemblance between her and her sister, Asta.

Violet spotted Grace right away. "Hey, Aunt Grace."

Grace wasn't married to the girl's Uncle Lukkas, but he was the only one who cared about that. Grace had been around before Violet was born and remembered being the first victim of her biting stage.

"Hey, Violet. Food's here."

"Great, I'm starving. I probably won't eat again until I get home tomorrow." Violet picked up her glass and did her swirl and sniff routine. "Really, Grace? A Malbec, with salad?"

"Look around, Violet. We're in a mall in Montana. Trust me. It was the best option on the list."

"At least you didn't order a vinaigrette dressing. That would have been a real disaster," Violet chided.

"Drama much?" Grace teased back.

"If I wasn't starving, this conversation wouldn't be over," Violet said and shoved a forkful of salad into her mouth.

Grace sucked her teeth, making a *tsk* sound, and shook her head. "Well, it's three now. The plane doesn't leave until six, so you've got some time. You'll be in Seattle overnight, and Jack's on the crew. He says you owe him money."

Violet picked up her glass with a snicker. "It's not money I owe him."

"Naughty girl." Grace brought her hand to her chest, feigning shock, and they both laughed. "It's good to see you. I wish it wasn't only in passing. Thanks for doing this for me, by the way." Grace lifted her glass, and they clinked.

"No problem. Not sure why you couldn't have waited for the jet, though. I was heading back tomorrow anyway."

"Had to get in under the radar. Can't have anything traced back to the family on this one. Not sure what this group wants from me yet."

"Jesus, Grace, are these the same people that were watching you in Italy and Scotland?"

"And Russia too."

"Well, be careful."

"Mmm," Grace mumbled, swallowing her food and picking up a bag. "Give this to Lukkas for me, please." Grace handed her a boutique shopping bag with black and white stripes tied with a pink bow. "Here are your crew credentials for the flight. The flight suit is in the backpack under the table, and you have the wig, right? I don't think anyone will believe my hair was that color when I left."

"Did you really take the time to buy his face wash?" Violet asked, pushing the badges aside in the bag.

"I had time to kill."

"There's something wrong with you."

"Probably." Grace pulled three twenties out of her pocket and placed them on the table. "I gotta go, sweetie. See you in a few days."

"Is that all the cash you have? Here, take this." Violet shoved a wad of bills into her hand.

"Honey, they don't use euros here."

"Oh, wrong wallet." Violet snatched the euros out of Grace's hand and replaced them with a bundle of fifties.

"Thanks, Violet. Do you have enough left for the cab?" Grace didn't really need the money, but there was no point in trying to refuse it from her.

"Yes ma'am. See you in a few days."

Grace left the restaurant first, scanning the area as she headed toward the exit. It was coffee time.

There wasn't anything special about the strip mall café on the other side of town. The place was practically empty. It was nearly four in the afternoon. Too late for the lunch crowd and too early for the evening crowd. It was the perfect time for an appearance. Grace walked in and scoped out the place. Just two cameras inside, one on the door and one on the cash register. Standard alarm system. Oh, and the smoke detector was also a camera. Suppose they thought they were hiding it. Eight customers, three employees. The barista working at the register was the one she was looking for. A customer reading a paper was watching; pretty sure he was a sentinel. Everyone else was on a phone or laptop minding their own business.

"What can I get started for you today?"

"I'd like a large honey latte, extra shot, low foam, please. I'm here to see Ben."

"Yes ma'am. Will that be all?" Barista Boy looked nervous. He didn't ask who Ben was. Good sign.

"Yes, thank you."

"That'll be $5.98. Please have a seat over there and we'll bring it to you."

She paid cash and sat down at the table he indicated, right in the camera's line. She expected him to go to the pay phone afterward. Instead, he took a cup of black coffee to the man reading the paper. He had his back to her and talked to the man for longer than the usual time it took to deliver a coffee. She had to give Lukkas credit. This was definitely the right place. Barista Boy went back behind the counter. The second barista took the order slip from him but didn't start right away. Sentinel Man was texting now. She figured she had fifteen minutes, tops. Barista Boy finally brought her coffee out in a house cup.

"Thank you. Can I get this in a to-go cup, please?" That made him squirm a little.

"I thought you were here for a meeting. Sorry, I thought you were staying."

"I don't think this will take long," Grace replied, watching him plaster on a customer service smile and take the cup back to get her a to-go cup, slowly of course. A few minutes later, he brought the drink back to her.

"Thank you. Do you have a restroom?" Oh, was that relief she saw on his face?

"To the left of the bar and down the hall," he said.

She picked up her coffee and walked to the restroom. Taking her time, she freshened up, washed her hands, and did a quick check to ensure she had nothing on her that could identify her or where she came from. A little less than ten minutes had passed since she entered the restroom. That should have given them plenty of time to respond. She walked out the door, past the counter, and straight out of the store, making direct eye contact with the camera. To let Lukkas know she was okay, she gave a nod and a quick smile. The newspaper rustled behind her, followed by footsteps. She turned right and walked to the side of the building.

"Here we go," she whispered to herself. She stepped into the alley and took a few steps. The sentinel was so close behind her she could feel the heat of his body on her back. She looked up and saw the older of the four men from the photo lineup step out at the end of the alley at the same time the man grabbed her arm.

"Ma'am, would you mind coming with us?"

All she could focus on was the man ahead of her. His face was stunning, if that word could be used to describe a man. Of course, he was handsome, but that was far from it. His eyes shone bright blue and clear, drawing her focus to them. He was, for lack of any other thought in her brain ... godlike. All she could imagine was that he had the summoning face of an angel. She melted out of the sentinel's grasp, drawn to the man at the end of the alley. In the blink of an eye, she was standing inches away from Ben Olsen, knocking him off balance. Reaching out to steady him, she touched his shoulder, her eyes locked with his.

"I know you. How do I know you?" Had she said that out loud or to herself?

"We would like you to come with us, please." The sound of Ben's voice jolted Grace out of the trance she had found herself in. It was unexpectedly deep, raspy, authoritative. She wasn't sure what adjective she should use here. Whatever it was, it pulled her out of her haze and into the present moment.

"That's why I'm here. At your invitation, I assume, since you've been following me for months. Or at least trying to." An attempt to be clever ended as a complete failure. The words that came out of her mouth sounded more condescending than anything else. Oh well, gotta go with it, she thought.

"We've been looking for you for a long time. I'm ..."

"Ben Olsen," she cut him off. He turned his head, cutting his eyes at her, and reached back, opening the side door of a van behind him. There were no windows and there was a wall between the cargo area and the cab, which obliterated any visibility from the back. There was comfortable seating, a small table, and a snack bar. Strange choices for a van, until she assumed they spent a lot of time in it. It looked more like a mobile meeting room than a kidnap van. Safe enough, she thought as she stepped inside.

"And you are?" he asked.

"You don't know who I am? Surprising," she said in an amused tone.

"We know a great deal about you. We don't know what you prefer to be called these days."

She was willing to play along with his little game, for now.

"You can call me Grace."

"Well, what do you think you know about us, Grace?"

Was he fishing or trying to distract her during the ride? Probably both. It didn't matter to her; it was just a curious thought.

"You at least appear to be a global, paramilitary operation interested in the more interesting inhabitants of this world. You capture and/or recruit those with special skills and abilities outside the normal range. It's almost like you're fighting a war that the average person can't or won't see. Am I supposed to be your next acquisition?"

"I would say that is a fairly accurate assessment. How did you figure all that out?" Ben said, ignoring her question. He hadn't expected an answer.

"A girl has to have a few secrets, doesn't she?"

"I didn't think you'd give up your sources. I would like to know how you knew who I was, though."

"Well, you're sloppy. When I accept a mission—"

"Mission?" he asked.

"It's rude to interrupt. When I am asked to help someone, I do a little before and after watching." That was a stretch. She had CCTV and people to do the watching for her. "You have shown up quite a few times in the last year. Plus, your sentinels are totally obvious. Give them a tablet or a laptop or *something*. Nobody reads hard copy anymore. None of them run away or assist when things happen; they only watch. They don't even live stream like the popular kids do. They don't fit in nearly as well as they should."

"I'll make a note of that." His tone was deliberately mocking. "Have you ever considered we wanted you to see them? That we might have been trying to get your attention?"

"Sure. I also considered you created some situations I might be interested in. But the facts remain: you see me, you follow me, and then I lose you. I do what I do and then I go home, and you don't know how or where I disappear to. You also don't mind having someone else do the hard work for you. You don't mind getting the occasional package tied up with a bow. The fact is, you're looking for me, and if I hadn't come to you, you never would have found me."

"You are aggressively honest."

"Both words are matters of perception. Now, what is it you think you know about me?"

"We don't know anything about your life now, your name, where you live, your attachments, or all of your abilities. The one thing we do know is every detail of who you were before you lost your memory." The arrogance that poured from his mouth shattered the attractive illusion he had been projecting.

The look on his face told her he thought he had the upper hand. He did not have any idea what she was capable of. When she got her answers, she would be the one to decide it was over. He could be as smug as he wanted. When she was done, she was done, and he wouldn't be able to do anything about it.

After thirty minutes, the ride was over. She heard electronic doors, not like a roll-up garage door, more like a solid sliding door. The van stopped. Someone pulled the slider open to leave her facing a single set of industrial-sized elevator doors. The magnitude of the garage area was indeterminable in the darkness. It sounded cavernous. She could hear distant sounds, and every click of her boot heels on the polished stone floor echoed. The elevator opened in a flood of bright light, giving her an amusing thought about the seven levels of hell making her snicker lightly. As they entered the elevator, she caught an image in the reflective steel wall of Ben's smile as well. She thought the hell reference must be a common thought among people entering this place.

CHAPTER THREE

The room was brightly lit, containing a conversation area with two oversized stuffed chairs, one end table, an ottoman, and a sofa off to the side. There was no coffee table between the furniture. It was a deliberate decision to remove any visible barrier that would create separation. The only other furniture was a small bar-height conference table with four upholstered swivel chairs around it. Not your typical interrogation room, although that's exactly what it was. Grace sat in the chair farthest from the door. Ben sat across from her.

"How did you do what you did in the alley? When did you know you were capable of such a thing?" he asked, cocking his head slightly to one side.

She had considered not telling him. Then she decided it was better to give him something if she wanted him to reciprocate.

"At first, it only happened when I was afraid. It took me a long time to learn to control what I was doing. I can move through things, or let them pass through me, when I am calm. When I'm angry, I become hard as a stone. It's like my skin gets too tight over my insides."

"What do you mean by that?" Ben looked more curious than puzzled, but the tone in which he said it sounded like he was trying to goad her into an argument.

"Well, to be more specific, I've found I can control the vibration of particles without adding or removing heat. This means that I can control the density of myself or other objects by changing the vibration of the atoms within the object to move faster or slower." She stopped talking and looked at him with an expression of disbelief on his face and thought, *You are such an arrogant ass.*

Ben had looked down at the notes he was taking but abruptly looked up at her, appearing amused. "Well, that was kind of unproductive."

"What was?"

"You called me an arrogant ass."

Looking him dead in the eye, she thought, *I never said that out loud.*

He raised an eyebrow, so she knew he heard her, but showed no other movement.

She continued in her head, *What is our connection? I can passively share thoughts only with people I am connected to. Otherwise, I have to push the idea to them, much like texting. If I don't hit send, it's just typing. Since we just met, I shouldn't have this connection with you.*

"Yes, we have a connection. I can't tell you much more yet. I'm asking you to trust me a little." His tone was calm to the point of cajoling.

She wanted to trust him. This was the closest she had come to finding anyone who knew about her past, but she needed more from him as well. It was his attitude that was bothering her.

"Okay," she said hesitantly. "I'll trust you until you give me a reason not to. As long as you give me something in return."

Ben nodded, and Grace continued. "I don't need you. You were the one hunting me, and you would never have caught me if I hadn't come in. Now tell me how we first met. No lies or I walk."

"How do you think you're going to leave? You don't even know where you are." His amused expression provoked a flash of anger in her.

"I don't need to know where I am." In a split second, she was no longer in the room.

Ben panicked. He had just found her, or rather she had found him, and now she was gone. She was right. He had no idea how to find her. He had searched for almost a year and there was barely any trace. Every time he thought he had a lead, she was gone long before he got there. How could she have gotten out of this room? She couldn't have ported. There were blockers on this entire floor, and he wasn't sure she remembered she could open a port, but she shouldn't be able to do this either. The modulating energy in the walls should have kept her in. He jerked the door open and stumbled through her, landing on the floor in the hallway. She reached down to help him up. When he grabbed her wrist, it was as solid as his in her hand.

"How did you do that?" he asked.

"That's what I was telling you. I'm not sure of the physics, but I can control the density of myself and the objects I come into physical contact with. I walked through the door."

"But I didn't even see you. You were invisible," he said, unable to understand how she could perfect that skill in such a primitive place without knowing who she was.

"No, I wasn't invisible, just fast. When the atoms inside of me are moving rapidly they become loosely connected, and I can move faster than you can see. When I am at my densest, I move much slower, but I'm still faster than other people. It's not magic. I can't turn invisible, although I could probably come close." Grace walked back to the oversized chair in the middle of the room, sat down, and gestured for Ben to do the same.

"Or are you asking me how I got out of this room with an enchanted limestone floor, a daemon trap on the ceiling, an electronic seal on the door, and random energy disruptions through the walls?" she asked with a combination of condescension and mockery.

How could he answer such a question? For the first time in his long memory, he was speechless. The floor had a rug covering it, the ceiling had a drop panel, and the barrier was invisible. She couldn't have seen any of it. He had expected none of it to work on her, except the modulated energy in the walls, and there was no reason it should have, but how did she know it was there? Had she used their connection to read his thoughts?

She hadn't read his mind. That wasn't the kind of telepathy she had. Limestone was visible at the edges of the floor and Ben used an electronic panel to access the door when they entered. The modulating energy in the walls vibrated as she passed through, and the pentagram was a strategic guess.

"I'm not a daemon, and I'm not a witch. I don't really know what I am, but what I do know is that this thing humans like to call magic doesn't seem to work on me. Can you go through that door, or is that little conjurer's trap holding you in?"

"Those things weren't meant for you. We bring all kinds of beings into this room. A bio-coded lock allows me to go through that door, but only *after* I open it," he replied.

"Well, I guess that's fair. We both seem to have a lot to tell each other." Now it was her turn to stall. She wanted to see how much he was willing to share with her and how far he would go to get her information. She hadn't come all this way to leave empty-handed. "Got any decent coffee around here?"

"We do. How else do you think I survive living down here?" Ben seemed relieved that she was just proving the point that she could leave whenever she wanted, and she learned that they lived in this facility. He tapped a spot behind his ear and asked someone on the other end to bring in two honey lattes with an extra shot and light foam, without thinking of asking her what she wanted. Seems he was paying attention in the café. Either that or Sentinel Boy told him before he got there. "That's okay, isn't it?"

"Works for me," she said, although she thought it was presumptuous of him to order for her. "And now it's your turn. Where did we first meet?"

"I'll wait for the coffee, if you don't mind."

"I don't mind at all. I don't have anywhere else to be."

After about ten minutes of silence, the coffee was brought by a dark-haired, green-eyed young man from the pictures. He was wearing a black V-neck T-shirt, black tactical pants, and black boots. That seemed to be the uniform of this place because Ben wore the same. Comfortable but utilitarian, with no signs of rank, so it didn't seem to be a standard military facility, which confirmed her first assessment. The second he stepped into the room, a sense of connection shot through her. She stared at the young man. He looked up and locked eyes with her, giving her a quick smile before looking away. She was sure now. There was familiarity in his unusual green eyes. The thought that this was her Aleksander unnerved her. He left the room quietly. How was it possible? Was this a test to see how she would react? Of course it was a test. All of this was a test.

After he left, Grace forced herself to focus on the situation. She refused to let this man toy with her emotions. With a deliberate movement, she picked up the ceramic cappuccino cup. Ben flinched, giving her an internal sense of satisfaction after the stunt he pulled with Alex. She didn't feel any marking on the bottom, so there was no clue where it had come from. She thought they were still in Montana. The drive hadn't been long enough to have gotten them out of the state. She sat quietly for a moment, allowing something else to occupy her thoughts. Some people here might have the same abilities as she had. How had they been able to hide from her for so long if they didn't have advanced abilities? Could she really escape if she wanted to, or were they just making her think she could? Had they slipped something into her drink to allow them to track her? If she could get away from this place, it might be better to stay away from home for a while. She needed to make a plan for that scenario. Her thoughts were interrupted when Ben spoke.

"I understand you have no memory of the time before you woke up here. Where and when did that happen?" He hadn't forgotten the question; he was avoiding it.

"Nice try. How did we first meet? How long have we known each other?"

Ben knew he had to answer her question, or she was out. No bluffing this time. With a sigh, he sank back into his chair.

"We were young, the time between children and adults. My mother knew your father from early on. They ran into each other at a harvest festival, and we were there with them. They talked for hours, and we ended up exploring the festival's entertainment together." Ben tried to answer her without giving her too many details.

It was obvious what he was doing. She just wasn't sure if she wanted to call him out on it yet. "So, you're like me? The age thing, I mean?" She was tentative about her question. Frankly, she was afraid of the answer.

"You don't even understand half of it. We still have to find out a few things about you: what you remember, how long you've been here. There's a lot we can't piece together yet."

"You mean we have to start in the middle and work our way out." This was a statement, not a question. "I'll tell you, but I need to know one thing first."

"Okay."

"Are they really my sons?" Grace asked as she tried to feel his heart race or see his breathing grow rapid. Neither of these things happened. The question didn't surprise him.

"Yes. They are your sons." He watched her carefully as her bottom lip began to quiver.

Her eyes were welling up and she was shaking. Hearing those words released a surge of emotion. Ben leaned forward, reaching for her hand. She pulled away, closed her eyes, and took a deep breath, as if to brace herself. Almost at a panic pace, she could hear him thinking, *Don't run, please don't run.*

She exhaled quickly. "I'm not going to run. I thought it would be rude to throw up on you." She knew he hadn't said it, but that didn't mean she hadn't heard it.

"Wouldn't be the first time," he said out loud. She opened her eyes and laughed nervously, unsure if that was an actual answer or if it was an attempt at humor.

"Are you ready to continue?" Ben asked, taking a sip of his coffee and wrinkling his nose. It was far sweeter than he liked. How could she drink something so disgusting?

Grace sat up straight and cleared her throat. "Yes, what was your question?"

"What is your first memory of this place?"

She wanted to talk. Talking now would take her mind off the idea that she had abandoned her own children or been taken from them. It would also show Ben that she was open to an exchange of information.

"My first memory is of waking up in a temple somewhere in Scandinavia at the foot of a statue of a goddess. I was wearing a simple linen dress and this amulet." She pulled out the amulet around her neck.

"It's impossible for me to remove it. My past was a complete blank, and I had no memory of who I was. I had knowledge. I could speak, I could understand, I knew the names of things. It was as if only the pieces that made me who I was were missing," she recounted, knitting her brows together.

"The attendants charged with taking care of the temple found me. They thought I had been sent as some kind of gift. They said I had appeared out of nowhere. I stayed with them for several months, learning their ways and assisting devotees who came to worship. I also heard voices telling me to take away their pain. At first, I didn't understand what that meant. I thought I was crazy until one night, a little girl, spinning around like little girls do, fell into the fire. They doused her with water to extinguish the flames. But it was too late; the damage was done. This tiny little thing was screaming as her flesh was peeling away from her bones. I wrapped her in a blanket and carried her inside. On my knees before the goddess, I begged her for help with the child. That's when I began to feel the child's pain. Somehow, I drew her pain into me, and she stopped crying. I stared into her little eyes and felt my flesh searing and my bones burning with excruciating agony. She smiled at me peacefully before she died in my arms. Then my own pain slowly faded away. That's when I understood. That's when I knew what I was here for. At least I thought I did."

Grace was momentarily saddened by the memory. "After that, I understood how I could lay hands on the sick and injured, allowing me to absorb their pain. People from all over came to the temple to die in peace. I didn't know how to heal them, but I could at least offer them peace before they passed on. They called me the Bearer of Pain. I stayed there, performing my duties for twenty years before anyone, including myself, noticed that I didn't appear to be aging."

"How long ago was that? I mean, do you know what year it was?" Ben asked in an unsympathetic tone. He was digging for something.

"They didn't really keep track of the year the same way then. And the calendar was different too, so I figure I woke up around 336."

"You mean seventeen hundred years ago, 336?"

"Yes. You don't seem shocked."

"I'm a little confused because the time lines don't quite add up." Concentration narrowed his eyes for a moment. "Our people age differently. I think I owe you at least an explanation for that part."

Ben wanted to blurt everything out right away. He didn't like to keep things from her. He never had. Without her memories, he didn't know if she would be able to understand everything, and he couldn't risk trying to restore her memories just yet. He thought it would be too much for her to process all at once. "Do you need a break?"

"I want to know what you mean by 'age differently.' Are we not immortal?" she asked.

Ben rubbed the back of his neck. "Our bodies age at a nearly imperceptible pace. I'm not sure I can explain it any better than that right now," he said. "We should really take a break."

Grace didn't want to push him. It would be better to agree for the moment and keep the opportunity to get more information. "I need more coffee and maybe a washroom."

"Want to stretch your legs? I'm sure most everyone is off duty by now. Do you know how to use a cappuccino machine?" There was that charming smile again.

"I'm sure I can figure it out," she answered. She had no idea who this guy was or why he was wavering between smug and charismatic. He seemed familiar, but that didn't always mean he was her friend. Why would her boys be with him if he wasn't? He said they knew each other, but in what context?

Ben held the door open for her. "The dining room and kitchens are on the other side of this floor. This is the top level where we do assessments, have recreation areas, and visitor services."

"Visitor services? What is that, show and tell for the weird and secret?"

He chuckled at her question. "I never thought of it that way. Yes, I guess it is. I'm sure you've come across some things you can't explain. You probably already suspect that not every life form on this planet is from here."

"I have my suspicions about many things, including the idea that I am not from here."

"There's a lot to talk about when we get back to the room. The restrooms are located down this hall. We'll go to the kitchen after."

"Wait. How long have you been looking for me?" It hadn't occurred to her to ask that question before. Had they had to eliminate other planets before coming to this one?

"Honestly, we didn't even know you were alive until recently. I've only been here a little over a year."

"How is that possible? What about the boys?"

"We refer to them collectively as The Sons or The Three. They're a little old to be called boys. They've been here for about five years. I'm sorry, this is getting really complicated and off track. Can we start again after we get some more caffeine?"

"All right, give me a minute." Grace entered the restroom, while Ben waited in the hall. This was more of a swanky spa locker room than a regular bathroom. "Wow, this is pretty nice."

"Thank you, Grace. What do you need assistance with today?" Grace jumped at the calm mechanical voice surrounding her. It was a surprise that shouldn't have been. Of course, they're equipped with some kind of interactive services in a facility like this. What one would be doing in a restroom, she wasn't sure.

"I just wanted to use the toilet and wash my face."

"There are sanitized towels in the cabinet to your right." A door slid open, illuminating the cabinet and revealing several sizes of clean towels and other linens. Grace took a small towel and a washcloth.

"Personal hygiene items are in your assigned locker. Please follow the lighted path on the floor."

"I have an assigned locker," she said aloud to herself as she walked around a row of doors on the left, following the lights to the next row.

The mechanical voice took the statement as a question. "Yes, Grace. Please continue to follow the lighted path."

The path ended at a door illuminated by a ring of lights.

"How do I open it?" There was no lock, no handle; the entire front was smooth. When she leaned forward to examine it, the locker popped open on its own to reveal an array of toiletries and hygiene products.

"Thank you … um, what do I call you?"

"I am IDA, Interactive Digital Assistant. Please let me know if there is anything else you need."

"Thank you, Ida." Grace grabbed a toothbrush, toothpaste, soap, and a stick of deodorant to freshen up a bit. As she walked toward the line of sinks, the overhead lights brightened to higher levels, making her wonder if the lights were following her or leading her.

As she was walking back to the locker, she heard Ben's voice over the speaker. "Are you going to be much longer in there?"

"Almost finished," she answered in a slightly elevated voice. "Ida, please open my locker." The locker popped open, and Grace placed the items back inside. "Where do I put the dirty towels?"

"Please follow the lights on the floor." The lights led to an opening in the wall near where the clean linens were. "You may drop them into the opening. Enjoy your evening, Grace."

Ben was standing in the middle of the hallway, waiting for her.

"You could have warned me about Ida."

"I didn't really think about it. I guess I'm used to her," Ben said, scratching his head. He looked tired.

Grace wondered what time it was. As they walked toward the kitchen, the lights came up in front and dimmed behind them. She hadn't noticed before the locker room that Ida had been adjusting the lighting during their walk. They came to the dining area first. Several long tables with upholstered chairs took up the center of the room. Surrounding those were high-top tables that sat from two to six diners each. Overall, it was sleek, black and white, glass, and steel. It was modern and inviting at the same time. The kitchen itself was as she expected—industrial, restaurant style, and very well equipped. The cappuccino machine was an advanced piece of technology. Grace looked at Ben with a raised eyebrow.

"Maybe I spoke too soon about figuring this out."

Ben grabbed one of the oversized cups, placing it under the machine's nozzle. "Ida, please make me a black coffee, strong, no sweetener."

"That's cheating." Grace looked sideways at Ben.

When the first cup was full, Ben placed a fresh cup under the nozzle. As he started to order, Grace stopped him, "Ida, I would like a plain cinnamon cappuccino with an extra shot of espresso, please." She turned toward Ben. "I'm a big girl, Ben. I can order for myself."

"I'm sorry, I thought you liked honey lattes."

"Because I ordered one in the coffee shop where you picked me up? I do like them. I like lots of things."

"I'll remember that. You hungry?"

"Not meal hungry, but I could snack."

Ben pulled some cheese and fruit boxes out of the walk-in. "Will this work?"

"Perfect," Grace answered, walking out of the kitchen, sipping her coffee with Ben following behind her.

"Do you know where you're going?"

"Ida's lighting the way." She motioned to the ceiling, wondering if he had gotten so used to the interactive automation that he didn't notice it anymore.

"Well, I guess I have," he replied.

"I have to stop this. I forgot you can hear me."

"It's not my fault. You're the one who isn't filtering. Do you know how to block it?"

"I can, but I have to think about it when I'm tired."

They were back at the door of the interrogation room.

"Let's try it my way this time." Grace unexpectedly grabbed Ben's arm and pulled him through the closed door.

"HVAÐ Í FJANDANUM?! How…?" the words trailed off as Ben leaned against the wall, unintentionally flipping off the overhead lights and leaving only the wall sconces and a lamp near the chairs on.

"I told you, whatever I touch, I can control as an extension of myself." Grace bit her lip, wondering if she had gone too far. She wasn't sure why she was being so aggressive with this guy. She just felt the need to get back at him for something.

"Size doesn't matter?" He was flustered but recovered quickly.

"Size always matters. Just kidding, sort of. Larger things take more effort. The biggest thing I've ever tried to phase was another person and his horse. The first time was an accident."

"And how exactly would you accidentally phase a man and his horse?" Interest took the place of Ben's annoyance.

"It was during a raid in one of the old provinces of Norway or Sweden. I'm not sure which one it was in that century. Borders were more fluid back then. I was moving around from temple to temple, so I wasn't always sure where I was. Anyway, during the raid, we were riding away and got pinned against a boulder that blocked our way out. I squeezed my eyes shut, and when the horse backed up, it went through the rock. After that, I could do it whenever I wanted."

"You still could have killed me. What if it hadn't worked this time?" Ben challenged irritably.

"When I grabbed your arm, I could feel every cell in your body, the boxes, your cup, even the coffee. I wouldn't have done it if I had any doubts."

The grimace on Ben's face conveyed his doubt. Grace shrugged and went back to the sitting area. Each of them took the same seat as before. Grace kicked off her boots so she could curl her legs under her in the chair.

Ben propped his feet up on an ottoman he had pulled out in front of him. "Let me know when you've had enough. I have a place for you to sleep when you're ready."

"I think I can go on for a few more hours. What about you? You look kind of rough."

"I just got pulled through a solid object, so yeah, I'm sure I look pretty rough."

He had been up since 5:30, as usual. Plus, he was still trying to wrap his head around the door thing. Adrenaline and caffeine were all he had to keep him going, but he didn't want to miss the chance to find out as much as he could. There seemed to be some missing time between when she left and when she showed up here. She was right about the calendar, though. It could be a simple miscalculation of time equivalents here and on the other side of the universe. It could be other things. Time wasn't always linear.

"I'm good for now."

"You took that better than I thought you would. The guy on the horse freaked out a little more. Horse seemed to be fine with it though."

"So, you were trying to scare me?"

"Not really. I was looking for your threshold for the unusual. I didn't think you'd mind. How many people can say they passed through a solid object?" Now she was just goading him because she could.

"I'd appreciate a heads-up next time, if that's not too much to ask." Probably because he was tired, it still annoyed him she had done that without asking. He understood what she meant about feeling free. He felt like he could have dissolved into nothingness. The only thing restraining him was her.

"Ah, isn't that cute? You assume there's gonna be a next time."

"I'd like to give our researchers a demonstration. How else are we going to find out how you do what you do? Isn't that what you wanted?"

"True." That was part of what she wanted. "I didn't think you were going to ask me to risk a human life for a demonstration." She had a very serious look on her face.

"Since I'm not exactly human, that shouldn't be a problem," he replied. "It's late, let's get back to your story," he said in a more serious tone.

"Wait a second. Didn't I have these abilities before?" She never considered the possibility that she had never had these abilities before.

"You have always had telepathy and the phasing thing, just not at the level they are now. You can heal injuries, too. Not diseases. Just the injuries the body is capable of healing on its own. I didn't think you'd be able to do the other thing here. You had centuries of lessons before, and honestly, you were never great at it."

"Oh," she grimaced. "So, you were scared I was going to bond you to the door. Sorry," she apologized. Knowing that, she wasn't sure how well he would take the other thing she could do. "There's another thing, too."

"What's the other thing?"

"It's connected to the rest of the story in the temple. Let me finish that part, and then I want you to tell me the rest about the aging thing. Does that sound fair?"

"It does. Let's pick up where we left off." Ben leaned back in his chair with his coffee and fruit.

Grace pressed herself down into her plush chair as well, staring into the darkness of the room beyond the reach of the lamp. "I had been in one temple or another for about five hundred years. Many attendants had come and gone. Clan leaders and kings who had learned of me through their seers had summoned me. They had brought me to battles, to birthing chambers, to dying royalty. These were my missions. They always returned me, usually with a substantial donation to the temple. I saw myself as helping people; the attendants saw me as a way to keep the religion relevant. I didn't see any harm in it. The old gods were fading into myth. Christianity was spreading. I enjoyed having a purpose. I enjoyed being one of the few who remembered the old gods when their power was strong.

"It was strange for me because I saw the gods as friends, not gods at all. For me, they were the only ones who were constant because everyone around me was dying in such a short time. And they spoke to me almost as clearly as I can talk to you, at first. Mostly Frigg and Freya. At least I thought it was them who were talking to me. It could have been anyone. Or I could have been legitimately insane. They told me where I was needed. I stopped hearing Frigg a long time ago. I stopped hearing Freya more recently. Now I look for my own missions. It feels like I have been left behind again. I apologize for rambling." She looked at Ben, who appeared to be mesmerized by her voice.

"No apologies necessary. I understand what it's like to feel abandoned," he said, dropping his eyes to the floor. "Go on."

"Yes, the other thing," she sighed, shifting to make herself more comfortable. "The temple I was staying in came under attack, sometime in the ninth century. There was a Christian force of around a hundred men who attacked in the middle of the night. We were peaceful. The temple housed the old, the sick, and the infirmed. It was a slaughter. The only warriors we had were a few temple guards, maybe twenty. I was afraid, not for myself but for the helpless.

"When I heard the commotion, I went outside. A soldier swung his sword at me. I put my hands out, and he screamed, falling to the ground, writhing in pain. The pain poured out of me and into him. My hands tingled with energy, and I could see waves of it moving from my hands to him. I looked out over the entire compound, and I pushed that pain into all the soldiers. Every one of them fell to the ground, where our guards slayed them. They were completely immobile, except for contorted twitching. They died where I forced them down. I had taken all the pain I could generate and unleashed it on them. After that, we took everyone we could and ran. We left the temple in Denmark and went back to Norway, where we met a seer who said he was there to guide me." Grace locked eyes with Ben.

"Are you afraid of me yet?"

"No."

"You should be. I scare myself sometimes."

"How do you cause someone else pain?" he asked.

Grace bit the inside of her cheek, twisting her face as she attempted to summon the words it would take to convey an explanation. "Well, I control mass by controlling the energy of the particles within it." She paused. "I guess what I'm doing is exciting their nerve endings into stimulating pain. That's the best way I can explain it."

"Can you control the amount of pain you inflict?"

Grace winced. "Yes."

"Has it ever gotten away from you?"

"Not since that day. I can be extremely precise with it now."

"Show me." Ben surprised her by saying this.

"No, I don't want to hurt you." She shook her head and narrowed her eyes at him.

"Come on, I'm asking for it."

"In more ways than one, but I still don't want to hurt you." She used sarcasm as a defense. She really didn't want to hurt him.

"Make it small and precise. Make my hand feel pain."

"If you want it small and precise, I'll make your left little finger feel like I'm poking you with a thin needle."

"Okay, I'm ready."

She shifted her eyes to his hand. His finger felt like it was being pricked with a pin. He made a short inhalation sound.

"More. Make it feel like you're cutting the back of my hand with a knife." Now he pushed the breath out and felt exactly what he asked for.

"Is that enough?" She didn't want to keep doing this to him. It was a minor representation of what she could do.

"Give me a single second of everything you have." He wanted to know how much she could inflict.

"No, you'd stop breathing, your heart would stop beating. A single person isn't built to handle that, not even you." She was adamant.

"I was built to handle it. I can't be harmed."

"That's not true. Your skin is impervious, not all of you. I've felt every cell in your body. I know that I can kill you and I refuse to give you the level of pain you're demanding."

"Come on. Stop acting like my nursemaid. I know I can take it." He wouldn't back down from her, and he was so arrogant. He thought he was invulnerable, but she knew he wasn't invincible to her.

"No!"

"What? Are you afraid you'll lose control, or do you know you can't really hurt me?" he taunted, deliberately leaning toward her.

"Half. I'll give you half," she finally agreed, wincing and sliding back in the chair, mostly because she wanted him to stop. "But I know you'll regret it."

"I doubt it," Ben snorted.

Grace closed her eyes for a split second and his body involuntarily contorted just before he passed out.

Shit, she thought. At least he's still breathing. *Why did I let him push me like that?*

She was angrier with herself than with him. No one pushed her buttons like that. It had happened so fast, too. How could he know exactly what it would take to make her lose her temper so quickly?

Within a few minutes, he had started to come around. She had sprinted across the complex to the kitchen and back with an ice pack and a towel before he stirred. As she leaned against the side of his chair, she wrapped her arm under the back of his neck and lifted him up to wipe his face with the cool towel. The color returned to his cheeks, though his eyes were still unfocused.

"Ben, you're an idiot." The irritation was clear in her voice. "I could have seriously hurt you!"

"This isn't the first time you've told me that." He actually found it funny.

"That I could seriously hurt you or that you're an idiot?"

"Both." His fingers and legs twitched and tingled like they were coming out of a deep sleep. At least he wasn't feeling pain any longer. That was some serious power, and she hadn't even touched him.

She could hear him laughing in his own head.

"Stop laughing! It's not funny!"

"Admit it, it's a little funny." A breath caught in his throat as he tried to sit up. "I'm sorry. I won't ask you to do that again. Looks like it hurt you as much as it did me." Ben knew he had crossed a line with her. He didn't want to hurt her, and he knew she had never enjoyed inflicting pain, even on him. At least that hadn't changed.

"I'd like to get some sleep now. At least a few hours." The words had come slowly because the experience had drained her both emotionally and physically.

"I could use a few hours myself. We can finish this tomorrow."

"You mean today?"

"Yeah, today. Come on, let me show you to your room."

The two of them walked to the elevator, taking it down to the fourth level. When they entered the hallway, it looked like any other apartment building. At the end of the corridor, a door opened when Ben placed his hand over an electronic panel. It was a nice apartment—open floor plan, kitchen at the end. Not at all what she expected from an underground steel and cement facility. The entire back wall was an electronic display of windows, with a view of mountains and night sky.

"You're the door on the left. I'm on the right. See you in a few hours."

"Thank you." Grace nodded and walked through the door into a large bedroom with an attached bathroom. The bathroom was stocked, as was the closet. There were a few pairs of jeans, a few shirts, and a nightgown. The dresser had underwear and socks, all in her size. She took it at face value because she was too tired to do anything else. She pulled on the nightgown and climbed into bed. Before her head hit the pillow, she was out.

CHAPTER FOUR

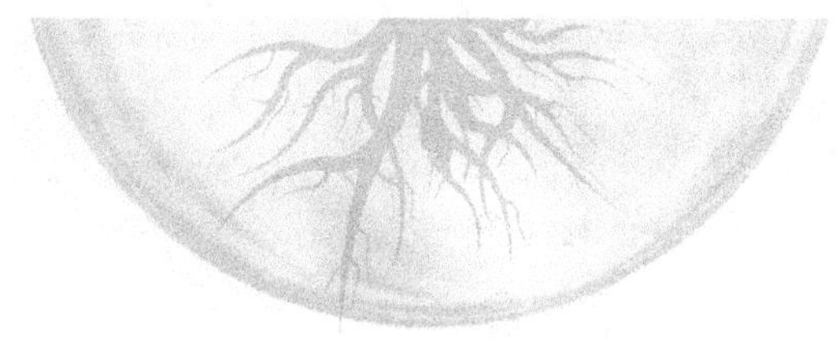

Who the hell was knocking on the damn door? Grace awoke in a haze, realizing she wasn't in her own bed.

"Ugh. I'm up!" She crawled out from under the warm covers and walked through the door blindly. "Crap!"

Ben was on the other side, and she had walked right through him.

"Sorry," she mumbled, grabbing the cup of coffee out of his hand and taking a big gulp before she noticed he wasn't alone. They were staring at her. She turned to apologize to them and reconsidered, taking a second gulp of coffee before heading to the kitchen for a refill.

Ben turned to the three men in the living room. "And … this is Grace. Grace, these are—"

"Seriously? You're going to introduce me to my own sons? Aleksander, Erik, and Mikkel. Guess what? I even know which one is which, do you?"

"Grace, they're our sons." Ben's statement came at her like a slap.

"They're … they're what? Did you say ours … as in yours and mine?" She pointed back and forth between herself and Ben. It was far too early for that level of thinking. She couldn't have heard him correctly. She rubbed her forehead, then sat down on the floor, took another gulp of extremely hot coffee, and looked at Ben.

"Explain this NOW!"

"Do you think you could get dressed first?"

"Hand!" She reached up as he reached down to pull her off the floor. "I just need five minutes by myself."

Grace escaped back into the bedroom in a state of panic. It made no sense. None of this made sense. She did not know what she was expecting to find in this place, but this certainly wasn't it. It took her a few minutes to calm down, to convince herself that she hadn't heard him right. Eventually, she emerged from the room, fully dressed. They were all sitting there, calmly staring at her. There was an empty chair with her cup of coffee on the table next to it. She crossed the room and sat down.

"What the hell is going on?"

Mikkel had a big grin on his face as he leaned against the back cushion of the sofa with his fingers interlocked behind his head. "Now this feels like home."

Grace and Ben snapped simultaneously, "Shut up, Mikkel!" Then they looked at each other with shocked expressions.

"Grace, this is important. Tell me how you recognize them as your sons."

"When you tell me how the hell they're *your* sons," she snapped back.

"When you're done, I'll tell you everything, but first I need to know how you know. Do you remember them?"

"How could she not know who we are? We're unforgettable!"

"Shut up, Mikkel!" Grace and Ben shouted again in unison.

Grace looked at The Three. "I have a feeling this is a theme."

"Yeah, Mikkel is the annoying one," Erik joked.

"Shut up, Erik," Grace and Ben said in unison for the third time.

Mikkel burst out laughing, leading Alex and Ben to follow suit. It was a surreal situation that ended with the men focusing on Grace.

"Why are you looking at me like that?" Grace asked.

"We're just waiting for your answer," Erik said calmly. "How do you know you're our mother?" He hadn't found anything about the situation funny.

Grace turned to the three of them. "Honestly, I don't know. I can't tell you anything about any of you. What I can tell you is that I feel you. I feel your consciousness, I dream about you, and I think I always have. It's something about your energy that I feel drawn to. It's like I can sense it vibrating between us. There is absolutely no doubt that you are a part of me. And I can't deny the eyes. I've never seen another person with the same green as mine, and now I see three sets sitting in front of me."

"All right." Ben rubbed his chin and considered her answer. "We need to hear the rest of your story. Tell me about your life after you got here."

"That wasn't the deal. You go first." Grace nodded to Ben, and when he glanced in her direction, her stomach growled loudly.

"Let's have this conversation on a full stomach. Erik, you're cooking," Ben instructed.

Erik got up and walked to the kitchen and the others followed, taking seats around the counter. Ben poured coffee for everyone, and Erik set the plates out. Grace's stomach was churning, but it wasn't because she was hungry. She wasn't even sure she could eat.

Ben knew he couldn't avoid this conversation if he wanted her to stay. "I have to start with how you got here."

"Go on." The coffee vibrated in Grace's trembling hand. One thing she needed to focus on was that no matter how plausible his story was, there was no way to know if it was true. The way he told the story was what she had to focus on, not the sentiments of it.

Ben began his tale. "The realms were on the brink of war. Every world chose sides. We thought our people were united, and we were, except for one, who tricked my brother into killing me to keep me out of the battle."

"Did you just say he killed you? Like you're dead? Now? You're dead now?" Grace sneered.

"Do you want to hear this or not?" Ben retorted and The Three snickered.

"Oh, do go on," Grace replied snidely.

"All of my brothers were noble warriors, so keeping me off the battlefield wasn't much of a loss in that regard. My gift was that I could unite people and bring them together in a way that the others couldn't. It was jealousy, however, that got me killed. Once I was out of the way, my essence was claimed and taken to the underworld to wait out the conflict. There was a deal made between Hel and my father for my return when it was over."

Grace interrupted. "This sounds familiar." She squinted her eyes and tilted her head with a perplexed expression.

"Are you remembering?" Ben asked hopefully, drawing the attention of The Three.

Grace looked over at Ben, shaking her head rapidly. "No, not like that. I remember hearing or reading something. Never mind. Go on."

Ben continued. "When I was gone, you took my place and rallied our people to fight, putting you squarely in the sights of our enemies. You were poisoned soon after, and it was made to appear that you had died of grief. They burned our bodies together on a single ship. Freya claimed your essence for Fólkvangr, as was her right of first choice with all warriors."

"I was a warrior? And I'm dead too?" Grace interrupted again.

"You could say that," Mikkel interjected.

Grace shot him a sideways glance. "What is that supposed to mean?"

"Ignore him," Ben said, annoyed. "You were definitely a warrior." He shot Mikkel a look. "Do you mind if I finish now?"

"Oh, don't let me stop you," Mikkel replied.

"As I was saying, my mother collaborated with Freya to send you here to protect your essence from destruction. With our kind, the destruction of the body isn't usually the end of the person. The essence is taken to one of the three holding places and can be restored if it hasn't been damaged."

"You're telling me that the mythology of the Norse gods is true, that your people are gods of some sort?" Grace was cynical. This was ridiculous in her mind. The association between his recounting and her being the person he was talking about wasn't connecting in her mind.

"No, we are not gods, more in the category of deities, which doesn't really mean the same thing here as it does out there. None of us are gods, not the Greeks, or Romans, or any of the other worshipped species. Many advanced civilizations spread throughout the universe have all visited this world at one time or another. We live immortal lives. That doesn't mean we can't die, just not of old age or common disease. It's considered inorganic immortality. Our essence survives our organic material, but some means can still destroy it."

"Then why do we look older than they do?" she asked, pointing to Erik and Mikkel.

"We age, just at a very slow rate. Our bodies are stronger, they heal faster, and many have various abilities. If we find that our physical form is no longer useful due to age or injury, our healers can move us to another. Our people have the technological ability to harness a person's essence or energy and place it into another vessel, which is optimally grown from a bit of their original genetic material. If there is no material left, a purely synthetic vessel can be created, though it may not have the same appearance. The stories or mythologies, like most, are loosely based in fact before being distorted and romanticized into fairy tales. Those aren't factual accounts of our lives."

Grace looked at The Three, who all appeared completely bored, as if that was their hundredth time listening to this information. It probably was.

"I'm struggling to understand the idea that your mother grew an adult version of me from my genetic material, restored my essence, bound my memories, and dropped me on a strange world to protect me. Is that kinda the gist of what you're saying happened? Why would she take my memories?"

Alex broke the silence. "You always had some unique abilities, not that you used them very often. But if you'd known who you were and what had happened, you would have found a way back. Even without being able to remember, you're still exactly who you were. You're unstoppable."

Grace smiled at Alex, not sure what to make of his intended compliment.

She turned back to Ben. "Why can't you just take this necklace off? Wouldn't it be easier if I could remember all this on my own? And what would have been so terrible about me finding my way back?"

All of it sounded ridiculous to her. Could she be from another civilization? What reason would they have to tell her a lie this unbelievable if it weren't true?

"Removing the amulet might not be as easy as you think. It may also scatter your energy throughout the universe for all we know. As for finding your way back, you were sidelined from the war, just as I was. The deal to get your essence back was you had to remain out of play, off the field. We had rules. You had to agree to the terms, or it wouldn't have happened. You were fully aware that you would remain here until the end of the Great War. Only my mother and Freya knew of your whereabouts. If you had made your way back, your agreement would have been severed, and you would have been dissipated. Many people lost their lives in the war, and I'm thankful that you weren't one of them.

"There's a possibility that some others are still out there, but finding them now would be an impossible task with our limited numbers. Only a handful of us made it out before our world completely imploded. The one surviving ship could only save one hundred and six. The Three had already been sent here years before, so, including you, we may be the last one hundred and ten of our people left in this universe."

After taking a deep breath, he continued. "I have told you as much as I can for now. It's your turn to tell us the rest of your story."

"Are you sure you want to hear this?" If Ben was the father of her children, he might still be her husband. Or at least something close to it.

"Just tell us." Ben tried to look stern, but it didn't work.

Grace thought for a minute. "It starts where I left off this morning. The seer who came for me was the king's seer. He trained me as well as he could to control my abilities. One morning, he told me of a prophecy. And, no, I don't know where the prophecy came from. For all I know, the king could have told him to tell me himself. Anyway, the queen had died. The king needed a new wife to raise his sons. He also wanted to use my abilities in his service, which I'm sure was the real reason for this revelation." The last bit she said sarcastically.

"It was a partnership of necessity, during which I became bound to the king. When he went into battle, I took on his pain. I, too, became a ferocious fighter. The pain strengthened me. Alongside his sons, I led his wars and won his conquests. After many years at his side, I watched him die as I took his pain one last time. My feelings never grew to care for him as a wife should, but he made me feel like I was part of his world. It was the feeling that I had a purpose, that I belonged, even if only for a short time. The only things he gave me that mattered to me at that point were his children. I raised his sons to be strong, resilient men, then kings in their own right. Finally, I had to watch each of them, one by one, grow old. I wept for them as I watched each one take his last breath and leave his world for eternity." Grace blinked as a tear ran down her cheek, clearly reliving the intense emotional pain of watching the children she had raised die. She took a cleansing breath and wiped the tear away with a trembling hand, brushing against her flushed face.

"Out of all the death I have witnessed, those were the hardest." She looked at each of her sons in turn. "No parent should ever have to face the death of a child, at any age. I had less than a hundred years with them. Even though I didn't give birth to them, they were as much mine as I could have had here."

Mikkel looked at Grace with unexpected sadness. "I'm sorry you had to go through those things with no one to turn to. You should never have been sent to a place where you had to lose everyone you cared about." He shot Ben an angry glare.

That memory always made her emotional. She had buried it deep, and it had been difficult to bring it up from that dark place. She must have picked up on everyone's feelings as well as her own. The intensity of their connection was strong. All she could do was push it back down and focus. Staying in control was the best way for her to get through this.

Ben didn't know what to do. In all the time he had known her, he had only seen her cry a handful of times. It broke his heart to see her upset. He put his hand on her shoulder, but she brushed it away, not wanting his pity.

"You shouldn't have been here alone for so long. We searched half the universe, narrowing it down to this planet, but we still couldn't find you. The amulet hides you from our sensors," Alex said in a vain attempt to comfort her.

"I'm here now." Wiping away the additional tears that had escaped her eyes, she regained her composure. "Tell me how I move forward from here. Tell me what you want from me." A flash of irritation took her over, stiffening her body. Too much was at stake and time was running out. She would only be here for the rest of today and tomorrow.

"How did The Sons get back here?" she asked, pressing her back against the chair.

"We had a bridge of sorts, a portal between worlds that could open for travel from either side. There were many bridges, all connected to our home world. Each sent travelers through a portal controlled by Heimdall, but they were all destroyed during the Great War. The Three crossed over before it all began. The rest of us who escaped had to take a transport ship to get here," Ben replied.

"Oh, yeah. The Bifrost right? I remember that one," Grace said.

"You remember?" Mikkel asked.

"I remember reading about it," she shrugged, embarrassed she had phrased it in that way.

"Mikkel, stop," Ben ordered.

"So, you sent them here as some kind of advance party to prepare for the worst-case scenario?" Grace guessed, thinking it was a sound strategy.

"I didn't send them because I was in Hel. They had been looking for you off and on for quite some time. They were sent here for another reason, and they made the plan to find you on their own," Ben explained.

"Oh," Grace said suspiciously. There was a lot he wasn't telling her, and it was beginning to irritate her. She wanted to keep him talking, though. There was a lot more she needed to know, and this was a topic she could address with The Three later. Ben must have seen her skepticism as he continued.

"Whether the war was won or lost, we were always going to come to look for you. Odin had sent them away as punishment for some unknown slight against his authority. They contacted our allies, outfitted this facility with everything we would need, and then started looking for you."

Random questions were firing through her brain. "How did you know how to look for me once you arrived here?"

"We have telepathy with each other and with you. Even with your memories erased, we were still able to contact your subconscious mind, and we could hear you sometimes when you were asleep. It was mostly an image flash or a word here and there, but nothing we could understand," Erik explained.

Grace realized they had been trying to contact her for years. "I thought I was dreaming of you. You've been calling out to me for five years. You've been here for five years? I thought I was going crazy hearing voices in my dreams."

"Your kind of crazy has nothing to do with hearing our voices," Mikkel interjected, as an obvious inheritor of her sarcasm.

"No way I can deny you're mine," Grace retorted with the same sarcastic tone. "What about the necklace and my memories?"

"There are two issues with removing it. The first is we think all your memories will flood back at once, which may drive you insane," Ben said cautiously.

"I'm almost afraid to ask this question. Exactly how many years are we talking about?"

"Well, we can agree that time is measured differently here than it was in our world, right? A year is an orbit around the sun and all, and since we had a much larger sun there, a year here was not a year there. Does that make sense?" Ben was flailing badly.

"I don't remember the span of a year there, so can we go with an approximate number in years here that I understand?"

"Five hundred thousand, give or take." Ben had the look of someone waiting to be struck.

"I need a drink." She stood up quickly. Her eyes were moving side to side as if she was reading something. You could literally see the wheels turning. She didn't want to know the answer to her next question. It was inevitable; it wouldn't go away, no matter how hard she tried to ignore it. Ben handed her a shot of clear alcohol, which she slugged down in one gulp, finishing the glass upside down on the counter.

"You said we met pretty young."

"Yes," he answered.

"Are we still married?" she whispered, leaning toward him.

He wanted to give her an answer that wouldn't make her feel any obligation toward him. "Well, in our culture, both yes and no. We have each met the 'till death do us part' burden of a normal bonding." At this point, he looked directly into her eyes. Grace saw from her periphery that The Three glanced suspiciously at each other.

"I'm not expecting anything from you. I understand you have a life here and I also understand you don't remember me. It's not my intention to push you. All I ask is that you don't shut me out."

"How long?"

"How long what?"

"How long have we been married?"

"Off and on, we've been together pretty much all of it, at least four hundred and fifty thousand years."

Grace stared at the floor for an uncomfortable amount of time. Minute tremors ran through her body. When she raised her head to look at Ben, her eyes were wider than normal.

"I'm sorry. This must be so hard for you." Grace's eyes filled with empathy. She didn't want to feel sorry for him. Hell, she didn't want to feel anything for him, but she couldn't help herself.

Ben didn't expect that from her. Her kindness was one reason he had been drawn to her so long ago. He should have known she would be more concerned with his pain than her own.

Ben lowered his gaze to view her hands. "It is hard watching you, while I remember every minute of our life together, knowing you don't even know who I am. I can't imagine how hard it is for you having all of this dumped on you at once, not knowing who we are."

"I know them. It might not be the details of their lives, but it's enough for now." Grace's answer was sincere.

Alex took a step forward, drawing her attention. "Deep down you know us. A hundred years or a hundred thousand won't change anything. We're still us and you're still you, regardless of whether you remember the specifics of us."

She could only nod. A moment passed before she turned back to Ben. "What was the other reason? Not removing the necklace, I mean."

Ben understood she was taking it all in and avoiding the issues of their relationship. He couldn't blame her. He would have done the same.

"The second reason is because of the loss. You are tied to our people, our world. We don't know what level of physical pain, mental anguish, and despair you would open yourself up to. Most of our people are gone in one way or another. Many of their essences have been destroyed. The rest are missing, and we don't know if they are dead or not. You may be opening yourself to the pain of millions simultaneously. The better way would be to reduce the binding slowly if we can, so we can see if there are any issues."

"You said your mother placed this to hide and protect me. Does no one else understand how it binds?"

"Her journals and logs are gone. We won't know until our technicians can look at it, study it."

Grace stepped back from him. "I can't stay here for months, or years, while you figure this out." She was not about to abandon her current life to this place. Cold ran down her spine while heat rose in her chest. Escape plans were already forming in her mind. As much as she wanted to be connected to these people, to understand who she was and where she came from, the facts were that the old world no longer existed and the only connection she needed here was with her sons.

Ben clearly saw the panic rise in her face. "No, no, that isn't what we meant at all. We aren't trying to keep you here. We can scan it, examine it, take some measurements, and work on some theories. It will only take a day or so. You can come back periodically, for a day or two, whenever you want, so we can test out some things. It is completely up to you, on your schedule. We all have time here," Ben blurted. He meant all of it. He didn't want to scare her away. Time was the one thing he had on his side. He could wait as long as she needed.

"I can stay today and tomorrow. After that, I need to go home. I need time to process all of this."

Only two days. That's all the time he had to connect with her. It's not like he thought he could convince her to come back right away. He did think he had more time, though. Once she left, he didn't know when he would see her again.

"Let's get our research department started, then." Ben finally uttered a coherent idea.

"All right, let's go." Grace wasn't sure she wanted the binding to be broken anymore. She didn't like the idea that they would be able to locate her without it. She had built a very comfortable life for herself. These memories and feelings were going to complicate things. It could take years for them to figure it out. She did, however, need to see what this facility was all about, to know what she was up against.

The Three headed off to perform their assigned duties for that day. Grace and Ben made their way to the lab two floors below them on level six. Nothing there was what she had expected. The lab was immense, accentuated with walls glazed in a rich golden-blue color. There were large sections that appeared to be cycling through the most inviting outdoor scenes. Morale was clearly important to people who spent most of their time underground. The lighting was bright without being too intense. The obvious star attraction of the room was a piece of equipment that looked like a large round glass shower without the parts for plumbing. Surrounding the top was a ring with thousands of tiny sensors attached to it. As they entered the space, everyone turned to stare at her. From the looks on their faces, she was sure they knew her, or at least who she was.

Ben came in behind her. "Everyone, this is Grace."

Grace realized that she needed to be introduced. Even though he had told her in the van, the thought hit her like a brick. Everything about this place made her feel uncomfortable. Out of all the things she had dreamed about when finding her people, the reality of this place was far from the options her imagination had presented. She didn't feel like she was being welcomed home. Quite the opposite, in fact. They appeared suspicious of her.

"Ben, what was my name?" It was clearly not Grace. That name had been chosen for her.

"Nanna." He had expected this question, just not at this moment.

"Yeah … I think I prefer Grace." Her current identity was one of the few things she had to hold on to.

He smiled and whispered, "Me too."

"If I remember my mythology correctly, that would mean you're actually Balder, wouldn't it?" she asked with a nervous smile. No wonder she reacted to him the way she did in the alley. She had been married to the god of beauty and light. *Great,* she thought, rolling her eyes, then hoping he hadn't heard.

"It does." His answer didn't seem to portray having heard her.

"I think I'll stick with calling you Ben. A new life calls for a new identity and all."

"I had to pick something. Balder doesn't exactly fit here, does it?"

"No. Not anymore. Not with the end of the old world." She shrugged, wanting to appear disconnected.

It was a cold, hard action. With that simple gesture, he realized, nothing would ever be the same. They would never be the same. It was truly a new beginning and a finite ending to their old life.

An obviously eager, small but sturdy woman, who held out her hand to Grace, approached them as quickly as her short legs would carry her. Grace reached out to shake her hand, but the woman reached past her and pulled the amulet out of Grace's shirt.

"Ooohh, I have waited so long to see this!" Grace stepped back on her right heel but was aware enough not to phase out. "Sorry!" The woman dropped the amulet and took Grace's hand in both of hers, shaking it fervently. "I'm Seshet. I've been looking forward to meeting you all day."

"It's ten in the morning," Grace said, scrutinizing the woman before realization set in. "Oh, you're the Keeper." Grace had expected someone older, more refined.

"Yes, I am. I've read what little there is about the amulet. I never thought I'd get the chance to see it in person."

"If you can get it off me, you're welcome to keep it." Grace regretted that sentence the second it passed her lips. She hadn't conclusively decided if she wanted it off yet.

"Really!" That seemed to be the best thing this woman had heard in her entire life. "Let's pop you into the scanner and get started."

Grace thought this woman was far happier than anyone living underground should be.

"Take it down a notch there. What exactly does this thing do? I expected you to scan the necklace, not my entire body." Grace waved her hand at the scanner.

Ben looked at Seshet quizzically.

"It's perfectly safe. It's not like we can take it off to scan it. We need to do a full scan to see how the connection between Nan—oops," Seshet giggled, "Grace and the amulet works. Is it physical, metaphysical, genetic, magnetic, or some other thing that binds it to her?" Seshet spoke hastily.

Grace thought she needed to lay off energy drinks. Ben stifled a laugh when she thought about that. He had heard her … again. Which meant he had also heard her a minute ago. Why was she unable to block him?

"What do you want me to do?" Grace asked unenthusiastically.

"Remove your shoes and step into the center of the circle," Seshet instructed. "This will only take a minute."

Grace looked at Ben. It clearly amused him to see her being ordered around in that way. Grace frowned, showing she was far less amused. Hopefully, this thing would give her some answers she wanted. The downside was that this group would have those answers first. It was a risk she was willing to take. Removing her shoes, Grace stepped into the machine.

"Okay, you can close your eyes. The lights are pretty bright." Seshet was almost giddy.

"Do I need to hold still?"

"It doesn't matter." Seshet tapped the control screen a few times. A ring of lights turned on at the top of the glass. The chamber shut, and the light ring began whirling, descending, and creating a grid pattern. The machine had completed the whole process in under two minutes. As the front piece of glass receded, the ring lifted back up.

"All finished, you can come out now," Seshet ordered without looking up from her digital pad. "The next thing we need is a quick blood sample, and we're finished for now. It shouldn't take more than a few hours to go through the data. After that we should know if we need to run any more tests. Rena here will draw your blood when you're ready."

"Well, that was a lot less painful than I thought it was going to be." Grace was relieved by the lack of invasiveness of the initial examination. She sat at the blood draw station, where Rena filled three vials.

"Why don't you two get some lunch? We'll call you when we're finished with the initial analysis." Seshet was annoyingly eager and awkward.

"Are you hungry yet, or would you like to see the training room?" Ben asked.

How often do these people eat? she thought. "Training room, please."

"Okay, the training room is on level two." Ben grinned at Grace, obviously having heard her … again. He turned back to Seshet. "We're headed up."

Seshet mumbled something and waved him off dismissively, which annoyed Ben. Grace noted that it didn't seem to be the type of treatment he was used to getting from his subordinates.

They took the elevator up to the second floor. The training room was as impressive as she had expected. About half a dozen people were working out; only two were sparring. There were all kinds of advanced weight training equipment, cardio stations, two sparring rings, and tons of weapons, most of which she was familiar with and a few of which she did not know how to use.

"Sweet!"

"What would you like to do first?"

"Spar."

"Of course you do. I don't want you to hold back. You can't hurt me with any weapon, so make all your strikes true," Ben said confidently.

"Only if you do the same," Grace countered.

"I can hurt you. You're not invincible to a blade," Ben countered. He didn't remember her as being an adept fighter and thought he would take it easy on her at first.

"You're not fast enough to hurt me. Matter of fact, you can't even touch me unless I want you to," Grace smirked at him.

"I'll remember that. Pick your weapon," he smirked.

"I'll go old school: short broadsword and shield." It had been centuries since she had hung up her sword and shield. She felt nostalgic rubbing her fingertips over the well-worn braided leather hilt. The weight of the weapons felt good in her hands.

"I think I'll take the double-headed axe." Ben pulled the axe from the wall. In one fell swoop, he spun as the axe passed right through Grace and her shield.

Instinct took over. Ben's attack awakened something in her that had been dormant for a long time. She countered, slamming her newly solidified shield into him and knocking him onto his back. She plunged her phased sword into his right thigh and phased it again, returning it to its solid state as it passed through his leg. He screamed in pain as it pinned his leg to the floor, rendering him incapable of moving from that spot. A weapon had never injured him like that before. His skin was impenetrable, unable to be broken by a blade, but this blade had ripped him open from the inside.

Grace pulled the sword out and threw her weapons to the ground. Ben screamed again as blood sprayed up the front of Grace's shirt, filling her nose with the unmistakable metallic scent she was so familiar with. She touched his shoulder, pulling his pain into her as she pressed her other hand against the wide gash in the front of his thigh. Everyone in the gym looked at them in disbelief.

"Get a medic up here NOW!" Grace screamed to the crowd that had gathered to watch.

"I'm sorry! You told me not to hold back. I knew something like this would happen! I told you I could hurt you!" She pressed down harder on his wound, wincing at the pain she was inflicting on herself that he didn't feel.

He leaned forward, his head cocked to the side inquisitively. "I've never seen so much of my blood before." Ben poked at the wound curiously.

"Just shut up, Ben!" Grace shouted at him, slapping his hand away. "Where the hell is medical?!" Her heart was racing. Her mind was screaming in a frenzy of confusion. *Skreyja!* Grace cursed herself for her stupidity. *I could have killed him! What was I thinking?! Can I not control myself for one minute around this idiot?!*

He put his hands on her arms. "Calm down. I will be fine. Your mind is screaming so loudly."

He looked at the crowd that had gathered. "I think everyone can hear you," he admonished through clenched teeth.

The Three ran in. They certainly heard her panicked mind screaming. She was unsure of what was happening. Her composure never faltered this badly. When things went wrong, she was typically the one who remained calm and took charge.

"This isn't helping, Mother, move. Father, stop talking," Alex ordered. "Erik, get an ETA on medical. Mikkel, throw me that towel."

Ben pulled Grace to his left side as Alex wrapped the towel around his leg and compressed it. She let out a slight gasp of pain and Alex realized she was the one feeling it and let up a little.

"No, press harder," Grace demanded. "Use your belt to stop the bleeding."

Erik yelled, "Two minutes!"

Alex took off his belt and created a tourniquet over the towel around Ben's leg, watching his mother for a reaction. It was still bleeding profusely, but the arterial spray had stopped. Aside from the initial sign, Grace did not show him any weakness to the pain.

Three medics ran in with a gurney. When the first one saw that it was Ben who was lying on the floor, he stopped cold and got knocked over by the other two rushing in behind him. Alex dragged them back to reality. "Get over here!"

The medics loaded Ben onto the gurney. Alex and Erik each took one of Grace's arms and pulled her up from the floor. The four of them followed behind the medics into the elevator. Grace limped, trying not to show how much pain she was in. Medical was four floors down on level six, the same level as the lab.

Grace, what's wrong? Lukkas's voice broke through. She felt a moment of relief at hearing him. It had been more than a day since they had spoken. It was softer and quieter than the surrounding voices as the medics shouted at each other.

I'm fine. I hurt someone. It was an accident, but it's being resolved. I'm sorry I alarmed you.

I never heard you like that before. You startled me. Are you sure everything's okay?

Yes, there's a lot happening here. I'll explain everything when I get home. I'll be coming, as planned, the day after tomorrow. There are people I am connected to, Lukkas. I need to keep you away until I'm sure what's going on. I'll call you when I'm on my way.

Lukkas was gone. Grace had enough to deal with here, and she thought it best to shut him out. These two parts of her life needed to be kept separate for now. She desperately wished she had never left home. None of this would have happened if she hadn't come. Ben would never have been hurt. It seemed like people always ended up hurt when she was around.

Mother. It was Alex.

Yes. Grace responded out of instinct. Although it should have felt foreign to her, the term was oddly comforting.

Where were you? He had heard her conversation.

She was out of sorts and obviously hadn't hidden the conversation as well as she thought she had. What she said wasn't meant for him to hear. She hadn't meant for anyone to hear her.

I was talking to someone else. He knew I was out of sorts and was checking on me. Did the others hear it? I don't think I could be able to explain it to everyone right now.

No, it's only me. I pushed in. I see that you're in pain and you're confused. You don't understand your connection with Father because you don't remember him. I understand how hard it's been for you coming here.

Please, Alex, I can't do this right now.

Alex squeezed her hand and lowered his head as they proceeded forward. The doors finally opened. There were two healers who immediately grabbed the gurney with Ben. Their expressions were those of complete confusion. They were thinking, *How was this possible? He couldn't be hurt.* Alarmed thoughts were always loud and difficult for Grace to block out. The group followed the healers down the corridor opposite the lab and were instructed to wait in a small room to the left of the hall. As they sat down, Grace felt a sharp, searing pain in her right leg and let out a soft moan.

"Are you okay?" Erik asked.

"Yes, I'm fine. I didn't expect them to probe his leg like that." She made an exaggerated frown, masking the pain that was becoming more severe. "Wuss!" she huffed, breaking the uneasy feeling in the room. The Three smirked back at her.

"Just because he can't feel it doesn't mean he doesn't need anesthesia!" she yelled into the back. Grace sat with her eyes closed, concentrating on her breathing as they lasered to stop the bleeding and melded the muscle together. Immortal pain was incredibly more intense than mortal pain, except that most immortals have a much higher tolerance for it.

A healer emerged from the trauma room. "Grace, I am Dian. You need to come with me. We are unable to cut through his skin and it's crucial we know what he is experiencing. He told us you were somehow blocking his sensation?"

When Grace rose from her seat, Erik and Mikkel stepped up beside her. She motioned for them to stay while she followed Dian into the treatment room, limping the entire way. The healers glanced at her, unbothered by her appearing soaked in blood.

Tao spoke. "We don't know how this works. We need to know what he is feeling. If we don't make sure the nerves haven't been severed, we'll never be able to get back in again to fix it." They were using a small electrode to touch different areas on his feet and lower leg. "We can laser the muscle, but we don't have any way to close the wounds. Our healing instruments won't work on his skin."

Grace looked at Ben. "I can give him back enough sensitivity to tell you what you need. I can't do anything to make the surface healing instruments work, but when you're ready, I can bring him into phase with me so you can sew through his skin."

"Grace, let me have all the pain back. They can give me anesthesia."

Tao looked up. "We already tried that. Your body must see it as some kind of poison because you expelled it."

"Lucky him," Grace spat sarcastically. "Ben, you've never felt pain like this before. I'm telling you, you have no threshold for it. Besides, it's my fault, which makes it my burden. I will only give you what they need you to have," she said, taking a seat in the chair to his left.

Ben reached for her. She didn't need to touch him to return his pain. After staring at his outstretched hand for a moment, she begrudgingly gave him hers, along with some of the pain. Just a small amount, enough for him to tell them what he was feeling. Once they had lasered and melded the insides together, she held him in phase with her while they stitched his external wounds. By the time they finished sewing him up, Grace was exhausted. It was hard for her to keep her eyes open any longer. She had never held someone in phase for so long. It had been nearly an hour, which she found to be a ridiculous amount of time for a few stitches. Her phasing usually happened in moments, not hours. When she was dozing off, the healers let The Three into the room. Grace sat up, trying to show them she was fine, but there was no hiding the fact that she had a problem. Her form would become blurry around the edges, making it difficult for them to discern the boundaries of the chair from her body. She was phasing in and out, seemingly at random. Concerned, they called the healers back.

"We'll get the shaman. We don't know how to stop this," Dian said.

A few minutes later, Seshet came bouncing in with one of the staff shamans. "Oh, isn't this exciting?"

"Exciting?" Erik growled. "My father, who has impenetrable skin, has a hole through his leg, and my mother is unable to maintain a solid form. There's something seriously wrong with both of them and you find that exciting?!"

Seshet backpedaled. "Maybe exciting was the wrong word. It is incredibly interesting. It's unexplainable. Grace, I'm sorry to ask, but I need to scan you again. It would help tremendously to understand if we can compare your previous scan to one of you now."

Alex stepped between Grace and Seshet. "She can't even stand up."

"We have a scanner she can lie down in. We must hurry before she recovers."

Seshet glanced at Erik's glaring eyes and scowl. "You think it's insensitive. My only motive is scientific. We don't know how to help her unless we can see what is happening."

"Well, I think sleep would help a lot. I feel like I've been running continuously for weeks." Grace wanted to sleep for the next twelve hours, at a minimum. As she finished her sentence, a nurse came in with a wheelchair to take Grace to the lab.

"It's okay. I want to know how this happened. Help me into the chair," Grace replied, giving in to Seshet's demands.

Before Ben could raise an objection, Grace cut him off. "I need to do this."

Mikkel was the one closest to Grace, and he lifted her from her seat to the wheelchair. Alex instructed Mikkel to go with her while he and Erik stayed with Ben.

"This is different." Erik looked at his father's leg. "How did it happen?"

"We were sparring. I swung an axe, expecting her to duck, but instead she phased, and it went through her. When she brought her sword down, it was still in phase when it went through my thigh. It solidified inside my leg, tearing it from the inside out. I had told her not to hold back because I didn't think there was any way she could hurt me. Looks like I was wrong about that," Ben said with a chuckle. "It was a ridiculous accident. You heard how she lost it when she realized she hurt me. We were just killing time. Neither of us expected it. Do you think she'll recover?"

"I hope so," Alex sighed. "Are you going to be okay?" He was worried about both of them. There were far too many years in his memory when the two of them were each other's fatal weakness. It was never a question of if they would hurt each other, but how often and how badly.

"Please!" Ben scoffed. "You have all had worse injuries."

"Yeah, we have, but you've never been injured at all, except for the time you died," Alex replied.

~~~~

Grace wasn't doing quite as well as Ben. Seshet had to scan her several times because of her uncontrollable phase changes.

"I need another blood sample."

"Yeah, Seshet. Good luck with that," Grace replied tersely as Seshet grabbed her arm. Having a new favorite guinea pig to torture made the woman absolutely thrilled.

"Mikkel, please check on your father." Grace had noticed his discomfort as he watched Seshet stab her arm several times without finding the satisfactory purchase of a vein.

"I can just check in with Alex," Mikkel responded, pointing to his head.

"I prefer you go see for yourself. I'll be there soon," Grace countered.

"Yes, ma'am," Mikkel replied, slowly backing out of the room.

"Oh well. I guess that isn't happening," Seshet remarked to herself after missing Grace's vein several more times. "Let's get you somewhere you can sleep," Seshet sighed loudly, sounding disappointed for the first time since Grace had met her.

"Finally."

The nurse returned with the wheelchair. He lifted her off the machine as if she weighed nothing. As he was setting her down, she phased solidly, which made him drop her the last few inches. She went from barely twenty pounds to over two hundred in an instant.

"Sorry," she grimaced. "I can't control that right now."

"It's okay, I just wasn't expecting so much weight for your size. Let's get you to a bed." He wheeled her back into Ben's room and helped her into the bed on the other side of the open divider. The nurse turned around to face The Three.

"She'll probably be out for a while." Then he turned to Ben. "You should get some sleep as well."

Ben noticed Grace was already asleep. "I could use a little shut-eye," he shrugged.
~~~~

Erik stood up first. "We'll check on you later." He grabbed Mikkel and Alex by the shoulders and motioned for them to get up.

Ben lay on his side and watched Grace sleep for a while before finally drifting off himself.

A few hours later, Grace woke up groggy. The rough pillowcase, smelling strongly of bleach, clung to her cheek, which was coated in a thin layer of saliva. Although she'd only slept four hours, she felt much better, and her thoughts were becoming clearer. The nurse from earlier came in to change Ben's bandages.

"Hey, sunshine." He shook Ben's shoulder until his eyes opened. "Good to have you back. I'll get this cleaned up and be out of your way in a minute. Those stitches are going to leave such a nasty scar. I don't know why they didn't use surgical glue."

Grace blinked and wiped the remaining slobber off the side of her face. "Say that again." Her mental wheels spun as she narrowed her eyes at the man. The nurse returned her scrutiny with a blank stare. What they had done had made sense. She would have done the same. "Can you please call one of the healers in here? I have a question I need to ask."

As the nurse nodded and left the room, Seshet stepped around the corner. "I was wondering how long it would take you to figure it out. Don't be angry with the healers. I saw an opportunity I had to take."

"To test my limits. I'm sure I would have done the same."

"Besides, you had a fail-safe, didn't you, Grace?"

"And I wondered how long it would take you to figure that out once you took my blood." Grace knew they were going to find it. They still wouldn't be able to tell where it came from.

"I got the preliminary blood test results as you were coming down in the elevator. Like I said, I couldn't pass up the opportunity. I'd like to thank you for making that happen," Seshet said smugly.

Ben opened his eyes. "Anyone want to fill me in on what's going on here? Start with the opportunity, then we'll discuss the fail-safe."

Seshet looked nervous as Grace spoke. "They could have used surgical adhesive on your skin. Instead, Seshet saw an opportunity to test my limits. It's logical I would have done the same if I'd have thought of it. No hard feelings," Grace said.

It was apparent Ben had hard feelings about the incident as he raged at Seshet.

"It isn't up to you to make that kind of decision, Seshet. Nothing concerning Grace is your decision!" His face was red with anger.

"I couldn't risk you saying no. The data is too valuable," Seshet raised her voice at him unexpectedly.

"I would have definitely said no! Testing Grace's limits can only be done with her permission. I'll take this to the ethics committee."

"Who do you think authorized the test?" Seshet crossed her arms and leaned smugly against the doorframe.

"They'll get their own taste of my disapproval then," Ben sneered. "No more anything without her consent. Am I clear?"

Grace took the opportunity to interrupt. "This is what I came here for, to find out about my past and understand my abilities. Maybe not behind my back, but this is what I came here for." They both looked at Grace. "I already told you I have no hard feelings. I would have done the same. It's a cleaner experiment than if I had known. She didn't create the circumstances. I did. I was the one responsible for your injury. And she's right, I came in with a fail-safe."

Ben looked hurt. "What do you mean, a fail-safe?"

"She has vampire venom in her system. That's why she gave us a three-day time limit. That's how long it stays in the blood: three to four days. Smart girl. If we had killed her, she'd have come back with all the abilities she has now, plus all the standard vampire enhancements. Win-win for her." Seshet was impressed by the thought Grace had put into making contact with their group.

The women looked at each other with what appeared to be mutual respect.

Ben was confused and angry with both women. "What in all hells is wrong with you two?" he sneered.

The women both shrugged.

"We're the ones being rational," Grace replied.

Seshet turned to Grace. "Where did you get the vampire venom?"

Grace blinked slowly at her. "I have sources. What else did the tests tell you?"

"Come by the lab in the morning and we'll go over the results. We should finish compiling the data by then. I'm the one who needs to get some sleep now." Seshet cocked her head toward the door without breaking Grace's gaze. Grace raised her eyebrows and nodded back.

"Touché."

Grace turned her attention to Ben. "Who do we talk to about getting some food around here? Aren't you hungry?"

"Sure. Why not?" he moped.

"I'll send the nurse back in," Seshet said as she left the room.

The nurse came back to finish changing Ben's bandages. When he was done, he took their dinner order and left.

"Were you going to tell me about your fail-safe?"

"No."

Ben looked at her, expecting more. Grace stared back at him, silent.

"Why did you do it?"

"Come on, you really have to ask? I didn't know what I was getting myself into. You would have done the same thing if you had the chance."

"No, I wouldn't have."

She looked at him with that stop-lying-to-yourself look.

"Okay, well, maybe I would have. It surprised me."

"Ben, think about it from my perspective. I don't know you. I don't know anything about this organization. All I knew was you were hunting me, and I didn't know why. Now, if you had the opportunity and access to venom, would you have done it?"

"Okay, yes. I see your point." Ben still looked a bit disappointed. "Now that you know we're not trying to kill you, do you still have to leave the day after tomorrow?"

"Nothing has shown me you don't intend on killing me. It only shows you want to experiment on me first."

"I wasn't the one who did that!" Ben yelled at her.

"No, your employee did, and your ethics committee approved it. And yes, I have to leave the day after tomorrow. I have a schedule, and it's not just about the venom. I have an exit plan. If I miss my transport, I have people who will be concerned."

Ben clenched his jaw, turning away from her. He was angry, but not with Grace. "How do we find you again?"

"You can reach me by simply calling from here." She tapped her temple. "I'll come back when I'm ready, but I need time to process everything first. I'm also not ready to let you into my life outside of here after only a few short days. You'll have to wait and earn my trust."

"Time is one thing I have in abundance. I can wait until you decide you want to be here."

In Grace's opinion, it was arrogant of him to make such a statement. "You say that as if you think I'm going to run back into your arms. What makes you think I don't have someone waiting for me at home?"

"Maybe for the next fifty years. What are you going to do after that?"

Fortunately for Grace, a server came through the door with their meal. She did not want to finish this conversation.

"So, who had the steak and who had the salmon?"

While they ate, Grace steered the conversation to the lighter side for the rest of the evening. They talked about general, safe, getting-to-know-you stuff. Sometime around two a.m., Grace dozed off again and Ben pulled his device out to get some work done.

CHAPTER FIVE

At six in the morning, a new nurse flipped on the lights. "Morning folks, let's get this day started." Ben popped up immediately; however, Grace was far less of a morning person, opening only one eye.

"Coffee, where do I get coffee?"

The nurse looked at her, smiling far too broadly for this time of morning. "We have some at the monitoring station. I can get you some after I change Ben's bandages."

Grace got up, ignoring the nurse, and walked to the door. Nurse Irene, as her name tag showed, opened her mouth to say something when Ben caught her arm. He shook his head in warning. "Let it go."

Grace returned a few minutes later carrying two cups and handed one to Ben.

"Thank you. I almost thought you brought both for yourself."

"This is my second cup," she said, lifting the one she was drinking.

Nurse Irene finished with Ben's leg. "This is healing a little faster than we expected. Those stitches should come out tomorrow."

Grace looked over. "They need to come out today."

Ben was confused. "Why?"

"I already told you I'm leaving early tomorrow, and they won't be able to get them out. They can use the surgical glue if they need to keep it sealed."

Irene opened her eyes wide. "Oh, I'm not sure anyone had considered that."

Grace looked at her cynically. "Uh-huh, I'm sure they didn't consider that stitches would make me stay longer. Tell the docs today, or he's going to be living with those."

Ben was fed up with the staff's ridiculous denial and didn't want to hear any more of it. This was his facility, and he was in charge of it. "Where's Seshet?"

"She'll be in the lab at eight. How about you guys get some breakfast, then you can get cleaned up?"

"I get the shower first," Grace pronounced between sips of coffee. "Ooohhh yeah, you can't shower with stitches." Grace looked at Ben with false concern. Then she turned to Irene. "Can I get some clean clothes?"

"Sure, we'll have some brought up."

"She has some in my apartment. I can have one of The Three bring them down," Ben replied harshly, irritated at Irene's dismissal of his demand to see Seshet.

"Done. I just asked Alex to bring them," said Grace. Ben and Irene turned toward her. "What? Did you want him to bring you something, too?"

"Since you asked, can you have him grab my gym shorts and a long-sleeved T-shirt?"

Grace looked away for a second and giggled.

"What?" Ben asked with indignation in his voice.

"He wants to know if you mean your old man pedophile shorts."

"Ha … ha. They're the only ones I have that won't cover my stitches. Unless you'd rather have my junk hanging out while they remove them."

"Pedophile shorts it is!" Grace announced cheerfully. "He'll be down in a few minutes."

Irene quickly picked up the rest of the bandages, giving Grace a nervous glance, and left the room.

"She's acting like she's never seen a telepath before," Grace said.

"I don't think that's what made her uncomfortable, Grace. Not everyone here is like us and it's taken them a while to get used to us," Ben explained.

"Them? Well, what is she?"

"She's a human, but she's also an elemental. Mostly she uses herbs and energy, so she has a hard time with something she can't touch."

"She can't touch energy."

"She can feel it. Not the same way you can, but she uses it to heal," Ben defended Irene's ability. Despite being irritated by her response, he still valued her contribution.

"So, what is this facility for, besides housing refugees from the universe? You have humans working here and it's clear that Tao is not from Asgard, which means he's not Æsir or Vanir. Seshet is an Egyptian. What other rogues are hanging around?"

"That's a long explanation. Why don't we save it for the next time you come?"

"Sure, I understand we have to work on building some trust before we reveal our secrets to each other. I've only known you for two days, and you can't be sure that I'm the same person you knew, either. It's been a long time."

"It's not that I don't trust you, Grace. It will take more than a few hours to explain. There isn't enough time today with everything else."

"Now that we have restored our connection, we can talk while I'm at home. We both need time to process all of this. I need time to see…"

"You both need time for what?" Alex unintentionally cut her off as he came in with the things they had requested.

"Digestion." Grace smiled and took her clothes from him. "Shower time." She closed the bathroom door behind her, leaving Alex and Ben alone, but she could feel them staring at the door.

"What did she mean by that?" Alex asked.

Ben shook his head and shrugged. "Here," he called, reaching for his clothes. "Let me get out of this gown and into something normal."

Alex threw the shorts at Ben, who, feeling no pain, instinctively jumped up to put them on. Alex winced, looking at him.

Grace sternly passed the thought, *I would appreciate a warning before you do something stupid like that. Once they get those stitches out, I am terminating this link and giving your pain back.*

Ben sat back down on the bed and yelled "Sorry!" through the door. He finished pulling up his shorts and pulled on his T-shirt. "We need to be at the lab at eight for your mother's test results."

Alex nodded and asked, "Wheelchair or crutches?"

"I don't need them. I can walk."

"You're not the one who is going to feel it. Wheelchair or crutches?"

"Crutches are fine."

"I'll have a nurse bring you some." Alex pressed the call button on the side of Ben's bed.

When Grace came out of the bathroom, breakfast was on her tray. Ben was already eating and had fresh coffee brought up as well. Twenty minutes later, the three of them were moving to the other side of the level where the lab was. Grace realized that her life was going to change no matter what she learned. She was hoping for as little disruption as possible. When they turned the last corner, Erik and Mikkel were waiting in the hallway. After sharing a silent moment of acknowledgment, they all entered the lab without further discussion.

Seshet was standing at the front of a long table on the right side of the room. Behind her was a digital board with changing scenery. "Good morning, all. Do you want the good news or the bad news first?" Her voice was as cheerfully irritating as it had been the day before.

"Well, that's not very scientific of you, Seshet. Good and bad are matters of perspective, not fact." Grace mocked her mostly because she could. "Why don't we categorize the information as desirable and less desirable based on our perspective?" Grace then plastered a huge fake smile on her face.

"And how am I supposed to know what your perspective is, Grace?" Seshet returned the comment with the same hyper, exaggerated energy as before.

"You're not. That's the point. You can't decide what is good or bad for someone else," Grace smirked. "What news would *you* like to start with?"

Seshet huffed, straightening the lapels on her jacket. "I'm going to lay out the facts of the situation first. Once I'm finished presenting each section, you can ask questions. Does that work for everyone?"

The group collectively nodded to show their agreement.

"Then let's take our seats. Ben, I have you over here in the recliner. Dian said to keep your leg elevated to keep the swelling down. When we finish, I would like to have your stitches removed here so we can monitor both of you during the process."

The way Seshet was fawning over Ben was sickly sweet to Grace. It made her wonder where the attitude from last night had gone.

"As long as you do it today, I don't care where you do it," Grace said.

"The lab is fine, Seshet. Thank you," Ben said in a tone that apologized for Grace's curtness. She didn't understand when Ben's attitude had changed. He was ready to throttle Seshet less than an hour ago.

"Excellent. The first piece of information I would like to present is that the amulet is bound by blood. Ben's blood. I think Frigg set it up so that if he never found you, no one else would be able to find you, either. She constructed it to obscure you from all location trackers. Does everyone understand that the purpose of the amulet was to hide Grace?" Seshet asked in the condescending tone of a preschool teacher.

Everyone showed their understanding by nodding.

Erik raised his hand.

"You have a question?" Seshet asked.

"How do you know they sealed the amulet with our father's blood?"

"If your mother hadn't been able to stab him, we wouldn't have known. The scan showed a blood seal. When we loaded the sample of your father's blood yesterday, the data filled in as a match," Seshet answered. "Any further questions?"

"No," Erik responded.

"Then I'll continue. The less desirable information, from my perspective," Seshet said, cutting her eyes at Grace. "The amulet has nothing to do with Grace's memories. It does not hold her memories, it does not block any memories, it does not block her connection to your people in any way. The sole purpose of the amulet was to hide Grace from being located. Period. Are there questions about what exactly the amulet does or doesn't do?"

Grace had two questions. "If I let Ben remove the amulet, will the protection end, or would I be able to use it again?"

Seshet pondered the answer for a moment. "We have no idea."

"Okay. My second question is, what did you do with the rest of Ben's blood?" Grace studied Seshet's body language.

"The sample utilized in the analysis process was spent. There is none left."

"And the blood on the floor in the training room and on the towels and my clothes?" Grace continued.

"Ida identified it as a biohazard and sanitized it. Any more questions about the amulet?"

"I'm not finished yet. How do I know you didn't save any of his blood?" Grace continued. She couldn't shake the feeling Seshet was lying.

"Why do you care if they have any of my blood or not? I thought you wanted the amulet off?" Ben pushed.

"Because I want to be the one to make that decision when and if I decide to take it off," she countered.

"If there isn't any left, how do you think you're going to get the amulet off when you want to?" Ben asked.

Grace moved her finger up and down in front of him. "There's about seven liters right there that I can get to anytime I want."

Ben swallowed. He didn't like the way she got to it the first time.

"Excuse me. Are you sure *none* of her abilities are tied to the amulet? Would she lose anything other than protection if it were removed?" Erik asked.

"No. We can find absolutely no connection to her abilities whatsoever. As far as we can see, it cloaks the wearer, making them appear invisible to any detection. Are there any other questions?"

Ben was the next to question Seshet. "So, how does she get her memories back?" This was important to him. His goal was to have control over the order in which her memories returned.

Seshet took a breath. "We don't think it's possible. As far as we can tell, her memories have been extracted. She may have bits and pieces hiding in there somewhere, but we do not detect the type of brain activity in her that exists in the rest of your people containing your oldest memories. Whether they were completely erased or rendered dormant somewhere hidden, I do not know."

"Could the amulet be concealing the location of the memories? I don't think Queenie would strip those away from her permanently," Erik asked, referring to his grandmother by the name he had always used for her.

"Possibly. Whatever the case, we do not have the ability currently to restore any of her past. Her memories were also what kept her attached to the others. She felt nothing about their deaths because the connection to them had already been severed."

"Then how is she still attached to us? Aside from the memory part, we have a telepathic connection." Erik asked.

"That's the easiest question to answer. Blood connects you. Even with Ben— not incestuously; you're not brother and sister or anything. You must have created a blood bond in the past, most likely in some sort of ceremony. It was probably before your skin became impenetrable."

"My skin was impenetrable long before I met Grace. My mother knew a painless way to extract my blood. Not the way Grace did it, of course. The blood bond used to be part of the binding ceremony. No one remembers the old ways, I guess."

Seshet continued, "The whats and whys don't really matter at this point. What does matter is that Grace can't currently recover any memories. We have other ways for you to learn about your past and your people, if you wish. We have some historical texts that we can download for you."

Ben added, "I have memory prints and pictures. I even have some recorded clips I salvaged if you would like to see them."

Grace's face went blank. "That's too much for me right now. Let's leave memories and history for another trip. Is there anything else about me you can share with the class, Seshet?"

"There is nothing remarkable about your physiology for your species. You are primarily what we refer to as an evolved humanoid. Your brain centers are active in accordance with your advanced abilities and intelligence. You have excellent health, excellent muscle tone, low blood pressure, low cholesterol. You consistently achieve all above-average marks, as expected. Introducing vampire blood and venom into your system also gave us the additional opportunity to confirm some theories we have been studying about how that process works. I mean, we have blood and venom samples from other vampires. We just never had access to those elements suspended in the blood of a living humanoid. We have two vampires here, but neither will take part in a study. They tell us that most pure-born vampires mate with other pure-born vampires. Keeps the population down, plus they avoid mating with their food." They all just stared at her. "That was a joke."

Her statement visibly appalled Grace. She thought Seshet was probably working with a couple of rogues looking to make some quick cash. No respectable community member would say something so disgusting.

"Seshet, you're straying a little off topic, I think. Is there a point to all this?" Erik asked.

"Oh yes, sorry, the point. Our current research has shown us that vampires are the only biologically immortal humanoids native to this planet. Their venom is very similar to that of the *Turritopsis dohrnii* species of jellyfish, which I'm sure you all know is immortal as well, although it didn't originate here. They regenerate whenever they're near death. Not like they can regrow a body part if it's been chopped off or something, but they can heal it if it's still attached and …"

"Seshet!" Ben shouted, irritated with her blathering. "Is. There. A. Point?"

Grace didn't understand what was going on with this conversation. The Three were frantically scribbling notes onto their devices and Ben was irritated.

"Of course, there is a point," she sneered. "We never understood the process of turning. Why do some who are bitten turn while others don't? We knew what happened, but not how it happened until we connected the dots after seeing the way Grace's blood kept the vampire blood and venom separated. Vampire venom and vampire blood are miscible, and when they mix, it creates a virus. Humanoid blood cells are an ionic compound, like seawater. When someone introduces venom into the bloodstream and vampire blood is added, the human blood keeps the two separated. That's the reason the victim has to die, allowing the blood and venom to mix and resurrect the body like a beneficial virus."

Heat rose in Grace's chest. "Why do you care about any of that? How does another immortal species affect you at all?"

"We need to know how to kill them. The only way we have found to kill the virus that keeps them alive is to burn it, which is why the only way to make sure a vampire is dead is to burn the body. Not that I'm condoning killing vampires for sport or anything. At least not if they haven't shown any aggression toward us."

Alex interrupted. "That's really great information. If we run across any vampires, we need to know the best way to deal with them. The same goes for skinners, werewolves, Energy Essentials, or any other species with abilities. We need to understand the weaknesses of what we're up against. Most things stay dead if you take the head and burn it. This is valuable research, Seshet. I'll get it out to the teams."

Mikkel and Erik nodded in agreement.

Grace tried to hide how disturbing Seshet's assessment was to her. She had been trying to hide her community. Now it was her fault their weakness was exposed. She tried not to reveal how alarmed she was by this conversation, but the sickening feeling in her gut forced her to speak up. "What are you talking about? Vampires won't come after you if you leave them alone! What is going on here?"

Ben looked from a horrified Grace to The Three, who seemed excited by this new information. "You should probably get back to your duties. We'll call you if we need anything. Seshet, can you get everything set up so we can get these stitches out?" He waited for them to leave.

"We should have this conversation in private," he said to Grace.

"About you coming to someone else's planet and immediately planning how to annihilate them? What the fuck is wrong with all of you?"

"No, that's not what I meant," Ben defended.

"That's exactly what Seshet just said!" Grace spat bitterly.

"Look, we don't know who might come after us, and we don't know who they are going to bring on their side. We don't know who destroyed our world, but we need to find out. And we need to find a habitable world where we can go. The type of force that attacked us is a force this world would never survive." Ben paused before adding, "Our world didn't survive."

"How does that have anything to do with you making genocidal plans against a species that doesn't even know you exist?" Grace challenged. She had lost the rage after his explanation, but not the resentment.

"These forces had an army of species we knew nothing about. We can't exclude the possibility of any species being associated with them. We have some fighters they had with them captive here, so we can study them, interrogate them, learn how to destroy them."

"Vampires have nothing to do with that. They weren't involved with destroying your planet because they can't get off this one. And do you really think bringing captives to a vulnerable world is a good idea? What if they can be tracked back here?"

"This facility has blockers. They can't be traced here," Ben said.

"We don't need you bringing your war here," Grace scolded.

"We prefer not to bring any war anywhere, but if they find us before we can find somewhere else to go, we need to do what we can to prepare."

"By killing innocent people that have nothing to do with you?"

"I just said we don't want to kill them. We are only trying to assess the strengths and vulnerabilities of every species on this planet. I'm trying to keep our people safe," Ben defended.

"By looking for ways to kill everyone else?"

Ben shook his head. No matter what he said about it now, he would never win on the subject. "We're not going to agree on tactics. The only other thing I want to say is with whatever might come for us, if the amulet does nothing other than protect you, I'm not taking it off you."

"I think that should be my decision." Grace didn't want to take it off right now, and she didn't like being told she couldn't.

"Good thing it isn't your decision, then." Ben would not budge on this one. "It's not only about protecting you."

"Meaning what, exactly?"

"If there's something out there that has a way of finding us, not being able to see someone with your abilities may be an advantage we can't pass up."

"What makes you think I would put myself on the line to protect your people? I don't even know you! It is not my responsibility. You've obviously done something heinous enough to make someone destroy your entire world, and I refuse to be dragged into it!" Her voice was angry, but not loud enough for the others to hear.

"That's not fair, Grace. I'm just trying to protect what's left of our people."

"Then you should want to take this from me! Reproduce it and protect whoever you want. But you're delusional if you think I'd go to war for people I know nothing about." Grace pulled the amulet forward.

He looked at the amulet she had shoved into his face. "Knowing my mother, it probably can't be reproduced. A blood bond wouldn't work for mass production." Ben ignored the rest of her statement and turned his eyes to the table. Her declaration had hurt him, even though he knew it couldn't be true. He knew that if they were attacked, she would come forward. That was who she was. *She doesn't know the people she saves on her little missions, but she does it anyway because it's the right thing to do.*

"You already have blockers. If they could figure out the cloaking technology, I'm sure they can figure out another way to seal it so your enemies can't remove and use it. What about a device that goes under the skin?" Grace suggested. She didn't like that she was starting to empathize with his predicament after he had offended her so effectively.

He snapped his head around to meet her eyes. "That's a pretty good idea, actually. Huh, maybe a device that can be bonded inside a person's body."

At that moment, Seshet stood up and waved them to the other side of the room. "We're ready to remove the sutures."

Ben got to his feet before Grace handed him the crutches.

"Let's get this over with," Grace said, loud enough for everyone to hear. There was no reason for the others to know about their argument. She lowered her voice as they approached Seshet. "I'm serious, though. You have no right to expect me to fight for you."

Ben clenched his jaw. He understood he didn't have the right to ask her, but he still expected she would come.

Dian had set her station up inside a makeshift sensor field. "We're going to do the front first, then you'll turn on your stomach and we can do the back of your leg. Hop up on the bench."

The bench looked more like one of those anti-gravity loungers with the footrest separated from the seat area but still attached with a space in between. Only this one could also lie flat.

"We're going to start by cutting the tops of the stitches so we can apply surgical glue. After the glue dries, we'll focus on getting the stitches out. Grace, we won't need you for this part yet. You can have a seat on the chair to his left and then we'll switch sides when he turns over. Does that work for everyone?"

"Yes," Grace acknowledged.

"Fine," answered Ben.

Grace had already decided she needed to learn to hold phase longer. She also was interested in seeing how strong she could become at phasing others with her, so this was an opportunity for her to practice with little risk. Dian cut the first fifteen stitches, applied the glue, then used a small handheld UV light to dry it. She repeated the procedure with the remaining fifteen stitches on the front of Ben's thigh.

"Okay, Grace, you're on."

Grace took Ben's hand and phased him enough that Dian could pull the stitches straight up through his skin and the glue.

"Wish I could bottle some of that. This is the easiest stitch removal I've ever done. No tugging, tearing, or bleeding." She examined one stitch. "Actually, there's no blood at all. Interesting," she said to herself.

"It's even better when you're removing a fishing hook."

Ben and Dian chuckled. Grace shrugged, still trying to shake off the earlier interaction. "Well, it is."

A few of the staff had difficulty hiding their amusement at the remark.

"That side's done. Turn over." While Ben complied with Dian's orders, she and Grace changed sides.

"Grace, I have a question for you. During the process of phasing Ben, do you only reduce the density of his skin or does the density of his entire body get reduced?"

"For the front side, I fully phased only the skin on his right thigh. When I concentrate, I can be very specific. I didn't know how much you needed yesterday, so I partially phased his whole body so the stitches would stay in place, which is probably why it drained me so quickly."

"Can you do his entire body for a few seconds before you isolate the area? We would like to see if it makes any difference on the scan."

"Sure, no problem. I can only do it partially, though, or he'll fall through the table."

Seshet added, "Can you hold for about thirty seconds? We want to make sure we have usable material."

"Sure."

"Do you mind moving this along a little faster?" Ben asked. "This is not the most comfortable position to be in, you know."

"Uncomfortable for you, is it? Ooh, we can't have that, now can we?" Grace replied sarcastically.

"Maybe I was a little hasty. Go on, take all the time you need," Ben matched her tone, giving her a side-eye over his shoulder.

Dian finished drying the last of the glue and was ready to remove the stitches on the back of his thigh. "I'm ready, Grace."

Grace reached across and lifted Ben's shirt to place her left hand on the middle of his back. "I'm making his skin porous over his entire body." Grace picked up a metal probe as she spoke, sliding it about a half inch into Ben's lower back.

Dian pulled a few stitches, which slid out of the holes they were sewn into. "Why isn't he bleeding like he did when the sword went through his leg?"

"The sword was in phase when I put it in his leg and I made it solid before I pulled it out, ripping the skin and muscle with it. When I'm holding his body in phase, it allows anything to pass through," Grace explained.

"Oh, I get it. It's like water and ice, right? Same compound in different states, liquid versus solid. You're speeding up and slowing down the molecules without breaking the component."

"Almost. There are three states: gas, liquid, and solid. The natural state is solid. This is like the liquid state, but not as messy."

"Interesting. And you can perform this on an entire object or only part of it?"

"I disapprove of being referred to as an object," Ben interjected.

Grace rolled her eyes, ignoring him. "Next, I am localizing the phase to his thigh." Grace showed the probe no longer broke through the skin on Ben's back, but Dian could still extract stitches in the same manner she had before.

"Last, I'll make the skin on Ben's thigh fully permeable, or in our analogy, the gaseous state."

Now Dian could pull the clipped stitches straight upward through the skin and glue as she had with the front of Ben's leg. Grace held this phase for only a few minutes until all the stitches were out. The removal had been a much shorter, calmer process that hadn't drained Grace at all. Dian finished up by wrapping his leg in clean gauze. Grace removed her hand so Ben could sit up.

"Ready to feel your battle wounds so you can heal without hurting yourself?" Grace wanted his permission to return his pain. Although she had no obligation to get his consent, she believed it was the right thing to do for her own morals.

"Whenever you are."

Grace locked eyes with him, reached out, and touched his shoulder. His eyes grew a little wider. He put his hand over hers and squeezed it gently before she pulled away. Inhaling deeply, he paused. She could see it hurt. Hell, she knew it hurt. She felt it herself for an entire day.

"You all right?" she asked.

He exhaled fast, with intention. "Yeah, I'm okay."

"Up for some lunch? I'm starving." The procedure hadn't made her tired, but it expended a lot of her resources.

"I could eat."

"Crutches?" she offered.

"Let's take the wheelchair for a spin."

"Wuss," Grace said, smirking at him.

The attendant brought over a wheelchair and helped him in. Grace let the attendant push Ben's chair to the dining hall on level two. She was not about to be the one to bash his leg into anything. Accelerated healing was a characteristic of their people. He'd be up on crutches by evening and probably ready to work it out within a day.

Ben was the center of attention in the dining hall. Everyone had to lay eyes on him to believe that he was injured. They also wanted to lay eyes on the person who hurt him, which made Grace uncomfortable since some clearly knew her from before. She didn't recognize any of them and felt she made them more uncomfortable than they made her. She was never more interested in leaving a place, as she was in getting out of there as soon as lunch was over.

"I could use another coffee," Grace said.

"I could use a shower."

"I'd have to agree."

The attendant piped up, "We took a shower seat down to your apartment, crutches as well. The glue is set, so you can shower when you're ready."

"Thank you. You can leave us at the apartment."

"I'm not helping you in the shower." Grace looked at him with mild displeasure, at which he laughed.

"Don't worry, I'll be fine with the crutches if you can at least get me to my room."

When they got to the apartment, he couldn't reach the pad to open the door. He told Grace to put her palm against the sensor. She did, and it opened. She looked down at him suspiciously.

"You want to come and go as you please, don't you?" His answer was satisfactory, although she would prefer her own apartment if she came back. She thanked the attendant and wheeled the chair into the entry. The crutches were waiting against the wall inside the door. Grace handed them to Ben, then helped him to his feet.

"Have you ever used crutches before?"

"Just this morning."

"With pain?" Grace added.

"Nope. Have you?"

"Nope. I'll walk behind you in case you get a little off-balance. At least to your bedroom door. I know you won't be putting any weight on your leg when *you're* the one who can feel it."

He was a little off-balance, although less than she expected. At his door, he slipped against the frame while turning the handle.

"Come on. I can at least get you to the bathroom door."

"I'm not so sure that's a good idea." He looked embarrassed.

"There is nothing in here you could have that would surprise me—exotic porn, a bondage dungeon, bunnies, or kittens. How bad could it be?"

Before he could say anything else, she pushed the door open. It was much worse than she expected. The room was enormous. The bed was oversized, even for a king. Everything was extremely ornate, gold, and silk, in hues of reds, oranges, and yellows. There were beautiful tapestries on the walls. The entire back wall was a digital screen filled with a gorgeous view of mountains and a huge red sun in the distance. It was fit for a gilded palace.

"It's a reproduction of our bedroom back home." His face was nearly scarlet. He was only going to let her see this when she started regaining her memories. "I wanted you to have a piece of home if you got your memories back."

"I think that is very considerate of you. I have one question, if you don't mind?" She swallowed hard as her eyes scanned the room.

"I don't mind. Go ahead."

She looked at him as if she had a piece of live tentacle squirming in her mouth. "Do you like it?"

He looked at her with an expression of relief. "I'd rather be back in Helheim."

They laughed hard enough that Ben lost his balance and needed to brace himself against Grace's shoulder.

"This is horrible. Did I pick this stuff out?" she asked, appalled that this may have been her taste at any point in time.

"Actually, I think someone already decorated it when we moved in."

"And we never thought about changing it?"

"I never thought about it at all. I think you didn't want to offend my mother. The entire palace was decorated in this style."

"This is hideous. You should change it to something you like."

"I've never thought about how I would decorate anything."

"What about the rest of the apartment? It's pretty modern, sleek; it seems more you."

"The Three did that for me."

"Do you like it?"

"It suits me. Yeah, I guess I do like it."

"Then you should redo this room in that kind of style."

Ben hobbled over and sat on the edge of the bed. "I'd start with getting rid of this monstrosity."

"Whatever you want. It's a fresh start."

"Are you only saying that because you have no intention of coming back?" He let loose the real elephant in the room.

She knew he was asking if she was coming back to him and not the facility in general.

"Probably not. Even if I got my memories back, things between us would never be the same."

"Are you with someone?"

"I can't even imagine how hard this has to be for you," she replied, avoiding the question.

"Grace, I realize this has been overwhelming. I just want you to be honest about what my chances are. Are you with anyone now?"

"Yes." This was very difficult for her. Lukkas saved her and she loved him for that. She also felt a very strong draw to Ben. Was it something like muscle memory, or was it a real connection? She didn't know. Time was what she needed to deal with all of this, a lot of time. She couldn't wait to get out of here and think.

"You didn't mention if we had a chance or not. You know I can wait for you, Grace. I have time. I just need you to tell me if I should."

She couldn't look at him. She didn't want to see the disappointment on his face, so she looked up at the ceiling. He already knew. He had guessed earlier, but this confirmed it for him.

"He's an immortal," she mumbled.

"He's a vampire, isn't he? That's how you got the venom and blood. It's also why you got so angry in the lab, isn't it? How long have you been together?"

She looked at him, then down at the floor. "I have been with him on and off for just over seven hundred years."

"Off and on? So, you're not mated to him?"

"He wants to turn me for us to be mated. I never wanted to turn."

"But you let him inject his venom and you drink his blood as a backup plan. If you get killed on one of your missions, you'll turn and take the option?" He sounded angry and disappointed.

Grace raised her voice a bit. Not yelling, but louder. She was angry that he would question her about finding something to hold on to.

"You're damn right I did. I had *no one*. I had been here completely alone for *a thousand* years, not having any idea where I came from or who I was. He was the only constant I have ever had. I was broken before I met him. I had lost everyone I had ever cared about, and it kept happening over and over again. What did you expect I would do? While away my days grieving for a life I didn't know I had lost? Spending my time looking for mortals I could be with for a few years before they die on me again and again? I would have been miserable and probably insane. What kind of life were you hoping I would have here?"

Ben looked at the floor. He didn't want her to see he was close to tears. "I didn't want to think about it, I guess. I have never wanted you to be unhappy, Grace. It would just be easier if you could remember you had a better life with me."

"But I can't." She had a hard time seeing him sitting there, looking devastated. She could feel his sadness. "I can only see who you are now. I see you're a decent man. Knowing you better is something I would consider, but I can't offer any hope of us being together. I'm sorry Ben, I'm with someone else."

Grace left the room, crossing the apartment to the room she slept in the first night. It seemed ages ago. It was only two in the afternoon, but she was so emotionally tired. Her head was throbbing. It was too much, and she couldn't take any more. Her mind needed to shut down. She took off her jeans and boots and climbed into bed.

"Ida, please make sure I am up by midnight. I need transport back to Helena at 2 a.m."

"I set your alert for midnight. Transportation will meet you outside the elevator doors on the garage level at 2 a.m. Is there anything else I can help you with, Grace?"

"Please turn out the lights."

CHAPTER SIX

It seemed as if she had shut her eyes for only a few seconds before Ida was telling her to wake up. She couldn't believe it was midnight already. The clothes she wore when she arrived had been washed, folded, and placed on top of the tall dresser in her room. She lay in bed staring up at the ceiling for what must have been an hour. When she was ready, she changed without showering, anxious to get out of this place as quickly as possible. Ben was sitting on the sofa reading with his leg propped up when she opened the bedroom door.

"There's already a pot of coffee made. I put a take-away cup on the counter for you."

"Thank you. You're not coming?" Grace didn't want him to accompany her. However, she wanted to make sure he hadn't intended to do it.

Ben hadn't slept at all. He thought a lot about what she said to him, and he wasn't upset anymore. He knew the loneliness must have been horrible for her. He didn't know how he would live without her by his side even after so long apart. Knowing she was safe was the only thing that kept him sane during his time in Hel. He had only now realized that her time here alone was her hell. He should be grateful she had found someone to get her through it, even if it meant she would never be with him again. At least she was alive.

"Not sure I'd do well with the trip," he said, rubbing his leg and avoiding eye contact. "Be safe. Let one of us know when you get home."

Even though he was making a show of rubbing his leg, she didn't know if he meant because of his leg or because of her. She wasn't sure she wanted to know at the moment.

"I will."

Grace walked toward the sofa from behind. That's when she saw it. Just the bottom few inches of his forearm above the wrist. He had been wearing long-sleeved T-shirts the entire time she had been there. They both had several tattoos. She had seen the ones on his back and legs, but this one gave her a knot in her stomach. She walked around in front of him, inducing him to look up at her. Her eyes were enormous, focused. She dropped to her knees, reached down, and pulled up his left sleeve. It was a phoenix rising out of flames. How did he have this? It looked older than hers. The flames looked burned in. But they couldn't be.

She only got hers a few hundred years ago. She didn't remember exactly when or even why, only that the design had drawn her in. Hers didn't have the flames but otherwise it was the same. Neither of them knew what to say. He had seen hers and thought it too strange to explain, so he kept his covered while she was there. He thought she had enough strange in her life already.

"I didn't want you to see that. I couldn't explain it," he said as she ran her fingers over the scarred flames on his wrist. She felt a long pull from her gut and immediately let go of his arm.

"What are those from?" Grace asked awkwardly.

"Those were a gift from Hel. Part of the deal with Hel. She couldn't do anything to harm my essence. I woke branded with flames, and of course, Hel denied having anything to do with it. While I was there, they were made from actual fire. I had the tattoo added soon after as a show of disobedience to her. She would ignite my flames at random, inappropriate times." Ben actually chuckled in a bittersweet way at this memory.

"I don't understand. If you didn't have a body, how could she have done that to you and how could you have gotten a tattoo?"

"Everyone taken to the halls of the fallen—Valhalla, Fólkvangr, or Hel— receives a new body to prepare for Ragnarök," he answered.

"What made you pick it? The phoenix, I mean." Grace didn't know why she asked that question. She didn't want the answer. She didn't want to be having this conversation at all. The last thing Grace was looking for was another gut punch of familiarity, yet here it was. A powerful urge bubbled up from the depths of her mind.

"I was dead, in Hel, had literal flames on my skin, and was awaiting rebirth back into the living world. It was a pretty simple choice," he answered.

She ran her fingers over the flames one last time. Her stomach flipped again. She couldn't stop looking at his arm. She pulled her hand away almost too quickly and stood back up.

"I have to go, Ben. I can't be late." She stumbled to her feet, bumping the table and nearly knocking his leg off.

He winced as he watched her pick up her cup and race out the door. Emptiness came over him like a cloak as he wondered if that would be the last of her he would ever see.

Grace felt like she was going to throw up any second. She took several deep breaths and rushed to the elevator. She stood in front of the doors for a short time, wanting to regain her self-control before she headed up to the garage level. Her eyes rose to the sound of the lift chiming its arrival and she stepped inside, uncertain whether this would be the last time she would be in this place. The doors to the elevator opened to the empty garage. Grace stepped out into the still darkness, her footsteps echoing against the smooth stone. Headlights approached from her left, blinding her as they got closer. The van stopped a few feet in front of her. She was expecting to be guided into the back again to leave. Instead, the passenger door swung open. When the light came on in the cab, she saw Alex was her driver.

"Where to, lady?" he asked, winking at her.

She smiled back at him. "There is a twenty-four-hour gym off the fifteen freeway," she answered, climbing into the passenger seat.

"That's your exit point?"

"Not as much of an exit point as it is a starting point. My credentials and schedule are in a locker. After I pick those up, I head to my exit point."

"Nothing around here is twenty-four hours. How are you planning on getting in if it's closed?"

"Oh Alex, did you forget who I am? I'm going through the side wall. I'll reach through the locker door and pull out my stuff. No one will ever know I was there."

"I can't even comprehend what it must be like to be in your brain," he said, shaking his head.

"Lucky you, Alex. I've been doing this for a very long time. I'm good at disappearing."

"Let's get you disappeared then," he replied as he drove out the sliding door. On the other side, once it was closed, it appeared to be a seamless rock face. Something mechanical slid out of the base of the rock, combing away the tire tracks, then vanished back into its hidden spot.

As they drove, Alex asked Grace the question she knew was coming. He had already hinted at hearing part of her conversation.

"Mother, who is Lukkas?"

"He's an immortal I'm with. Your father already knows about him. He does *not* know his name and I would appreciate it if you didn't tell him. I want to talk to Lukkas first. It has to be his choice if he wants to be known to all of you."

"When you say immortal, you mean vampire, right?"

"Yes, I mean vampire." Grace looked at Alex and rolled her eyes.

"I'm glad you haven't been alone here. I was always concerned that they sent you away alone." Alex sounded remorseful.

"I am a little surprised you support me being with someone else."

"I can't say it's not awkward. I've never seen you with anyone else. It's strange, but I do understand. It's not like I'm a child. I'm over two hundred thousand years old. I recognize the need to be connected to someone. Naturally, you'd seek an immortal. I get it."

"Well, thank you. I appreciate your position. You should probably not bring any of it up to your father. He's not taking it very well." Grace was sad about the way it came out with him.

"I didn't imagine he would, although he really has no right to tell you how to live your life."

"What's that supposed to mean?" Grace turned her face toward Alex and cut her eyes up to look at the side of his head. He didn't turn to meet her gaze.

"Well, I … um. I just mean no one has the right to tell anyone else how to live. Don't you agree?"

"I suppose," she answered, certain he was holding back yet another thing she likely didn't want to know.

They drove for fifteen more minutes while Alex answered some questions she didn't want to ask Ben. As they passed the front of the gym, she saw a sign on the door. The gym was closed. Opening crew wouldn't be in for two more hours. She laughed to herself. At least she didn't need to worry about anyone being in the locker room.

"Here's your stop. You need anything else, or are you good?"

"Just a hug, if you don't mind?" she asked hesitantly.

"Mind? I've been waiting for one forever," he said, reaching across the seat.

She leaned over, meeting him in the middle. "I'll reach out when I get home. It'll be twelve to fourteen hours from now. Tell your brothers I'll keep in touch. I should be back in three to four weeks under a less covert travel situation."

"If that feels right," Alex said, releasing her. "Let one of us know if you need more time. See you when you get back," he answered, unsure if she would ever come back.

Grace got out and waited on the sidewalk a few minutes for the van to pull away. There were no street cameras on this side of the building. She looked down the length of the wall and found her mark. Violet always used a tiny dot of violet nail polish as her marker. Grace leaned against the wall, making sure no one was watching on the street, then slipped backward through it. The locker had the same small violet mark on it. Grace reached in and pulled out the small satchel. Everything was there: IDs, a passport, air crew credentials, and a lot more cash than she would need to get home. She still had almost all her cash left from the trip here. She stuffed everything back in the bag except for the phone, which she placed in her jacket pocket. After slipping back through the wall, she started walking, looked around again, and phased out so she could move faster.

Five minutes later, she was behind an abandoned furniture store near the last bus stop outside the airport. Right on schedule, the next pickup was in fifteen minutes. She put her crew lanyard around her neck as she walked over to the group of people waiting at the bus stop. She stood at the back of the group, noticing most of them worked at the airport. A few others looked like travelers. Nobody talked outside of their small groups. Maintenance grouped together, security was on the other side, and the airline staff was in another group. It was easy to tell what each group did based on their tag colors. Grace's tag was plain white, which was basically no access outside of the crew areas. The digital barcode gave specific information on where they were from, headed, and allowed to go.

When the bus pulled up, Grace stepped forward to be in the middle of the pack, not wanting to appear out of place. She kept her head down, making herself insignificant. Holding her coffee cup in the crook of her arm and her bag in her left hand, she dug out the correct change before taking a seat near the middle of the bus. She leaned against the window, scanning the reflection to see if anyone was watching her. Nothing suspicious here.

The bus made several stops at the airport, long-term parking, short-term parking, two at the front drop-off points for airlines, then finally three stops at different crew terminals. Grace's was the last stop at the air freight crew gate. Three others got off at the stop with her. Each held up their badges to be scanned. The guard had them wait for the tram so they could be dropped at their specific hangars. One of the other crew members tried to start a conversation with Grace. She replied in French, pretending she understood little English, forcing the men to talk among themselves until the tram pulled up.

Once she arrived at the second hangar, she headed toward the light over the open door. Jack and one of his brothers were unbuttoning the plane, readying it for departure in an hour. They had customs services at this airport, but Josh preferred to make the extra stop at Sea-Tac instead of going directly back home, even if it wasn't the weekly scheduled route. She always wondered about his connection with the place, but it wasn't her business to ask. Hopefully, if she returned later, she could take one of the vineyard's private jets instead. She'd have to see how her new information was going to go over with the family first. Grace was in her own head and almost didn't notice Josh standing in the doorway right in front of her.

"Hey, Pops! I am so happy to see your face!"

He wrapped his warm arm around her shoulders, pulling her inside. "Glad to see you in one piece. How was the trip?"

"I don't even know how to answer that. What's for breakfast? I'm starving."

Josh was familiar with Grace speak for 'I don't want to talk right now.'

"Dehydrated eggs or frozen waffles?"

She scrunched up her nose in displeasure at the suggestion of powdered eggs.

"Frozen waffles it is," Josh chuckled.

The flight back was uneventful. Grace couldn't sleep at Sea-Tac like she had on the way in. She stared at the wall, lost in her own little world. The last three days were breaking into her reality, hard. She contacted Lukkas to let him know she was coming home. Otherwise, she was unusually quiet for the remainder of the flight. She had so much to tell Lukkas and some things she didn't want to tell him that she still had to let him know. She was right about one thing when she started this trip. Her life would never be the same.

CHAPTER SEVEN

Grace could see Lukkas sitting on the hood of the SUV as Josh's truck pulled into the gas station. She let out a deep breath she hadn't realized she had been holding. The tension visibly escaped, allowing her body to slump lower in the passenger seat. He was a sight for sore eyes. He was her light after such a huge amount of dark and twisted over the last few days. She just wanted him to hold her. Sinking into the familiarity of her own bed was also something she was looking forward to. After this insane excursion, all she wanted was a fraction of normalcy.

Lukkas watched Grace get out of Josh's truck slowly. He anxiously slid off the hood of the SUV, wiping his sweaty palms on his pants. She looked defeated, tired. His posture was stiff as he anticipated her approach. Their short communication about an accident continued to disturb him. She grabbed him immediately, hugging him so hard she nearly knocked him over. He felt her body release all its anxiety as he wrapped his arms around her. She buried her face in his chest, taking in the comforting sandalwood scent that had become so familiar. Lukkas and Josh looked at each other uneasily. Josh shrugged. Grace hadn't told him anything. Their conversation from the time they met in the hangar's doorway until now was nonexistent. Josh was sure whatever it was couldn't be good.

Finally, Grace loosened her grip a little to look up at him. "I wanna go home, Lukkas. Take me home."

Lukkas kissed her on the cheek and guided her to the passenger side of the Land Rover. He opened the door, letting Grace climb in. He waved to Josh, and both men got into their respective vehicles and drove away. Grace reached over to take Lukkas's hand, sitting in silence the entire two hours home. She wouldn't let go of his hand. She couldn't let go. In this beautiful, tranquil setting, everything she had just experienced seemed surreal. Was it all some mad dream? This wouldn't be the first time Grace had wondered if she had lost her mind. Where could she even begin telling anyone what happened?

"We're home, Grace." Nothing. "Grace, we're home," Lukkas repeated, nudging her side.

"Good," she mumbled, unbuckling her seatbelt. He started to open the driver's side door when she placed her hand on his arm. "Lukkas, I want to tell you what happened, but there's just so much, I don't know where or how to start."

"Can I ask you something?" Lukkas asked in a cautious tone.

"Anything."

"Are you staying?"

"Yes, I'm staying." She turned to look at him. "This is my home. That has not and will never change."

He kissed her on the forehead. "I love you too," he said, smiling at her as if she had said it first.

She returned a smile, although hers looked sad. "I need a shower," she said, pulling her collar away from her. Her clothes reeked of the sanitized nothingness of that place, and she wanted them off.

They got out of the truck and were halfway up the front stairs as the entry door was flung open. The whole family was there, minus Violet, of course. Asta was out first, followed by her mother, Vivienne, then Galin, Mrs. B., and Vito trailing behind. Asta had Grace by two inches, yet she somehow managed to wrap her entire body around Grace like a toddler.

"You're back! We were so worried," Asta proclaimed, hugging her tightly.

Vivienne pried Asta off Grace. "Don't say that to her!"

"We were concerned," Vivienne said, greeting her in the Italian way, grabbing her face with both hands, then kissing her on each cheek. She looped her arm around Grace's, leading her into the house. "You must be starving."

It was mid-afternoon and the last thing she ate was almost twelve hours ago. "I am hungry, Viv, but I desperately need a shower first and a drink wouldn't hurt."

"Excellent. Go get cleaned up and we will see you back down here at three for a late lunch. Lukkas! Open Grace a bottle of the Pinot Noir. Go on, everybody move!" Vivienne was undoubtedly the one in charge of the family. Galin may have wanted everyone to think he was, but even he knew better.

Grace went upstairs while the others scattered. Galin followed Lukkas to the wine bar in the hall. "Is she okay? She doesn't look okay."

"I think she is. She hasn't said anything other than she's not leaving. She said she learned a lot and didn't know where to start."

"I'll tell Asta and Vivienne not to grill her over lunch. We have to let her tell us in her own way. Pushing never helps." Galin had been married long enough to have gleaned at least that amount of wisdom.

"Thanks. See you at lunch." Lukkas headed upstairs with an open bottle and two glasses.

Lukkas walked into their room. He had moved into Grace's room as a surprise for her while she was gone, although he was sure she hadn't noticed yet. He could hear the large shower in the corner of the bathroom running. Grace didn't notice him when he walked through the open door. The showerhead was on the far wall with a tile wall on the right, glass on the left, and open on the closest end to him. In front of the open area was a tile bench, and the center of the shower had a trough-style drain that ran the width perpendicular to the glass wall.

Grace had her back to him, leaning on her hand, letting the steaming hot water run over her hair and face. He took off his shoes, rolled up his pant legs, and sat on the bench, pouring two glasses of wine, placing one on the seat, and sipping the other.

He quietly watched her. Her dark hair extended down the middle of her back between her shoulder blades. She was average height, with smooth olive skin. She had muscular thighs and curved hips. Her waist was average and her body firm with the long musculature of a runner. She was fit, not too thin. He didn't like women too thin. It wasn't healthy. She had several beautifully done tattoos. Her body was a work of art and he enjoyed watching her. He thought back to the first time he saw her.

The year was 1324, and Lukkas had been traveling with his brother through northwestern Denmark, near Ribe, where he was born. They had been separated while making their way back to their village. A group of religious fanatics attacked him, but not because he was a vampire; they hadn't realized that yet. They attacked him because he was a pagan. The sheer number of attackers overpowered him, and although he killed most of them, he sustained severe injuries in the exchange. It had been some time since he had fed, so he wasn't healing as quickly as he should have been.

The men, upon realizing he wasn't altogether human, staked him between two trees and tortured him. They had broken many of his bones, shot arrows through his torso, and started peeling his flesh away from his body. He was losing so much blood that he would die of exsanguination before long. There were only six or seven men left alive of the mob that had attacked him. He felt he had done well and had no problem meeting his end in that manner. He was slipping in and out of consciousness. Each time he awoke, the men resumed their torture. He chuckled at the thought that he was supposed to be the monster, which earned him a boot to the face, rendering him unconscious again.

The last time, he awoke to the remaining men writhing on the ground with their bodies contorted, screaming in pain. He heard something moving behind him. What could be coming now? Had his brother found him? Then *she* walked into his view.

She reached forward, grasped a handful of hair, and pulled up Lukkas's head to make sure he was still alive. She could barely discern his blood-covered, beaten face as one belonging to a man. Through the red haze of blood, he noted she was average, not remarkably beautiful except for her eyes. Large deep-green eyes stared steadily into his swollen ones. Long dark hair framed her oval face. She had a look that he had never seen before. He felt strangely drawn to her, with no explanation as to why. She lifted her free hand slightly from her side when the men's screams suddenly stopped.

"Do you wish to be saved?" she asked in a voice barely above a whisper, without breaking eye contact. He didn't reply. He didn't understand why a human would want to save him.

"I know what you are, and I know how to save you. I need your acceptance of my terms," the stranger demanded, tightening the grip of her fingers in his wet, sticky hair.

"What do you mean, terms? Who sent you?" His words were barely above a whisper from weakness. He was confused. Once she leaned forward, he didn't understand her scent. It wasn't completely human, but it wasn't animal either. It was something he had never smelled before.

"I will take away your pain and I will let you drink from me," she said calmly.

"And what do you want from me in return?" It was difficult for him to speak as he choked on the blood pooled in his throat.

"You cannot kill me, you cannot turn me, you will be my savior."

"Doesn't look like you need my salvation. Who sent you?" He was still confused.

"I don't know. I was told to come here and save the wronged man." Her voice was soothing, but he had more questions.

"You don't have time," she answered, a question he hadn't yet asked.

He felt a need to consent no matter what the cost. If this was a deal with the devil, he would make it. He wanted to live.

"I accept."

She pulled back her hair from her neck, moving her body against his. "Feed from me."

He hesitated only long enough to take in her scent more deeply. He drank and she, in turn, drank from an open wound on his shoulder in a way he could only describe as completing a circuit. As they drank from each other, he began to feel her. He could simultaneously feel himself drinking from her and feel what she was feeling, as he pulled her warm blood into him. His pain diminished, and he began healing more quickly than usual. She was speeding up his healing faster than ever before. His blood was in turn replenishing her, allowing her blood to regenerate as quickly as he could drain it. If she were human, she would have been long dead from the amount he had taken from her.

"Stop," she commanded.

He pulled back, licking the remaining blood from her neck. His wounds were closing as she watched. She began cutting him from the tethers, laying him on the ground so she could reset his bones. He felt her touching his skin, but he felt no pain from the broken bones. Their connection allowed him to sense that she was the one who felt it. His skin was healing quickly. His bones would take longer.

She sat on the ground next to him, needing a few minutes to recover. His pain was excruciating, making her shake. She was panting. She had never taken in that much from one being before. His species was strong, though not as strong as she was. His life was limitless, without time. He was the closest she had ever seen to what she was, yet different.

The pain had begun to dissipate. She tried to stand when he reached out and stopped her, pulling her down against his chest, whispering "Thank you" into her ear. "I've never needed saving before."

She ignored his comment, pushing herself away from his grip. "We need to move. Can you sit?"

She sat up, facing him. He pushed himself off the ground and saw her eyes roll back. He understood it was causing her suffering as she said, *Stop.* She couldn't have said it. Her mouth was closed. *It's not your imagination. I can hear you and you can hear me. It's a bond of blood that will survive for eternity.*

He looked into her eyes. Thinking the words, he asked her, *What do you mean, 'eternity'?*

She smiled, then spoke. "I'll tell you as we walk. We must start moving before they wake up. I didn't kill them; I only gave them enough of my pain to make them sleep. Then I gave them some of yours because they deserved it."

She pulled her bag over to Lukkas, taking out clothes for him to change into. "You can't be covered in blood. Change quickly." She stood, turning her back to him.

He wasn't astonished she had clothes that would fit him. It felt like it should happen that way. He changed, took a sword from the ground, and the pair began walking. He didn't know where they were going, only that it didn't matter.

"What is your name and what did you mean by eternity?"

"I have no name. I have been in this world for a thousand years as a servant to the gods. I do not know where I came from. I have always been and will always be. I was sent to you, and we are bonded from now beyond death. Eternity."

"No one has ever given you a name. What are you called?"

"Most commonly I am referred to as The Bearer of Pain. When addressed, it is Bearer, Queen, or Mother."

"You can't go through life without a name," he said, taking a moment to think. "You are my saving grace, so that is what I'll name you."

"Grace," she whispered. The name was easy in her mouth. "I like it."

~~~~
~~~~

"Where are you?" Grace was standing in front of him in a towel. "Lukkas?"

"Sorry." He handed her a glass of wine. "I remembered the first time we met when I gave you your name. I don't know why I was thinking about that. I hadn't thought of it in forever," he said, rubbing the top of his head where her hand had clenched a fistful of hair so long ago.

She ran her fingers through his hair, pulling his hand down. "You saved me too, you know." Then she kissed him, sliding onto his lap. "I don't know what I would do without you. I was so lost and alone until I found you."

He hugged her firmly. "I love you. I even moved in with you without a ceremony." He smiled a huge shining smile and rubbed her thigh. She got up, taking a drink from her glass, mirroring his smile.

Lukkas was right. She hadn't noticed.

"You know it's better this way. We're both already immortal, plus look at everything we would lose. If we had a turning ceremony, you could never feed from me again and I know you like that. We can still wear the rings if you want. I'd even go along with a binding if we weren't already bound for eternity."

"It's old-fashioned, I get it. It's just the way of our clan."

"You know as well as I do that the only purpose of a turning is for a human to be made immortal. That doesn't apply to our case. Besides, two vampires can never have a life as good as ours because we're symbiotic."

He sighed, knowing she wasn't ready to be turned. "I want the rings," he said, shaking his head at her. He had given in to her argument, for now, but he hadn't given up. He usually gave in eventually, if for no other reason than to stop the debate.

She jumped up and down like a giddy schoolgirl, kissed him on the mouth, then went to get the box. Within ten seconds, she was back, standing in front of him. The idea of rings didn't matter to her at all, but it was an enormous step for him, which thrilled her. She still wasn't sure he would ever fully accept her as she was. In this moment, after the days she had had, she didn't care. She needed this bond to cope with all the unbelievable things she had witnessed.

She opened the box, took out his ring, then handed hers to him. He took the box out of her hand and put it down on the sink. They had picked these out years ago: exquisite black bands with a ring of platinum around each center. She wanted more than anything to belong to someone. To have an equal partner.

He took her left hand, placing the band on her ring finger. "For eternity," he said with a grin. Then it was her turn to do the same.

She repeated, "For eternity." They shared a long, passionate kiss. She stretched up to whisper in his ear. "Seal it with blood."

He leaned in to drink from her, at the same time pulling out his pocketknife. He made a slight cut in his own neck, letting her take in his blood as well. Their wounds healed, and they kissed again.

He smacked her on the rear. "Now go get dressed, Mrs. Eliassen. If we're late, Viv will come up and drag us down."

"Yes sir, Mr. Eliassen." Grace went to her closet, an enormous grin indelibly plastered on her face, and threw on some black jeans, a black-and-white polka-dot blouse, and a pair of black ankle boots. "I need to dry my hair. Give me ten minutes."

He sat in a white club chair next to her vanity, sipping his wine and watching her. She was so happy it made him happy, too. He only wished he could have changed her mind about the ceremony. He always believed she would make an extraordinary vampire.

<div align="center">~~~~</div>

Lunch was a little uncomfortable. They were all watching Grace, expecting to hear about what had happened. She wanted to talk to Lukkas in private for most of it first. She decided to give them a little, enough to keep them at bay for a while.

"Lukkas must have told you not to ask me questions, and I appreciate not being interrogated on my first day back. I *am* going to tell you what is going on, just not right now. I can share a few details, then the rest of it I want to discuss with Lukkas first."

Everyone looked around the table.

Galin asked, "What can you tell us?"

"Let's start with three things and see how you guys wrap your heads around it. Fair?"

Everyone nodded.

"First thing is the amulet I can't remove. It's like a cloak that keeps anyone from locating me while I am wearing it. It has nothing to do with my memories or my abilities. The only thing it does is keep me hidden."

"Why can't you take it off?" Asta's question was a little more than Grace wanted to share, but she would try to provide a vague response.

"The one who placed it on me sealed it with blood. Only the blood that was originally used to seal it can remove it. The rest is complicated and starts an entirely different line of questions I don't want to answer right now."

"How in the world are you supposed to find blood from nearly two thousand years ago?" Galin asked.

"That's not something I really need to worry about. The second thing I wanted to tell you is that I'm technically much older than any of us expected."

This time, it was Lukkas who spoke. "What do you mean by 'technically,' and how old are you?"

"By technically, I mean the people I come from have bodies that aren't completely immortal, like yours are. They do age, only at an astronomically slow rate. What they do have is the technology to take the energy essence, or as we refer to it here, soul, and place it into a new shell created from the original body's genetic material."

Grace looked at each of them for acknowledgment of understanding mixed with disbelief before she proceeded.

"As far as my age, this is going to sound incredible, but I'm, in terms of Earth years, about five hundred thousand years old."

"Excuse me?" Lukkas had nearly choked on his wine. "What do you mean by 'Earth years'?"

The others began blurting out different questions simultaneously, with each attempting to be heard over the others.

Grace raised her voice to calm them without screaming. "You people are vampires, and you have a difficult time with the concept of life on other planets? This is the part you're going to have a hard time with?"

She searched their faces once again. Their eyes were enormous as they gave each other glances.

Grace continued. "I come from a world on the far side of the universe. My people have been coming here for eons, as well as deities from other planets. When I needed to be hidden, my memories were removed, and they sent me here."

They exchanged confused expressions between them before looking back at Grace. Vivienne took this moment to speak. "So, when you say *your* people are from another

world, how do you know that?"

"I know because the people who were looking for me are the people I came from. I have connections to them."

No one spoke for several minutes. It was a lot for anyone to think about.

Lukkas broke the silence. "What do they want from you?"

Grace shrugged. "I don't know. There was too much information and not enough time. They want me to come back when I have thought about everything. I'm not sure I want to know."

"You'll need to find out what they want from you. Now that they know you're here, I can't see them leaving you alone." Lukkas was rational, and he was also right.

"We still have a lot to discuss. I think I'd like to walk the grounds for a while. Lukkas, are you coming?"

"Yeah." He stood up and took her hand. She saw he had a lot more questions he didn't want to ask in front of the family.

They walked around the vineyard, ending up at the west tasting station. It was a small shelter with tables and chairs set up. Three sides were open. The far side had a bar and several wine refrigerators. They had painted it green, matching the leaves and summer grasses. Old vines grew up the six-by-six posts around the outer edges. Lukkas opened a bottle of spring Riesling, then they walked to a bench at the junction of a path that surrounded the retention pond. They had a breathtaking view of the hills to the west. If it was any other day, it would be enjoyable.

The sun was moving downward toward the horizon. Shortly, it would set, spreading golden, orange, and pink hues across the water. This time of year, the evenings grew cooler rather quickly. Grace slipped on the sweater she brought with her, pulled off her shoes, and took a seat on the bench. Lukkas sat beside her, handing her a glass of wine.

"Thank you." Grace smiled at Lukkas. "I know you have a lot of questions for me. Before we get started, I have something I want to say to you."

Lukkas was a little apprehensive. He wasn't sure where she was going with this. "Okay, what's on your mind?"

"I need you to understand that I am choosing you. You're not a consolation prize or someone I'm settling for. I love you and I am choosing to be with you. I will always choose you, even if I get my memories back."

"There's no way you can be sure of that," Lukkas said, shaking his head.

Lukkas's tendency to be obtuse was exasperating to her sometimes. He hadn't even noticed that was the first time she had told him she loved him. He said it often, yet she had never felt free enough to reply in kind.

"Yes, I can be absolutely sure of that. I learned something while I was with the others. The way I came here was a choice. When I came here, I could have stayed where I was and waited to be brought back with the others."

Lukkas seemed relieved. "What do you mean, brought back with the others? Don't get me wrong, I'm happy you want to be here with me. I love you more than I ever thought I could love anyone, and I love our life here. I just don't understand what you mean by you chose to come here."

"When I told you about how we can transfer our energy essence to a new shell, I also told you we can die. You were born a pagan Dane in a city of Christians. I know you've heard the myths of the Norse gods. They're not special or unique compared to others. They are simply another species from the other side of the universe."

Lukkas narrowed his eyes, and his forehead wrinkled. "Are you telling me that you come from gods? The same gods my people worshipped for thousands of years?"

"No, Lukkas. I already told you, they, we, are not gods. Some of the mythology is based in fact, while most of it is nothing more than human fantasy. When one of us dies, our society has set options about where our energy goes. If you are a warrior, Freya has first choice, Odin second, and the remainder of the essences are held by Hel in the underworld. Freya took my essence to her hall, Fólkvangr, which is the battlefield where warriors train awaiting Ragnarök, which is the final battle. Odin's hall is Valhalla, which is the one most people know. Hel's hall is Hel, with one 'L,' or Helheim, but it's just another holding place, not like the hell Christians understand."

Lukkas nodded. "I'm with you so far."

"Anyway, Freya claimed my essence. Frigg asked her to restore me to my body, but Freya said that she had taken me out of play. It was only right that I couldn't return until Ragnarök. She said the only way she would allow Frigg to restore me was if they sent me somewhere that I could remain out of everything. They gave me the option: stay in Fólkvangr for an unknown length of time *or* have all memory of my previous life removed and come here. I came here, and I chose to have my memories removed. I don't know why, but if that was my choice, I had a reason to want to change my life. So, I know I would not make the choice to return even if I remembered. Sending me here without my memories was a wise decision. I found a perspective that I don't feel I have ever understood before. I wanted to tell you that."

"I'm glad you told me. Now that you have found them, what do you want to do?"

"I don't know. I'm torn about it. Their world was destroyed. That's why they're here. Only one hundred and ten are here, including me. The rest are dead or scattered throughout unknown parts of the universe. I don't have any idea what they want from me. I don't think they even know what their options are at this point. From what I can tell, they are in recovery mode. They aren't even sure if there is still anyone hunting them, which is why they want to keep me hidden if they are being tracked. They said I could be a valuable resource if necessary. That's all the information I got about that." Their motives perplexed Grace and her face showed it.

"Wait, what do you mean they *want* to keep you hidden? I thought you didn't have a choice in removing the amulet because it is sealed with blood thousands of years old. If Frigg put it on you, does she have the means to take it off?" Lukkas was questioning if she was telling him everything.

"Frigg is dead, her essence is gone. She sealed the amulet with blood, but it wasn't her blood, it was her son's. He is the only one who can remove it and he refuses to. He was my husband before we both died. I didn't want to say it like that, but you need to know. I don't know him, so honestly, I don't feel any emotional attachment to him, and death ended the marriage. Even though we were both restored, the vows are broken." Grace was very matter-of-fact in her explanation.

It still made Lukkas jealous. He didn't want to show Grace any kind of negative reaction when she was being honest with him. Against his instinct, he introduced a little levity to the conversation.

"Tell me if I got this right. You are a Norse goddess, a warrior, a widow, and an alien? That's a lot of labels," he said, chuckling a little, hoping to lighten the mood.

Grace couldn't help but smile and close her eyes. "You're such an ass. How about we just stick with: I'm yours? The rest of that crap doesn't even matter." She was relieved he had reacted the way he had.

"Since you're taking that so well, I should probably tell you that those three young men, the triplets, are my sons."

"Alrighty then. Should I ask who their father is?"

"Ben Olsen is Balder, Frigg's son, and their father. And I referred to them as young men because of how old they look, but they're twenty times your age. Calling them 'the boys' isn't appropriate. They refer them to as The Three, or The Sons. Sort of surreal, isn't it?" She was still a little mind numbed by everything. She thought this was probably enough for him to deal with for the moment and wasn't opposed to continuing the conversation later.

Lukkas thought otherwise.

"How do you know they are really your sons and they're not just telling you that to manipulate you?"

Grace's back stiffened against his words. The thought that they were manipulating her was a fear, although her link to The Three was an absolute in her mind.

"The only explanation is that I have a bond with them. After talking to them, it's clear they are who they say. I can communicate with them the same as I can with you. All of that, plus they have my eye color, cemented it as a fact for me."

"That's a lot to take in. You seem to be doing all right with it, at least on the outside."

"The wine helps a lot," she laughed nervously. "Do you want to take a break and head back to the house or crack open another bottle and keep going?" Grace hadn't realized they had finished an entire bottle already. The sun had dipped below the mountaintops in the distance, setting the sky ablaze with color.

"That depends. How much more do you want to tell me?"

"All of it. I don't want to hide anything from you. It'll take a while longer if you're willing to listen."

Lukkas smiled. "Another bottle it is. I have nothing but time."

Lukkas walked back up to the tasting shed to grab another bottle. She couldn't help but think how lucky she was to have him. He was everything she could want in a partner: patient, loyal, loving, rational, and calm. He never overreacted and didn't smother her. She couldn't exactly say he didn't have a hot temper occasionally. He just never had one with her. She only hoped she was as good for him. Sometimes she wondered. Her emotions could overwhelm her at times, and at other times, she could be totally detached. The ability to cut herself off from feeling anything concerned her. Is that how she was before? She had been questioning herself a lot today. She, however, never questioned Lukkas. It also didn't hurt that he was pretty to look at.

Lukkas came back to resume his spot on the bench with a fresh, chilled bottle. "How about you tell me about the accident that had you so freaked out?"

"Oh, I'd forgotten I lost it a bit. It was a stressful day. I had just finished up with my scan to see how the amulet had been bound to me. It was a pretty slick scanner too; you stand up in it like a spray-tan booth. The sensors move down in a circle around you from the ceiling. They read everything from basic vitals to specific genetic anomalies. The capabilities are amazing. They found your venom and blood mixed with mine, too. Oh, and by the way, do you know how the combination works to turn someone?"

"Not specifically. I understand the mechanics of it. I have a feeling you're going to tell me anyway, aren't you?" He understood what to do and wasn't engrossed in the rest.

"Not if you're not interested. I'll tell Asta, she loves all the scientific stuff."

"Okay, so you had finished getting scanned. What came next?"

"They had to wait for some results, so I was going to get a tour of the facility. Ben asked me if I wanted lunch or to see the training room. Of course, being me, I picked the training room. It was a top-notch facility too, surpassed my expectations. The back wall next to the sparring rings had weapons I hadn't seen in centuries. We agreed to spar. He told me to go full on because there was no weapon made that could injure him. I picked a short broadsword and round shield, just like I had back when we met. He pulled a double-headed axe off the wall and swung it flat side, hoping to catch me off guard. I phased, letting it pass through me. I sent him backward with a blow from my shield and plunged my phased sword into his thigh, where I made it solid again. It was complete instinct.

I wasn't even trying. It ripped a gash all the way through his thigh, close to the bone. That's when I freaked out. Thoughts of me killing my benefactor in *his* facility were going through my head. It was intense."

"Uh, yeah, I can imagine so."

Lukkas asked a lot more questions about the visit. Grace told him everything about their technology, her interactions with each person, and everything she was told about herself. She also told him they knew about him. Not him specifically, but that she was in a relationship with a vampire and had been for several hundred years.

"It's up to you if you want to come with me when I go back. I want to take some time before I contact them again. I want to dig up as much information on them as I can."

"You're damned right I'm coming with you. I'm not letting you go back there by yourself. Something doesn't seem right, though. You said The Three had been here for five years preparing the facility."

"Yes, that's what they said."

"How did they know what was coming five years before it happened? They kind of skimmed over that part, didn't they?"

"I'm usually far more perceptive about that kind of thing. Ben told me they had been sent here as a punishment by Odin. He didn't actually say what they were preparing the facility for."

"They were probably banking on your being too overwhelmed to catch on to the finer details, hence the reason you're not going back alone. They won't catch you off guard if you're prepared for it. I'll make sure of that."

Grace's wheels were spinning again. "It really makes me wonder what the angle is. Was it only a lack of time, or are there things they're intentionally not sharing with me? All this sends me back to the question of why I made the choice to leave."

"It's best not to think too hard about it right now. It was only a matter of time before something was going to screw our lives up again. It always happens, remember 1460?" Lukkas howled at the memory, making Grace laugh until she was nearly crying.

"We've survived some rough times and a lot of amazing times too. These last few hundred years alone have been phenomenal for technological inventions. All our businesses thrive. We do what we want and don't answer to anybody. There's still always a price. Even your mission to save people one at a time has a price."

Lukkas's last statement offended Grace. She indignantly stated, "I don't charge anyone for my services. I've never turned down a job because someone couldn't or wouldn't pay. I only take what's offered. People hold greater value on things they personally sacrifice for. Only the currency has changed. If they're reluctant to offer a sacrifice, I know what kind of people they are. I'm satisfied knowing they'll get what they deserve, eventually. And sometimes I get to be the one to give it to them."

"Watch out, honey, your deity is showing," Lukkas joked.

Grace didn't think that was something to joke about.

"You mean my truth is showing? Everyone deserves a chance to be a better person. It's their choice if they want to take it or not. It's my choice to show them there are consequences to their actions."

Lukkas was amused. "And who shows you the consequences of your actions?"

"Other than you, nobody's had the nerve to show me my flaws," she replied with an exaggerated arrogance.

They both tried not to take themselves too seriously. Neither was perfect, and they were very aware of it. They understood that with immortality, there could also come a reduction of humility and empathy if you let it. They'd both seen it and tried hard not to let that happen to them. Grace, especially, tried to help protect innocent souls. She had a soft spot for those who had a hard life yet still gave to others. A person could have noble intentions yet perform unspeakable acts of violence in the accomplishment of that goal. It was an illusion to think you could provide peace through aggression and conquest.

The wine seemed to have an effect on Grace. Her mind was wandering to philosophical questions, which she thought couldn't be good for anyone.

Lukkas was still laughing. "Snap out of it, Gracie." He snapped his fingers in front of her face. Even though he didn't want to drop the subject, he felt that she had had enough for tonight.

"Stop calling me Gracie!"

"And she's back. Speaking about saving the world. While you were gone, we looked through the postings. There's a snatch and grab that looks interesting if you need a break."

"That should take my mind off things for a day or two, anyway." Grace sounded relieved to discuss something routine.

"You deal with things better when you're working."

"True, gotta stay busy. Tell me about it." She looked at a new mission as a relief.

"Basic kidnapping. Father is Joel Rosenblum, a network security guy for an up-and-coming biotech company in Virginia. Someone took his daughter, Sarah, from her school this morning. Ransom is to load a program, providing undetected external access into the internal network. Standard inter-sector sabotage. Standard clauses for law enforcement: any hint, and the girl will be eliminated."

"Any idea where the girl is being held? Proof of life sent yet? Drop site for the program?"

"Slow down a second. Nothing conclusive as to the location of the girl. Cameras at the grab site show nothing. They left her phone and school tablet at the scene. Dogs couldn't pick up her scent outside of her school. Local traffic cameras and CCTV didn't pick up any unusual traffic. All cars check out as parents. All the buses that went through the gate were assigned to that school and all the drivers accounted for. Nothing out of the ordinary. It's like she simply vanished from the spot she was standing in."

"Who do we have that can go to the school and look for other exit points?"

"Already on it. Tomorrow, we should have a clearer understanding of how she was removed from the grounds. In the meantime, the father's company has set up a virtual server with fraudulent data. It should be ready to deploy tomorrow afternoon. They have given him three days to load the program, starting today. He received a video. She isn't being restrained, says she's being treated well. Lots of wildlife sounds in the background, which are being analyzed to narrow the location. All we can determine is she's in a country environment, likely pretty far out, so no reason for keeping her tied up."

Grace thought for a few minutes. "I guess there's nothing left to do tonight, then. I'm ready to head back and get some sleep."

CHAPTER EIGHT

Morning came way too fast for Grace's taste. She reached over to the other side of the bed to find it empty and cold. Lukkas was a morning person and had probably left hours ago. She got up and went to open the doors to the terrace, to find him reading the news on his tablet. When he heard the doors unlatch, he started pouring her coffee. She crossed the balcony and sat in the chair opposite him, taking a few sips from her cup.

"Mmmm. Thank you. Any news on the girl?"

Lukkas put his tablet down on the table. "After analysis of the soundtrack, they have narrowed it down to about a dozen possible locations. I've got our guys looking into satellite imaging now to see if any have suspicious activity. You should probably shower up. I've got a private jet waiting at the airport to take us to the area. We'll have the location by the time we land."

"You're coming on this one?" Grace was a little surprised. She preferred for him to keep his exposure low, especially after the events of the last few days.

"I've set up a meeting with one of our distributors in the area for this afternoon. It's an opportunity for me and a cover for you." He could be very pragmatic when he wanted to be.

"Are you sure you're not just coming along to monitor me?"

"Partially. I'm uncomfortable about your recent contact with the Aseer. I have an uneasy feeling this may not be what it looks like."

"Æsir," she corrected. She would not argue about him coming. It was a relief that he would be close by. She had been more than a little concerned about the timing of this incident as well. "Okay, let me get cleaned up then. Should I pack a bag?"

"Already done. The Board is also having an open reception tonight in D.C. I've RSVP'd us and booked a room at the hotel. I packed your red dress."

"And what shoes?"

"The black stilettos with the red soles and crystal-studded ankle straps." He grinned at her.

She smiled back. "I knew I kept you for a reason."

~~~~

The jet landed in a private airfield near the eastern coast of Virginia. Lukkas pulled out his phone to make a few arrangements. One call was to his contact working on the location of the girl.

"Yep, here he comes."

He hung up as the limo driver boarded the plane. Lukkas spoke with him for a few minutes as the driver turned over a folder and a set of keys.

"We found her location. Here are the coordinates. Let me know if you run into any problems, otherwise I'll see you tonight at the reception," Lukkas said to Grace, tossing her the keys.

"Sounds like a plan," she said as she caught them. "What are these for?"

"That's a surprise," he said, with a grin.

As they got off the plane, Grace spotted a gorgeous black Ducati motorcycle with two helmets.

"Ooh! You never fail to impress." She grabbed Lukkas and gave him a hard kiss on the cheek before popping over to the motorcycle in the blink of an eye. "See you tonight!"

Before he could say anything back, she was pulling onto the service road. Lukkas stood there, watching her until the dust trail had disappeared. It seemed like lately this was becoming a routine view, watching her leave. Worrying wouldn't change anything, but he couldn't help but feel this might be a mistake so soon after the latest expedition.
~~~~

It only took her about forty-five minutes to get to the coordinates Lukkas had given her. She pulled the bike over, covering it with some branches to obscure it from the road.

The farmhouse was remote. It was a white two-story with a wraparound porch on the first floor. Red tin roof. Pretty standard for that area of the country. Nothing around for miles, flat land, hills a couple miles to the north and west, no cover for approach. There was surveillance and a laser grid several feet deep and eight feet high throughout the perimeter. Four guards were visible outside, two dogs and at least three other people were inside. There was more going on here than a snatch and grab. How much security did they need for one ten-year-old? The ransom they were asking wasn't high enough to warrant this type of security, either. It was a bait trap if she'd ever seen one. If she had any sense, she'd turn around and leave. Of course, there was no way she was actually going to do that. It appeared that someone else was looking for Grace.

"Time to play," she said audibly to herself.

The only concern she had was staying downwind from the dogs, so they didn't catch her scent. Dogs can always tell if you're there even if they can't see you. Everything else was a walk through the field, literally phasing out and walking through the field as quickly as she could. She easily passed through the laser grid and tall grass. She stopped momentarily on the side porch, feeling where the people were inside the house. Their energies were all human except for the dogs, of course. The girl was upstairs in one of the back rooms. Grace moved through the side of the house, up the dark and narrow stairs near the front door, past a guard, and through the wall of the bedroom.

The guard looked around, feeling a breeze blow down the hall. After he had checked the corridor, he thought someone must have opened a door or window and remained unconcerned.

Once in the room, Grace solidified. It was a generic room with beige walls and more beige carpet. The twin bed had a pink ruffled bedspread and matching ruffled curtains. The girl was across the room, sitting at a small white desk, playing a computer game. She turned around to face Grace.

"Hi."

She didn't seem scared at all. She was an average-sized ten-year-old. Blonde hair, brown eyes, and freckles. She was wearing jeans and a pink T-shirt with cartoon characters on the front and a matching headband. "Are you an angel too?"

Grace was curious. "No, honey, I'm not an angel. What do you mean, 'too'?"

"The angel who brought me here has been looking for you for a really long time. I'm supposed to call when you come. Are you the one they're looking for?"

"I'm not sure, honey. My name is Grace and you're Sarah, right?"

"Yes."

"Who are you supposed to call? The angel?" Grace was getting more interested in who this "angel" was.

"The angel and my dad. They're waiting. They said your name was Nanna. I thought you'd be like a grandma."

"Well, it used to be Nanna, but I like Grace better. You're supposed to call your dad? So, no one has kidnapped you then?" Grace spoke in an amused tone.

"No, they said I could help. You wouldn't hurt a kid and they really want to talk to you. I like Grace better too." Sarah spoke in a very matter-of-fact manner.

"Before you call your dad, what can you tell me about this angel?" Grace sat on the floor close to Sarah's desk.

"I'm not supposed to talk to strangers."

"That is an excellent rule, but they told you I was coming to see you, so shouldn't that make it okay?" Grace asked.

"I guess so."

Sarah approached Grace slowly, sitting on the floor in front of her. "The angel's name is Amitiel, Aahh-*mee*-teal." Sarah stressed the pronunciation. "I call her Ami. She says she's not exactly a girl or a boy. Where she's from, everyone is a ball of light, and she can look like a boy or girl. She said she doesn't care how you think about her, and she never lies about anything."

Sarah leaned toward Grace, held her hand up to the side of her mouth, and whispered, "Sometimes it's annoying."

"Well, that makes complete sense. Do you know why Ami is looking for me?"

"Ami said you've been friends for a really long time. She came to see you at home, but you weren't there. She's been trying to find you since then." Sarah spoke with the tone of a miniature adult. "Can I call my dad now?"

"I think that's an excellent idea."

Sarah stood up, went back to the desk to pick up her cell phone, and dialed a number.

"Dad, she's here. I told her Ami was looking for her. Okay, I will." She put the phone back down. "You should stand over here." Sarah pointed to the area next to her beside the far wall.

Grace moved to the area the child indicated. At that moment, two people appeared in the middle of the room with a light breeze similar to what Grace had created when she passed in front of the guard. One was Sarah's father, Joel. The other was the most stunning creature Grace had ever seen. Tall, androgynous, thin and straight, thirty-something, with over-cropped, tightly curled jet-black hair. Surprisingly, there were no wings to be found. Ami spotted Grace and rushed at her.

"Nan! What in all the hells were you thinking of, disappearing without telling me? Do you know how worried I've been?!" She grabbed at Grace. Shocked by her charge, Grace phased, and Ami shot right through her, nearly running into the wall. Grace spun around, solid again. Ami looked at her, laughing hysterically.

"I forgot you could do that. I can't believe I finally found you." She approached Grace slowly and hugged her so tightly she couldn't breathe.

Grace felt absolute love and concern from Ami but was still in a state of confusion.

"Uh, hi?"

"Sorry, sorry, sorry. I forgot for a second you don't remember me. Can I show you how to open your memories now?"

"What do you mean, open them up? How do you know where my memories are? They said nobody knows where they were," Grace asked.

"I don't have them, you idiot. They're locked in your head." Ami tapped on the side of her own head. She spoke aggressively like only family ever speaks to each other. She even craned her neck while looking at Grace like she was completely stupid. "Who the hell told you they were gone? They've always been in your head." She overstressed "always."

Grace had almost forgotten there was a child in the room. She looked over to Sarah and then back at Ami. "Let's slow this down for a minute."

She looked back at Sarah. "Sorry for the language."

Sarah shrugged. "It's okay. I'm used to it." She went back to playing her game, completely unfazed.

Grace looked at Joel next. "Hi, I'm Grace, and you must be Sarah's father."

Joel shook Grace's hand. "Yes, ma'am. Joel Rosenblum. I'm not actually an IT guy, I'm a genetic engineer. I own the company I said I worked for in the ad. It's an honor to meet you, Your Highness."

Grace scrunched up her face. "I'm not royalty. Well, not anymore, I guess. At least I don't think so. Anyway, Grace is fine." She let go of his hand and gave him a sympathetic smile.

"Grace, huh? Where did you come up with that? Not that it isn't ironic. You're the clumsiest person I know."

"I'm not the one who almost face-planted the wall," Grace chided.

"Well, I wasn't exactly expecting to go through you, now was I?" Ami smacked back.

"Probably not." Grace took a breath. "So, now other than your extremely exuberant quest to find me, what are you doing with a biogenetics engineer?"

"Oh, Joel, he's trying to figure out what the differences are between mortal humanoid species and immortal humanoid species. His goal is to improve health and life expectancy for people of this planet." Ami looked at Grace like it should have been a given that she knew this information.

"Please stop looking at me like you think I'm stupid, Ami."

"Well, stop acting stupid and let me show you how to unlock your memories so we can have an actual conversation."

Grace thought Ami was either a very close friend or someone super annoying who thinks she's your best friend. She hadn't decided which yet.

Grace's expression changed to be slightly sad. "I'm not sure I want them back. What if it changes the perspective I have on the life I have now? I have a family and a life I love. What if I find I still have feelings for Ben?"

Ami's face twisted. "Who's Ben?"

"Balder. He goes by Ben here."

"That's not funny! He's here and you've seen him? Believe me, the only feeling you have left for him is contempt. Was it him who told you that your memories were lost? Oh! How convenient!" Ami exclaimed.

Grace felt almost ashamed. "I've only seen him once a few days ago."

"How did he find you when I couldn't?"

"By being overly conspicuous. His people kept showing up in places where I had been. Sometimes within minutes. I wanted to know who was hunting me, so I found a way to contact his group." Now Grace knew her gut was right. Something was off about him.

"I was the one hunting for you first! And what do you mean, 'his people'? They're your people too. Why are they even here?" Ami was very suspicious of his motives.

"He said Ragnarök had taken place. Asgard was attacked by an unknown species and their world was destroyed. They had escaped with just over a hundred people." Grace was also getting a suspicious feeling now.

"He is so full of crap. Not about the war. That really happened, but it wasn't an attack by an unknown assailant. It was a rebellion. The other realms were sick and tired of being ruled in absentia. They were conquered worlds, and the Æsir were supposed to protect them, but they left them to fend for themselves while forcing them to pay homage. They plundered those planets for millennia, leaving them with no support or defenses. Six of the lower realms banded together and destroyed the palace, but most of the rest of Asgard is still there. Odin and his little minions have always invaded sovereign worlds because he loves the conquest but not the actual ruling part. Now they're all dead and there's no one else to blame but him." Ami was ranting and pacing.

"So, I guess that means no one is following them or hunting them?" Grace was coming to some harsh conclusions.

"Not likely. I can't speak to the intentions of the others, but odds are if Balder—or, what did you call him? Ben?—is here, he doesn't intend on leaving. I wonder if they registered with the Council? Remind me to check on that," Ami said, pointing at Grace.

"What's the Council?" Grace raised her eyebrow.

"Ugh! You are making my life *SOOO* hard. It's where we first met. The Council of the Divine. They're the ruling body of The Everything?" Ami stepped closer to Grace. "No? Nothing?" she sighed heavily. "This is a protected, emergent planet. If there is a delegation from Asgard here, whether their world still exists or not, they need to register." Ami sounded exasperated, like she was reading from a tourist brochure, and Grace felt it.

Joel was sitting quietly on the other side of the room, excitedly observing the conversation. The two immortals didn't even acknowledge his existence.

Grace took in a deep breath, blowing out hard. Meeting Ami was so much different from meeting Ben. Grace immediately felt she could trust her. Maybe not trust her to keep her mouth shut, but definitely trust her to tell the truth. There was no pretense or hesitation in her words as she blurted out everything that crossed her mind.

"Okay, Ami, I only have one more question before I decide if I want to open my memories. Why do you think I would have nothing but contempt for Ben?"

With a sneer, Ami said, "Well, that's an easy one. Two, actually. First, you've separated from him more than once. Last time you said it was for good. Everyone who knew him adored him, but with you he was a control freak. His ego doesn't allow him to have an equal partner. You two had epic battles that didn't end with your separation. You loved him almost as much as you hated him. And, second, he was the one who had you poisoned."

"What did you just say? Ben was the one who had me killed? Are you serious?"

"Yup."

Grace felt deep, raw anger welling up. "You think maybe you should have led with that one?"

Ami shrugged. "That wasn't the order the events happened."

"Why in all the hells would he have poisoned me?"

"The Council was going to be voting on erasing humans from Earth. Well, Earth and like a bunch of other planets. It's not a big deal. They've done it before, a few times actually. It's a simple reboot. It could be just humans, or they could erase everything and start fresh. So, some of the pantheons saw the current iteration as another failed experiment and wanted to start over. The species they created was steeped in greed, killing one another, becoming rebellious and corrupt. Blah, blah, blah, whatever. Like those assholes have any right to throw stones about greed, corruption, and murder. I think it's hilarious, because they weren't being worshipped anymore, they were being emulated.

"Anyway, you were advocating for humanity to the point where you even told your delegate you would volunteer to provide guidance. Balder, or Ben, or whoever he wants to be, had already died and was rotting in Hel. He still thought he had the reach to control you and forbade you to go. You told him to stick it, so he had you poisoned so you would rot along with him. He was pretty pissed when Frigg and Freya conspired to get you out. They were going to send you here without any consequences, but Ben reminded his mother that he wouldn't always be in Hel and he would make her life miserable unless she took your memories, sending you away blank. She agreed but then added the amulet, so he couldn't send anyone after you in your debilitated state."

Ami had spoken swiftly and had barely taken a breath. It reminded Grace a little of the way Seshet had spoken, except without all the overt enthusiasm. Ami sucked in a deep breath and was about to go on when Grace stopped her.

"I've heard enough. How do I get them back?"

"Oh … um, well, sit down." Ami pulled Grace toward the foot of Sarah's bed.

"Wait! How'd you find me?" Grace asked suspiciously.

"I had a friend who was really close friends with Frigg, and we were talking when he asked me if I had heard any news about you. And then he said that you were here. I asked him why he hadn't told me centuries ago, 'cause he knew I was looking for you. He said he found her journals after she died but didn't read them right away, but this was before the war, so now he's gone, too. And then I told him I was already working on a project here with Joel on extending mortal human life expectancy. And then he said …"

Grace cut her off again. "Okay, Ami. Never mind. It doesn't matter." Grace made a mental note not to ask Ami anything if she wasn't prepared for a minute-by-minute monumental dump of sheer word vomit.

"Okay." Ami stopped talking like she hadn't just had a manic episode and reached out to touch Grace between her eyes. "Ah, there. Hold on, this is going to make you dizzy. Do you feel the line I'm pressing in?"

Grace felt a warm sensation stretching deep into her brain that tingled and itched.

"That's where they are. All you have to do is imagine turning the lock and opening the door."

"That's it?"

"Uh-huh."

Grace scrutinized Ami, who sat there and stared back at her. She closed her eyes, following the warm vibrating line into her mind. As she concentrated on the spot, it glowed inside her closed eyes. She visualized turning the lock and pulling the door open. As she did so, an ocean rushed forward. Grace's head swam as she watched hundreds of thousands of years of memories slamming back into her head. She didn't just get dizzy; she passed out cold, falling back onto the bed.

Grace's eyes fluttered open to Sarah sitting next to her head, leaning over uncomfortably close to her.

"Her eyes are open!" the girl yelled into Grace's face.

Ami moved Sarah out of the way.

"Sorry. Guess I didn't account for the amount of stuff in there. You've been out for over an hour. Can you sit up?"

Grace sat up slowly. "Can I get some water?"

Joel opened the door to find the guard standing outside.

"Can we get a bottle of water up here?"

A few minutes later, the guard was back with the bottle.

Ami opened it for her. "You okay? Got a headache?"

Grace looked a little groggy as the room swirled around her. "I'm okay, no headache, just a little, um, I guess the right word is 'full.'" She rubbed her eyes and shook her head violently from side to side. The action seemed to make the room stop its churning motion.

"So many things make sense now. And I am SO ANGRY," she growled through clenched teeth. "How do I get in touch with the Council?"

"That's easy. I can get us in to see them in the morning. Give me a minute." Ami ported out and back in seconds. "All set."

"Ami, you don't think The Three knew, do you?" Grace asked tentatively.

"Knew what?" Ami asked deadpan.

Grace didn't want to believe her sons knew. In her restored memory, she and Frigg had hidden it from them, but she didn't know if they had found out another way. She also didn't want another twenty minutes of a droning answer from Ami. Her overwhelming need to know won out, and she asked.

"Knew about Bald—, I mean Ben killing me?"

"I don't think they could have known when it happened. After you were gone, though, everybody knew. Odin was actually proud of Ben for doing it. He thanked him for getting you out of his hair over resetting a batch of planets filled with mortals. But then, after Frigg resurrected you, Odin got furious with her because she wouldn't tell him where you were. She made him look bad in front of the Council because he had to vote against resetting a group of planets that he initially supported. She said you were on one of them and that he would never be able to find you. The realm was already angry with him. Hell, the Council was angry with him, too. If they found out that they had dissipated you on a rebooted planet he voted for, well, he wouldn't have had any supporters left."

Grace pulled out her phone, and glancing at the time, she realized she had to get back for the reception this evening. She had been gone far longer than she had expected. Lukkas would be losing his mind.

"*Skitur!*" Grace exclaimed. "I have somewhere I need to be! Ami, what are you doing tonight? I don't want to end this conversation and I don't want to lose touch with you again." Grace had remembered Ami. As flighty as she was, literally and figuratively, she was, in fact, Grace's best friend.

"Nothing that can't wait," Ami answered.

"Wanna go to a party? Not like old times, though." Grace shook her head fervently at Ami. "My husband's distributor is hosting. We can't embarrass him. You got a dress or a suit? Whichever you're feeling. Black tie."

"Sounds like fun." Ami would go anywhere Grace asked. She was overjoyed to have her friend back. "Wait, you got a husband?"

"What, you expected me to be a hermit living in a cave somewhere?"

"No. Doesn't it bother you when they die, or by that time are you ready for another?" Ami could be very brash.

Grace looked back at Ami impertinently. "Until five minutes ago, I didn't know any more than what I learned in less than two thousand years on a primitive planet. I would have been quite satisfied with a regular mortal." Not true, but Grace didn't like being called out. "And besides, I didn't pick a mortal for a mate."

"What's that supposed to mean? If someone on the Council or registry knew where you were, they would have been obligated to report it. They don't like untraceable deities roaming around, mixing with delicate little humans. He's going to be in a lot of hot water." Ami was now the impertinent one.

Grace started laughing. "He isn't a reportable immortal. He's a vampire."

Ami perked up. "Oooh! A nouveau immortal! I haven't met any of those yet. We were waiting to see how they acclimated to their new status before the Council recognized them. Maybe not for another five thousand years or so. I can't wait to meet him."

"Port home and get some clothes. I've got to get my motorcycle back and then we'll go to the hotel. Are you going to wipe these two?" Grace was pointing to Joel and Sarah. It was protocol for angels to wipe most of their earthly contacts.

Ami waved it off. "No, he's approved, and Sarah is one of our potentials, so she'll have to learn about us at some point anyway. The exposure's good for her. Now wait here. I'll only be a second."

At that, Ami disappeared with a slight suctioning sound of air collapsing into the space that had been filled only a second previously. That left Grace, Joel, and Sarah alone in an awkward silence.

Joel's voice cracked slightly. "Grace, will you be taking part in the study?" He swallowed hard, looking nervous.

"I'm not sure I'll be able to. I have a bit to sort out with the Council, and I'd also like to talk to Ami about it."

Grace was less than interested in being poked and prodded, since she had already succumbed to that recently. How she wished Ami had found her before she had gone looking for Ben. If she'd only waited a few more days, she would have known the truth. She wanted to see Lukkas, and she wanted to talk to the Council. Ami appeared between her and Joel, holding a garment bag and a small travel bag.

"Give me just a minute to talk to Joel and we can leave."

CHAPTER NINE

Grace and Ami walked into the hotel lobby. It was a very luxurious hotel near the center of Washington, D.C., that had often seen a variety of the rich and famous. Instead of a gift shop, it had a jewelry store. The art in the lobby was museum quality. The hotel restaurant was a signature eatery of an award-winning chef, and the furniture throughout the space cost more than Grace's last house. It was modern, sleek, and impeccably clean, decorated in tones of blue and gray splashed with deep orange. She asked Ami to wait while she went to pick up a room key. She had already checked with Lukkas to see what room they were in. Grace could have just phased or ported into the room with Ami, but she preferred to keep up normal appearances, especially with places where they were in solely to be seen. Ami had spent enough time in the human world to understand the necessity of not freaking out the general population. They went up to the room, and Grace turned to face Ami.

"Don't embarrass me."

"Would I do that?" Ami looked offended.

"You would, and you have. He's not a zoo animal. Don't examine him as if he were."

"I'll behave. I promise."

Grace opened the door to the suite. It was the size of an average one-bedroom apartment with an entire wall of windows along the back. Lukkas wasn't in the living room, but she could hear music coming from the bedroom.

"Wait here for a minute. I need to make sure he's dressed."

"I don't mind," Ami said.

"I wasn't worried about you," Grace said, giving Ami a nod before disappearing into the bedroom.

"Hey, honey."

Lukkas had recently showered and was wearing a pair of gym shorts with no shirt. "Hey. Did everything go okay?"

Grace had a wide grin that hid a juicy secret. "Not like I expected. But pretty great result overall."

"I'll bite. What do you mean by that?"

"Well, it wasn't a kidnapping at all."

"Really?"

"It was a very old friend who had been looking for me since I disappeared. And by very old, I mean someone way older than me, who I have known most of my life."

Lukkas was suspicious and curious. "Another one?" He narrowed his eyes. "And how do you know this is true?"

Grace stepped toward him, widening her already huge smile. "Because they showed me how to get my memories back. And, by the way, I'm still choosing you."

"Are … are you serious?" Lukkas stuttered, leaning back against the dresser.

"Completely. And I've got a surprise for you. Put a shirt on."

He grabbed a shirt and followed Grace into the living room.

"Lukkas, this is Ami. Actually, Archangel Amitiel. Ami, this is Lukkas."

Lukkas was dumbfounded, sniffing at the air to take in the unrecognizable bouquet. Ami was intrigued.

"*He's* a vampire?! Are you screwing with me? He's so pretty." Ami walked around Lukkas, touching his torso.

Lukkas watched her cautiously, lifting his arms as she moved around him. He was unsure if there might be a screw loose there. "Um, hello."

When Ami reached up to touch Lukkas's mouth, Grace pulled her hand away and snapped at her, "Ami, behave yourself. Sorry Lukkas. She's never seen a vampire before."

Ami immediately sulked like a scolded child. She was of considerable age yet seemed so innocent. "Sorry. We're all curious about your kind. You're the first immortal species that has occurred innately in eons."

"Well, you're the first angel I've ever met, so I guess we're even. I didn't know you were real, either. Do you have wings?"

"Of course I have wings, silly."

"Can I see them?" Lukkas asked with a bit of shock and excitement.

Ami looked around the room at all the breakable objects and shook her head. "They won't fit in here and Grace will get mad at me if I break something."

"Oh. Well, it's nice to meet you, then."

Ami timidly reached out and shook his outstretched hand. "Very nice to meet you, too."

Grace found their exchange amusing. "I think it's time for us to get ready, don't you, Lukkas? I invited Ami to the reception."

"Did you tell her what kind of reception this is? She isn't going to lose her composure with everyone, is she?" Lukkas glanced at Ami, noting her odd behavior.

"I haven't told her yet. She'll be fine once we get a few drinks into her."

Lukkas looked at Ami cautiously. "Ami, this is a reception sponsored by distributors of clean blood. Most of the people in that room will be vampires. You don't really have a discernable scent, but you smell more like Grace, so you should probably say you're related to her."

Ami stared straight at Lukkas. "I can't do that. I can't lie."

"She literally means she is physically incapable of saying anything that she perceives to be untrue." Grace was unsure what to do. She hadn't considered Ami's scent.

"Can you just not say anything about who you are if anyone asks? I mean, if I introduce you as Grace's cousin, can you not correct me?"

"You can lie all you want. I am not required to correct someone else's untruthful statements," Ami replied with a neutral expression.

"Won't that open another entire line of questions? Introducing her as a relative would have them asking what I am and where I come from," Grace asked.

"We can push off that conversation by telling people it's complicated. It's eventually going to come out now anyway, isn't it?" Lukkas questioned back.

"I guess that's true," Grace agreed.

"Okay then, we're agreed. Ami, you say nothing about who you are, and we will keep you out of anything other than general social conversation." Lukkas wasn't too concerned about questions at this party, since it was at a public venue. Everyone would be covert with their conversations.

"What's clean blood? I would like details, please," Ami asked.

Lukkas and Grace looked at each other. "You can take this one, Lukkas. I'm going to get ready so we're not late." Grace quickly disappeared into the bedroom.

Lukkas turned around as Grace shut the door, then completed the circle, stopping in front of Ami. "Well … um, clean blood is a synthetically produced blood product that we make to replace human blood."

"Why do you need to replace human blood?"

"Blood is our food source," Lukkas answered.

"Oh. Why wouldn't you want to feed on humans?"

Lukkas couldn't help but smile at her, since the way she asked was just as interesting as the question itself.

"Because it can hurt them if we're not careful. We've matured beyond the need for that. Some vampires still feed on humans occasionally, but we don't want to kill to feed, so we created clean blood."

Ami's face contorted while she thought about her next question. "Why don't you drink the little bags that humans use in their healing centers?"

"It's expensive, difficult to obtain, and there isn't an adequate supply to support us and human needs. Our product is less expensive if you count the cost of expired blood that has to be disposed of each year. CB is practically colorless and to humans, odorless and tasteless. It doesn't need refrigeration if it is properly freeze-dried and sealed, and it doesn't require crossmatching. It keeps us from feeding on humans, while it's also beneficial for the human species."

"Why would humans need it?"

"Some of the human uses would be for remote humanitarian missions and military field hospitals. Any place, really, that doesn't have refrigeration. Our scientists have been working on this product for close to a century, but it's only gone into wide distribution for about half of that time," he explained, ready to take questions.

Ami appeared to be thinking about what he had said. Her question was not quite what he was expecting. "How are you involved with it? How did it start?"

"In the seventeenth and eighteenth centuries, we were overpopulating. Vampires were running around uncontrolled, rampantly attacking people and animals to survive. As a result, we were hunted nearly to extinction. The surviving clans formed a governing authority to set rules ensuring our survival. We are now thriving in every facet of business, banking, science, technology, industry, and government. We have fully integrated into society, although we keep our uniqueness behind the scenes. As far as my involvement goes, I'm an investor, to start. The wines we produce contain CB. It's not harmful to humans but they don't require it to live, so we keep sales mostly to vampires." He picked up a bottle, pointing to a stamped gold "CB." "Anything with this stamp contains CB. Does that answer your question?"

"Yes," Ami nodded. "How many things contain CB?"

"We have hundreds of products that contain CB. Any vampire can receive it for free in powder form, but you'll see tonight that we like our varieties."

Ami tilted her head to one side. "Let me know if I'm correct in my assessment. In only the last two to three centuries, your species has formed a government, enacted basic laws, blended into human society undetected, and created a humane, mostly autonomous food source. Are you socially responsible to all members of your species too? I am trying to understand the evolution and structure of your society." Ami was succinct in her question.

The question caught Lukkas off guard due to its complexity. He thought for a moment about how to answer. "Yes, to a degree. We assist with financial support and education for any member who's in need. We live in clans and are reportable to our regional representatives. The laws related to behavior are strict to keep our populations in check. Our priority is to provide resources and support to members in need, rather than allowing their behavior to harm the community. We take care of our own and we discipline our own."

Ami cocked her head, taking a step forward. "What specific type of governance have you formed? If I am understanding correctly, you have formed a closed society operating within the parameters of an open society."

Talking to Ami was like conversing with an incredibly precocious six-year-old. There was a line between inquisitive and inquisitor. Lukkas was also not entirely sure he could divulge information about their society to others. He hadn't realized he was sharing so openly with Ami, either. It wasn't his normal behavior. He felt a subject change was in order.

"This is getting a little beyond light conversation. I'm sure we could get you someone more knowledgeable to speak with about our governing structure at another time. We should probably start getting ready for the reception." Something about being in her presence made him feel sharing with her was almost compulsory, as if she was summoning the truth to come forward from his lips against his will. He would need to ask Grace if that was one of Ami's abilities or if it was only a reaction to her innocent demeanor.

"You can change out here if you don't mind. I'll be in the other room with Grace. Let us know if you need anything." The more he thought about it, the more he realized he needed to report this contact, so the Regent and Board could decide on an appropriate course of action before moving forward with their interactions.

When Lukkas walked into the bedroom, he knew something wasn't right. Grace wasn't there. She had been there. He could still faintly smell her.

"Grace?" he called, looking in the closet and bathroom. "Grace?" he called a little louder. She suddenly appeared behind him with a *whoosh* of air pushing toward him from the spot.

"What? Why are you yelling?" she answered calmly.

"Where were you?"

"You forgot to bring my earrings." She snapped the back on the one in her left ear and held out the other for him to see.

"You didn't answer my question. Where were you and how did you get those earrings if I forgot them?"

"Well, you know how I can phase through things? Right?" she continued, putting on her other earring.

"Grace. That doesn't explain how you now have on the earrings that I left on your dresser at our house, four thousand miles away, and got back here within minutes." He pulled off his shirt and began to dress.

"That's quite a bit more interesting. You know, phasing was something I figured out how to do from instinct and fear. Then I learned to control it, and, well, it's kind of like that."

"Um-hum. Go on." He gestured with his fingers in a pushing motion while he stepped into his tailored tux pants. It was the way she would explain what she had done that he was interested in. He had already figured out the *what* of what she had done, not the how. It was entertaining to watch her flounder a bit.

"Most of my people have the ability to open these small ports in this dimension, through another, and back into ours in a different location. It only works for the specific planet I'm on, but I can move through all the iterations in the multiverse for that planet. I just can't go to another planet or galaxy. A few others can, but I don't have the math skills for those calculations. For off-world travel, there are devices that fold space. They're kind of like a mass transit system, but you need a port platform on each side."

Grace always talked too much when she was nervous. She had thrown a lot at Lukkas in the last few days. She was afraid it was all going to come crashing down on him and he would want to leave her, yet she still could not stop herself from rambling.

"Grace, are you trying to tell me you can teleport? I might not understand the process, but I do know what it's called," Lukkas said in a condescending tone.

"Asshole. You enjoy watching me squirm, don't you?" She finished applying her lipstick, giving him a playful side-eye in the mirror.

"Absolutely." He grinned back while attempting to tie his bow tie. "Now, please give me a hand with this."

"Come over here. Let me fix you," she replied to his reflection in her mirror.

He moved toward her as she stood. "Grace, I have always accepted that you are different. You are beyond me in experience, intelligence, bravery, and gratitude. You have always been exceptional in what you can do and who you are. Now that your mind is open to things you didn't even know were possibilities, it makes me even more drawn to you. As smart as you are, you are so incredibly insecure. Have I ever given you any reason to doubt me?"

Grace was staring at the tie. "No. I know you love me. I'm worried it will all be too much for you."

"Fat chance of that. I want to know everything. If there's something I don't understand, I'll ask. You can't get rid of me that easily."

"Good to know," she sighed, feeling her confidence return. "Ami and I have an appointment with the Council of the Divine tomorrow. You should probably set something up with the Regent for tomorrow as well. We have a bigger picture to look at now and a lot more to discuss between the two of us."

"Ivan will be at the reception tonight. I'll set a meeting with him and see when the Board is available." Ivan Novak was the Vampire Regent and head of the Board of Representatives, which was the governing body of all vampires.

"Your leadership is the Council of the Divine?"

"I'm not sure how much exactly I can say to you about that right now. That's part of why I need to meet with them. You're considered an emergent species, which we are supposed to restrict contact with. However, you are also an immortal species, which we normally observe and evaluate prior to inclusion in the Council, which comprises all the immortal species in this universe."

"All? How many are there?"

"Species or universes?" she asked.

"Either?"

"I can't really say. What I can say is that vampires are the only natural humanoid immortals indigenous to Earth, and as far as I know, you are only in this iteration of Earth. I really can't discuss it any more until I find out if I have violated any restrictions with the Council. I'm sorry, Lukkas."

"No, you're right. I think we both need to have some discussions with our respective leadership. Although you've been living under ours since its inception. I think you should be part of the discussions with the Regent as well."

"I do have a lot to explain, don't I? Can you make the meeting for the afternoon since I'll be out of pocket in the morning?"

"Sure, I'll see what he has available on short notice." Lukkas adjusted his jacket sleeves on his cuffs. "Ready?"

"Not at all, but we should do it, anyway."

When they went out to the living room, Ami was standing still, staring at the wall. She had picked a beautifully fitted white silk suit with a deep V-cut in the front, black lapels, and cuffs. Her neck was adorned with a diamond lasso-style chain that extended to the base of the neckline. Ami was a classic, stunning beauty; delicate, while still having a look of strength. Her appearance awed Lukkas, at least until she opened her mouth.

Ami swung around. "Finally. Let's go." She was extremely eager.

As they went down in the elevator, they reiterated to Ami about discretion being necessary, at least until they had the chance to speak to the Regent. She agreed, saying she would do her best. Grace had heard that one before. Ami's curiosity always got her into interesting situations. Grace was secretly hoping Ami would say something, so she would be the one to spill and Grace wouldn't be blamed for letting the divinity issue out of the bag.

"This is going to be so much fun!" Ami exclaimed.

Lukkas thought to himself, *What could go wrong?* He decided to brace for the impact he could see coming. It was going to be quite a night.

The elevator doors opened. He could already hear the din of conversation from the banquet room at the end of the grand hall. It was apparent the staff heard nothing, but with his species' heightened abilities, he could hear everything, which also meant most of the attendees could hear them exiting the elevator as well.

Lukkas inhaled, pushing it out quickly before opening the doors to the reception. All the guests within twenty feet of the door turned to look at the interesting trio. Everyone was familiar with Grace already. Lukkas realized Ami's scent was going to be of more interest than he had realized. Ivan was halfway across the room to the right near the bar. Lukkas wanted to get to him as quickly as possible to set the meeting for the next day, as well as out of respect for his position. They traveled through the crowd, attempting to have as little conversation as possible on the way. Finally, they were within approach distance of the Regent.

Lukkas extended his hand to meet Ivan's as a strange thought entered his mind: *A vampire, an angel, and a goddess walk into a bar ... I know there's a joke in there somewhere.*

"Lukkas, it's so good to see you. It's been too long." Ivan completed his handshake, then turned to Grace. He placed his left hand on her waist, pulling her toward him simultaneously, raised her left hand with his right, then kissed the back of it gently. "Grace. It's always lovely to see you. I see you've added a particular piece of jewelry to this hand. I guess that ends my chances of stealing you away from this very young man." Ivan had always been attracted to Grace and immensely enjoyed flirting with her, especially in front of Lukkas. Grace also enjoyed his flirting, but they both always knew who she was going home with.

Grace leaned in close and whispered in his ear, "You can't imagine how old I am." She flashed him a wicked little smile.

He returned an intrigued expression. The two shared a similar dark sense of humor. Could this be some kind of witticism he was not yet privy to? He seemed to be her closest match in intelligence since they had known each other, and they often shared banter that included riddles and puzzles.

"I've brought someone I'd like you to meet," she continued.

Ivan looked over at Ami, obviously enchanted by her radiance. He had let go of Grace's hand but still had his other hand on her waist.

"Ivan, this is Amitiel. Amitiel, this is our Regent, Ivan Novak."

Ivan reached out with his free hand, taking Ami's right hand, and pulled her in close. He lifted her hand to his lips, kissing it, lightly breathing in her scent. "It's lovely to meet you. How do you know Grace and Lukkas?" He raised an eyebrow, intrigued by an unknown aroma.

Ami smiled a lovely, confident smile and whispered, "I've only met Lukkas tonight, but I've known Grace for over four hundred thousand years. You can call me Ami. I'm an archangel and this is the most interesting group of people I've seen in millennia."

Grace gave Ami a disapproving look. "Ami."

"What? You said I couldn't say anything until we met the Regent. He's the Regent."

Grace and Lukkas looked at Ami, then at Ivan. Lukkas thought he took that well.

"Well, that didn't happen the way I had it planned. I think we should move this conversation to a more private setting, if you agree," Lukkas suggested. He extended his hand toward the door in a gesture to let the Regent pass in front of him.

Ivan appeared unfazed, although Grace could feel him slightly unnerved inside. Fortunately, it didn't appear anyone had paid attention to the exchange, which was odd to her, given the group's exceptional hearing. Ivan released Ami's hand and slid his around her waist as well, keeping her as close as Grace while guiding them forward past Lukkas.

"Ladies, my penthouse should be more appropriate."

Lukkas followed behind to the end of the hall, where he moved in front of the trio to summon the elevator. The ride to the top was tense. Grace passed a thought, telling Ami not to speak again until Grace gave her permission. Ami had followed Grace's instructions exactly as she had given them to her. If she hadn't wanted her to say anything at all, she should have just said that. She didn't understand people's reasoning for not being truthful all the time. When the elevator stopped, Lukkas exited first. There were two guards who both looked at him but didn't move. They had their Regent's scent and realized there was no threat. One guard opened the doors, letting the group into the room. When the guard started to enter the room behind them, Ivan told him he wouldn't be needed inside and to make sure no one was allowed to enter.

The penthouse was large, with a view of the city. The carpet was white throughout. It was four times the size of Lukkas and Grace's room. The furniture was luxuriously stuffed, covered in leather and suede. The lighting fixtures were chrome and crystal: modern fixtures for an impeccable room. Ivan steered Grace and Ami toward the ample sofa. He removed his hands, took off his jacket and tie, and unbuttoned the top two buttons of his shirt.

"Let's get more comfortable. This appears that it could take a while."

Grace took off her shoes and dropped onto the sofa, leaning against the arm with her legs curled under her to the side.

"Lukkas, pour me a scotch, please. Ladies, would you like something?"

Lukkas pulled off his tie and jacket, then headed to the bar to pour drinks.

Grace looked over the back of the sofa. "Wine please, red for me and white for Ami." Lukkas nodded at her. Ami had wandered over to the windows and was staring out into the city. "Ami, are you going to sit down?" Grace raised her eyebrows at her.

"I'm fine." She continued standing with an impassive look on her face.

Grace insisted as she glanced at Ivan. She knew he wouldn't sit until the ladies had been seated first. "We would be more comfortable if you sat down."

Ami headed for one of the oversized chairs opposite the couch, sitting straight with her hands on her knees until Lukkas handed her a glass of wine. He handed the other to Grace and went back to the bar to retrieve the scotch.

"Bring the bottle," Ivan directed as he sat on the sofa close to Grace, putting his feet up on the coffee table. He pointed Lukkas to the chair across from him, next to Ami.

Ivan was about fifteen hundred years old but only appeared to be thirty-five or so. He was an attractive man. Slightly under six feet, very fit, tan skin, neatly kept medium-length light-brown hair, and very dark brown eyes. He took a glass of scotch from Lukkas, then placed his hand on Grace's ankle. They had always been physically comfortable around each other, although it made Lukkas visibly uncomfortable. For Grace, Ivan's presence always provided a clarity and confidence in her she seldom had around others. Ivan turned toward her and spoke.

"So much said in one brief sentence. You want to tell me how exactly you could know our lovely Ami for over some quarter million years?"

Grace tilted her head toward Ivan. "Actually, it's closer to half a million of this planet's years, if we want to be accurate." She smiled a little. "I'm a five-hundred-thousand-year-old Æsir and I got my memories back today." The shy smile on her lips broadened into an expansive, wide grin that came as close to emanating light as he'd ever seen.

Ivan had known all about Grace's past, or lack of one. He had shown interest in her from the first time they had met when he joined Lukkas's village for harvest. To his chagrin, however, she had been spoken for. As much as he had wished to, it was a line he would not cross, although it didn't mean he couldn't occasionally balance on it.

A huge smile swept over Ivan's face in response to her excitement. He tapped Grace's ankle twice. "I *always* knew you were extraordinary."

He looked at Lukkas. "How long were you planning on keeping this from me?"

Lukkas shrugged. "Don't look at me. I just found out an hour ago. As soon as we got dressed for the party, we came straight to you." He took a sip of the smooth, single-malt scotch, drenching his throat in warmth. "I haven't even heard her story yet."

Ivan looked at Ami next. "What about you, Ami? What's your story?" He paused to let Ami respond. She looked at Grace with wide eyes. "Well? Are you going to answer me?"

Grace nodded approval toward Ami.

"Grace told me I wasn't allowed to talk anymore until she said I could," Ami blurted quickly.

"When did she tell you that? I didn't hear her say anything."

Grace looked at Ami. "Go ahead. Tell him whatever he wants to know."

"In the elevator. We don't have to speak to talk to each other."

Ivan studied her blank expression. He turned to Lukkas next.

"Grace has telepathy with Ami, me, and a few others," Lukkas replied to the unvoiced question.

Grace corrected him, *Actually, I found out I have it with anyone I choose.*

Ivan still appeared unflustered. "Interesting." He turned his gaze back to Ami. "This is going to be a much more engaging night than I had planned. Ami, what did you mean when you said you were an archangel?"

Ami spoke, holding a neutral demeanor. Emotional highs and lows were reserved for times of investment, not times when she was merely recounting droll information. "In a monotheistic religion such as what some humans practice with Christianity, there are three major categories of beings: God, angels, and daemons. An archangel is a kind of angel who is the strongest of all created beings. They are the highest-ranking members of God's creations. We are chief messengers, protectors of humanity, and the brightest of all the angels. You couldn't look at me in my true form outside of my body. Well, not the two of you, anyway." She looked between Ivan and Lukkas. "Grace has seen me without my shell, but it would probably kill you. Her energy is brighter than mine, so it doesn't affect her at all."

That bit of information seemed to throw Ivan off slightly. He took a large swig of his drink, then looked at Grace.

"So," he paused to phrase his sentence, "you're a goddess?"

Grace rolled her eyes and spoke in a slightly agitated tone.

"Ami, you're so dramatic." She looked at Ivan and Lukkas. "I'm not a goddess. Æsir are higher-level beings. When we first started exploring the universe, we were labeled as gods because of our advanced technology and immortality. Once your species advances and branches out, you'll be thought of by non-immortal beings as gods too. I mean, you'll have to learn to open portals and fold space to get across the universe or travel between dimensions, but that shouldn't take you more than a few centuries."

She raised her hand to her lips, realizing how condescending she sounded. "Oh, sorry about that." She grimaced, feeling heat creeping up to her face and blushing a light shade of pink. "You may get a little help now that you've been exposed to us, if the Council allows it. You'll still have to develop some biological advances to use more of your cognitive abilities. That's something difficult to teach. Mostly those develop over time and with practice."

"Council?" Ivan looked around at the others.

Ami spoke up. "The Council of the Divine. They are an interdimensional governing body of divine entities. It's sort of like your United Nations, except on an interdimensional scale instead of international. All the immortal species have a representative for each dimension they are worshiped in. Grace and I are going to see Earth's subcommittee in the morning to report the unregistered Æsir delegation."

That got Lukkas's attention. "Ben's delegation is unregistered with your government?"

Ivan's interest had also been piqued. "Who's Ben?"

Ami was more than happy to answer that question. She wasn't a fan of Ben, even if everyone else who ever met him thought he was Mr. Wonderful.

"He's Grace's narcissistic ex-husband. In Asgard, he's known as Balder. He's the one who killed Grace and had her sent here with her memories locked away."

"He's not a narcissist." Grace looked disapprovingly at Ami. "He does rightfully have a large ego, though."

Lukkas had become noticeably angry. "Why are you defending him?"

Grace leaned forward. "Lukkas. Honey, look at me. It wasn't permanent, as you can *clearly* see. He didn't destroy my essence, and he didn't do it himself. While he was in Hel, someone else poisoned me on his behalf, but his mother resurrected me in a new physical body. If he hadn't done it, I never would have left Asgard, and we would never have met. He did us both a favor."

Lukkas sighed and shook his head. "I don't have to like it, but you're right. If you hadn't come here, we never would have met."

Ivan had lost a little of his composure. This discussion of deities, mythologies, and death or non-death was being bandied about as though they were discussing paint colors.

"Lukkas, can you hand me the bottle, please?" Lukkas complied. "Thank you."

Lukkas had calmed down less than Grace had thought. "I'd still like to kill him."

Grace looked at him. "You can't. He would kill you without breaking a sweat, and I don't want to see that happen."

Ami said cheerfully, "I can."

Grace glared at her. "Ami, you are *not* helping. They would send you to your Hel dimension for eternity, and I just got you back. Neither of you is going to kill him. Is that clear? I'm the one he killed, and I am perfectly fine. Better than fine, actually. I'm glad he did it."

"Lucifer would kick me out of hell after a century, tops. I irritate him." The last sentence Ami said mockingly, rolling her eyes.

Ivan's mind was spinning. He adjusted his position, sitting up straighter, taking on a diplomatic air. "Angels, daemons, deities, dying without dying, essence and shells, and an unregistered delegation of powerful immortal beings amongst us. That is quite a lot to digest." He shook his head. "What does that mean for our community? What are our options at this point? Can we meet with the Council?"

Grace was unsure. "I don't know, Ivan. I'm concerned about it too. There is no one more invested in this community's survival than I am. I will do everything I can tomorrow to set up a meeting for you, as well as find out what sanctions they will place on the Æsir. Unfortunately, I think the Council will punish them all for Ben's lack of responsibility, and as much as I don't want to see that happen, I believe it's unavoidable."

"Grace, we're depending on you. I don't want to bring this to the Board until I hear from you, but you will need to be with me when I brief them. I'll call a meeting on Monday. Lukkas, I want you there as well."

Lukkas nodded. "Yes, sir, text me the time when it's set."

Ivan nodded in agreement. He next looked at Ami, appearing deep in thought. "Ami, I would also invite you to attend if you are willing."

The invitation quite flattered Ami. "I would very much enjoy that. Your species has piqued my curiosity and I have many questions. I've never had access to a newly developed immortal race before, and I find this exciting."

Grace stood up. "I, for one, need a refill."

Lukkas stood up quickly. "Here, I'll get it for you."

Grace handed him her glass and sat back down. Ami had barely touched hers, but Lukkas offered a refill anyway.

Ami emptied her glass in one gulp. "Yes, please."

Ivan had enough to think about for one evening. "Doesn't seem like there is much we can do until tomorrow. Let's turn the conversation in a different direction, shall we? Ami, what's heaven like? That is where you live, isn't it?"

"No!" Ami scoffed at the assumption. "Heaven is for humans. We take care of heaven and provide for the souls held there, but angels reside in a different dimension. You wouldn't be able to pronounce it, so you can just call it 'angels' home.' None of us have human forms there, so when we go to heaven, we need to dim ourselves and take on human appearances. As an archangel, I don't take care of them. That's a job for low-level angels."

"That's much different from what I've heard before. You said another dimension. People talk about it like it's in the clouds. How do you get there? Where is it really?"

That question clearly amused Ami and she began to laugh. "No, it's not in the clouds. It's another dimension right here, in the same space, just like heaven and hell. We simply open a port and move through."

Ivan was confused. "I'm not sure I understand."

Lukkas had been listening as he poured the drinks. He crossed back to the seating area and handed Grace her glass.

"Do you mean they exist in a multiverse?" He handed Ami her glass and took his seat. He was also interested in the concept.

Grace decided to take the explanation. "Exactly. We refer to it as The Everything. Let me give you an example. You've all heard about people seeing ghosts, right?" Ivan and Lukkas nodded. "Some people believe that means they haven't crossed over. They're stuck here, but that isn't normally the case. They are creating thin spots between the dimensions. You can see them, but they seldom have corporeal form and very few can affect objects or communicate effectively in this dimension. Sometimes they are in heaven and are trying to help or protect people. Some are in hell and are trying to come through to cause problems. Either way, they have figured out a way to manipulate energy and manifest here."

Ami added, "They're usually dealt with by their respective deities when it's discovered they are crudely tearing holes between dimensions. Altering dimensional space incorrectly can have devastating consequences for the natural balance between all time and space."

Ivan was beginning to understand. "Huh. So, who decides where the soul goes after the body dies?" He looked at Ami for an answer.

"That depends on what they believe. All the pantheons have set up dimensions for their souls to go to. Whoever has the most souls at the end wins."

Ivan followed up, "How do they win souls?"

Ami replied, "The human has to pick them. Some are baptized in a specific religion, and some sell their souls for worldly possessions. It's different for each one."

Lukkas asked, "Wins? Wins what?"

Ami shrugged. "I don't know. I wasn't there when they made the wager."

Lukkas and Ivan exchanged glances.

Ivan added, "What about atheists?"

Ami hadn't really thought about that before. "I don't know. They must go somewhere. Maybe there's another entire dimension just for them. Energy doesn't simply cease to exist. I'll ask Archangel Michael. He'll probably know. He's very smart."

Ami paused for a few minutes. "He's not answering. I'll have to ask him later. Okay, now it's my turn. I thought you couldn't go into the sun. How are you so tan?"

Grace and Lukkas both stifled a laugh while Ivan gave a hearty chuckle. "It seems we've all been misinformed. It's true all our senses are heightened, but the sun isn't an issue except when we're newly turned and getting used to our enhanced abilities. Our skin can be sunburnt more easily, but we just use sunscreen like everyone else. If we get a sunburn, we heal quickly once we are out of direct sunlight. I was already tan when I turned, so I kept my natural coloring. I do know several vampires who like a nice, even spray tan." Ivan's eyes glinted with amusement.

They continued chatting for another half hour. Grace had never seen Ivan so open. He was normally quite sophisticated and guarded around the other vampires. She wasn't holding anything back either. If this conversation wasn't allowed, Ami would be told to wipe them after their Council meeting tomorrow, so there was no harm in speaking openly.

Lukkas sat back in his chair, taking it all in. He had the most to lose if the meeting tomorrow didn't go well for Grace. In his mind, there were limited options. The Council could let them be to develop naturally, they could destroy them altogether, or they could bring them into the fold. Either way, he wasn't entirely sure they would allow Grace to stay. In his assumption, with her knowledge, she could influence their natural evolution. He had always been pretty good at assessing and adapting to situations, and he was sure this would work itself out. He didn't want it to work out in a way that separated him from her.

Ami and Ivan had gotten into some existential "what if" scenario. Grace was in her own world playing over the events of the last week, looking for details with a new perspective. She realized Ben had been trying to gain her trust to get her back under his control. He lied to her about when they had met. True, the events happened, but it was his brother who caught her eye. The three of them had explored the festival together. His brother had courted her for some time, and Ben was always trying to win her over. Ben wouldn't take no for an answer and went to Grace's father to arrange a marriage. Her father agreed, which angered Grace immensely. She was never sure if he really cared about her or if she was only a trophy, another conquest he had won over from his brother. She thought about how they had used her subconscious connection against her. They experimented on her in a way she wouldn't have agreed to if she had remembered. That's when it hit her.

"Ivan? Excuse me for interrupting."

Ivan was slightly embarrassed he had gotten so carried away with the conversation he was having with Ami. He very much enjoyed debating, in a world where there were so few able to keep up their end of a discussion.

"Oh, no, Grace. My apologies for dominating the conversation."

Grace was wondering how she should phrase the question. "Do you know of any vampires who are currently unaccounted for?"

Ivan thought that question was odd, completely out of left field. "Not that I'm aware of. Why do you ask?"

"Could you check, please?"

"Of course." Ivan pulled out his cell phone and made a call. "Now, why do you ask?"

Grace was uneasy. "It's just a feeling I have. When I was at the compound before I could remember, I heard something about them having two vampires there who didn't want to take part in something. They said they had many different species at the facility, and I never considered they may not be there voluntarily. I've been rethinking with a different viewpoint."

Ivan was concerned if they were taking his people to perform experiments on. "We should know soon. I've put out orders for each clan to do a thorough all contact."

As soon as Ivan ended his sentence, Lukkas's phone rang. It was Galin.

"Yes, we're fine. I'm at the reception with Grace. No, we don't know why he would have done that. I'd suggest you collect your regional report, so you can send it. You don't want to be the last holdout. Okay, see you in a couple of days."

"I apologize for lying to my brother. It's not something I usually do. I didn't want to give him any inclination that I knew any more than he did," Lukkas said to Ivan.

Ivan shook his head. "No apologies necessary. I appreciate your discretion. At least we know they're actually checking. Grace, what is the scenario if they are performing experiments on our members?"

"It's hard to tell. There are a few different options. If they are illegally holding vampires against their will, it gives us some leverage to request sanctions. It also gives me leverage to have the Æsir facility inspected if they're performing experiments on immortals without consent."

Lukkas questioned her conclusion. "Don't you already have leverage on the sanctions? They performed an experiment on you without your consent."

"I don't count. I'm still a citizen of Asgard. The Council does not interfere with sovereign pantheon dealings. That is considered a domestic issue. Unless the egregiousness of the action has implications that affect the rest of the Council, they cannot get involved."

Ivan's phone rang. He spoke for only a few moments before hanging up. "Only about twenty percent of the clans have reported. So far, none missing. It could take hours to receive all the counts. What time are you going before the Council?"

Grace looked at Ami, who answered, "Five-thirty."

Grace's eyes narrowed. "In the morning?"

"Yes."

"But it's almost one now. Ivan, can you please call me with the results as soon as you get them? I need some sleep."

"I want you thinking clearly tomorrow, so I don't want to wake you in an hour or two. I want you to call me as soon as you get up, and I'll have the answer for you then."

His consideration warmed Grace. "Thank you, Ivan. I only have your office number since you changed your mobile. Do you want me to call that?"

"I'll text you. I have a feeling you're going to need it often in the future." Ivan picked up his phone and, within a few seconds, Grace's alerted.

"Hopefully for better circumstances than these," Grace said.

Lukkas held out a hand to Grace as she got up from the couch. She picked up her shoes and carried them over her shoulder. They were nearly at the door when she realized Ami hadn't moved.

"Ami, we're leaving."

Ami got up. "Ivan, thank you for the conversation. It was very informative."

Ivan still wasn't completely sure what to make of Ami. "It was lovely to meet you. I hope to speak to you again soon."

The trio took the elevator one floor down to their suite. When they arrived, Lukkas asked Ami, "Do you mind sleeping on the pullout? I can call service to set it up for you."

"I don't need to sleep. I'll go home and be back at five." When Ami finished the sentence, she took a step forward and vanished.

"Guess I'll have to get used to that."

Grace shook her head. "That's not the shocking part. You'll have to get more used to the porting in. I promise I'll try to give you warning before I do that to you."

CHAPTER TEN

The alarm was blaring when Lukkas jolted up on the other side of the bed. "What the fuck?"

She groggily opened her eyes to see Ami standing at the bottom of the bed, staring at them. "Told you porting in was harder to get used to. Ami, how long have you been standing there?"

"I don't know. I couldn't figure out what time it was from home, and I didn't want to be late."

"Ami, watching us sleep isn't appropriate. Go wait in the living room. I'll be out in a few minutes." Grace slammed her alarm off, then turned to Lukkas. "I've never been able to get Ami to understand personal space."

Lukkas got out of bed, shaking his head. He picked up a pair of sweatpants from the chair. "I'll make coffee."

He pulled them on and left the room.

Grace went into the bathroom. Hair, face, and clothes were all she had time for this morning. She finished up, grabbed her cell, and called Ivan.

He sounded groggy too. "I've got the reports back. We are missing two clan members, one male and one female. They are a mated pair. She's from one of the old South American clans and he's newly turned, less than two years ago. Someone abducted them from their hotel in California. The clan didn't report them missing because they thought they were just taking a few extra days to tour."

The news had confirmed Grace's suspicions. She didn't think any vampire would voluntarily help Ben's group, especially without letting their clan know what they were doing. Clans were extremely tight-knit. Even a rogue would likely not submit to being experimented on for money.

"I need you to be sure, Ivan. The Council will need proof."

"I know. We sent some locals to check their hotel room a few hours ago. All their things were still there. There was a small amount of the male's blood, and no one at the hotel had seen them in over two weeks. Someone else had paid for their room in cash for the entire month. The CCTV was already overwritten, but we've got a sketch. Text me your email address so I can have everything sent over to you."

"I'm so sorry, Ivan. I give you my word I'll get them back."

"I hope so, Grace. Call me after your meeting."

She hung up the phone and texted Ivan her email address. When she went to the living room, Lukkas and Ami were sitting at the kitchen bar. Lukkas was attempting to explain the concept of personal space. It wasn't working out the way he expected. Grace picked up the coffee he made for her, swallowing half in one gulp.

She told them what Ivan had said before hearing the chime of her email. The woman was Olivia Santos. Grace knew her parents and had been her blood nurse as a newborn. She was from Brazil, roughly eighty years old. The man was Zane Santos. Also Brazilian, who had just turned twenty-six under two months prior. They had been in California delivering a customized luxury private jet from their clan's company to a business buyer. They were going to take a brief holiday afterward, but should have returned three days ago. Ivan had attached pictures and the sketch of the man who paid the bill. No one recognized him, which wasn't surprising. They likely used someone random off the street to pay.

Grace ported back to the vineyard to pick up Lukkas's file on the Æsir. She softly closed the door to Lukkas's office and printed the email, hoping it would buffer the sound enough that no one would come to see what the noise was. She wrote Ivan back, asking him to locate the man so they could find out who sent him to pay, grabbed the printout, and ported back in under five minutes, just in time for her and Ami to leave. They had to get to the Council in a roundabout way. Since there were no port platforms on Earth that Grace was aware of, and they could only go to other Earth dimensions to find one, they ported to Ami's home and picked up a platform from there.

They appeared in the chamber outside the Council hall. It was much like a church vestibule, long and narrow with ornately carved cushioned chairs and benches lining most of the walls. At the far end, there was an area set up with beverage service. There were two doors in the center of each of the long walls. A scribe was waiting to escort them in.

"Five minutes early. That will be appreciated. Follow me. I will make your announcement." The scribe turned curtly toward the chamber door.

"Wait," Grace said, halting the scribe's progress.

He turned back, tilting his head to one side with a disdainful sneer. "What?"

"We have a second piece of business to address," Grace said.

"That is highly unusual. Give me the specifics and I will tell you if you may present it in this session."

"I have knowledge of two immortals being held against their will for experimentation without authority."

The scribe lifted one eyebrow, tapped a few notes into his device, then spun back toward the door. "Very well, follow me."

They followed the scribe into the chamber. It was set up like a large courtroom with viewing areas, a large table in front for council members, and seating across the table for those giving testimony. There was only one person waiting to hear their case.

The scribe announced, "I present the Archangel Amitiel and the Æsir Goddess Nanna, goddess of undying love and joy and the protector of peace. Please pay respect to the head of the Subcommittee for Earth on Ethics and Justice, Egyptian Goddess Ma'at, goddess of truth, justice, harmony, and law." Grace and Ami both nodded their heads slowly with respect. The scribe took his seat to the right of Ma'at. "Please be seated." He pointed them to the opposite side of the committee table he had sat at, facing forward.

Ma'at proceeded. "Thank you for coming early. I appreciate timeliness." She directed her comments to Grace. "I have been told you have some information to report to the committee. My apologies. We were unable to have a full panel; however, we deemed the information of considerable importance. I would also like to ease any trepidation you may have about your own situation, Nanna. Frigg reported you to us before her death under seal, not to be opened until you were located. I offer my condolences for your loss. I assume you are in full knowledge of your history now?" She nodded her head toward Grace, allowing her to answer.

"Yes, madam. Thank you for your sympathies. I should also like to inform the committee that I am no longer known by the name of Nanna. I am using Grace Eliassen now."

"Note for the record, we will now address the Æsir citizen formerly known as Nanna Nepsdotter by the name of Grace Eliassen." Ma'at turned back to face Grace and Ami. "Now, I understand there are two specific pieces of business you wish to address the committee with. We will address each topic separately. The first item for discussion will be the disposition of an unregistered delegation that has taken up residence on a protected dimension of the Terran planet, commonly known as Earth. We will entertain any physical proof along with any corroborating testimony of witnesses. What proof do you have as to the delegation residing as mentioned?"

Grace pulled a folder out of her bag. She took out the date-stamped pictures Lukkas had given to her the night before she flew out to Montana. There were many shots that could easily place them in several countries.

"These are photographs showing at least twenty known Asgardian citizens over the past year on this planet. They are each labeled with the names they are using. I also have hearsay as to the length of time they have been here in excess of the dated photographs. I am an eyewitness to the facility they are residing in, as well as the location of it. There is also at least one other immortal involved, although I do not know if her pantheon sanctioned her actions or not." Ami was unusually quiet, and Grace was thankful for that.

Grace watched Ma'at as she went through each of the photos. It was obvious that she recognized many of the faces. Bringing up Seshet was going to be a touchy subject with Ma'at, as they were both part of the Egyptian pantheon.

Ma'at placed her folded hands on the photos. "These will be entered into evidence in the case of the unregistered delegation. We will begin by taking an accounting of the facility location and how you came to know of this specific location. Please state the country where the facility is located, so we may provide a map for the coordinates."

"Montana, United States. If you have a detailed map of the area, it is approximately thirty-five kilometers southwest of Helena."

Ma'at ordered the scribe to produce a map of the area, which he did within less than twenty seconds. He dragged his tablet screen into the middle of the table, creating a three-dimensional holographic map between the women. Grace found the location by pinching at the middle of the area and pulling outward, revealing the exact entry point for the facility.

"This is the main entry point for vehicles. Behind this façade wall is a large parking level. Straight in twenty meters is a central elevator. There are twelve levels on the elevator keypad, but I don't know how many are in use."

Ma'at studied Grace's face for any type of deceit. "How are you aware of this facility?"

Grace understood the suspicions that she could be acting in consort with the other Æsir. It was reasonable since she was one as well. The Council was not the most trusting group of beings. Some of their own members were also far from the most trustworthy.

"Before I restored my memories, people had been following me. I noticed specific people appearing in areas where I was working shortly after or while I was completing my assignments. I confronted a small team and was voluntarily taken to their facility. They initially took me to level one, the visitor's level. There is at least one interview room, shower facilities, a dining hall, and a kitchen. Level two contains training facilities. Level four is housing, and level six is the lab and medical facility. I don't know what is on any of the other levels. The interview room is where I learned who they were, why they were here, and that I was one of them. They also performed some tests on me, mostly with my consent, but there was one specifically harrowing test I did not consent to."

Ma'at raised her hand. "Stop right there. I understand you gained access to the facility and you learned several things, which we will discuss. However, you are still Æsir and whatever they did or didn't do to you is irrelevant. That is a domestic issue, and we will not be involved in any way. What I need to hear from you is why they are here, how long they have been here, and what their intentions are."

"Yes, madam. When I was at the facility, I was told by a man introduced to me as Ben— who you can clearly see in the photograph is Balder—that they had set up the facility approximately five years prior to the incident that ended

Asgardian rule. It was something they apparently foresaw. After the incident, a small contingent of one hundred and six came here to meet with The Three, who had set up the facility along with assistance from the human community and at least one other immortal, Seshet."

Ma'at flipped her hand up quickly, which Grace was understanding meant to stop talking. "Seshet? Who told you that Seshet was helping them?"

"No one had to tell me. I had several conversations with her. She is the one who performed the testing on me."

Ma'at contemplated for a moment. It was obvious she did not know Seshet's involvement. She was smoldering.

"I'll need to check the rule of law. Because she was acting under Asgardian authority, it still may not be an issue." She turned to the scribe. "Decree that Seshet will be compelled to appear before Osiris, head of the Egyptian pantheon, for testimony with charges pending for aiding and not reporting, and possible charges for experimentation on an immortal being without consent."

Grace spoke out of turn. "Multiple immortal beings."

Ma'at snapped her head around at the outburst. "That is to be determined in another line of questioning once this topic is exhausted. Now, what can you tell me about their intentions?"

Graced shrugged. "Their intentions are unclear to me. Ben told me this was a short-term solution, and they were looking for something more permanent. I do not wish to assume what he means by a more permanent location. I don't know if it will be on this planet, another planet, this dimension, or another. Much of what he told me was untruthful, and I do not know if I would believe any information about their plans or their numbers."

Ma'at turned back to the scribe. "Decree that Balder/Ben will be compelled to appear before Kali, head of the Committee for Earth in the current dimension, to explain his action in neglecting to register, as well as provide plans for future habitation and governance. There will be no formal charges for this testimony; however, a penalty for non-registration is anticipated. In the absence of the Asgard Representative Tyr, who cannot be located, he may bring an acting representative for his pantheon."

Ma'at returned her focus to Grace. "I have one last question on this topic. How many members of the Asgard pantheon are you able to verify at the facility?"

Grace thought about how to phrase that answer. Less than twenty was a minor penalty. She saw about fifty onlookers during the stabbing incident, some from the pictures, but they may not all be part of the delegation. She had seen at least twenty she recognized in the facility and the photographs. Ben told her there were one hundred and nine, but could she believe him?

"According to Ben, there are one hundred and nine individuals here, including The Three. I saw approximately fifty total people at the facility myself; however, I do not know if they were all from Asgard. Reasonably, some would be human, humanoid, or synthetic support staff working at the facility. In retrospect, I recognized at least twenty faces, several of whom I can name in the photographs. I cannot pinpoint a specific number of Asgardian citizens in the facility."

Ma'at addressed Ami. "Amitiel, do you have any firsthand knowledge of the population inhabiting the Asgard facility?"

Ami appeared disoriented, as if someone had just woken her up. "No, ma'am." Ami was clearly listening, but something was off.

Ma'at took the tablet from the scribe to make some notes. When she finished, she handed it back, pointing to something she had written. The scribe sat the tablet on the table.

"Excuse me for a moment. Would anyone like refreshments?"

"Coffee." Grace immediately spoke prior to Ma'at breaking protocol.

Ma'at looked up at him. "Bring a carafe."

Ami, remaining aloof, didn't answer.

Ma'at spoke. "Amitiel, leave us for twenty minutes." Ami made eye contact with Ma'at, stood, then vanished without speaking.

"Grace, I wanted this to be off the record. I don't know if we will make formal charges against Seshet or not. I would like you to explain to me what experiment she did not receive your consent for," Ma'at explained.

Grace described the sparring incident, Ben's injury, and the entire ordeal with the surgery and stitches. She also explained that she had given explicit consent for the scanning and blood work.

Ma'at's mouth was slightly agape. "Wow! You seriously cut through his skin? I didn't think that could happen."

"He was pretty surprised himself. I didn't know it was that big of a deal at the time. Other than him giving me his word, there was no possible way I could hurt him with my blade."

"That's something you probably shouldn't share with his enemies," Ma'at said, raising an eyebrow.

Grace leaned forward. "Isn't it?" She sighed and sat back. "Okay, I wouldn't, even as angry as I am with him. I don't really want to see him eliminated. I would like to see him suffer a bit, though."

"There's plenty of time for that. I'm curious. What were the test results?"

Grace snickered, shaking her head. "What they told me and the actual results appear to be different things. They told me the amulet only masked my position, which I believe. They also said it was bound with blood and only Ben could remove it. That I now know to be untrue. Frigg did bind it with Ben's blood, but I remembered her telling me that anyone in his direct line could remove it. I prefer for now to keep it. The second part was absolutely not true. They told me that my memories had been removed completely. Ami showed me yesterday where they were locked away in my mind and how to retrieve them."

"So, you've only had your memories for …"

Grace finished Ma'at's sentence. "About eighteen hours."

"You should still be lost in a maze of confusion. I mean, that's half a million years of memories slamming in all at once. I wouldn't be able to put together a coherent sentence for days if it was me."

Grace smirked, "I was at a party last night. I think you could pull it off."

They laughed, and Ma'at reached across the table and patted Grace's hand. "Next time invite me to the party."

"If I had known you were here, I would have. Almost two thousand years have passed since I've been up to date. I don't know where anyone is. How's your husband doing? You still together?"

"Thoth? We're still going strong. He's doing well. Always reading something. We took a little time last year to hop out to sector eighty-four to visit Jur. It was a historic trip for him, but it was a paradise vacation for me."

"I have a lot of catching up to do." Grace had known Ma'at since before she and Ben divorced the second time. They were friendly acquaintances.

They both heard the scribe approaching the door. Sitting up straight, Ma'at winked. "Here we go."

Their personas instantly reverted to professional grade.

The scribe set the coffee in the center of the table, pouring two cups and placing one in front of each woman. Grace reached for the sweetener while Ma'at took the cream first. Then they switched without speaking. It was a rhythm they had conducted before at hundreds of council sessions. The familiarity of the motion had overtaken her before she realized she took her brewed coffee black now. She made a slight grimace at the cup before bringing it to her lips and deciding it was better to drink it than make a fuss. It certainly wouldn't be the worst thing she'd ever had.

A short time later, Ami ported back in. The scribe was scowling.

"Porting is not allowed in these chambers!"

Ami snapped back, "I was told to port out and be back in twenty minutes. I was following instructions. If I wasn't supposed to port back into this chamber, I should have been told where I was supposed to port."

Ma'at stopped the argument. She had forgotten how literal Ami was. "It was my mistake. I should have been clearer. Ami, in the future, porting is allowed when leaving the chamber. When porting back in, you are required to port to the vestibule to limit disruptions."

Ami replied, "Yes, madam. Thank you for clarifying." As soon as Ma'at looked away from her, Ami smirked at the scribe, who stuck his tongue out in return.

Ma'at closed her eyes for a moment and tapped the table. "Now that we are all back, we will proceed with the second item of discussion. Let it be noted that your complaint was amended to include the possible kidnapping and illegal detainment of two immortals by the Asgardian delegation. Is this correct?"

Ami had returned to her catatonic state.

Grace replied, "Yes, that is correct."

"We have had no pantheons report on anyone missing. Where did you come by this information?"

"While I was at the Asgard facility, Seshet informed me they had two immortals I know for a fact have been missing for several weeks. I do not believe these two would be there of their own accord without communicating with their families." Grace was choosing her wording carefully, attempting to get more information across before she had to tell Ma'at about vampires.

"Once again, I will state no pantheon has reported missing members. What would make you believe they are not there voluntarily? And how would you know anything about other immortals missing for weeks, much less their families, if you couldn't remember any of them?"

Grace pulled out the files she had on Olivia and Zane Santos, sliding them across the table to Ma'at. "They don't belong to any pantheon. Their clans have reported them missing and there were signs of a struggle in their hotel room, along with some of the male's blood. There is a male and a female who have been missing approximately three weeks."

Ma'at opened the file on Olivia. Her mouth fell open and her eyes widened. "Vampires? Grace, how are you involved with vampires? This is against protocol. We can't get involved in this."

Grace spoke quickly. "Yes, you can. You have an obligation to all immortal beings, not just Council members. Our charter states that *all* immortal species are obligated to regulation and protection of the Council. Nowhere does it say there are any exclusions if the immortal is not a member. We are obligated to protect them, and it is illegal for them to be held or experimented on without their full knowledge and consent. Even if the vampires weren't included under the protections, Ben and Seshet are illegally holding immortals regardless, and that is criminal behavior under the Council Charter. We just want them back."

Ma'at stood up and began pacing, shaking her head. Grace noticed again that Ami had no reaction to the tension. Grace clenched her jaw at the realization of what Ami was doing.

Ma'at stopped. "What do you mean by *we* want them back? How are you involved with them?" She was raising her voice, which was out of character for her.

Grace stayed as calm as possible. "My mate is a vampire. I have been part of the community since it started."

"I don't know what to do about this situation, Grace. This is unprecedented. I must get the Council involved." Ma'at addressed the scribe. "Call an emergency meeting of the subcommittee. Three hours." She turned her attention back to Grace.

Before Ma'at could speak, Grace stood and leaned forward with her weight resting on the table under her hands. "You can start with getting these two back. The rest we can deal with later when they are out of a dangerous situation. Then you can decide what to do with the community and me."

Ma'at took her seat. "This would be so much easier if they weren't an emergent species. If they were further along in their progression. We just don't know enough about them to decide whether to advance their development."

Grace dropped back into her chair. "I can bring in their Regent. He and my mate are the only two who are aware of my situation. And if the two young vampires hadn't been kidnapped, the Regent wouldn't have become involved at all. Please, have the Council hear him out. He's willing to work with you to get these people back. If you don't think they're ready, put them on probation. You can always have him wiped if you have doubts about what he says." Grace was certain Ivan could convince them to give the vampires a chance to prove themselves.

Ma'at chewed her lower lip as she was assessing her options. "This is what is going to happen. The Regent and your husband will appear in this chamber as soon as possible. I don't know yet if they will be questioned or if we will decide their fate without their testimony. That is something for the subcommittee to decide."

"You," Ma'at said, pointing to Grace, "will take Amitiel and a retrieval squad to the facility. Our squad commander will serve notice for Ben and Seshet to appear. They will also compel Ben to turn over the vampires. You will all come back to these chambers. Until we can decide, no one with any knowledge of these events can be exposed to the general population. You will be an observer in this situation. I am only letting you go because you are familiar with the facility. Do you understand?"

Grace gave Ma'at a short, curt nod. "Yes"

Ma'at continued. "*Observer*, Grace. Do not aggravate the situation. You are only being allowed to go because I feel our squad will face less aggression if you are there. If the situation escalates, find the vampires and return here. Do not engage in any physical altercation. If an altercation ensues, that is what the squad is for. Am I making myself clear?"

"Yes, Ma'at."

She continued. "As for the rest of it, I don't even know where to begin. You are clearly influencing an emergent species. Because of your lack of knowledge about other immortals until yesterday, it was impossible for you to provide them with any developmental support. I honestly have no idea what the Council is going to do about your situation now since you would be an obvious influence and in clear violation of the charter."

Grace didn't reply. She nodded solemnly and sighed.

Ma'at looked at Ami, who was still staring ahead. "Amitiel, do you understand what your role is in this situation?" Ami didn't respond. "Amitiel!"

Ami appeared scattered, looking to regain her composure. "Yes, madam. I understand."

Ma'at suddenly realized what Grace had figured out twenty minutes earlier. "Amitiel! Are you broadcasting?! Who is hearing this?"

Ami became defensive. "Council meetings are open unless they are posted as private. I'm not doing anything wrong."

Ma'at was livid. She balled her fists at her side as her face reddened. "Who are you broadcasting to?"

Ami didn't like being yelled at. She crossed her arms and lowered her head. "Ivan and Lukkas."

"Who are Ivan and Lukkas?"

Ami looked down at her hands. "Ivan is the Vampire Regent, and Lukkas is Grace's husband."

Ma'at closed her eyes and growled, "Go get them immediately and bring them directly back into this chamber. Do not port into the outer chamber. Do not let anyone see you." She opened her eyes and Ami was still there, appearing confused.

"But you told me earlier—"

Ma'at cut her off. "NOW!"

Ami disappeared with a *whoosh* of air.

Ma'at turned on Grace. "Did you know she was broadcasting for them?"

"Nope. I didn't know how this was going to go, and I certainly didn't want Ivan to hear anything he didn't understand. Lukkas, on the other hand, has put up with me for years, so he doesn't jump to conclusions when he doesn't understand something."

Ami ported back into the chamber with Ivan and Lukkas in tow. Both men stumbled as she dragged them forward, like she snatched them up without saying anything. Porting could also be disorienting if you were not prepared for it, so it surprised Grace that neither of them was puking. Lukkas had changed into jeans and an Oxford shirt, thank the stars. Ivan was still in his tux pants and shirt from the previous night. His appearance made Grace realize he hadn't slept at all.

Ma'at stood. "Gentlemen, please come forward. Grace, Amitiel, you are dismissed. Ami, you will be dealt with when you return. The squad commander is waiting for you in the staging area."

Ma'at sat and addressed the men. "Now, what am I supposed to do with you?"

Ivan and Lukkas looked at each other, then back at Ma'at.

Ma'at continued. "Which one is which?"

Ivan answered. "I am Ivan Novak, Regent of the vampire race. This is Lukkas Eliassen, one of our most distinguished citizens."

"I, as I am sure you have already heard, am Ma'at, head of the Subcommittee for Earth on Ethics and Justice. Ironic, isn't it, since you've been involved in an action this morning I would consider unethical?" Ma'at paused, letting her eyes scrutinize the men, making them visibly uncomfortable.

Ma'at continued after resting long enough to unhinge their confidence. "It will be my job to recommend if the committee should hear your argument or decide your progression without your testimony. I will be asking some very specific questions and I expect specific, truthful answers." She again paused momentarily, letting Ivan and Lukkas nod in agreement.

"You may take your seats," Ma'at directed, waving her hand toward the two seats opposite her position.

"Which of you has known Grace the longest?"

Lukkas answered. "That would be me, ma'am. Over seven hundred years. Ivan met her a few weeks after."

"And how did you meet?"

Lukkas explained about the villagers in the woods, how Grace found and saved him, and how he gave Grace her name.

Ma'at concluded even then someone was interfering with the progression of the vampire species by sending Grace to save Lukkas. "Did you know at that point she was not from this sphere?"

"No, I understood she was different, immortal but not afflicted with the requirements of our species. And she smelled different. Not a vampire, also not entirely human. When I drank from her, I had gained strength and healing abilities uncommon for even natural-born vampires."

His statement intrigued Ma'at. "Explain what you mean by natural-born vampires. I thought you only procreated by turning humans."

"No ma'am. That is not correct. We can reproduce among ourselves."

Ivan saw she was looking for further explanation. "If I may?"

"Yes, Ivan, please explain."

Ivan wanted to clarify their evolution. "The first of our species were like animals. Their actions were driven solely by primal instincts. All they were concerned with was feeding and pleasure. As we incorporated some more enlightened humans into our kind, they were able to determine what the actual needs and capabilities of our species were. A few vampires had been born, but they hadn't understood it was from a purely vampiric union. In fact, so few had been born that we concluded the women were already with child when they were turned. It was unknown then, but our species' gestational period is only one hundred days."

Ma'at's face shifted minutely, showing the slightest hint of surprise at the abbreviated length.

Ivan continued. "The first birth that couldn't have been a prior pregnancy didn't happen until much later in our timeline. Research spanning several hundred years has shown that female vampires are only fertile for a few days every half to full century, during which they can bear offspring. We've adopted the practice of keeping our populations small after the seventeenth- and eighteenth-century exterminations. We rarely turn humans unless they are being taken as a mate. And even then, humans must go through an arduous assessment process before we accept them to be turned. We need to ensure they are mentally stable and fit in with our new society. Most vampires less than three hundred years old are naturally born. We restrict each mated pair to two children. For another child, the Board's approval is subject to strict conditions and endorsement from their clan."

"What about mating with humans? Does your species have children with humans?"

Ivan furrowed his forehead. "Those are two different questions. For us, mating is for life. If a vampire chooses a human to be mated with, as part of the mating ceremony, the human must be turned. The human and sire become bonded. The only exception we have ever made was Grace. She and Lukkas haven't had a mating ceremony, but even if they had, we would never give her approval to be turned. She's already immortal, and that's the basis for the ceremony, and we don't know how turning would affect her natural abilities." Ivan glanced at Lukkas before continuing.

"Even if Lukkas had requested a mating ceremony, the Board would never have allowed her to be sired as part of it." Ivan would never let Lukkas put Grace at risk. She was too valuable to the community in ways that the others did not know of.

Lukkas looked shocked at Ivan's statement. He didn't think it was the Board's business if he and Grace decided she should take the turn. Ma'at noticed his cheeks flushed with anger and made a note that this may be a point of contention.

"As far as a male vampire procreating with a human female, that has always resulted in the mother's death and the children aren't always immortal. They all have the thirst, but some don't have the ability to regenerate. Many have mental issues as well. A human male has never successfully seeded a female vampire. We ended the practice of mixed species with our new government, and we heavily punished the practice, as it is not ethical for the mother or child."

Ma'at leaned in. They seemed to have a sense of conservancy for the species, as well as an ethical code beyond their infancy. She wondered how much of that was from Grace's influence. Even if she didn't directly have memories, she was still a far more developed species.

"Ivan, how did you come to form your existing governing body?"

"There was a time when we were conspicuous and careless. We started off as a predatory species, seeing humans as only a food source. We had lost our own humanity, becoming heady with our power and immortality. Our downfall was because of arrogance. It shouldn't have been a surprise when humans began banding together. The predators became the hunted. We came to realize we needed to change to survive. Some of us had known of other clans and had occasionally worked and socialized with them. Lukkas, Grace, and I had known each other for a few centuries, and we had a different view of our situation than some of the other clans. We wanted a more symbiotic relationship with humans. Most vampires in our area didn't hunt humans any longer. We survived on animals, and when we needed to feed from humans, we would refrain from killing them. Some of us had learned a way of entrancing them that would allow us to make them forget our interaction or change what they remembered. We brought our clans together, with two other local clans, to discover a way to keep from being hunted. We decided on a few basic rules of conduct. When discussing survival, we found out that each group knew of clans the others were not familiar with. We sent envoys to invite each clan's leader to meet for discussions. Each of those clan leaders knew of more clans. We ended up with over a hundred representatives from all over the world when all was said and done."

"And they all agreed to your terms?" Ma'at asked.

"We agreed to create the terms. Grace suggested we set up a structure by region and helped define boundaries. They would appoint a representative for each clan. We chose regional board members from the local leaders elected by clan representatives. The Board of Representatives then elected me as their head, or Regent. We hold elections twice a century, but the representatives seldom change."

Ivan was well spoken and quite charismatic. He was calm and direct. Ma'at believed he would testify well if it came to that. Since she was recording, the committee may not find it necessary to speak to them. If the committee appointed her to advocate for them, she needed to assess how advanced their abilities were.

"You clearly understand how momentous this could be for your species. We need to assess your progression and determine if you are ready to be aware of or included in the Council. This will probably take place over the next few months or even years. The next few questions will determine if I am going to advocate for you with the subcommittee or let them determine your fate without further input. My first question is regarding the entrancing you had previously mentioned. Do all vampires have this ability, and can they perform it on anyone?"

Because these questions were regarding the entire species, Ivan would be answering most of them. "Yes, this ability is present in all vampires, to some extent. The more one practices, the sharper this skill becomes. As for the ability to entrance anyone, we have had success with humans, of course. It depends on the skill of the one performing the entrancement and the strength of resistance in the subject. Some of us have skills sharp enough to entrance other vampires."

"I will require a demonstration. Scribe, step forward."

The scribe looked irritated and afraid simultaneously.

Ma'at reached over to touch Ivan's hand and placed a thought inside of his mind. *Tell him to walk around the table twelve times clockwise before he takes his seat.* Ivan nodded in reply. Telepathy seemed to be an ability not specifically attached to only Grace's species.

He placed his hand on the scribe's shoulder, looking into his eyes. "I will not hurt you. Are you all right?"

The scribe answered, "Yes, I am well. I am not concerned about being hurt as much as being embarrassed."

Ivan was assessing the man. He was strong but not exceptionally intelligent. It would be a bit harder than it would be with a human, but Ivan could easily entrance this one. He locked eyes with intense concentration and pushed deep, whispering, "When you return to your seat next time, circle the table clockwise twelve times before you sit. You will not physically be able to seat yourself until you complete the task." Ivan backed off, changing his demeanor back to neutral.

"Are you sure you're okay? You look a little pale."

The scribe answered, "I assure you, I am fine. Please proceed."

Ma'at and Ivan exchanged a look.

Ma'at said to the scribe, "I think it has been enough for now. Take your seat."

The scribe turned around, walking past the short side of the table back to his seat. He pulled out his chair, then pushed it back in and proceeded around the table. The next time around, he attempted to seat himself again but could not.

Ma'at found this terribly amusing. "Scribe, take your seat now."

"Yes, madam." He tried to turn around to take the shortest route back to his chair, but he couldn't. He didn't even appear to be fazed by the odd behavior, continuing to circle the table like it was the most natural thing to do. Each time Ma'at would tell him to be seated, he would reply, "Yes, madam," and continue his journey. When he had completed his task, he sat and made a note that they did not complete the experiment. Ma'at took his tablet, scribing the statement herself and signing it. When she handed it back to the scribe, he put his head in his hands.

Ma'at chided. "It could have been much worse. Be grateful I wasn't in a better mood today."

The scribe looked up warily. "Yes, thank you, madam."

Ma'at thanked Ivan for the demonstration, directing him back to his seat. "Would you be able to entrance someone more powerful? Have you ever been able to entrance Grace?"

"I've never tried. Lukkas, have you ever been able to entrance Grace?" Ivan was curious himself about Lukkas's abilities.

"Not me. I can't even talk her into anything she doesn't want to do. If I could entrance her, there are many times I certainly would have. Ivan has honed the skill far better than I. He may at least be capable of planting a suggestion with her."

Ivan was not pleased with the idea that Lukkas would want to entrance Grace for his own purposes.

Ma'at looked at Ivan. "Try it with me. I warn you, though. Nothing embarrassing."

"I can certainly try. May I?" He gestured a request to approach Ma'at.

"You may."

Ivan walked around the table and knelt in front of her chair. He reached out, taking Ma'at's hand and looking deeply into her eyes. She had immense intelligence and quite a bit of power. He engaged her in some light conversation while attempting to press more deeply into her mind. After a few minutes, he believed he had it. He pressed in with all he could muster and whispered something to her, then backed up slightly.

"It seems you may be more of a challenge than I had expected. Thank you for your patience."

Ma'at nodded to him as he rose to take his seat back. "I applaud your attempt."

As he sat, he remarked, "I must compliment you on your breathtaking tiara."

Ma'at appeared confused. "I'm not wearing a tiara." She reached up to find her emerald-encrusted choker was, in fact, sitting atop her head. It clearly impressed her. She had no memory of the suggestion, nor of removing her necklace or placing it on her own head.

"That is a very powerful ability. There may be potential for your species yet." She replaced her necklace firmly back around her throat. "I hope I will not find this on my head again."

"No. It was specifically a onetime suggestion. It was very taxing to implant. A longer-term suggestion likely wouldn't have taken effect. I clearly need additional exercise with my skills."

Ma'at found Ivan even more charming and humble than she had before. He was skilled at getting into and out of the entrancement without tipping his hand. She was searching for an appropriate descriptive word for him. She thought he was smooth, like a well-aged whisky.

They spoke for another two hours. She questioned them about their basic abilities: speed, strength, intelligence, hearing, sight, smell, and, of course, entrancement. She also asked about other skills and was told if they had a certain skill as a human, it would be exponentially enhanced as a vampire. Musical abilities, for example, would be enhanced by having better dexterity and more pronounced hearing. Ma'at was also interested in the CB products and their reasoning behind developing them.

By the time they were wrapping things up, she thought the squad ought to have returned. The subcommittee would be meeting in the main committee room in a few minutes. Her examination of the squad's activities would have to wait until the Council was in session.

She had the scribe show the men to a comfortable waiting room. She didn't need them sitting around the chamber and she also didn't want to let them go just yet. The scribe was instructed to tell them it was in case she needed their testimony. Realistically, she wanted to keep them here, so they didn't speak with anyone about the Council.

CHAPTER ELEVEN

While Ma'at was interrogating Ivan and Lukkas, Grace and Ami ported into the staging area. Commander Vaeweth was standing on the platform. There were usually only a handful of Jur in this sector, but today there were two thirteen-person squads plus the commander. It made her uneasy, wondering if they were expecting resistance or ensuring there was none. Jur were uniquely qualified for this type of work. They were quick, quiet, and extremely strong. Mind probes didn't work on them, and they could withstand multiple hits from energy weapons. They also had the ability to endure extreme heat and cold.

When Grace turned, Vaeweth was staring at her. She and Ami proceeded toward him. He was solid and muscular with dark, thick skin, white-blonde hair cropped military style, and gold eyes. She extended her hand. He grasped it with a very firm handshake.

"Grace," he stated, nodding at her.

Grace saw his eyes were highly unusual. Around the gold center there was a reflective gold ring, which almost appeared to be lit.

"Commander," she nodded back. He released Grace's hand and extended it toward Ami, who glared at him.

"Ami, don't be rude."

Ami complied, reaching out to shake the Commander's hand.

Veins protruded from Vaeweth's temples. "I'm not going to have any trouble with you this time, am I, Amitiel?"

"No, Commander. I've been told to do whatever you say."

He didn't trust her. She was a wild card who did what she wanted. He didn't like wild cards. He liked an integrated team that did exactly what he planned for them to do. It seemed to him Grace had some influence over Amitiel. He would have to find a way to use that to keep her in check.

"We took your location information and were able to pull a set of original blueprints for the facility." He led them to a digital table where the facility diagram hovered as a 3D hologram. "They built it initially as an end-of-world bunker. We've made the adjustments to the layout based on your testimony. I'll need you to show us any details we didn't place correctly."

Grace looked over the image and pointed out a few differences she could see. "That is as accurate as I remember. They're also using an AI called Ida."

Commander Vaeweth's jaw twitched. "That information is helpful. There are still too many unknowns for my liking." He called up one of his team members to relay the information about Ida. It was a known AI platform, so they would concentrate on trying to hack through it as he continued speaking to Grace.

"The outer walls are over a meter thick reinforced concrete sandwiched between carbide-reinforced sheets. We've staged a mock-up in the training bay. They have the facility on lock. There's no way to port in without a code. We've been trying to hack it with no success so far. The info on the model of AI should help. We have no way to breach the wall without causing undue attention, so if you have any better idea than blowing the crap out of the place, I'd like to hear it."

"Show me the mock-up."

Grace looked at the wall, then peered back over her shoulder at him. She stepped forward and easily phased through it, then turned around and returned.

"You mean like that?" The room went silent as everyone stopped what they were doing to watch her.

"Where have you been all my life? Can you pull a team through that?"

"I certainly hope so," she replied.

"If you have any doubt, we'll find another way. I don't want my squad placed in any danger."

"Let's see how many I can handle. I can start with four with gear and we can add from there." Grace was confident. Remembering the past gave her insight on how to use her skills. That was another thing Ben had lied about. She always had a high aptitude for phasing, though she seldom used it.

Vaeweth circled up the squad. "Listen up. I know you all saw what happened. I want three volunteers to step forward. Everyone else take a knee and pay attention. Grace, it's all yours."

Grace stepped into the middle of the circle. "We are going to drill phasing through that wall for the next hour. We are going to make sure everyone gets through this wall safely. To accomplish this, I need unbroken physical contact. It's like an electrical circuit. Any break results in everything downstream not being connected. Understood?" She looked at each fighter for a nod or a thumbs-up.

"I need everyone who is right-handed on my right and left-handed on my left, so they have their dominant hand free for defense if necessary. Take your weak-side hand and grip the harness of the person next to you. Wrap it in if you have to, so there's no chance of the chain being broken. If you break contact with the person closer to me, do not attempt to step through the wall. It could result in you being permanently embedded in the wall or killed. This isn't some fun little *jävla* trick. You need to pay attention." She looked up and down the line.

"When I give the command 'Ready, Step,' quickstep forward. Once the end fighter on your side has cleared the wall, peel off. Continue the pattern into your designated formations and proceed with your mission. Is everyone clear?" She looked up and down the line again, getting a thumbs-up from each fighter.

Commander Vaeweth was growing less apprehensive about Grace. She wasn't just some random woman looking to grind an axe; she was tactical and mission oriented.

Grace exited the circle, facing the wall. "All right. You four step up on your dominant hand's side of me. I need to be close to the center, if possible, for the first few runs, so two lefties and two righties." She was missing something. They had nothing to grasp on her. "Commander, can I get a harness, please? I don't need anyone losing a grip on me if they get disoriented."

Commander Vaeweth pointed at one of the kneeling fighters. "Up!" The fighter took off quickly. She was back inside of a minute, handing a harness to Grace.

"All right. Tag up. By the time we finish drills, everyone should be used to the feeling of phasing." Grace continued buckling the harness straps and pulling them snug.

Commander Vaeweth grabbed her left-side harness, with another fighter on his left and two more on Grace's right. She made eye contact with him and spoke to him without speaking. *Ready?*

He wasn't sure if he had really heard her or if he had imagined it. Jur were skilled blockers and others being able to initiate a telepathic conversation was not a normal occurrence, but he still replied in his own mind, *Hells yes!* Grace smirked and he knew she heard him. Who was this woman and where in all hells had she come from?

"Ready! Step!" Grace commanded. The line proceeded forward through the wall seamlessly. Grace felt a minimal amount of drag and the soldiers didn't seem to be affected much by the process. She was confident she could pull most, if not all, of the fighters and gear through safely.

"Good run, everyone! Add four more," Grace ordered. Four more fighters stepped up, three on her right and one on her left. "I need one of you to go weakside, so I have another on my left. I felt some hesitation on the first run. You need to stay in step with me straight through, so I don't have drag."

She readied herself, glancing up and down the line. "Tag up." She looked up and down the line while they all took a firm grip. "Ready! Step!"

This run was much better timed. She felt only a slight drag since they were all in step. They kept adding fighters until she was up to twenty. She was starting to feel the heaviness of pulling. It wasn't overwhelming, but the repetitiveness was wearing on her. It would be easier if she had more time between runs. She wasn't sure she wanted to attempt all twenty-seven under her own power.

"Ami." Ami had been standing at the back of the bay, watching for the last half hour. Her attention was now on Grace. "I need a power boost."

Ami tilted her head to the left. "What am I supposed to do? I don't know how to phase."

Grace shook her head. "I don't need you to. I need to draw on your energy to boost mine. Grab a harness and stand on my left." Ami came forward as Grace instructed. Grace wrapped her left arm under Ami's, taking her hand. "When I give the command to step, I want you to push your energy out to me. Got it?"

"Yes." Ami nodded.

"All right. Everybody on line. Tag up." She scanned the line. "Ready! Step!" She felt a tremendous burst of Ami's energy. Everyone pulled through easily. They could have pulled twice as many with Ami's help.

"Yes! Okay, for this next run, I need everyone to line up on their dominant side." There were only five left-handed fighters lined up on her left, plus Ami. That made twenty-two on her right. With Ami's boost, it wouldn't be a problem. They drilled, breaching the wall for the next twenty minutes until she was satisfied and the fighters were as comfortable as they could be with phasing.

Commander Vaeweth called everyone around to go over the procedures, giving Grace a rest period before they left. They would send one team to drop through the main elevator shaft. There was a set of emergency stairs on each end of the parking level and two recirculating ducts twenty meters on each side of the elevator shaft. They would drop their own block on entering the parking level to prevent anyone from porting out, even if they had the facility code. The plan was to disable the elevator and lock down the stairwell doors, leaving one team topside to collect anyone trying to escape. They brought containment cubes that expanded to hold anyone who was uncooperative. They would breach down to the sixth level. The control center should also be on that level from the original plans.

Commander Vaeweth planned to have Grace on his team so she could phase them through the command center bulkhead if it was locked down. He also wanted Ami with his team, so he could keep an eye on her and so her stupidity didn't get any of his fighters killed. His primary goal was to find Ben and Seshet and bring them back to the Council. His secondary goal was to find the two vampires.

Grace's goals were opposite in importance. She didn't really care at this point if they brought in Ben and Seshet. Her priority was to retrieve the two innocents. She was hoping Ben wouldn't be arrogant enough to resist. In her mind, he should have seen this coming. Maybe not her specifically, but someone.

Vaeweth was seventy percent optimistic about the plan. There were a lot of variables. He would have predicted a better outcome if he had another twenty-four hours to prepare, but he didn't.

"Everyone! Take a break. Get your shit together and be back here in fifteen." He walked toward the head, past Grace and Ami.

Upon the Commanders return, everyone was ready. They gathered in a semicircle, and he addressed them one last time. "I want everyone on line in the breach position. We will all port together. Once we appear outside the facility, we will be exposed to whatever surveillance or sensors they have in place. I expect ninety seconds before we meet resistance. We need to penetrate the wall within three seconds of porting. Is everyone clear on your position, team, and mission?"

The fighters shouted in unison, "Sir, yes, sir!"

"Tag up!" He assessed the line, ensuring all were in place. "Ready! Port!"

They swiftly transported the line to the established coordinates outside the facility's entrance. Grace didn't hesitate once she felt the port close.

"Ready! Step!"

In the blink of an eye, they were inside the facility. The teams peeled off. Commander Vaeweth's team, including Ami and Grace, headed to the elevator shaft. Two of the fighters pried open the doors and dropped in. The elevator had been stopped on the fourth level. They descended quickly down the sides of the shaft, leaving the rest of the team behind on the main level. Using the external brakes, the pair forced the elevator down three additional floors so the ceiling would be even with the opening for level six. The remainder of the team dropped in as the others engaged the break locks. When they were in position, standing on top of the stopped elevator, the fighters pried open the doors to the sixth-level hallway. Alarms blared loudly. The moment the lab workers saw the Jur fighters, they immediately surrendered. Two Jur secured the hallway, lining the technicians along one wall.

One of the fighters announced, "We are not here to harm anyone. Please sit along the wall until we finish our business, and you will be free to go. Where are Ben and Seshet?"

One worker pointed toward the command center at the far end of the hall. Commander Vaeweth's team headed down the corridor to the command center. Grace looked directly into the camera above her head. She was so pissed, she was calm.

Ben was watching the monitor. As soon as he saw Ami, he realized Grace had her memories back. He did not want this fight with her or with the Council. He knew he should have registered, but he thought they would be long gone before anyone realized they were here. Not registering was a minor infraction, and he thought he might get a pleasant invitation from an envoy if they found them. He wasn't expecting it to be a full-scale attack. He had obviously miscalculated.

When Vaeweth's group arrived at the door to the command center, it was locked. Grace hit the intercom. "I know you're in there. I'm giving you the chance to be courteous and open the door. You know it won't keep us out."

Ben took a deep breath and nodded to one of his sentinels to buzz them in. Vaeweth came through first, followed by Grace, then the other two Jur, and finally Ami. On Ben's side, there were six sentinels, Ben, The Three, and several operators at the panels. Upon seeing The Three, Vaeweth realized if they decided to fight, not a single Jur would survive the encounter. The sentinels drew down on the Jur team. The Jur stayed on task. Vaeweth ordered the operators away from the control panels, imparting a confidence he was internally lacking, while the sentinels yelled at the Jur to drop their weapons. The two fighters were yelling back for them to drop theirs.

Ben knew it was a fight the Jur would not win, even with larger numbers, but said nothing. He looked at Grace with disdain. "It didn't have to be this way. I want you to remember you started this. I just wanted you to come home."

Grace boiled. She flashed so quickly she didn't even know she had done it. She was inches from Ben's face with her hand inside his chest, holding his heart. She growled low, but loudly. "ENOUGH!"

Everyone in the room froze.

She had a look of pure hatred. Her tone was guttural, calm, and terrifying. "Unless you want me to make this hand solid and rip your vile, lying heart out of your chest, you will hand over the vampires you kidnapped. NOW."

Ben shot a questioning look at Seshet, who audibly gulped, taking on a tinge of green to her skin. He signaled for the sentinel closest to the door to go get the vampires. One of the Jur fighters escorted her. The rest lowered their weapons, and someone turned off the alarms. Ben said nothing, unwilling to move even slightly. He had never been afraid of Grace before. She never wanted him to be afraid of her before. Things change. She had changed. She stared daggers at him, never moving her hand from the grip it had on his heart.

Commander Vaeweth moved past her slowly to the microphone. "Attention please. The Council representatives request your cooperation. As long as you follow instructions, you will not be harmed. We ask that you remain in your quarters or in your general work area until our visit has concluded. Thank you." He never took his eyes off Grace and Ben. This standoff was intense.

"Mother?"

"Shut up, Mikkel," she and Ben said simultaneously. Only this time, no one thought it was funny.

Commander Vaeweth instantly made the connection he had missed. He had heard the stories, and he was glad he wasn't on the receiving end of that rage. He continued with his mission, observing the scene while moving toward Seshet.

"You are being detained for the crime of unauthorized experimentation on immortal beings and failure to report an unregistered delegation. You will be detained until you are called to appear before Osiris." Then he whispered as he placed binding links on her wrists, "Oh, and just so you know, Ma'at was publicly embarrassed by your actions."

Seshet swallowed hard. Angering Osiris was one thing, but Ma'at could find ways to torture her even after death.

Vaeweth turned his attention to Ben. "You are being called to testify before Kali, head of the Committee for Earth in the current dimension, to explain neglecting to register as well as provide plans for future habitation and governance. You have no charges pending at this time. You will receive Council assistance as necessary to relocate and reestablish your pantheon. In the absence of your pantheon representative, you may bring one Asgardian citizen with you as support. I will not be binding you at this time."

Ben looked at Grace's arm sticking out of the middle of his chest, as if to say he didn't think that would be an issue.

Vaeweth lightly placed a hand on Grace's free shoulder. "Grace. You should let go now. You're only making things worse for yourself."

Grace never took her eyes off of Ben but replied loudly, "Don't worry about me, Commander. This is a domestic issue. The Council doesn't get involved with domestic issues. Isn't that right, Ben? They didn't do a thing about it when you had me murdered, stripped of my memories, and sent here, did they?"

"No," he almost whispered. A slight tinge of guilt washed over him. It wasn't enough to subdue the arrogance that he felt for doing what he felt he had to. But he was sorry he had taken it so far. There was no going back now.

The Three looked at each other. They all felt guilty. They knew their father had been planning something. After centuries of hearing his unsupported threats to keep their mother in line, they didn't think he'd actually do anything. Alex was the only one who attempted to tell her she should be careful.

This information dumbfounded the sentinels. They had always been told that she died of grief, and they had sent her here without memories as a solace for her. That's what the explanation had been to all the Æsir. They now understood where her anger was coming from, and they did not want to be caught in the middle of this feud. All they wanted was to find a new, safe home for their families.

Grace continued to dominate control of the room. She continued speaking in a low, terrifyingly monotone voice. "Why did you come here? Of all the planets and all the dimensions you could have chosen, why here? And don't lie to me. I've had enough of your lies to choke me."

He was afraid to lie to her, but he was afraid to tell her the truth, too. "I came here to find you," was all he was able to say.

Grace was doing everything in her power to remain calm. She flexed her fingers, pressing them against the back of Ben's heart. All eyes in the room were on her.

"You've done everything you could possibly do to make my life miserable. You tricked my father into agreeing to make me marry you when I was involved with your brother. You controlled everything in my life, from what I wore to who my friends were. You spent all your free time with your adoring fans, and I always supported you. I gave you children. I never said a word against you to anyone, even when I knew you were with other women. I even grew to love you in some sick and twisted way. I did everything you ever asked of me until I couldn't take it anymore! The last time we separated, I thought I was finally free, but you never took your thumb from my back. I was only a conquest for you. I was just another trophy for you to bring out on display at your whim. You treated me like property. Your own mother felt sorry for me to the point of helping me get away from you and now you've tried to ruin the only happiness I've ever had. You shouldn't have come here."

Ben was growing uncomfortable with her tightening grip. "I thought if you didn't remember the bad parts, we could start over. How can I make this right?"

A wave of sadness overtook her. "You can't. There is no way for you to undo what you've done. You need to find a world to make your own for your people. You need to find someone you can be happy with. I want you to let me go." She slid her hand out of his chest. Turning her back to him, she walked through the wall into the hallway.

Ben bent forward, bracing himself on his knees. He ran a hand through his hair as his lunch threatened to purge itself from his stomach. He straightened himself, contemplating what she had said. It was never his intention to make her feel the way she did. He could never make it up to her. What he had done to her was as much torture for him as it was for her. One day, he hoped he could make her see why he had to treat her so harshly when he was fully aware she didn't deserve it.

Alex got up to run after her. One fighter raised his weapon. Vaeweth pushed it down and let the man pass. He ran around the corner to see her sitting on the floor with her back to him, hiding her tears.

She heard Alex behind her and wiped her face. "I'm sorry you had to hear that. Your father is a good man. He loves you and your brothers, and he would do anything for you. He just wasn't a good husband for me." She was clear. There was nothing left for her to be angry about. She was doing everything she could to let it go. Anger had never served her well, and she was distraught that she had let it take over so completely with Ben.

"We never saw how unhappy you were. We didn't know any of that. Why didn't you explain what was going on? We would have understood."

"Alex, there wasn't any point. I didn't want to poison your memories or taint your image of your father. He's still a righteous man. He will make an excellent ruler for the Æsir. You need to support him in that. You understand I'm not coming back now. I can't come back."

"I know," he said sadly, bowing his head. "You'll stay in touch, won't you?"

"Of course. I'm not abandoning you. I'm just not going with you. You're all grown men now. It's about time you got families of your own."

"Like any decent, moral women would have us?" he said, letting a grin slip over his lips.

"You're such an asshole."

"And that's why I'm your favorite," he said, helping her off the floor. They walked back into the command center.

Vaeweth asked, "Are we ready to move out?"

Grace side-eyed him. "You should get the codes and port them back. I'm not leaving without the vampires. They're the only reason I came."

"We'll all wait. My team doesn't split up. We all come in. We all go out."

Seshet opened her mouth for the first time since they arrived. "I have the codes. It will be easier to port a group from the platform in the lab."

Vaeweth didn't like or trust Seshet. He had an additional little surprise for her. "Amitiel, please escort the prisoner to the port. Set up the appropriate codes to unlock the block. Take Paneth with you. He has the coordinates to the detention and can check the device for tampering. Do not let her out of your sight. Do not take off the binding rings. You are authorized to use any force necessary to ensure she doesn't escape."

Ami was thrilled to be useful. "Yes, Commander. I will perform my duties exactly as you have instructed." Ami was also hoping Seshet would step out of line. It would give her an excuse to cause her pain for what she did to Grace.

Seshet, on the other hand, did not look happy about this situation at all. Ami was unpredictable and reckless. Seshet was afraid, especially with the way Ami was smiling. Ami placed a hand on Seshet's shoulder, causing a shudder to run up her back.

"Shall we?" Ami grinned even more broadly, pushing her into the hallway. Seshet flashed Vaeweth a pleading look. He replied with a wave and the three of them disappeared down the hallway.

Commander Vaeweth addressed Ben and Grace. "Are you two quite finished?"

Ben replied, "Yes."

Grace replied, "My intent was to de-escalate and control the situation. I apologize for the rest of my actions."

Vaeweth contemplated his answer. "I can't condone your method, but you accomplished your objective."

Grace checked her watch. They had been in here for just under twelve minutes. "Can you check the status of the hostages? I don't want to be here any longer than we need to. These people are scared enough."

Vaeweth tapped his comm. "Spear Bravo, status." He listened for a few moments, nodding his head. "Spear rally point level six lab three mikes."

"We'll all meet up at the port in three minutes. Ben, you are authorized to bring one advocate to the Council with you. Who do you choose?"

Ben looked at Grace, more from habit and instinct than anything else, and she nodded to Alex.

"Alex," he said.

Vaeweth signaled him to come with them. He looked at the others in the command center. "Our apologies for the interruption. Your people will be returned to you after the Council inquiry. You may carry on normal operations once we clear the port."

Erik and Mikkel stood up.

Erik answered, "I will ensure you have no resistance."

Ben directed Erik to maintain standard operations. "We will have a clearer plan when I return. Make sure everyone understands we will cooperate with any Council representatives in the future."

"Yes, sir." Erik returned order to the command center as the group exited toward the lab.

When they got to the platform, the remainder of the teams were filtering in. The sentinel and fighter were exiting the elevator with the two vampires. Olivia recognized Grace from some events she had attended. They had never met again after Olivia had turned one, but she knew who she was. Grace approached them.

"Olivia? Zane?" They looked disheveled, tired, and hungry. Especially Olivia, whose skin was showing signs of dehydration.

Olivia answered, "Yes, Miss Grace. How did you find us?"

"Let's not worry about that now. We need to get you somewhere safe. How long has it been since you fed?" Grace was concerned about her.

"Not since they took us. I've been on CB for decades. They kept putting humans in our cells, but we wouldn't feed. They gave Zane a few blood bags, but they tried to force me to feed on the living. Our venom was extracted after they took our blood. I was afraid if I fed, they would try to turn them. I didn't take any of the food or water they offered for fear they would contaminate it with human blood."

Grace spun around. "Find those samples and take the data they have collected."

Vaeweth signaled to one of the fighters to comply.

Grace brought Olivia and Zane over to the squad. "Ami, as soon as we port, I need you to go to my hotel room and get the two bottles with the CB mark on them. There is also a bag of supplements in my travel bag."

"Got it." Ami remembered the bottles of wine Lukkas showed her with the mark.

Commander Vaeweth pulled Paneth aside. "Is the port good to go, or do you think someone has tampered with it?"

Paneth answered immediately, "Looks legit to me, sir."

"There's one way to find out for sure. Seshet, you will go through first with Amitiel. Amitiel, if it is a trap, or it doesn't port to the platform, shred her."

"Absolutely." Ami was far too eager about the possibility she would get to rip Seshet apart.

"Take this comm so you can report back as to where the port lands." Paneth was handing Ami his comm.

"I don't need that. I can let Grace know."

Paneth took his comm back, unfazed by the remark. Most of the Council's citizens had telepathy of one type or another. It was the reason the Jur were trained against it.

"Well then, I guess we're ready for the test run. There will be custodians waiting to take Seshet when you land. Step in." Vaeweth wanted to get out of here as soon as possible. "Turn off our block."

"Done," Paneth acknowledged.

"Paneth, activate the port."

Ami and Seshet instantly disappeared.

"They're on the platform. It's clear," Grace reported to Vaeweth.

Vaeweth responded, "Everyone, get in position." He waited until everyone was inside the port area. "Paneth, activate."

They appeared on the detention platform as Seshet was being led away, and Ami was already gone. The outcome of the mission left Vaeweth feeling satisfied. He did, however, need to address some issues with the execution.

"Ten by ten, squad!" The squad celebrated the end of a safe mission with howling, back slaps, posturing, and chest bumps.

"Get the vampires to waiting room one. Grace, you and Ben are expected in the vestibule outside the main Council chamber. It was a pleasure working with you." He extended a hand to Grace.

She shook it firmly. "The pleasure was all mine. Thank you." She stepped back and ported to the vestibule without waiting for Ben.

Ben shook his head and ported along with Alex. Grace was already at the coffee bar with her back to him. She finished pouring her cup and sat down at the far end of the room near the chamber doors. Ben grabbed a bottle of water and sat directly across from her. Alex sat at the opposite end of the room, as far away from both of them as he could get, finding the situation extremely awkward.

Grace closed her eyes and tried to communicate with Lukkas. He either was somewhere he couldn't hear her, or he couldn't reply. Either scenario made her uncomfortable.

They had been sitting there for at least thirty minutes when Ami appeared. Grace perked up immediately.

"What took you so long? Is everything all right?"

Ami sat next to Grace. "They're fine. I got them what you asked for. They are fed and have been taken to somewhere they can clean up. I stayed to make sure they didn't need anything else. They need to sleep, but overall, they're healthy."

"That's a relief to hear. The news of their safety will bring comfort to their clan." Once Grace had finished speaking, she began a nonverbal conversation with Ami.

Are they with Lukkas and Ivan? Did they say what happened while we were gone?

Ami replied, *They are with Lukkas and Ivan, but there were others in the room attending to Olivia and Zane. They didn't say what happened.*

Are they okay?

Yes.

Do you know why Lukkas isn't replying to me?

Ami sighed, *They're in the white waiting room.*

Oh great, Grace thought to herself, they're being held in isolation.

After another hour, the scribe from earlier opened the chamber doors. He pointed at Ben.

"They are ready for you. Bring your representative."

Ben and Alex followed him into the chamber and the doors closed. The word "Private" appeared over the door and they could hear it lock. It was another two hours before the doors opened again. Alex walked back through, flashing his mother a tentative glance before he ported out. The scribe came through behind him.

"You're next," he said to Grace. Grace and Ami rose.

"Not you," he said, pointing to Ami. "Wait here."

Grace took a breath before following the scribe into the chamber.

CHAPTER TWELVE

Grace and the scribe moved forward in the courtroom-style chamber. He made the customary announcements, directing Grace to be seated at the table on the left directly in front of the full committee panel. Kali sat in the center of the panel, Ma'at at the end closest to Grace. There were only three others on the panel she recognized, including the newly appointed Asgardian representative, Ben. She sarcastically thought this must be her lucky day. Of course, Mister Charming had wormed his way into the seat left vacant by the missing Tyr.

Kali waited until Grace had taken her seat before speaking. "Grace, you are in a unique situation, which makes it difficult to decide what to do. We have come up with two options. The choice of which option to proceed with will be yours. The first option is to return to your rightful place with the Æsir. They are in dire need of leaders to help find a vacant planet that meets their requirements. They have a monumental task ahead of them rebuilding their civilization and they will welcome you back with open arms."

Kali paused, and Grace acknowledged her with a nod as she bit her tongue hard enough to draw blood. She needed to do everything in her power to remain detached and keep her mouth shut during this proceeding.

Kali continued. "Your second option is to remain here as a liaison with the burgeoning new immortals. They need guidance in their emerging society. While they are being evaluated, they will retain a provisional membership."

Grace's heart soared at those words. She couldn't believe what she was hearing. Would they really consider letting her keep the life she was so happy with?

To Grace's disappointment, Kali resumed speaking. "If you choose this option, you will only have disclosure of your true identity with the Regent. None of the others will know your purpose."

The words sank in. It was just another big "screw you" to Grace. Her heart dropped into her stomach. She would not be allowed to keep her life, no matter which option she chose. What she was understanding was she could return to the Æsir to be back under Ben's control, or she could stay here and only have contact with Ivan. She definitely didn't want to return with Ben. Any life here, no matter how different, would be better than returning to him. Beyond what it would do to her, she needed to know how her decision would impact the vampires.

Kali was sympathetic about her situation. She did not like giving Grace these options, but the vote had not gone in her favor. Neither choice would be one she thought appropriate. Some of the other members saw it as a privilege to even have a choice. They ruled their own pantheons with an iron fist, with no room for choice from what they deemed a subordinate. They had no concern about her feelings or how greatly it would impact her life.

"Do you have questions that may help clarify your choices?"

Grace had many questions, but the phrasing had to be perfect. A moment passed before she swallowed hard and answered, "I would like to understand what impact both choices will have on the new immortal society. If I choose to go back to the Asgardian pantheon, how will the vampires be guided? If I choose to stay and assist them, what will my role be and how will I affect their growth?"

Kali nodded. "Both excellent questions. If you choose to return to the Æsir, the Council will assign another liaison to supervise their progression. We will erase your existence from their population's memories. If you choose to remain as a liaison to the species, their memories will be rewritten, and they will only know you as the Regent's mate. You and he will receive additional memories consistent with what the community receives while also retaining your existing memories."

Grace paused, letting her words sink in. This seemed to be the pattern of her life. Whenever she found herself happy, she was being sold off to a man. Back to the Æsir so Ben could control her or become Ivan's mate. Why did it have to be as a mate? Why did they have to put her in a position of being subservient? She was resentful but glad simultaneously to have any kind of choice. She did care for Ivan. He would be understanding. He would give her time to mourn the loss of Lukkas. Her punishment could have been far worse. No matter how they phrased it as a choice, it was most definitely a punishment for a crime she had no intention of committing. Her heart was pounding, and her throat threatened to choke closed. She breathed slowly and swallowed down the emotions that were threatening to erupt.

"When do you need my decision?"

"You must decide before you can leave the chambers by the end of today. We will be in session for two more hours. Do you have anyone you would like to discuss your decision with?"

Grace thought about her options. Lukkas was the first one to come to mind, but he would only give her an emotional argument, and she couldn't deal with that right now. They would never allow her to go back to him in either case. She needed to put up her mental armor. Grace wanted to cry, but she couldn't display any weakness. She needed to be pragmatic and cold. She had to pack her self-serving thoughts up and push them into the deepest, darkest corner of her mind.

"I would like to discuss this with the Regent, if possible, as my decision will affect him as well."

Kali nodded. "That is an acceptable choice. Ma'at, escort Grace to the holding room. I will have the Regent taken over."

Ben spoke out of turn. "As her pantheon representative, I believe I have the right to participate in this conversation."

His outburst had visibly irritated Kali and she snapped her head toward him. "First, you do not speak out of turn in these chambers. Second, this decision will affect her choice to remain part of your pantheon or be transferred directly under Council jurisdiction. The decision is not yours. Grace, do you wish to have your representative involved in your conversation?"

Grace sneered at Ben, making her disdain apparent. "Absolutely not."

Kali looked at Ben smugly. "As you wish. Ma'at, remove Grace from the chamber."

Once they were in the vestibule, Grace saw Ami was no longer there. The moment the door shut, Grace's entire body collapsed. She slid down the wall as a lump formed in her throat. Ma'at stepped in front of the door.

"I have some information for you before we go."

Grace looked up at her on the edge of tears. Standing straight to gain as much dignity as possible, she asked gruffly, "Information about what?"

"The testing Seshet did on you."

"That's the last thing I give a shit about right now," Grace snapped at Ma'at.

"I know. But you still need to listen to me." Ma'at was trying to be empathetic, but there wasn't time. The information she had couldn't wait.

Grace sighed and wiped her eyes as Ma'at continued. An entire species' evolution depended on her choice. She didn't have the luxury of falling apart.

"The Council was already given this information. Kali and the ethics subcommittee, minus Ben, have decided it is something you need to know. We will not let Ben know you have been told."

"Now you're scaring me. What information do you not want Ben to know that I have?" Grace was apprehensive.

"We know where you came from." Ma'at wasn't sure what would be the best way to say this.

Grace glared at her. "We all know I came from Asgard."

"Where your mother came from?"

Grace's heart raced. "My father said she died when I was born. What difference would it make who she was?" She wasn't certain how much more news she could take.

"We don't know if she died or not, but we know from your genetic profile she was from Alfar lineage, which explains where some of your abilities came from. She could have been Vanir, or she could have also been Disir. They both have the same markers."

Grace bit her bottom lip. "If that is true, it only makes sense that they were hiding me. I must assume since I had Æsir features, my father brought me back to Asgard."

"You were born during the war with the Vanir. If either side had discovered your birth, they would have killed you and your mother. Freya and Odin hadn't yet made their pact that ended the conflict. The combination of the abilities from her line enhanced by your father's line makes you extremely unique."

"But I died. Ben had me killed. I thought neither race could die like that."

"Technically, your physical body would have regenerated as long as your essence was intact. If they hadn't burned your body immediately, you would have reanimated. Frigg must have discovered it when she grew your new shell. She had to code your profile. That's likely why she guarded you with the amulet."

Grace was still processing. She was calculating how to get ahead of this. "When was the Council told?"

"I found out when Seshet went before Osiris. She claimed she had removed the evidence and never revealed it to anyone. I'm certain she was keeping it as a bargaining chip. The Council was told when you were waiting in the vestibule. I could tell Ben already knew."

She grabbed Grace by the arm. "You can't go back to the Æsir. I'm saying this as your friend, not as a Council member. They believe you can destroy the essence of any living creature at will. Even immortals. You can also heal others as long as their essence is intact. I think he wants control of that power. The other members believe it would be beneficial for him not to know you have this information."

Grace was stunned momentarily. She realized Ma'at thought what she was saying was true, but Grace couldn't do any of those things. "Ben told me that first night in the facility that I had the ability to heal others. I've never healed anyone, Ma'at. If I could heal someone, don't you think I would have healed him when I ripped his leg in half, or was that just another test too?"

"I don't know," answered Ma'at. "Ben is ten steps ahead on this one."

A light bulb set off in Grace's head. "Ben must have threatened to expose me. That must be why my father forced me to marry him. Ben already knew back then. He has always wanted control of me. I'm such an idiot! I have never been able to figure out why my father would do that to me, knowing I cared for someone else. He said it was for my protection. His excuse was that Ben would inherit the throne some day because Odin found Thor too unstable to reign. It never made sense to me. My father died knowing I was angry with him."

This entire week had been overwhelming. Last week she was happily pruning vines, blissfully unaware. She would give anything to go back. It was emotionally and physically exhausting.

"I understand this is a lot to put on you on top of everything else. But you need to figure out a plan. It changes the game and you and I both know it is *always* a game. If you'd still like to speak with Ivan, I can take you, even though I think it's pointless. You really don't have a choice." Ma'at's words were harsh but truthful.

Grace nodded. "I would like to explain the situation to him. I don't know where to start."

"I'm sure you'll figure it out."

"Is it close enough to walk? I need a few minutes."

Ma'at frowned. "It's far. We should port at least halfway."

"Okay," Grace conceded.

They ported halfway, then walked with Grace deep in thought for the rest. She had already resigned herself to the idea Lukkas wouldn't be in her life. It would be hard to see him without him remembering what they meant to each other. Hopefully, the fresh memories would help lighten the emotional toll she was bracing herself for. She was guarding everything in her heart that she could. Forcing herself to shut off her emotions regarding Lukkas. She told herself it had been only seven hundred years. With her lifespan, if she was being realistic, that short time was equivalent to a summer fling. At the moment, it was an open wound that festered and oozed, but it would heal. She didn't even believe her own argument. He was something she wouldn't easily get over.

If Ivan couldn't go along with her choice to stay, she thought she may take her chances looking for the Disir. They were known for keeping to themselves and remaining neutral in disputes. It was a matter of chance whether they would accept her, imprison her, or kill her because she was a half-breed who dared to search them out. Her mind had wandered by the time they got to the holding room.

Ma'at stood in front of the door. "You're on your own from here."

"I'm ready." Her agenda was clear. Ivan needed to make the choice. It would be easier for Grace to plan her next move under the Council's jurisdiction than under Ben's. She had decided to stay, and if she couldn't, she would run with the knowledge they wouldn't be able to find her while she still had the amulet.

Ma'at patted Grace's shoulder before she ported out.

Grace pushed the door open. The holding room was set up as a waiting room with a sofa at the end of the space, two chairs on each side, and a coffee table in the middle. The other side of the room had a round table with four fabric chairs.

It was sparse. Ivan was standing in the middle of the room. He turned around, appearing relieved when Grace walked in.

"Ivan, how are Olivia and Zane? Have you seen them?" She was genuinely concerned for them, but posing this question first was part of her strategy to make Ivan more accepting of her request. They may force her to lose her family, but she would do whatever was necessary not to lose her entire community.

"Typical you," he smiled furtively. "Always concerned about everyone else. They're doing well. Thank you so much for getting them back for us. I owe you a great deal. What's going on? Have you spoken to the Council?"

"Let's sit down." She pointed toward the table. "The Council has decided to observe and guide your progress. They will assign you a liaison and you will be able to attend meetings as a provisional member. You will have rights to speak, but not any voting privileges."

"That's a relief. So, what else?" Ivan didn't feel as much relief as he tried to portray. As many possibilities as this news would open for his people, it would bring a similar number of challenges.

Grace continued. "They are going to reconstruct the memories of everyone except for you so they don't know the identities of the deities they have come into contact with. You will be the only one who will have knowledge of or access to the Council."

He sat back in his chair, crossing his arms. "That doesn't sound so bad. No one except for me, Olivia, Zane, and Lukkas have met any of them. Why do you look so concerned?"

"Including me. They are going to remove memories of me." Grace tried to appear unfazed, although Ivan could see the sadness in her eyes.

"Grace, no! How are they going to make everything that has happened make sense without you?"

"The only other option will place an immense burden on you. I don't know if I can ask it."

"Grace, what are you trying so hard to not tell me?"

"If they allow me to stay, they want to reconstruct the community's memories, so they know me as your mate. It would be the only way to explain my involvement in your events while keeping my identity and the Council's hidden."

Ivan didn't react, so Grace continued. "The community will know nothing more about my background than they knew last week. I will act as your liaison.

They will give us additional memories consistent with what they give the others, but we'll still keep our current memories too. Otherwise, I will be forced to leave, and you will be the only one on this planet who knows I exist. They will assign someone else from the Council to engage with the community."

"Grace, how can you think that would be a burden for me? I would do anything for my people. It's you I'm worried about. How are you going to interact with Lukkas? How are you going to make that choice?"

"Well, Ivan, I was hoping to get some help with it from you. I don't think I'll be able to see Lukkas at all. At least not for a while. This decision will affect you more than anyone. You won't be able to take a mate for possibly thousands of years. You'll be stuck with me until the process is complete. My punishment shouldn't be yours too."

"Grace, I can't give you advice and I can't help you with your choice. It must be your choice alone. What I can tell you is I think we would make an excellent team for developing the community. As far as taking a mate, I haven't had a wife since I was human. Being Regent is a hard life. I would never try to bring anyone into my life with my incredibly insane schedule. You would be far worse off than I."

Grace shook her head. "This community means so much to me, Ivan. All of you welcomed me unconditionally, even though I had no idea who or what I was. It's the first time I've felt like I belonged somewhere. I prefer to stay. I just don't know if it's the right decision."

"Grace, you can only play the cards you have in front of you and build the strongest possible hand. You can't bet on cards you wish you had."

"Ivan, did you just reduce my life to a poker reference?"

"Those are wise words, Grace. Take them for what they are."

She could tell he wanted her to stay. He had always told her the community would not have become what it was without her. She also knew he wasn't one to force his will on others.

She shook her head again, but this time with a wry smile on her face. "This could be the worst choice I've ever made. Well, second worst after looking for the Æsir," she added sadly. "If you agree, I'll need to inform the Council immediately."

Ivan reached out, placing his hand on top of hers. "How could you ever believe I wouldn't agree?"

"Thank you, Ivan. I don't know what I did to deserve a friend like you." Grace let out a relieved exhalation. "I don't know how long it'll take for the memories to be ready, but none of us can leave until they have finished. Tell Lukkas whatever you need to stall. He won't remember it, anyway." She shook her head remorsefully as she stood up.

"I'll ensure he's comfortable with the wait," Ivan promised.

"Thank you." She surprised him by leaning over and hugging him hard.

"Don't thank me until everyone is safe." He reached up and rubbed her back. "We can do this. Everything will work out."

She snorted, "Glass-half-full kind of guy, eh?"

"I know my hand. I'm pragmatically optimistic."

Grace released him, taking a step back. "I need to give them my decision. Someone will be in to take you back to the other waiting area." She avoided the term "isolation room."

"It'll work out Grace. Time is perspective."

She flashed him a tentative smile before porting out.

Grace had ported out of the room, but only to the hallway. She had a lot of thinking to do about how she was going to phrase her decision to the panel of egotistical deities. Before she realized how long she had been walking, Grace was back in the outer vestibule, to find that Ami had returned as well.

"Where have you been?"

Ami looked up. "They sent me to get the Fates to pull your thread, re-spin it, and weave it back into the fabric of time to alter memories of you. They had already seen your decision. By the time I arrived, they had pulled your thread. The community's memories should be complete shortly."

"But you left before I came out," Grace said skeptically.

"There was no reason for the message to wait. Your thread was going to be pulled no matter what choice you made."

The entire scenario made sense. It was much easier to pull her thread and weave it back into the fabric of time than it would be to rewrite individual memories of an entire community. The Fates had already known what they would be asked to do by the time Ami arrived. Grace was sure the only reason they sent Ami was in case the sisters turned down the request to make the alterations, and then the Council would have needed to find another way.

Ami continued. "Then I had to go to Mnemosyne to give the specifications for your and Ivan's new memories. Then I had to be the go-between because, you know, they don't work well together. I mean, really? They are all from the same pantheon, right? They all think that they're the most important. Their egos are ridiculous."

Ami's put-upon teenager attitude amused Grace. It brought a little lightness to the stifling she had felt since they had gotten back from the facility.

"Actually, Mnemosyne is from the Greek pantheon, and the Fates don't acknowledge any pantheon, because they believe all lower gods are beneath them."

Ami rolled her eyes. The pair sat in the vestibule for only a few minutes longer before the scribe opened the doors to usher Grace inside.

"You. Stay." He pointed to Ami.

This was it. Grace would give them her decision. She needed to be humble. Prior to making her statement, she didn't want to give Ben any public reason to be upset. She took her assigned seat, setting her expression to stone as Kali brought the panel to order.

"Grace, have you made your decision?"

"I have. It was exceptionally difficult. It was necessary to weigh how each species would be affected by my presence and lack of presence. I analyzed which group would be better enhanced with my skills or encounter more difficulties without them. I eliminated emotion from the equation. Injecting emotion would have created an impossible choice. I am devastated by the loss of Asgardian citizens. The toll was heavy on the community as a whole and I personally know many of the missing and deceased." Grace paused, giving due gravity to the situation the Æsir were experiencing.

"To their credit, they are an extraordinary, resilient species. Their technological advances are tremendous, as well as the strength of their leadership. The emergent species has none of these advantages. They are young, loosely bound with a tenuous central leadership. Assessing both situations, I believe I will have the most impact remaining with the new immortals." She glanced at Ben, who seemed unsurprised by her words, making her suspicious.

"My choice is to stay and be assigned directly under Council jurisdiction. I apologize if this is a shocking decision for anyone. My priority is to go where I can produce the most positive impact."

Grace appeared contrite. She glanced at Ben again, recognizing his look as being nothing less than livid, making her wonder if he was presenting that look to her or for the rest of the panel. What game was he playing here?

Ben once again spoke out of turn.

"I haven't had the chance to present the Æsir's case compelling her to choose to come back home."

Kali venomously spat at him. "I understand you are new here, but I have warned you once already about the rules of Council. Your lack of decorum is unacceptable. Speaking out of turn is unacceptable. You are not pleading a case. Her options were crafted per your specifications. She was given a choice of your contrivance. If she chose not to take the option you desired or speak to you about her choice, that is her prerogative. You had the chance to bring her back into the fold when you took her to your facility. Instead, you made the choice to be deceitful. You could not persuade her then, and by her choice, you are unable to coerce her now. You will be seated, and you will be silent." Kali then turned to the scribe.

"It is so entered her choice is to remain with the new indigenous immortal species. Have the appropriate paperwork drawn up removing the subject from the authority of the Asgardian pantheon and creating an assignment directly under, and reportable to, the Council of the Divine." She next turned back to Grace.

"You will report directly to the Council. We will assign your link within the next few days. Please proceed back to the holding room to await your contract and your additional memory upload."

Grace rose, nodding her head. "Thank you, Madam Chair. Thank you, Council. I am honored to be working with you on such an important endeavor."

She did not wait for any replies. She walked out of the chamber into the empty vestibule. Ami was once again nowhere to be found. The entire session had taken less than five minutes. It was bittersweet. All her target points had hit their mark. She had appeared altruistic, and most of the members appeared to have empathy for her, including some that believed she deserved no choice at all. Above all, she showed Ben she was done being toyed with. Rubbing his face in it was the only positive feeling she had after being gutted and emptied of her current life.

She ported back to the holding room, finding Ivan still there.

"That was quick. They haven't even come to take me back to the other waiting area yet," Ivan said from his seat on the sofa.

Grace plopped down beside him. "It went better than I expected." The gloomy expression on her face said something altogether different. "They should be here soon with the contracts and the memory uploads."

"Contracts?"

"Standard allegiance contract for me. I'll be moving from the Asgardian pantheon to direct control under the Council. The bonus for me is that Ben has already pissed Kali off, so I don't think he'll have quite the sway over them he thought he would. Many of them didn't look happy about the construct of the choices he insisted on."

Ivan adjusted his position. "I'm not sure I understand what sway he would have with them in the first place."

"Oh, that's right, you weren't there. Since Tyr has gone missing, nearly all the Æsir are dead and many others are missing, and Ben is now the Asgardian representative. As their representative, he will have the option to find a suitable replacement, but I don't think his ego will allow him to do that. Honestly, I don't think they should replace him. He is one of the fairest and most just rulers one could want, apart from anything regarding me."

"I understand his point of view somewhat. It's very hard to let someone move on without you. What I don't understand is after what he has done to you, how could you still be supporting him?"

Grace propped her elbow against the back of the sofa, leaning her head on her hand. There was a lot more to that question than what was said. "It's not that I support him. I clearly don't support the type of husband he was. However, when it comes to doing what is best for his people, no group could ask for a better representative. Regarding me, it's more that he lost a prize. He hasn't cared about me in a long time, if he ever did. He only wanted total control over me."

Ivan could see the subject was making her irritated. "I don't think I'm ready to dive into that dark rabbit hole with you. Tell me about the memory changes. How will they work and how do they get them in?" He adjusted to face her, reflecting her position.

"Do you mean for us or for the rest of the community?" She was glad to have something else to talk about.

"Both."

"Let's start with the community. You've heard of the threads of life, right?"

"Yes, it's poetic musing. What does that have to do with anything?"

Grace gave a slight giggle before answering. "Yes, it's a poetic musing. It's also a myth that has a tenuous connection to reality, so bear with me. The mythology is each individual's life is a thread. The threads are spun, and the cloth is woven. As each life ends, the thread is cut. The three Fates, or Moirai—Clotho, Lachesis, and Atropos—perform this task. In reality, they are more akin to what you would think of as historians. Instead of a cloth, each person's story or thread is woven into an infinite dimensional object compacted into a small sphere. The threads aren't physical, they're information composed of the energy expended on the thought or action. Follow me so far?"

Ivan nodded. "Yeah, I get the picture."

"Well, they're pulling my thread. It's easier to stick with that analogy. In that light, what's happening is they're fishing back through every thread my thread has touched since I've been here to see what the easiest way will be to make the alterations as they weave my thread back into history. They take anyone who is dead off the list. Everyone who has had only nominal contact with me or only knows me outside the context of my association with the community is off the list. They start with the fringes. Say, someone I was introduced to at a party with Lukkas once—after my thread is sewn back in, that single memory will change to me being with you or me being alone, or even me being absent altogether, depending on what type of contact their thread had with mine. Whatever fits best. You see how it builds." Ivan nodded as Grace continued to speak.

"After the memory alterations are written, it changes the community's memories organically. Ours are a little different because we're keeping our original memories. Mnemosyne is taking information from my thread and your thread from the Fates to craft memories for us. We'll each be fitted with a headset to stimulate the long-term memory centers of the brain. They will transfer the constructed memories via electrical impulses in moments. Our new memories will be more like movies we've watched a hundred times. You know, the kind you remember all the lines to. We'll have the visual and auditory information and even emotional responses to the images in places, but we won't have any tactile memories." She rubbed her fingers together to emphasize the point.

Ivan caught on. "So, if we have a memory of sitting at an outdoor café on the beach, we won't be able to taste the coffee, smell the salt in the air, or feel the sand under our feet."

"Exactly," Grace replied, pointing at his chest. "Unless it's your actual memory and I'm an add-in. Then I won't have those tactile memories, but you will."

Ivan added, "But not of you. I won't be able to smell your perfume or feel the wind brushing your hair in my face, but I'll remember our conversation."

"Yeah, that's how it works. Adding someone in is a little trickier than deleting someone, which is why it can't all be done at once through the threads. Some events, meetings, dinners, and so forth will be blended because we both attended. The rest will probably be yours with me as an addition. Since I was partnered for most of my time here, it wouldn't be practical for you to be added to mine. I'm just speculating, of course. She may surprise us both by giving us some completely different lives neither of us recognizes."

They had been waiting for some time before anyone came to check on them. When the door opened, a younger creature of a species unknown to Grace entered. It was possible she was a siren or sea nymph. She was petite with slightly green luminescent skin, large yellow eyes, four arms, and at least eight tentacles showing from under her long skirt. She appeared timid, probably not sure of the reaction she would get. Grace felt Ivan's shudder and placed her hand on his shoulder.

The girl cleared her throat. "My apologies for interrupting. They sent me to see if you needed anything."

Grace smiled warmly at her. "Do you have any idea how much longer we'll be waiting?"

She shook her head. "No. They did not give me that information."

"I think we're ready for some dinner, then. What type of food is available? Oh, and we should probably find out where the closest restroom is, too."

"You can order anything you want. Our kitchens are set up to feed all local species. And the restroom is directly across the hall."

"Thank you. What's your name?"

"Neylo."

"Thank you, Neylo. I think I'd like salmon and a Caesar salad, please. Ivan?"

Ivan had gotten over his initial shock. "I'd like a rare steak and a salad as well, if it's not too much trouble."

Neylo waved her arm. "No trouble at all. What species?"

"Excuse me?" Ivan questioned.

"What species would you like your steak?" Neylo asked.

"I think I'll stick with a standard bovine fillet." Ivan really didn't want to know what species he had the opportunity to select from.

"You got it. Anything to drink?" Neylo looked at the pair.

A thought popped into Grace's head. "You wouldn't happen to have any Shurian Spiced Nectar, would you?"

"We certainly do."

"Let's do a mini cask of that and some still water, too."

"Got it. Be right back," Neylo said, porting out with a slight pop, leaving behind a scent of saltwater. She immediately popped back in. "Sorry about that. I've been told it's rude," she said as she turned around and walked out the door.

Grace looked at Ivan and laughed. "You should have seen the look on your face." She laughed harder, close to the point of tears. She had to stop herself before she actually started crying because she knew she wouldn't be able to stop.

Ivan smirked at her. "It wasn't *that* funny. I've never seen anything that looked like … her? It was a her, right?"

Grace barely stopped laughing. "Sure. Some species have reverse or singular gender roles, but her appearance was feminine, so 'her' is likely appropriate, although it would be polite to ask."

"I'm glad my ignorance was amusing for you. I guess I need to be prepared for anything around here."

"You'll get used to it. It may take a few trips through other dimensions to see the full range of weird before it sinks in. Earth is only a tiny sample of life. You have an entire universe opening up. You gotta wrap your mind around it so you can get your people ready. We should start building a plan for that."

"Let's start fresh with that tomorrow. We've had a heck of a day so far and I'd really like a drink."

When their food came, they ate and drank. Ivan was surprised at how much he enjoyed the nectar. The hot beverage had the warmth and flavor profile of mulled wine, with notes of clove and cardamom. It also had a high percentage of alcohol and probably some psychedelics mixed in. Ivan felt drunk for the first time he could remember since he had been turned. He sat on the sofa, propping his feet up on the coffee table. Grace stretched out on the couch with her feet in his lap.

"You know Lukkas was always envious of you," she slurred.

Ivan snorted. "Why? He had you and his clan. I've always been a loner. For me, it's better to keep people at a distance, you know?"

She propped a pillow up behind her head, taking another swig. "Not of your lifestyle. Of how comfortable I could be around you. I'm not like that with people usually. But you never judged me. Not once. I felt like I didn't have to pretend to be anything around you. Do you remember the first time we met?"

"It was in a little village near Denmark. I hadn't seen Lukkas in maybe fifty years. We were in a hovel that passed for a house back then, catching up. You came flying in, barely dressed in only your linen chemise and an apron. Hair flying loose, bare feet, holding a basket of eggs and a bowl of milk." He could see her as if that previous version of her was standing in the room.

"You laughed at me. It wasn't out of outrage or embarrassment. You didn't look away as any decent male at the time would. You didn't judge me. All you did was laugh at me and it made me happy," Grace sighed.

"You were a free spirit. You were joyous."

Grace's expression saddened a bit. "And do you remember what happened next?"

"Grace, that was a long time ago. Things were different back then."

"Lukkas apologized to you for my behavior, told me to dress properly, and that I shouldn't embarrass myself in front of guests. Don't take that the wrong way. I know he didn't mean anything hurtful by it. He thought he was protecting my honor. I just always felt he wanted me to be more ... what's the word?"

"Tame?"

"Yeah, tame."

"Grace, you have a fire for life in you. You see the beauty in things others don't. You can't tame that."

"That's exactly what I'm trying to say, Ivan. You see me. You've always seen me. And you don't want to change me. That's why I think this partnership is going to work. I don't have the feelings for you I have for him, but we respect each other and we're comfortable with each other the way we are."

"I think we'll do well together. Before we get our new memories, there's something I want to tell you. I don't want things to get confusing or for you to think what I want to say didn't come from my own thoughts."

"Ooooo, sounds ominous." She took another swig. "Ok, I'm ready."

He put his hand on her ankle. "You know I didn't ask for this, don't you Grace? I never wanted you to be ripped away from Lukkas like you were. He was my best friend a long time ago."

She became serious. "I know. You didn't do this, I did. If I hadn't gone looking for my past, none of this would have happened. It's my fault, and I know I've put you in an impossible position."

"No, that's not what I meant. I'm not upset about the position you've put me in. Ever since the day you burst through the door in the village, I've thought of you as extraordinary. That's why I've never …"

At that moment, the door opened. Ma'at walked in with Kali and Seshet trailing behind them.

"Excellent, you're drunk. That'll make the memory transfer go more easily. No inhibitions." Ma'at was upbeat. That's when Grace saw Seshet.

"WHAT IN ALL HELLS is *she* doing here, Kali?" Grace growled, struggling to get to her feet. Ivan helped her up. He didn't know who she was talking about.

Kali stepped in front of Seshet. "Now Grace, calm down. She wants to apologize."

Grace raised her voice. "I'm not the one she needs to apologize to! She tested those kids illegally and immorally. They're infants. She's not even a hundred and he's only twenty-six!"

Ivan was instantly on his feet. Seshet poked her head around Kali.

"In my defense, we didn't know they weren't human when we picked them up. We've been experimenting on humans since there have been humans. They were going to be sent back with memories of a beautiful California vacation."

Grace looked at her with disdain. "But you didn't. When you realized what they were, you could have immediately sent them back, but you kept them. You starved them, and you tried to make them feed from and turn a human for you to further experiment on."

"I know. I'm so sorry. I have no self-control. I saw it as an opportunity to learn about them. I just couldn't let them go," Seshet whined, looking truly ashamed.

Ivan spoke unexpectedly. "Then hand it over."

Seshet stuttered, "H-h-hand over what?"

"All the data and samples you collected from my people. We do our own experiments on *volunteers*," he said, stressing "volunteers."

"How do you think we've been able to develop products to sustain us without humans? We no longer need them for food, or anything, for that matter. You're asking me to trust you after you have done this to my people. The very least you can do is hand over our data. Maybe at some point in the future we can share information, but today isn't that day."

Seshet opened her mouth to say something. Kali silenced her. "You are absolutely right, Ivan. We do need to trust each other. I personally will ensure we turn everything over before you leave here tonight. Is that acceptable?"

"Yes. Thank you. I very much appreciate what you're doing taking a chance on us. I understand you don't think we're quite ready yet, but I hope to prove you wrong."

"I also hope you prove me wrong," Kali said.

Ma'at exhaled a sigh of relief. "Well then. If everything is sorted, shall we continue?" She motioned to the table. Ivan, Grace, Kali, and Ma'at sat down to review the contracts while Seshet pulled a case in from the hallway and began preparing the data for transfer.

Ma'at and Grace reviewed the standard reassignment contract while Kali and Ivan went over the provisional contract conditions. Both contracts had dos and don'ts as far as disclosures, who to reach out to for help, Council schedules, and rules of Council. Grace had additional information on assignments as required related to her special abilities and assisting with training security forces. They both agreed and stamped their contracts with a bloody thumbprint.

It was time to upload the memories. The procedure made Grace a little nervous, mostly because she didn't trust Seshet. She was sure Ivan could hear her heart beating faster as Seshet placed the devices over their eyes.

There was a vibration, a flash of light, and then everything melted into darkness.

CHAPTER THIRTEEN

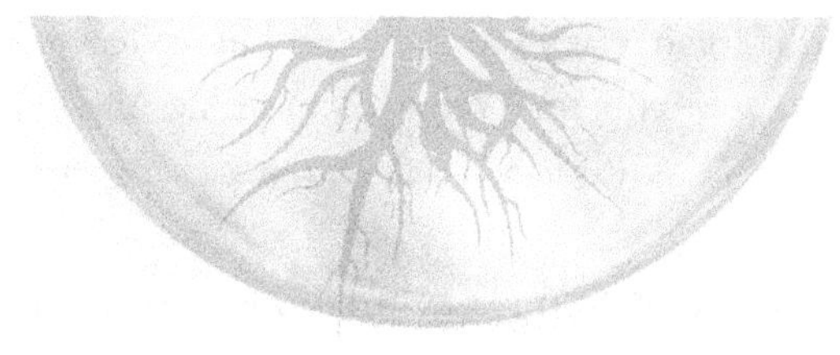

Grace woke to sunlight streaming through the tall windows on either side of the king-size bed in a room that was a blend of modern, with clean lines, and antique, with pale blue and white azulejo tiles inlaid full wall height behind the bed instead of a headboard. She recognized it. She and Ivan had bought the villa in Lisbon over one hundred and fifty years ago. They lived in it on and off since then. They had it fully remodeled ten years ago when they moved back after being gone for nearly thirty years.

It was Saturday, and Ivan would be at his favorite café on the beach. He was always up by five, so on Saturdays when they were home, he would walk through the intricately tiled streets watching farmers and fishermen bring their goods into town to sell to local restaurants and markets. It was the one day she preferred to sleep in, so she had never gone with him to the café. The memory was comfortable, realistic. It fit. It felt right, even though she wasn't certain it was.

She climbed out of bed, pulling a silk robe on over her thin nightgown. Her head ached a little. This must be what a hangover feels like, she thought to herself. She needed coffee. The perfect place to relax with a cup would be by the pool overlooking the city and the coast. It was her favorite place in the villa. She wanted time to go through her newly acquired memories. She opened the doors of the bedroom into a long hallway with clean white plaster walls broken up by two heavy arched wooden doors on either side. There were several skylights cut into the ceiling of the hall, creating oddly shaped shadows on the cool stone floor. The hall opened up onto the main living space, a huge room with a hand-tiled floor-to-ceiling fireplace across from her, a glass wall to her right opening out to the pool, and the kitchen to her left.

She turned the corner behind the large marble island. The antique chrome espresso machine was on the back wall. It was her favorite gift from Ivan. He had already prepped it for her as he usually did before leaving for the café. She turned it on, letting it run while she poured cold milk into the frothing pitcher. The familiar routine was enjoyable as she created a classic cappuccino sprinkled with cinnamon.

When she opened the glass door to the pool, she closed her eyes and felt the warm sun on her face. When she opened her eyes, she saw Ivan lying on the cabana bed with his tablet. As she walked toward him, he sat up, leaning against the pillows. She sat beside him, sipping her coffee. She handed him the cup. He took a drink and handed it back.

He leaned toward her, placing his arm around her shoulder. "How are those memories going for ya?"

"So far, pretty seamless. This is so much more vivid than it was in my mind." She closed her eyes, drawing a deep breath. "I can smell the sweet scent of the garden, chlorine from the pool, fish from the market down the hill, and the salty ocean carried on the breeze. The sun is warm and bright. I think this might be the most beautiful place I've ever been. Has this always been yours, or is it new?"

"It's been mine for about a hundred and fifty years. You remodeled it for me a decade or so back. Don't you remember?" He thought it had been an odd question for her to ask. She had remodeled it for him after she and Lukkas had come to visit and she simply couldn't get over his poor decor choices.

"I wasn't sure if that was an old or a new memory," she admitted, biting her lip.

"The additions are exceptionally realistic. It seems they dropped you into my life after all. We move between here, the country house in Scotland, and a cabin in the Rocky Mountains. We prefer to stay remote as long as we can get cell reception and Wi-Fi, of course."

"Oh, of course," she nodded. "I know I've been here before; it's all getting a little jumbled together. Aren't you usually at the café on Saturday morning?"

"Yup. I go every Saturday when I'm in the city. I wasn't sure how disoriented you were going to be waking up here, so I stuck around. You want to walk down with me? It's only seven. They'll still have breakfast till ten."

"I'd like that. Can we sit here for a little while until I finish my coffee?" She was a little disoriented. She had all her memories restored and now additional ones added all in the last few days. It was a bit of a challenge for her to separate reality from illusion. She guessed it didn't matter much. Reality was an individual's perception from their perspective, anyway. She made a decision to embrace her current reality and whatever memories flowed with it. She needed to commit to this world as it was now. Those who can't bend will surely break.

"We can stay here as long as you want." He pulled a pillow onto his lap to prop up the tablet and continued reading.

Once her coffee was gone, she got up. "Going to get cleaned up. You can pack the backpack." She leaned in and kissed him on the cheek before she realized what she had done. It felt like the right thing to do.

He pretended not to notice, believing drawing attention to it would have embarrassed her.

"It's already by the front door." He threw a pillow at her as she walked away. "Clean your hair out of the drain this time!"

"And leave you nothing to complain about?" she yelled back. "It's too late to wash my hair anyway. I'll just braid it. Give me fifteen minutes."

She washed her face, lingering on the image staring back at her from the bathroom mirror. Everything seemed to be in the right place. The top drawer to the right of her sink held all her makeup, with each type placed in its own section. She applied some eyeliner, mascara, and tinted lip moisturizer, then hung her face towel on the hook next to her sink. As she left, she turned back to throw the towel onto the floor. She had placed her hand on it before she remembered that was what she did at the vineyard. The family had maids, but it had still always bothered her to leave a wet towel on the floor. Lukkas used to tell her the maid wouldn't know what was dirty if she kept hanging all the towels back up. She smiled wistfully as she ran her fingers down the towel left hanging and walked out of the bathroom. She and Ivan had a cleaning woman who came twice a week to do the windows and floors, and a pool man who came once a week. Outside of that, they did everything for themselves. Grace preferred it that way. She disliked people cleaning up after her or doing things for her when she was clearly capable of doing them herself.

Before she got dressed, she made the bed, laying her robe over the chair next to it. She checked her outfit in the mirror, catching a glint of light from her left hand. She held her hand out in front of her and stared at a simple platinum hand-hammered wedding band. She remembered the ceremony as if it had actually happened. It was a half century after she rescued Lukkas. She had accompanied him back to the village where their clan was staying. They had become close on the weeklong walk back. When they had run into a group of people, he introduced her as his sister, and that is how they stayed. They were very close and absolutely loved each other, but in the way of siblings.

Once they arrived at the village, she met Ivan in the way they had remembered, but the change was that he courted her. They had their mating ceremony years after, but he never turned her. He told her he didn't need to ruin perfection. She had been standing there for a long time, staring at her ring.

"Grace, are you ok?" Ivan spoke softly, standing in front of her. He placed his hands on her shoulders, guiding her to the chair, kneeling in front of her. Her gaze met his. She wasn't distraught, she was calm. She was trying to make sense out of her path.

"They changed everything based on a question you never asked me: 'Would you do me the honor of allowing me to be your escort to the fire tonight?' You asked me that in the new memories, but not in the old ones. Is that something they made up, or did you want to ask me that before Lukkas saw me as anything other than a sister?"

"I wanted to ask you that question, but when you had left the room, Lukkas told me how you met. He told me he had already drunk from you. Back then, that meant he had claim to you. I didn't know the context until I came back the next year. By that time, you two had already grown close. I didn't want my interest in you to come between Lukkas and I, so I let it be. I let you two be happy, and I mostly stayed away. Looks like they built our life from one unasked and one unanswered question."

Grace continued after a moment of silence. "The funny part, Ivan, is back then I would have said yes. But if I had, neither of us would have become who we are. I never would have gone looking for my past and we wouldn't have all the possibilities in front of us we have now."

Ivan could see the processes churning through her head. "Look at you being a glass-half-full girl," he teased.

"Just bettin' on the hand I got dealt," she touted back. Grace wanted to get out of her head for a little while and let the memories take over in an organic way. "Let's go. I'm ready for a walk."

They left the house, opting to take the steep stairs and walkways down the slope into town. The road was winding, going far out of the way where the pedestrian walks went straight down. At the bottom of their street, they turned right into town. The sidewalks were narrow. The further into the city they got, the bigger and more intricate the azulejo became. Outside of the town, the streets were mostly asphalt paved. As they moved in closer, the walkways were square-cut paving stones that eventually turned into calçada on the sidewalks then on entire streets toward the old center of town. The paving was so incredible Grace had to be saved several times from walking through people as she admired it. That would have been quite difficult to explain. They came to the plaza at the end of the street. It was a full carpet of tile. She knelt down to touch the polished stones.

"I've been here hundreds of times with you. We sat right across there when they were laying this stonework in 1849. Touching the stones, hearing the sounds of the square, makes it all feel real."

Ivan was there for the stone installation. He was pleased he had her to share the memory with. "Grace, it's as real as you want it to be. We can visit every single place they have given you memories of, if that's what you want. I'd like to share all of them with you."

She looked up at him, reaching for his hand. She pulled him down to sit next to her on the ground. "You've had a very lonely, beautiful life. You've gone everywhere you've ever wanted and seen wonders I've never imagined. I've been consumed with being anything but alone for so long, I've neglected to do things that make life exciting. Lukkas seldom liked to travel without the clan. And my missions have always been in and out on the same day, with little time to explore."

Ivan felt her restlessness. "Grace, when I met you, you were the freest spirit I had ever met. I'm sorry you feel you traded love and stability for that freedom. I will make you a promise here and now. I will never stifle you. I will never hold you back. I will never ask you to do anything you don't want to. I will make sure from this minute forward your life is as much of an adventure as you want it to be. We can be two free, independent spirits roaming the universe together if you want to include me. You'll never have to be alone if you don't want to."

"No one has ever said anything nicer to me." She hugged his arm, releasing a strained breath from her lungs.

He wrapped his arm around her shoulder and hugged her tight. "We should probably get up if we're going to make it before breakfast ends. It's already eight thirty and I need to make it back home to finalize the list for the auction tonight. Were you planning to go with me, or did you want some alone time tonight? Maybe you could call Ami for a girl's night."

She hadn't remembered the auction being tonight. Ivan was very good at procuring art and had several clients interested in pieces at that evening's auction. She was sure he used entrancement to deter the other bidders. His warehouse was stuffed with things he had collected over the centuries. Occasionally, he would find something in high demand and sell it for a premium profit.

"Let's go. And you know how much I love strolling through the auction house. I would love to accompany you this evening." She stood and reached down to give him a hand up.

They walked the last few blocks to the café, and Grace realized how hungry she had become. She was starving and desperately needed another coffee. When they arrived, a slender older woman greeted them at the counter. Ivan kissed her on both cheeks.

"*Bom dia Consuela. É bom te ver de novo. Como você está nesta manhã?*" It surprised Grace that she understood him saying "Good morning, Consuela. It's nice to see you again. How are you this morning?" in Portuguese. It was one of the few languages she had yet to learn in her old life.

Consuela was happy to see him as well. "English, please! I need the practice," she said in a thick accent. "You're late!" she exclaimed, clasping him by the upper arms.

"My apologies. We had a very late arrival last night."

Consuela scanned Grace. "And who is your lovely companion?"

Ivan turned, reaching out to Grace. She took his hand. "I am fortunate enough to introduce you to my wife, Grace."

Consuela looked at him with surprise. "We didn't know you were married. Well! That makes perfect sense. You always sit alone, stay for only two hours, and take pastries when you leave. Why have you never brought her to us before now?" She released Ivan and grabbed Grace, kissing her on both cheeks, then holding her out to inspect her.

Grace smiled at her warmly. "Saturday is the day I like to sleep in. He comes here whenever we're in the city because he can't resist your pastries."

Consuela laughed a hearty laugh. "Your table is empty. I'll bring some out to you now."

Grace inserted, "And coffee, please."

"Of course, coffee! You can't have pastries without coffee. Go! Sit!" She shooed them outside and disappeared into the kitchen. Ivan took Grace's hand, pulling her toward the back and outside to a table in the far corner of the patio. She could hear Consuela telling someone in the kitchen that Ivan was here, and he brought his *wife*.

"That didn't sound like they got any additional memories of me."

Ivan shrugged. "No need, I guess. I always come early and alone. I don't remember them ever asking, although they tried to introduce me to their niece once. My response was a polite decline. I think they thought I was gay after that."

"That's pretty presumptuous. Why would they think you were gay just because you were alone? On second thought, any man would be lucky to have you," she said matter-of-factly.

"I never thought of it that way. Any man would be lucky to have me. I'm a catch."

"You know, if you're interested, I know a few very attractive guys that would be perfect for you."

"I appreciate that, but I think I have my hands full for the time being." He slid his sunglasses down, winked at her, and nodded his head in her direction.

"Well, if you ever change your mind, the offer is on the table."

"You'll be the first to know." He leaned over to pick up the backpack he had placed on the chair beside him. "You want to look at some pieces up for auction tonight?"

"I'd rather be surprised. Besides, I enjoy watching the people on the beach." She leaned back, kicking off her shoes to prop her feet on the railing. They sat in comfortable silence until Consuela brought out the coffee and pastries, trailed by an older man Grace assumed was her husband. Ivan stood when they approached the table. Grace took her feet off the railing and turned her chair toward the couple.

Ivan embraced the man. "Jaco, it's good to see you. I want you to meet Grace." He motioned Jaco toward Grace. "Jaco and Consuela have owned the café for what … twenty years now?"

Jaco answered, "We came here to retire, but who could pass up a place like this? We come in for breakfast, then the kids take over for lunch and dinner. Everybody's happy."

They spoke for a few more minutes before the couple left. Ivan went back to his work while Grace stared off into the crowded beach. She was trying to align herself with both sets of memories. Her line of work was much the same. She still specialized in rescuing kidnapped children. She still found some of her work on the network Lukkas had set up. Some high-end insurance companies hired her for cases where discretion was the highest priority and ransoms could run into the tens of millions of dollars, pounds, yen, whatever. She was called in for only the most troublesome cases. Her primary goal hadn't changed either. It was to have an educational program for newborn and newly turned in the community. Not standard schools per se. They needed more. They needed a network of caregivers and educators who would travel to the communities assisting the clans. Newborns for the last thirty years or so had been raised on CB. They never had the craving to drink from their human counterparts, but even an accidental bite could have grave consequences for the very young who couldn't yet understand.

There was already an informal network in place. Grace paid many of them out of her own pocket with the spending money Lukkas gave her. Wait, that didn't sound right. She tried to think about how she paid for the programs, but nothing was coming to her. She skipped that part, confident it would eventually come to her if she didn't push too hard.

The community needed something formal, both online and in person, but not a standard classroom setting. There was no way that would work for them, with only a dozen or so births a year and less than that turned. Every new member's education needed to be customized specifically for them. They were smarter. They retained information at an exponentially higher rate.

Grace had been lost in her dream of raising a new generation highly educated in hard sciences. They needed to be self-sufficient if they were going to advance the race. She had brought the idea up to Lukkas once before. He told her it was an excellent idea. He would do whatever she needed, but they wouldn't be able to help financially since all their money was tied up in the vineyards and other investments. The family helped other community members often. They just seemed more interested in maintaining what they had than advancing.

Other than the houses, Ivan had put all his money into CB when nobody else thought it had a chance. He was wealthy now, but for years he barely had anything. No, wait, they barely had anything. The researchers he employed did all the original CB testing on him. He believed in the race when no one else did. He believed they could be better. Her thoughts were still far more jumbled than she would like them to be. Her head still ached as she pulled her fresh memories forward, pushing down thoughts of Lukkas and her old life as much as she could. She remembered when Ma'at joked with her about being catatonic for a week, if it were her. Grace certainly wasn't catatonic, but thoughts were melding in confusing ways. She was hoping to gain clarity sooner than later.

She was staring at Ivan. He had felt her watching him for several minutes, and it was distracting to him. She was distracting to him in ways he hadn't imagined. Her scent alone was intoxicating. He raised his eyes to meet her gaze.

She reached across the table, grabbing his forearm. "I want to create an education system. We need members educated for survival, engineers, physicists, sustainable agriculture, alternative energy, mechanical engineering, trades, sanitation, water safety, even the arts. Everything it takes to create an independent society." She was talking so fast the words oozed together.

Ivan sat motionless for a few seconds, looking at her. He laid his hand on top of hers. "Ok, so let's build an education system. Where do we start?"

She didn't expect that reply. She sat up straighter, dumbfounded for an instant.

"Money. We have to raise funds. On this planet, it seems everything takes capital of some sort. I don't necessarily understand the entire concept of money. I've never really dealt with it."

Ivan suspected there was something quite wrong with her cognition. In this reality, she had always taken care of her own money. She was very good at it. "Grace, you have money. Quite a bit of it, in fact. Do you remember anything about your assets?"

Grace shook her head rapidly, as if the action would magically bring her senses to this reality. She couldn't grasp the new memories. Her eyes closed for a moment as she tried to pull the new thread forward. "Lukkas always took care of the money. He would give me some cash and a few credit cards after those were a thing. I can't see past that. Could they have left it out? I can't find any information on money." Panic had crept into her voice.

"It's okay. We'll work it out. Let's start at the beginning." His words were calming to her as he rubbed her arm.

"When you came to our village, you had a box with gold, silver, and gemstones. Do you remember what you did with that? You never gave it to Lukkas. You brought it with you."

Grace was searching, cramming the old memories down. It was making her headache worse. "I tried to give it to you, but you wouldn't take it."

"Then ..." Ivan didn't want to give her a clue unless he had to.

"Oh!" A broad smile crept across her face, allowing the pain in her head to subside a little. "I carried that heavy-ass box around for nearly fifty years until someone told us they had banks in Italy that would keep it safe, and I could take out what I wanted when I wanted it. And the bank gave me more money to let them keep it."

Ivan nodded. "And that was only the beginning. How do you remember getting paid for the insurance work you do?"

"Hmmm. Okay, Lukkas used to collect for me, so I never knew what I got. Honestly, I didn't care either. What did I need money for?"

"Grace?"

"Okay ... okay," she pushed a breath out, slowly tugging at the new thread again. "Now ... for the network jobs I get paid with cryptocurrency. I'm familiar with digital currency since it's pretty prevalent throughout The Everything. Insurance companies wire my payments to my Swiss bank accounts!"

"Gettin' warmer Gracie. How much do you typically get paid per job?" It was like baiting a cat. Ivan could see the light coming. His memories were easy to access, but she had gotten so many more than he had. He thought it was reasonable for them to be a little more difficult for her to work through.

It didn't even irritate her when he called her Gracie. "That's easy. Usually, it's ten percent of the ransom for insurance jobs and whatever the families can afford for the other stuff. Sometimes, in a special case, I'll do it for free."

"And what do you do with that money?"

"Mostly save it, but Lukkas has helped me invest some, too. Oh, he has me invest my money in things he used to invest in when he controlled my money. So now I get the profits from those investments instead of the family." She was seeing the pieces like they were a three-dimensional puzzle.

"Now, put it all together." She had to bring it out on her own for it to become real. Ivan had a considerable amount of patience in helping her discover things on her own.

She scanned him with a triumphant smile. "I'm fucking loaded. Like, heiress loaded. I can make this happen all by myself!"

"Well, not like you could run a small country loaded, more like you could support a medium-sized city, but you're right. You can make this happen. Scratch that. *We* can make this happen. I have a little money too, you know," he smirked.

She was so delighted she jumped into his lap, grabbed both sides of his face, and kissed him hard on the mouth. Then she let out a squeal, hopped up, and spun in a pirouette. "Ivan! I can't believe this. We're really going to make this happen. We have to start right away."

He sat staring at her with a huge grin. "Whoa … whoa … whoa there. Slow down a little. Let's wait a few days for your head to clear up before we plan. We want to have everything in line before we present it. We can put a proposal together next week and take it to the Board at the next session. It will be easier to have support from the community from the beginning."

She sat back down, settling herself into the chair. "You're right. Enthusiasm is fine, but we absolutely must get it right the first time. I'm so ecstatic." Grace twisted in her seat and smiled at Ivan. "By the way, thanks for not giving me the answer, again."

"I'll always be happy to be of no help whatsoever. Now, if you don't mind, let's walk. I have to complete these last few items and we have a flight to catch at two."

They packed the backpack and paid before leaving. As they walked, it occurred to Grace that they could easily port to the auction. "Ivan, you realize we don't have to fly, don't you?"

This amused him. "I realize you don't have to fly. Besides, I wasn't sure you were going. I won't be presumptuous with you. I booked the jet and I'm taking a few clients. It would be impolite of me not to fly with them."

She rolled her eyes. "Next time then. And I will teach you how to port, although I'm out of practice in the teaching aspect. I haven't taught anyone how to port since The Three, and that was a long time ago."

"How old are children when they learn to port where you're from?"

"We don't want to teach them too early. They escape easily enough without that skill. We usually wait for post-puberty, which, if they were here, would equate to around the fifteen-hundred-year to two-thousand-year mark," she estimated.

"Oh, so, children my age." He bumped her with his elbow. "Pedophile."

"Gerontophile." She bumped him back.

Grace and Ivan arrived home within thirty minutes. Ivan tossed the backpack on the floor near the sectional. "I'm going to finish up with the auction pieces. You want to hit the shower first?"

"Yup. Hey, what's the dress?"

"Better stick with business casual for the flight and dinner. Auction doesn't start till nine. I've booked a room where we can change. Black tie for the auction." Ivan's tux was already pressed and packed. He had several tuxes for different seasons and different occasions.

She continued down the hall to the bedroom and opened her closet. In this life, she was a shopper. She guessed she had to be with the number of events they attended. She wanted simple pieces that wouldn't wrinkle terribly. For the flight, she chose a pair of dark-blue pants paired with a white silk tank and topped with a blue and white pinstripe blazer. She grabbed a pair of white pumps and sapphire stud earrings for final touches. For the auction, she pulled out her black halter jumpsuit with a choker neckline, topped with a black chiffon overlay, and black stilettos. She mainly picked the jumpsuit so she didn't have to wear a bra all night. She'd keep the earrings, and her amulet would be a showstopper for this combination.

The amulet Frigg had given her was a platinum Ægishjálmr cut design caged over a full two-inch polished sapphire weighing at least twenty carats. A ring of raised runes surrounded the stone, and with the inscription band, the entire piece was about two and a half inches in diameter. She had it at least seventeen hundred years. Who knows how long Frigg had it before that? Nobody at the auction would believe it was ancient, if they even believed it was real.

When she came out from the shower, she dried her hair and did her makeup. They still had an hour before they needed to leave for the airport. Ivan was in the bedroom hanging her auction outfit inside of his garment bag. He had laid out her shoe bag and jewelry pouch on the bed.

"I wasn't sure which shoes you were taking since you pulled out three pairs. Bags on the bed. Car will be here at quarter till. Traffic's a little heavy. Seems like a lot of end-of-season tourists are leaving this weekend."

"Guess that means I have to put clothes on then. Shower's all yours."

"I told you I'd never ask you to do anything you didn't want to, but I don't think you can get through the airport without them. They have a dress code, you know."

Forty-five minutes later, the car pulled through the gates into the steep driveway. The trip to the airport was comfortable and not as long as expected. The airport was, however, quite crowded. They had a private jet, so at least they didn't have to stand in any lines. When they exited the car, private security met them. They didn't need it, but appearances could mean a lot. Their traveling companions were already in the VIP lounge when they arrived. Clients didn't normally attend auctions. This man wanted to see a few items up close before confirming his bid. She couldn't blame him for that. Nothing at this auction was going to be inexpensive.

The husband of this duo was talkative. They were from Norway, and he was interested in many of the Viking items being sold. Ivan had suggested that Grace was somewhat of an expert in Norse artifacts. She would be happy to assist him if he wanted a second opinion. He had made it clear that he had been studying Viking history his entire life and didn't believe she would know anything he couldn't discern on his own. That amused both Ivan and Grace immensely.

The husband said his wife wasn't comfortable speaking English, but she understood it well enough. She took little part in the conversation and Grace didn't let on that she spoke both Bokmål and Nynorsk dialects of Norwegian as well as Danish, mostly because she wanted to see what the husband was going to say behind her back. Also, because the husband was a typical spoiled, rich, entitled, arrogant jerk.

The flight was without incident, lasting only about two hours. After the plane landed, they were driven to the hotel they were staying at. The husband stated his wife would like to rest so they wouldn't be joining them for dinner. When they parted, Grace heard the wife ask if they were still going to dinner. The husband said they would order room service. He didn't want to eat with them because Grace and Ivan had the nerve to tell him they knew more about Viking culture than he did. Neither of them could understand how much of an expert he was, and it was rude of them to question him.

This time Grace laughed out loud. They didn't think she could have heard anything since they were already at opposite ends of the hall. "Oh Ivan. I would love to tell him who I am just to see him piss himself."

"Am I going to have to put you on a leash tonight?"

"Nah, I'd only walk out of it."

He shook his head. "Do you want to order room service or go down to the restaurant?"

"Let's eat in the room so I can take off my shoes and get comfortable." She opened the door. "I'm going to wear my hair up tonight, so he can see the tattoos in the middle of my back. Maybe I'll even let him try to remove my amulet to examine it. That'll give him the shock of his life. Might even stop his heart."

"You're aggressive tonight." Ivan hung the garment bag in the closet, taking out the clothes.

"I don't know why his superior attitude rubbed me the wrong way. Unfortunately, I've dealt with men like him far more often than I should have in my life. I can feel the anger welling up even thinking about him."

"I can't imagine how irritating it must be for someone to tell you how much you don't understand about a culture your species is responsible for. Would you please not do anything to him tonight? He is a client, and it could affect my reputation in the industry."

"Fine," she exhaled dejectedly. "But you owe me."

"Deal. Wait, what do I owe you?"

"Haven't decided yet." She flopped down on the bed after grabbing a menu off the table.

"Great. What looks good?"

They ordered, ate, and dressed for the auction. When Grace came out of the bathroom, Ivan could see a glow radiating from her he hadn't seen before. It would be difficult for Ivan to take his eyes off her tonight. They went down to the lobby to meet the car, but the other couple had already left for the auction house.

When Ivan and Grace arrived, they found the couple standing near a small exhibit, inspecting arm rings. The husband saw them approaching and told his wife he was going to test Grace to show her how knowledgeable he was and how little she knew. He asked Grace if she knew which arm ring was the most valuable. There were several gold and bronze bands, some with intricate designs, flat unembellished bands, and even a few spiral ones.

Grace immediately recognized most were from the tenth or eleventh century. She saw one she recognized intimately, picking it up. It was a loyalty band she had placed hundreds of times for the king she served in the ninth century. The client condescendingly told her there was one on the display that was much more valuable. He told her it was a tenth century design, and she should really pay better attention.

"The one you're holding has edges showing it had been cast and not hand hammered," Grace pointed to the back of the band she held. "See this rune. It's from the ninth century."

"I'll need to have that verified before I spend such a high amount," he said, pointing to the estimated value on the item card.

Grace flipped the card over. "Oh, look, it's in the description."

He huffed at her audacity. When he raised his head, he noticed her amulet in his eyeline. He wanted it. He thought it deserved a place in his collection. Even if it was a reproduction, it had to be at least a few hundred years old. He noticed the runes surrounding the outer band but would need an expert to decipher them.

"What a lovely necklace you have. Where did you get it?" The husband showed his curiosity.

Ivan watched her closely because of what she had said in the hotel.

"It's a family heirloom. I can trace it back to the fourth century. The story is Frigg gave it to her daughter-in-law for protection," she explained.

"It's so intricate and delicate. I don't think they used such hard metals for jewelry that far back. Have you had it dated?"

"I'm not sure the dating was correct. We have had the piece dated with the result coming out to three thousand years. Like I said, I'm only aware of it being about seventeen hundred." She was gloating now and wasn't sure why she had lied about having it dated.

"I'm surprised you wear it. It's a perfect display piece if it is actually that age. Has anyone been able to decipher the runes?" The man's condescension was becoming unbearable.

"It's always been worn, and I could never take it off. It would be tragic to keep something so beautiful in a box. And yes, I can actually read the runes. It says, '*May you be protected always—Goddess of Joy and Love—Frigg.*'" Grace lifted it as she read.

"But Frigg wasn't the goddess of joy and love," the man smirked.

Ivan spoke up, placing his arm around Grace's waist. "No, but her daughter-in-law, Nanna, was. That's who it was given to."

"Humph. Aren't you afraid of someone stealing it from you? The sapphire alone, regardless of age, must be worth at least a half million." The man was clearly affronted by her answer.

"No, sir, most people don't know what they're looking at. Others regard it as a costume piece, so I've never been bothered other than a compliment or two."

"Would you ever consider letting it out to a collection or outright selling it?" And there it was. The man made his motive apparent.

"Absolutely not. This piece will never leave my family. It was given with a promise of protection, and it will remain around my neck as long as I live." She smiled warmly at him as she rubbed her hand over the amulet.

He took a step closer. "If you ever consider displaying or selling it, I insist you give me first chance. It would privilege me to have it in my collection. May I take a photograph of it?" He was planning on verifying her interpretation of the runes. Some of them did not look explicitly Norse to him.

"Certainly." Grace held the amulet forward with the back of her hand for him to photograph without being in her personal space. He made her feel uneasy.

"I can't get a clear photograph. Could you take it off so I can get it into better light?"

The lighting in the entire space was excellent, gallery quality, since they were in an actual gallery.

Ivan pulled out his pocket square, placing it behind the stone. "This should reflect the light better."

"I'd prefer if she took it off," he insisted.

Grace started to reply, but Ivan stopped her. "I don't feel that is an appropriate question to ask of my wife," he stated sternly.

The client seemed to be offended by the statement. "Well, if you don't want to know anything more about it. I'm only trying to do you a favor. I have contacts that are very knowledgeable about these types of things."

If that were true, he wouldn't have hired Ivan to bid for him, Grace thought to herself.

"We're fine with what we already know about it. It's a family heirloom and I love it. What it means is what is important to me, not the value of it." Grace was trying very hard to be as diplomatic with her answer as possible. She felt like he had gone a bit too far. She had looked forward to him being envious of it, not being harassed about it.

"Whatever you want." He was flippant.

Ivan was a better diplomat than Grace. "If that's all, then. The auction will start soon. We still need to examine a few more items. Enjoy your evening." Ivan started walking away, nudging Grace along with him.

Grace opened a mental conversation with Ivan. *I don't know why he is making me so angry. I never get angry. I can feel my chest on fire and my head is splitting.*

I don't like the way he spoke to you. At the same time, he doesn't matter. You should try to let this go. I'm not comfortable with you having a headache either.

I wish I could push it down. It's clawing at me, and my insides are burning.

The man turned to his wife, speaking Norwegian. "I don't know who that little bitch thinks she is. She has no right possessing a piece like that. She has no idea about the cultural significance behind it. It's probably a fake, anyway. It's ridiculous hearing the story she made up. And did you see all her garish tattoos? It's so trashy. I can't believe we're associating with their kind."

Grace turned. She smiled, stepping back toward the man. In Norwegian, she answered, "Were you speaking to me?" Rage welled up, painfully ripping through her skull. It was blinding. Her eyes lit hot green from behind.

Ivan thought she would explode from anger. He felt actual heat permeating her skin. The light from inside her eyes was only a flash, but it was unmistakably emanating from deep within her. He knew something was wrong with her.

The man recoiled. Ivan smelled the bitter, pungent scent of his fear. He also feared she would slam the man with something deeply painful, or worse. He had never, even in his new memories, seen her angry.

She advanced on the man quickly as her blood boiled. The man's wife slipped back like a timid mouse cowering behind him.

Ivan used his contract recourse to reach out for assistance. He had never prayed in a Christian manner before. He placed his hands together and prayed for Ami. She immediately appeared between Grace and the man, instantly freezing the room except for the man, his wife, Grace, and Ivan.

Ami was caught off guard. "What the …? Oh. Grace?"

Grace didn't even acknowledge Ami was there. She walked right through her.

"You dare speak in judgment of me? You do not know what an insignificant piece of garbage you are." At this point, the man had dropped to the floor.

"Wha … *what* are you?" The man crawled backward, away from Grace.

"You speak of believing in the gods. You speak of culture and honor, yet when in the presence of one, you dare to treat them as if they were beneath you? I could extinguish you with a thought." This was definitely not Grace talking. She had never thought of herself as a god, even when she lived in Asgard.

"Please, please, I didn't know. I didn't mean to offend you!" he begged for his life.

Ivan stepped in front of her. "Grace!" Nothing. "Grace!" She was still advancing on him. Finally, he grabbed her arms, shaking her. "GRACE!" It surprised him when his hands didn't pass through her like Ami had.

She looked at him, noticing he was there for the first time. She didn't know where she was or what she was doing. Her skull felt as if it would split in half.

"Ivan? What's happening to me? I can't, I can't control the rage." She began to sob, and the amulet glowed. She tried to step back and instead ended up collapsing into him.

Ivan picked her up, sitting her down in the closest chair, ignoring the idiot cowering behind him, still begging for his life. He pressed the back of his hand against her forehead. The heat emanating from her singed his skin.

Motioning Ami to Grace's side, he turned to the man's wife first, taking her by the throat and staring into her eyes. "You had a pleasant chat with me and my wife. She had a headache and left to go back to the hotel."

The woman repeated the instruction in an emotionless whisper. Ivan let her go and knelt down beside the man, repeating the same motion. "We had a pleasant chat with my wife about the exhibit. You were polite and courteous. You will continue to be polite, courteous, and respectful to everyone around you. As you walked away to view another exhibit, you tripped and fell on the floor." The man repeated the instruction.

"Ami, take her to the Council and unfreeze the room." He let go of the man's neck, grabbing his hand before the room returned to normal.

"Sir, are you all right? You tripped on the edge of the display." Ivan pulled him to his feet.

"Clumsy as usual. Good thing I didn't have a glass in my hand. Thanks." His demeanor had completely changed. His wife rushed to his side, smirking a bit. She appeared to enjoy seeing him on the floor.

"He is well," she replied in English while brushing off the back of his suit.

Ivan patted him on the shoulder, waving a waiter over. "Let me get you a drink."

"Not sure I need another one, but since I've already embarrassed myself, why not?"

"Have you decided which piece you want me to bid on?" Ivan's enchantment had the desired effect, as it always did.

"I really like the ninth century loyalty band Grace showed me. Very historically significant."

"Excellent choice. Let me get the set finalized. Text me your top bid amount and I'll see you after the auction." Ivan quickly walked away. He was worried. He thought Seshet may have done something to Grace during the memory transfer. Calling Ami again would have to wait until after the auction.

Two hours in, he was wrapping up his last bid when he noticed Ami waiting on the side of the room. He didn't know how long she had been there. He had won the last item on his list and immediately walked over to her.

"How is she?"

"I'm supposed to bring you to her when you're finished."

"I need to confirm and sign the payment and shipping instructions for the items I purchased. It should only take a few minutes."

"We have time. They put her in stasis while they figure out what's going on. It's the only way to make sure she can't hurt herself or anyone else." Ivan did not feel any better after hearing that statement.

"Seshet isn't working on her, is she?"

"No, they have Beivve and Dionysus checking her. I don't know why, but they want to check you, too."

"Let me get this finished, then." As Ivan was walking to the confirmation area, the husband and wife clients approached him.

"Great price you got us on the band. Will they let us take it back on the plane, or will it be a few days?"

"I'm glad you caught me. For insurance, they are required to deliver items by courier. I only need to confirm the registered bids and delivery information. I apologize, but Grace and I won't be flying back with you tomorrow. We're going to stay a few days longer."

"I thought Grace went back to the room with a headache." The wife was repeating the entrancement. It seemed she hadn't had a problem with English after all.

Ami, who could never keep her mouth shut at an appropriate time, piped up. "Grace is in the infirmary. I'm supposed to take Ivan to her."

"Ami. There's no need to worry anyone. She'll be fine, I'm sure. I need to finish up so we can go."

The wife gasped at the news.

"No apologies necessary. Please, go quickly. We hope everything turns out for her," the husband answered.

Ivan pulled Ami with him. "Please do not speak to anyone else until we leave."

Ami shrugged. "Okay." It was a frequent request for her.

Once Ivan had finished, they quickly exited to the back of the building out of camera range. Ami ported them to the medical unit in the Council's dimension.

CHAPTER FOURTEEN

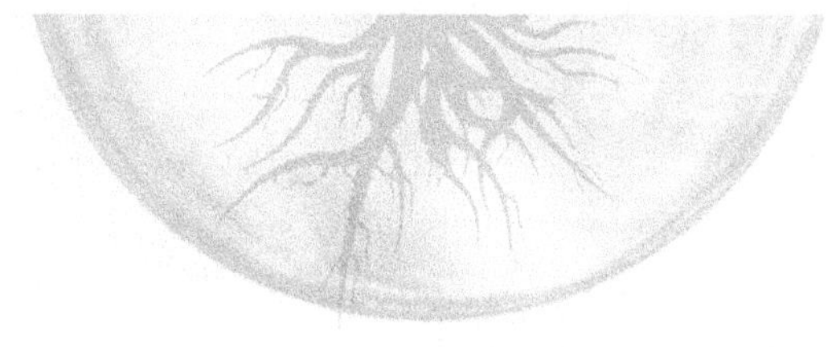

Ami and Ivan appeared on the port pad in an empty corridor with a door on either side of a plain white desk and two hallways on opposite sides behind them. They waited only moments before someone ushered them into the door on the left. They traveled down a wide hall into a room that defied his definition of a hospital. There were a dozen treatment cubicles separated by translucent walls that acted as data screens, and three-dimensional projections instead of monitoring equipment. Grace was lying on a raised padded platform that appeared to be floating. A light grid emanating from nowhere covered her from head to toe. Ivan didn't know what he was supposed to be doing. Ami spotted Beivve, a small, delicately framed woman with thick golden hair tied back. Her eyes were a huge watery blue that stood out from her very fair complexion. They started in her direction when The Three came in behind them.

Beivve moved in their direction, making a shushing motion to the group while she guided them toward a seating area behind transparent walls to her left. "Let's go in here."

When the group was inside, Ivan asked, "What's happened to her? Is she going to be okay?"

Beivve motioned to the chairs. "Let's all take a seat. I'm Beivve. We've done a full assessment of her. She's going to be fine. She needs to stay in stasis for a few more hours and she'll need a stress-free environment for a few weeks after. And by stress-free, I mean no antagonization at all."

They all nodded and agreed.

Erik spoke next. "What exactly happened to her? She's practically indestructible. I mean, I've seen her take a dagger to the chest and heal within minutes. Can we move her to a new shell?"

Beivve's eyes darted between each of them as she explained, "You all know her memories were opened a few days ago. That was a stressful event because of the sheer amount of information she needed to sort out." Beivve left out the part about the second memory upload. Ivan wasn't sure if it was because she wasn't aware of it or if she didn't know if everyone in the room knew.

"In simple terms, the biology of the shell had difficulty processing. Her essence attempted to escape. The amulet held it in and her shell overloaded, causing the lockdown when she passed out. Transferring her to another shell is not possible due to the amulet."

"Is there any permanent damage to her brain or her essence, and do we know if all her memories are intact?" Ivan needed to know for personal reasons and because of the impact it would have on the community.

"I can tell you there is no permanent damage. Everything physical will be repaired in time. Her essence remains intact, but it was attempting to remove itself from the shell when it shut down and trapped her in. As for the memories, we don't know what was processing in that specific area at the time it was damaged. It may be something as insignificant as one of the languages she knows, or it may be something major, like losing a time slot. We won't know until we bring her out of stasis." Beivve was optimistic about her outcome.

Ivan was noticeably upset. "I should have realized something was wrong. She was confused, mixing time periods and events, melding them together. She said she just needed more time to process. I shouldn't have listened to her."

Mikkel was angry. "No, you shouldn't have listened to her. You knew she needed help, and you ignored it. Who the fuck are you, anyway?"

Alex jumped to Ivan's defense. "He's the vampire, dumbass. And how was he supposed to know? It's not like she comes with a manual. And none of us has ever received a memory dump like she had. You would expect some confusion."

He extended his hand to Ivan. "Sorry, man. My brother can be a tool sometimes. I'm Alex. The quiet one is Erik, and the one with the big mouth is Mikkel."

Ivan shook Alex's hand and introduced himself. "Ivan."

Mikkel clenched his jaw, scowling at his folded hands. He wanted someone to blame.

"Well, who's at fault, then? Who's the idiot who thought it was a good idea to send her back to that primitive little planet without checking to make sure she was healthy first? She was one floor down from here yesterday and not one person had the brains to give her a once over?"

Beivve needed to calm the situation. She had a suspicion this was something Grace had done to herself, but she didn't know why.

"At this point, it doesn't matter. Would I have taken additional precautions? Possibly. We can't go back and change any of it. All we can do is deal with the reality of her condition now, and as far as I can see, it looks promising. If Ivan hadn't called Ami and gotten her to us immediately, who knows what irreparable damage she could have sustained? Ivan saved her, so you should be grateful. I'll keep you apprised of her condition. It will be a few more hours before she's awake. I'll let you know when we are ready to bring her out of stasis."

Beivve placed her hand on Ivan's forearm. "Ivan, see me before you leave so we can get a scan."

"Let me know when you're ready. I'm not going anywhere," Ivan replied.

"Not like he could if he wanted to." Mikkel was still pissy.

"Fuck, dude! Would it kill you to not be a douche?" Erik had become fed up with Mikkel's attitude toward Ivan as well. "Sorry, Ivan. None of us handle impotency well. Mikkel, least of all. He wants someone to hit or blame. He gets stupid when he can't fix whatever's broken."

"I completely understand that feeling. I should have told her to go back to your people and leave us to our fate. Maybe someone there would have seen what was happening." Ivan fully blamed himself. She wouldn't have had any memories added if she had gone home.

Alex's laugh was oddly out of place. "Do you seriously think you could have talked her out of staying here? She didn't want to return with our father in charge. Separately, our parents are both incredible individuals, powerful leaders, extraordinary warriors. Together, they are continually embroiled in battle. They are toxic to each other and everyone around them. She was never coming back. She would have disappeared into the abyss before she came back to us. There must be something she sees in your people if she chose to stay with you instead of just bolting off on her own. She did this to herself of her own free will. She knew there could be consequences placing this much stress on herself."

Mikkel stood up. "What makes you so sure of that, Alex? She wouldn't just abandon us."

"Because she told me she wasn't coming back. We're grown men. We need to have families of our own. She would be a port away if we needed her, but she wasn't coming back to live with us." Alex recalled the conversation in the hall outside the control center.

"Can you blame her?" Erik leaned back on the sofa. "I don't even want to be around us."

"It's not your fault. It's mine." Everyone turned to look at Ben walking through the door.

Who the hell is this guy? Ivan thought to himself.

"It wasn't any of you. I drove her away all by myself. I did everything to control her, I lied to her, and I treated her appallingly when she didn't bend to my will. Even when I had the chance to make it right, all I did was lie to her again. I constructed an impossible choice for her because I couldn't swallow my pride and apologize."

Ivan realized who this must be, having felt his regret. "You'll have another chance. She's going to wake up." Ivan held his hand out to Ben. "I'm Ivan. You must be Ben."

Ben shook Ivan's hand. "I owe you an apology as well. My actions disrupted your world, too. I never meant for things to go this far. I just can't stop with her. She's the only one who can infuriate me that way."

"She seems to have a profound effect on everyone she touches." Ivan actually felt a little sorry for him.

"I know I can't be here when she wakes up. My presence will only make her condition worse. I am going to call a truce with her when she's ready to see me. I need to concentrate on what's best for my people. A war with her isn't in anyone's best interest. We've lost too much already." The mantle of leadership, as well as the Council's disapproval of his past actions, seemed to have made an impact, however slight. Ami glared at him, harboring clear disdain as he spoke. "I know some people will never believe me, but I hope my future actions will solidify my words."

"I need to do what's best for my people as well. I'll let her know you would like to speak with her in a few weeks," Ivan replied.

"I'd appreciate it. Call me when she's ready. I won't come until she has been cleared." He handed Ivan a folded paper with his cell number on the outside. "When in Røros."

Ivan didn't let it show, but he was amused at the thought of an advanced species using twenty-first-century Earth technology, even if the reference wasn't quite on point.

"I should go. I only wanted to stop in to make sure she was going to recover and to assure you I wanted to stop fighting with her. Take care of her. She's not as strong as she lets everyone think she is." He shook Ivan's hand again, waving toward The Three before he left.

Once his father was clear, Erik walked over to Ivan. "I'd be careful believing him readily about our mother. He's always been overly possessive of her."

"He was sincere in what he said."

"I'm not sure if that's foolish or naïve."

"I could smell it."

"What do you mean, you could smell it?" Erik asked.

Ivan turned to face him. "Different emotions cause different hormones to be released. Fear is the most pungent. Joy is the sweetest. Your father reeked of regret and guilt. Whether that will change his attitude or actions toward her is yet to be seen. All I can say is he was sincere with what he said at the time he said it."

Ivan pulled his cell out to enter Ben's number.

Mikkel rolled his eyes and scoffed, "Those don't work here."

Ivan didn't look up as he answered, "I know. I was entering his number in case I lose the paper." He realized the paper had writing on the inside that was bleeding through. It was a note from Ben to Grace:

Grace, I'm sorry about the part I've played creating a lifetime of unhappiness for you. I've hidden a secret about your mother I've known since before we married. It was that secret that led to all the misery I have caused you. When you're ready, I will tell you everything. We've all lost enough.

Ivan stared at it. Great. The sentiment was genuine, but either way, it was a ploy of some sort. It was blatantly obvious that Ben didn't know Ivan. He would never hide it from her even if it led to her reconciling with Ben. Ben intended it for her and she would receive it when he was told she was fit to handle the stress it would cause her. It was her decision to make, not his.

Mikkel noticed he had unfolded the paper. "What's that?"

"It's a note your father wrote to your mother. I'll give it to her when Beivve tells me she can handle the stress of it." He folded it up and put it in his jacket pocket.

Erik grunted. "I knew he wouldn't have come here just to apologize. He's testing you."

"I know," was all Ivan said.

"Well, what does it say?" Mikkel could leave nothing alone.

"That's up to your mother to tell you if she thinks you need to know."

"But you read it."

"I did. From the contents, your father intended for me to read it." Ivan replied.

"He meant for Ivan to read it, idiot," Erik repeated, smacking Mikkel on the back of the head. "That's the whole point of it being a test. I'm sure he didn't expect him to tell us about it. Probably figured he'd keep it a secret or throw it away." Erik was still irritated with Mikkel.

During the exchange, Ami had wandered out of the room and was standing at Grace's side, staring at her with her lips pressed tightly in concern. Beivve motioned Ivan to the raised table on the other side of the room. He excused himself from The Three, who continued to snap at each other.

"We're ready for you. Lie down on the table. This will only take a few moments."

"You can scan through my clothes?"

"Yes, if you could take your shoes off to keep the table clean, that's all we need."

"What are you looking for?" Ivan inquired as he laid out on the table.

"Mostly to see if you have any of the same evidence of lesions. I want to eliminate the process of the upload as the cause." So, Beivve was aware of the upload he and Grace received.

"Lesions?" Ivan asked.

"We are theorizing the initial, unsupervised memory opening caused a lesion, a tear that was healing at the same speed it was opening. The second memory alteration may have sped up the tearing process, causing it to exceed the healing speed. If you have indications of tearing, then it was caused by the second process. If you have no indications, then my hypothesis is most likely correct, and it has another cause."

"I understand. Ready when you are."

"I'm finished. No evidence of lesions."

Ivan got up, sliding his shoes on. "What do we do now?"

"All we can do is wait," Beivve said.

"I guess I'm going to be here awhile. Is there anywhere I can get some water?" He took off his tie and jacket.

"I thought you only drank blood," Beivve stated innocently. She knew nothing about vampires.

"We eat food. We also have a synthetic blood substitute. I have occasionally subsisted on donor blood, but our community's primary source of sustenance is Clean Blood."

"Hm. Any way we could get a sample of it? For research?" Beivve asked.

"I'm sure I can arrange it. For now, can I get some water?" He didn't want to be rude, but he was very thirsty.

"Oh, my apologies. There's a refreshment station behind you. Enter what you want on the pad, and it will appear inside the area below. You can also select the voice button and speak into it if you don't know the languages on the panel."

"Thank you. Would it be all right if I stayed with Grace until she's brought out of stasis?"

"Yes. You can ask for seating at the convenience panel on the left side of her platform."

"Can I touch her? I mean, can I hold her hand? Will it affect the stasis?"

"You can. It won't affect anything unless she's removed from the table. I need to discuss these results with Dionysus. I'm sure he'll be entering in a dramatic fashion when we're ready to take her out of stasis. He's brilliant, and he's also a complete diva," Beivve said as she left the room.

Ivan got a glass of water and saw the alcoholic beverage category. He didn't understand how he could read the symbols on the panel. It astounded him when he saw they had scotch on the list. It had been a long day and a longer night. He was sure he would need several drinks in the next few hours. Satisfied with his choices, he walked toward Grace, glancing into the waiting area. Deep discussion embroiled The Three. Fine with him. He wasn't up for much conversation anyway. Ami was still in the corner, standing watch over Grace.

He nodded at her. She nodded back as he walked up to the service panel Beivve had pointed out. It was flat, unlit. He wasn't sure how to access it with his hands full. The pressure of him rubbing his elbow against the face caused it to light up. He pressed the microphone icon in the upper corner with the bottom corner of the glass water bottle he had just gotten from the other service panel.

"Chair," he uttered.

A muted voice replied, "Choose your category." There were several pictures lit up: barstools, desk chairs, occasional chairs. He scanned down to a selection of small recliners, choosing a gray anti-gravity chair with a small side table attached. It slid out of the wall, causing him to jump to the side. He set his drinks down and pulled it beside the platform Grace was lying on. He turned it opposite her so he could see her face when he reclined. After throwing his jacket and tie on the back of the chair, he sat down. Once he had reclined, he realized the platform was too high for him to see her.

"Ami, could you lower the platform? I don't know how it works."

She touched a lit section of the frame, releasing the magnetic lock and lowered it to an adequate level. "Like this?"

"Yes, thank you."

Ami returned to her corner.

"Are you tired? Would you like to sit down?"

"No, I'm fine. I don't need sleep."

"I rarely need much either. It doesn't mean you can't be comfortable."

"I'm comfortable."

Ivan let it go. It didn't bother him if Ami wanted to stand there. He took a gulp of water and a bigger gulp of scotch. With his free hand, he took Grace's, rubbing the back of her hand with his thumb. His brows sunk, knitting themselves together. What was she going to remember? If the additional memories were corrupted, would she stay, knowing she couldn't be with Lukkas and had no other memories to supplement? They surely wouldn't be able to give her new ones until she had fully healed.

Sitting there looking at her, the first thing that came to his mind was that Lukkas would never know what a raw deal he had gotten. He wasn't sure if he envied him or not. Aside from the guilt of Lukkas's loss, Ivan had even more guilt about his gain. There had always been something drawing him to Grace. She seemed to exude a hypnotic vibration, and he needed to be close to her. Ivan pondered the sensation for some time and landed on the comparison to her draw as gravity and he felt most comfortable being in her orbit, no matter how far away it was. Something about her just made him calmer, happier.

It was difficult for him to see her lying there, not knowing how her condition would resolve. It wasn't only about his feelings toward her. If she left, it may well be their species' ruin. He watched her for at least another an hour, and three more drinks.

Alex approached him. "Hey, Ivan, we need to go take care of a few things. Beivve said it would be at least two or three more hours. She's going to send someone to the facility when it's time."

"I'll keep an eye on her."

Alex patted Ivan on the shoulder. Then he stepped back so Ivan could see his face again. "You know, I wasn't going to say anything, but I see you over here struggling. I know about Lukkas, and I know about the choice my father forced on her. He was banking on her not having any feelings for you. If she didn't think she could care about you, she wouldn't have accepted the deal, no matter how much she wanted to help your people. I thought that was something you should know."

"Thanks Alex. I appreciate the gesture. I just hope she remembers me when she wakes up."

Alex walked back to his brothers. They walked through the exit doors and had ported before they closed.

Ivan stared and pondered. He couldn't necessarily say he loved her. What was love, anyway? A chemical reaction in the brain was what he had read. He did know he respected her a great deal. He trusted her and cared about what happened to her, and he truly liked who she was. For him, that much was huge. She and Lukkas were probably the only two people he felt he could trust as far back as he could remember. They were the two best friends he had. He couldn't help but feel a little sad that he had a part, no matter how small, in changing that alignment.

He closed his eyes and consciously thought, *Grace, I wish I could tell you how sorry I was about the way things are turning out for you.*

In response, he heard, *Sorry for what? You haven't done anything wrong. Ivan, why can't I see you? I can't move. What's going on?*

He opened his eyes to see she was still unconscious.

"Ami, did you see her open her mouth?"

"No."

He sat the chair forward. *Shhh, it's okay, I'm here. You're in stasis.*

"Ami, get Beivve now. She's awake in there."

What do you mean, I'm in stasis? Why? What happened? Grace didn't sound panicked, but she was definitely concerned.

What's the last thing you remember? Ivan didn't know how much to tell her until he knew what she remembered.

We were at the auction talking to those horrible clients. We walked away from them, then … she paused, *nothing.*

He took a chance that what he was going to say wouldn't be too confusing. *Seems like all the memory increases caused a small but manageable tear in your shell that was opening faster than you could heal. They had to put you in stasis, so your body could catch up with the flow of memories and allow you to heal.*

At that point, Beivve and Dionysus appeared with Ami. Ivan stood up. Dionysus pushed the chair out of the way. As it slid back through the opening in the wall, Ivan barely managed to grab his jacket. He didn't want to lose the letter he had stuffed into the pocket.

"What's going on here? I thought you said she was awake?" Dionysus complained, clearly annoyed.

"Her mind is awake. I'm talking to her now."

Dionysus hovered over her, attempting to make contact. Beivve checked her brain activity, and it did not respond to him.

Ivan, who are you talking to? It seemed Grace couldn't hear them either, since her body wasn't alert.

"Can you hear me speaking, or only my thoughts?" he said aloud. The monitor lit up when he spoke.

If you just asked if I can hear you speaking, I heard it. I don't hear anyone else in the room.

"That's okay. I'll relay the messages. I'm here with Beivve, Dionysus, and Ami. She can't hear any of you."

"Not even me? I can hear her," Ami said aloud. The monitor lit up again.

Yes, I can hear you, Ami. I didn't realize. When you aren't speaking, you are vacant.

"I can talk to her, too," Ami stated triumphantly.

How much longer do I have to be stuck in here? When can I go home?

"They're saying at least a few more hours. They want to make sure the tear is closed and won't reopen. Then you get a fun-filled, stress-free two weeks in the mountains." Ivan wanted to make sure he didn't say something incorrect, so he spoke out loud.

I miss the cabin. We haven't been back there since we caused that avalanche.

Ivan looked directly at Beivve. "You mean since you caused the avalanche?"

Semantics, we were both there.

"It appears we are confusing our hosts. Would you mind if Ami repeated what you say so I don't have to relay both sides of the conversation? They want to ask you some questions."

"Fine with me." Ami repeated Grace's words.

Dionysus wasn't sure why she was able to communicate when she should be too far under for her conscious mind to work properly. He wanted to ask some questions to test her memory. "I surmise your subconscious can speak to these two because you have a personal connection. I know your relationship with Ami. Who is Ivan to you?"

Ivan repeated his question to her.

The next words came out of Ami's mouth. "He's my husband, you idiot. Ami! I didn't say it like that."

Ami replied to Grace, "That's how you thought it." Then for Grace, "I wish there was someone else who could hear me."

Ivan snickered at the exchange before relaying Dionysus's next question.

"I'm trying to assess if there has been any memory loss. How long have you been married and how long have you known each other?"

Ami relayed, "Let's see, mated, almost what, seven centuries of time on this planet. We knew each other for maybe half a century longer."

Beivve entered info into the data system furiously. Ivan and Dionysus looked at each other with concern.

"Good, good. Now I'm going to ask you about others you are close to."

"Okay."

"What type of relationship do you have with Ben, Alex, Erik, and Mikkel?"

"Alex, Erik, and Mikkel are my sons. They were born on Asgard and ended up here after the destruction. Ben is a more complicated relationship. He's Balder, the father of my sons. I empathize with his situation since Ragnarök, but as much as I want to help, I don't trust him."

Ivan injected a question. "Let's go a little further back. What do you remember about Lukkas and Galin?"

"They are the first indigenous immortals I met here. I was sent to save Lukkas by whom I am now assuming was Frigg or Freya. I took him back to his village, his clan, where I met his brother, Galin. Ivan and I see Lukkas and Galin often and Lukkas is one of my best friends. If Ivan hadn't asked me to go adventuring with him, I probably would have ended up in a quiet farm life with Lukkas, which would have been fine at the time. Since I received my full memories again, I think it would have been quite sad and unfulfilling."

Ami started to speak for herself this time. "That's not how it …"

Beivve signaled for Ami to stop speaking much the way Ma'at had done with her. "Let's not contradict her. We are trying to assess how her memories are, not yours. Besides, you weren't there anyway. Were you?"

Ami was getting it now. "No, but she's told me the story before, and she didn't say it the same."

Ivan tried to cover. "Ami, people don't say things exactly the same every time. It's okay. Please, just repeat everything you hear Grace say."

"Okay."

"Next question. Grace, what do you remember about leaving Asgard?"

"I remember after Balder or Ben's death, he was sent to Hel. I was fighting with Odin over his idiotic proposal to reset a cluster of planets harboring mortal life forms. Ben sent me messages telling me to stop. He warned me I was making myself too conspicuous and I would become a target if I continued. Then he had me poisoned and made everyone believe I died of grief, of all things."

"Then what happened?"

"Frigg convinced Freya to claim me. She made the argument that since I always carried a dagger on my leg, I was in possession of a weapon upon my death and she had first right. Odin challenged her for the claim, but Frigg told him it was because of his stupid bet her son was already in Hel and he would not take me from her too. Odin released the challenge. Frigg and Freya decided I needed to be sent somewhere out of reach."

The questions went on for another hour. They brought in Alex to confirm many of the earlier memories. He was able to hear her, too. She seemed to have a full memory of everything from her life on Asgard and her uploaded memories with Ivan. Her original memories of Lukkas were altered or reduced in significance, which made Ivan wonder if she had intentionally increased the tear to remove the memories because they were too painful. Given her heightened consciousness of each cell in her body, he believed it was impossible for her not to have been aware of the lesion. She had been confused, but was it because of the tear or a result of her trying to eliminate her old life? He wasn't sure he wanted the answer to that question. He was suspicious, but it was something only she could answer and now she didn't even know.

Dionysus elbowed Ivan. "Did you hear me?"

"No, sorry. Go ahead."

"How many languages do you speak?"

How would he even know the answer before? Ivan thought. It was probably more of a cognitive question.

"Let's see, eighteen Earth-based languages, seven off-planet languages, and the language of the Ljósálfar."

Ivan confirmed the earth's languages, Alex confirmed the other languages. Dionysus found the confirmation to be satisfactory. He did want a further explanation about one item.

"And how do you come to speak the language of the Ljósálfar? You are Æsir, are you not?"

"I really don't know. I've always been able to speak it. My father is Æsir. He said my mother was as well, but I have heard many rumors that she could have been Vanir, which, if true, would explain the language. If not, I don't know how I speak it. I have no memory of learning it."

Her answer made Alex think. "That would explain why my brothers and I can read each other's thoughts as if they were our own. I thought it was an identical triplet thing, but it could also be an inherited ability if we are part Vanir."

"Since your mother may only be half, you could only possibly be a quarter. Bidirectional telepathy seems to pass to all Vanir. I don't know of other abilities that pass unconditionally." Beivve was thinking out loud as much as she was speaking to them.

"We've been scanned multiple times. No one has ever said there was anything unusual."

Ami passed a question from Grace. "Who scanned you many times?"

"Grandmother."

Grace responded, "So, the only one who ever scanned me until a few days ago was the only one who ever scanned you. I have an extra set of chromosomes. Do we have any of the results of your scans, or are they all lost back on Asgard?" This had gone from being a memory challenge to an ancestral search.

Beivve and Dionysus could see from all the monitors that her mind was functioning well, aside from the lost original memories. They stepped back from the conversation to do more research. At least the last hour or so would go by quickly for Grace since she was able to converse with the others.

Beivve came back to the group. "How do you know you have extra chromosomes? We haven't scanned for that." She was skeptical about how Grace could know that unless someone had told her. Beivve suspected Grace was more than what she believed she was.

"I just know."

"So, no one has ever confirmed it?"

"I don't think so."

Ivan then asked Alex, "Is there no one who can confirm your results or has any information that isn't speculation?"

Alex added, "Not that we are able to find. My grandfather, Nep, is dead. Frigg is as well. Odin and Freya are both missing. The only one who may have any answers would be my father, and I don't think it's a good idea to have them in the same room until she's back at full strength."

"Hello, I'm right here. I will be the one to make that decision, not any of you."

Ivan would always let her make her own decisions; however, this one wouldn't be up to her. "Ben stopped by to check on you. He won't come until Beivve deems it safe. He does not want to add any stress that may affect your healing. I'm certain he was being sincere."

"You can't possibly be sure. He's lied to me continuously since I've known him." Ami stressed the word "lied." Ivan was unsure if it was Grace's intent or Ami's.

"I'm sure. No one can change their base scent. It doesn't matter right now. The choice to speak with him is off the table until you're one hundred percent."

"You'll be back in fighting form in no time," Alex added, not wanting her to dwell on something she couldn't control.

"I prefer a no-fighting form. I'm tired of the anger and hate that plagues us. We all need to find a better way. I can only look forward, which means I have to let it go." She wanted peace, and she wanted to see her community thrive.

"We all have to let it go. A clean slate from today forward. Agreed?" Ivan suggested.

"Agreed." Ami, for Grace, and Alex replied simultaneously.

CHAPTER FIFTEEN

The cabin was more of a modern log home than a little cabin in the woods. It was remote, high in the mountains, and three miles up a dirt road. Not a neighbor for at least ten miles in any direction. They had over three thousand square feet, four bedrooms, and vast decks surrounding both floors, giving them ample space. At this elevation, the mountain air was crisp and cool when fall crept in. The trees were at the apex of color. Although it was still dark, the sunrise would be spectacular.

When Ami opened the kitchen doors, a refreshing breeze brushed her face and cleared the stagnant air that had built up from years of being closed. Ivan hadn't had time to send anyone out to clean before they arrived. Ivan lit a fire as The Three began pulling furniture covers off. It usually took their preferred service an entire day to prepare. With this group being ten times faster, everything should be perfect in just a couple of hours.

Ivan took a quick shower and changed into a pair of jeans and a long-sleeved green shirt with a flannel shirt on top. When they left, it had been just after four a.m. Grace was fully awake and healing as rapidly as expected. Beivve would port her in at seven after running some last tests. He wanted to ensure everything was flawless when she got there. He made a list of Grace's favorite foods before going out to check the rover. Every few weeks, the caretaker would come to perform maintenance on the property, drive the truck, and change the oil when it was necessary. As expected, the tank was full, and it started right off. With a satisfied smile, he pulled around to the front of the house to let it warm up.

"I'm headed into town. The closest twenty-four-hour grocery is just over an hour away. I'll be back before she gets here. Any special requests?"

"Yeah. Why don't you port?" Mikkel shouted. Erik leapt across the room like a basketball player making a half-court dunk and slapped Mikkel on the back of the head after the sarcastic comment.

"Ow!" Mikkel exclaimed, attempting to maintain his balance on the wobbling ladder beneath him as he rubbed his head.

"If you're offering, why don't you come with me? Someone as powerful as you can port the truck, can't you?" Ivan wasn't going to let Mikkel under his skin. Alex and Erik laughed at him.

"I can." Mikkel couldn't exactly decline now that Ivan had challenged him.

"Got coordinates?" Mikkel asked, climbing off the ladder. He hadn't been trying to be an ass. He thought himself quite funny.

"There's a GPS in the Land Rover. We should port close, then drive the last couple of miles." Ivan suggested.

"I know how to be discrete," Mikkel retorted, looking back over his shoulder as he followed Ivan out the door. "Have fun cleaning, suckers!" Mikkel's eyes widened when he saw the truck. Unlike the utilitarian vehicles they had at the facility, this one had all the options. "Oh, um, I need to drive in order to port the entire vehicle."

Ivan gave him a side glance. "Bullshit. I'll still let you drive, but I know you're full of it," he said, walking to the passenger side, leaving Mikkel to drive.

"Thanks, Pops," Mikkel said, smiling broadly.

Ivan just shook his head, thinking this man seemed to be mentally stuck in his eternal twenties. "Dude, you're ten times my age."

"Yeah, but you married my mother."

"You got me there. Drive on, son." He was starting to get Mikkel's sense of humor. He may be a little offensive sometimes, but he wasn't trying to be hurtful.

The comment also made Ivan wonder if Alex was the only one with retained memories. They all knew Grace and Ivan had their memories changed, but they may have thought that was only to change Grace's influence on the community.

Alex inferred Mikkel and Erik never knew Lukkas's name, so they probably assumed Ivan had been the vampire Grace had been with all along. Ivan needed to file that in the back of his mind for later.

"Okay, found the store. Is this a good place to port?" Mikkel was pointing to a dirt road about ten miles out on the map.

"Not that one. It's gated. Go the next one up."

Mikkel tapped on the road Ivan noted, pulling up coordinates. "Hold on to your hat." He drove forward toward the side of the drop. Mikkel glanced over several times, but Ivan didn't flinch.

Ivan felt a dragging sensation as they appeared seventy miles away from their starting point. This time he was expecting it, and the disorientation was severely reduced. The GPS flaked out for a few seconds before it continued routing them on their way.

"Now that's the way to travel. Man, I can't wait for your mother to teach me how to do that."

"She hasn't taught you in seven centuries. What makes you think she can teach you now?"

"You're forgetting, she didn't remember she could port until a couple of days ago." Ivan still remembered the night she told him on the sofa in the hotel. At least it confirmed Ivan's supposition that Mikkel thought he and his mother had been together the entire time.

"Hm. True," Mikkel contemplated. "I can still remember her teaching us with a gold rope. Erik got it first. He's quiet, but he's really smart. He catches on to most things first."

"Why a gold rope?"

"Because it's conductive. It's a safety line. It won't break off if the portal snaps shut as long as you each keep hold of an end, so she can use her connection to pull you through. I guess you could use copper or any other conductive, malleable metal."

"I may have some gold-braided cord in my warehouse. I should plan a trip next month to rummage around there for a few days." He was trying to recall other items he still had stored. He was sure he had some heavy drapery cords braided from gold thread.

"Why do you have a warehouse?" Mikkel never thought of storing things from his past. There was always something else around the corner. His grandfather used to keep old things, but he never saw the point.

"Mostly for things I've collected over the years. You can't imagine how much someone will spend on an old cup or painting these days. That old junk paid for two of our houses."

"Imagine that. Humans are strange creatures, aren't they? Holding on to things from a past they never lived in and can't possibly remember. Why would you want something someone else threw away?"

Ivan thought for a second before he answered, "Probably because they live for so short a time. They are looking for a connection to ancestors. They want to know how they lived, what they had, what they loved. But they don't want to know about the nasty stuff. The diseases, the lack of sanitation, the primitive conditions, and the backbreaking work it took for them to survive. They spent most of their time working to feed themselves. It even confuses me, and I was human once."

"Here we are. Not many people here this time of morning." Mikkel looked around the near-empty parking lot, wondering what type of people came to procure provisions at such an hour.

Ivan and Mikkel did their shopping as they discussed the frailties of humans. It took a while for him to warm up, but Ivan did like Mikkel.

"Is this your first time in a grocery store?"

"Yeah. We order supplies, which are delivered to the warehouse we pick up from. I've never had to get them myself. I have been to gas stations, coffee shops, and restaurants, but not anything like this. This place is enormous. Almost as big as our entire supply deck." Mikkel turned to look all around him.

"When we finish, we have to pay for all this before we leave. Do you understand money?" Grace told him The Three had been here for five years. He wasn't sure how often they were let into the human world.

"It took a while to figure it out. Every country has its own currency, too. That's the most confusing part. We work more on a universal credit system. I'm more comfortable with the debit cards than cash. The closest thing they have here is the cryptocurrency. Not many places take that yet, do they?"

"No, not yet. I think they will eventually. Fifty years ago they didn't have cell phones or debit cards at all, so I'm sure it's coming." Ivan had never thought about how confusing money could be. He had learned to convert currencies quickly through his travels.

"And these cell phone things are so huge. Our communication devices fit behind your ear. You can talk to anyone or look up anything you want in an instant. I have to say, I miss the speed of things. Everything's slower here."

Mikkel was warming up to Ivan as well. He wasn't at all what he had expected. "I have a question. You don't have to answer if you don't want to."

Ivan wasn't sure where this was going. "There's nothing about us I want to hide from you. Humans are another story. You need to be more careful with them. If they don't understand it, their first reaction is fear and to kill it."

"You were human. What makes you think differently? Wait, that's not the question I wanted to ask."

"That's okay. I want to answer that one first. Time. Time makes anyone think differently. Humans attempt to squash or destroy everyone or everything with different ideas. You couldn't imagine the number of wars based on religion or politics. Humans have difficulty setting their differences aside and working toward what's best for the entire race. They focus on the differences to justify why one group is better than another. They all think of themselves as the good guys. None of them ever want to believe they're the ones in the wrong. If one group can't persuade the other groups to accept their ways, they look for ways to destroy each other. It doesn't work. It'll never work, but they don't have the luxury of time to understand that. And they forget their history from generation to generation. Not what's sanitized and taught to their children, but the *actual* history of hatred and destruction." Ivan had thought about the futility of war often throughout his lifetime. Seldom was anyone ever better for it.

His words hit Mikkel. "Not just humans. Look at what happened to my people. After eons of peaceful coexistence, our world was destroyed. No discussions, no warning, well, except for the prophecy from a million years ago. But that same prophecy could have applied to almost any advanced race responsible for less advanced races. It seems ignorance isn't strictly a human quality."

"True enough. What was your real question?" Ivan was looking for a way to redirect the conversation since this one had turned a little heavier than he had intended.

Mikkel perked back up. "Who is all this food for? I thought you only drank blood. No way my mom's going to eat all of this."

"Total misconception. I get it all the time. Food is something we enjoy quite a bit. Personally, I love to cook. All our senses are heightened, including taste. We used food and alcohol to dull the blood cravings too. As a whole, we don't drink blood much anymore. Occasionally some donor blood. We mostly use a synthetic replacement that we've created. It's pretty inexpensive to produce and we provide it at no cost to any vampire who requests it."

"How do you pay for it?" Mikkel asked, bewildered. "Everything on this planet has a cost."

"We have several companies who add it to food items for resale. We charge the companies a small fee, so we don't have to charge individuals. It's a perfect sustainable substitute for humans too. We're planning to market it to organizations and governments as a blood substitute for remote locations. You can add it to just about anything or mix it with water and take it straight. Humans would rehydrate it and absorb it intravenously. I have some freeze-dried back at the cabin if you want to try it." Ivan was more than happy to share information if he was interested.

"I hate to admit it and if you tell anyone, I'll deny it, but I totally misjudged you. Not just you, but your entire species, I guess. I thought you would be …" Mikkel searched for an inoffensive word.

"'Animals' is the word you're looking for. Don't start worrying about being offensive now. I prefer someone straightforward. At least I don't have to guess what you mean," Ivan interjected.

"'Animals' works. I think I was looking for the word 'primitive.' You seem to be more forward thinking."

Ivan wondered if Mikkel had meant to give him a compliment or not. "Not all of us are that way yet. For the most part, we are. Your mother is working on a more formal education system for our young and a way to educate our older population in more contemporary ways. We all need to be on the same page if we're going to thrive in this new universe opening up to us."

"Ivan, you can't tell them anything about us."

"I understand, but what we can do is open their minds to a future that includes advanced technology and science. We can prepare them for a new experience that includes exploration and travel to nearby planets. Our survival cannot depend on human scientists. We also can't rely on the assistance of the Council for anything other than guidance. We need to make our own way."

"You are a very pragmatic thinker. You and Erik will get along."

"Thanks. You're not as big of a jerk as I thought you were when you first opened your mouth either," Ivan said, making Mikkel laugh.

"Don't tell anybody. You'll ruin my reputation."

"No problem. We should check out before this ice cream melts." Ivan turned the cart toward the cashier line.

They checked out, loaded the truck, and made it back to the cabin in a few minutes. The entire trip, which normally took three hours, took less than an hour. When they pulled up, Alex and Erik came out to help unload the groceries. There was plenty of time left to get everything put away and finish preparations before Grace got there.

When they were standing in the driveway, Ivan realized he had forgotten to check the water heater before they left.

"Anyone check to see how much propane is in the tank?" he asked before heading toward the front door.

They all looked at each other like Ivan was speaking a foreign language.

"Seriously, none of you know what a propane tank is?"

They shook their heads, looking at each other to see if anyone understood. Mikkel chimed in, "We had difficulty figuring out what to do with a plug when we got here."

Ivan grinned. "It's a rudimentary type of fuel. It's a different type of gas that is compressed into a liquid for storage. Once it leaves the compressed tank, it turns back to a vapor for use. It's highly flammable and explosive, so there's a tank in the shed about two hundred yards down the driveway. Electricity up here is very expensive and goes out often. I was hoping to add solar panels after I cut down a few trees that shadow the house, but I haven't gotten around to it yet."

"How do you refill it?" an inquisitive Erik asked.

"A truck comes out and pumps it through the valve on top of the tank. Want to walk with me to check it?"

Erik shrugged. "Sure."

Rusty hinges creaked as Ivan pulled the shed doors open. They inspected the outside of the tank for leaks, and Ivan wiped off the glass cover of the gauge. It was still half full. Ivan showed Erik the basic workings. He was interested in how old mechanical things worked. Ivan appreciated a curious mind since he had one himself. They returned to the house as the sun was lighting the horizon, and the early morning birds began chirping. The sky was turning that gray-orange color that comes just before the sun bursts over the mountaintop.

Grace should be home soon. That was an odd thought to strike him so naturally. He had always thought in the singular. He had spent most of his life alone. It felt good to think of being a partner to someone. It felt real for him to think of being a partner to Grace.

When he and Erik opened the front door, Ami, Mikkel, and Alex were in the living room.

"Finished?"

Alex raised a bottle of water over his head in a mock salute. "Done."

"Good. Who wants breakfast?" Ivan asked. Everyone chimed in with their own various affirmations.

The Three sat at the kitchen counter, Ivan was at the stove, and Ami stood at the end of the bar. He put everyone to work chopping and peeling. He ground fresh coffee to start a pot and heated the waffle iron and the flat top for the other items. This situation seemed like a family event. He had never had this kind of experience before and thought it was something he could get used to. He wanted to get used to it.

Within a half hour, he had started the second pot of coffee and was nearly finished cooking breakfast. The sun started peeking through the kitchen windows, creating bright streaks and long shadows across the floor. They turned at the *whooshing* sound of air being displaced.

"Now this is a sight worth coming home to," Grace remarked with a wide grin. She was glad to be here and happier that the four men in her life seemed to get along.

Alex was closest, picking her up off her feet in a giant hug. Erik and Mikkel followed. Ami shuffled over, cautiously hugging her like she was going to shatter. Grace squeezed her hard.

"I'm not going to break."

"Good to have you back," Ami whispered.

Grace sauntered over to Ivan, who was preparing her coffee. "You really know what a girl wants, don't ya, honey?"

The words struck Ivan as odd. Had she made that statement for the others or for him?

"Yes, I do." He bowed his head, emphasizing each word, holding out her cup. She took a sip, sighing with satisfaction. Placing her cup on the counter, she shocked Ivan by throwing her arms around him and giving him a quick kiss on the mouth. She pulled the back of his neck, so their foreheads were touching.

"Thank you. If it weren't for you, I would have been lost," Grace whispered.

"I'm glad you made it back. I don't know what I'd do without you." It sounded sappy, but he really meant it. He didn't know if he had always had such feelings for her or if the memories were responsible. It didn't matter because this was his reality now. He wanted to be with her and have the family he had passed up all these years. He didn't need to isolate himself anymore.

She stepped back, sliding her hand down his arm to intertwine her fingers with his. "The food smells delicious. I'm starving."

"Then let's eat. Beivve, will you join us?" Ivan extended his hand toward an empty seat at the end of the counter stretching the length of the kitchen to seat eight. Plenty of room for today's informal breakfast.

"Thank you. This looks wonderful. We can go over Grace's restrictions for the next few weeks while everyone is present." Beivve gracefully took a seat at the end opposite Ami. Grace and Ivan took seats at the end, closest to the doors, between Mikkel and Ami. The Three had piled food high on their plates. It seemed Grace wasn't the only one starving.

Once everyone began to eat, Beivve laid out the rules.

"Grace, I know you don't take well to restriction. In this case, I would highly advise you to consider reducing your activity for a short time. No porting at all until I can get another scan on you two weeks from today. No phasing either. It takes up too many resources and alters your physical composition. Your mind is still processing a vast amount of information. There are workers outside placing port blockers on the house. You should rest as much as possible for the first week and resume mild activity in the second. Even if your essence is able to recall everything, your healing process isn't complete. You may have spells of dizziness. From what we understand about elevated physiology, as long as you don't lose consciousness, that shouldn't be a concern. This hasn't happened to anyone before that we know of, which is why we are being overly cautious. Think of it as a vacation."

"How will I get in touch with you if I have a question?" Grace sounded like she was going along, but was she?

Ivan wondered if she'd be out hiking within two seconds of everyone leaving.

"Ami and your sons will take turns checking in. And Ivan obviously understands the emergency protocol."

Alex added, "And we'll give you both our cell numbers since we have no plans to be off world; you'll be able to call us without telepathy."

Beivve pointed directly at Grace, locking eyes with her. "Absolutely no telepathy. You need to reduce the amount of brain activity to the absolute minimum. I've heard that watching tel-e-vision is a mindless activity." Beivve said the word "television" as a question. She did not know what it was.

"Baking is relaxing," Mikkel added with his mouth full.

"And I'm not going anywhere," Ivan interjected.

"What about your board meeting?" Grace remembered they had set it for next week.

"We have internet. I'll remote in."

"What about …"

Ivan cut her off. "Stop. There is nothing I can't reschedule or do from here. I'm not going anywhere. There is nothing more important to me than you. Period."

"Guess I'm stuck with you then." She smiled at him.

"I guess you are."

Beivve was satisfied with the conversation. "I should get back. If you have questions, write them down so we can discuss them all at once. I'll check in tomorrow." She stopped before she walked out the door. Almost as an afterthought, she spoke loudly, facing the door. "Oh, and no sex!" After which she quickly exited and ported out.

Each of The Three groaned in disgust.

Mikkel complained, "I was just starting to like this guy. Why'd she put that in my head? I gotta leave." He tried unsuccessfully to port. Realizing he could not escape, he proceeded to the front door. "Love you. See you tomorrow." He was out.

The other two took that as their cue as well. Eric approached Ivan.

"It was nice to meet you. Thank you for being a stable presence in our mother's life over the years. We'll be back tomorrow since Ami has agreed to stay today. Please let us know if you need anything." He turned to Grace. "Mother, please do what you've been asked. Take care of yourself."

Alex shook Ivan's hand. "Anything you need, all right? Even if it's just someone to talk." He kissed Grace on the cheek. "Bye, mother. Get some sleep."

Ivan had the feeling Alex knew everything. He'd had an inclination on the medical ward, but he now felt certain he knew more than his brothers. He could tell Ami did, although she would say nothing to hurt Grace unless she asked her directly. Grace had no reason to do that. Although if she asked him directly, Ivan wouldn't lie to her either. He hoped she never asked.

"I could use a long relaxing bath. Seems like that can be the most pleasurable thing I'm allowed for the next few weeks."

Ivan hugged her, kissing her forehead. "There are clean towels on the sink. I need to finish washing the rest. Ami and I will clean up down here, so just yell if you need anything."

Grace hugged him back and walked across the living room. He watched as she climbed the stairs. He hadn't thought about sex before Beivve mentioned it. Well, he had, but not during this crisis. He was looking forward to having that experience with her, and yet he already remembered it. The dual memory set was somewhat confusing at times. He had been mindlessly cleaning when he realized Ami was staring at him.

"You know everything, don't you?"

"No, no one knows everything," Ami stated.

Ivan had forgotten exactly how literal Ami was. She had been unusually quiet through all the events last night and breakfast today.

"Why are you so quiet? Our last conversation at the hotel, you talked a mile a minute."

"I don't understand what's going on. I know everything from before she came here. I know everything from when I found her. After that, from the time we got to the hotel, it's all jumbled. From there to the facility the next day to the Council chambers, I don't understand. I know she's with you, but I thought I knew she was with Lukkas. What's right?"

"Ami, it isn't about what's right or wrong, it's about what she believes. If she asks you a question about those two jumbled days, you need to tell her whichever truth you feel she needs. Both sets of memories are true to those who have them, and at different times, they were both real, at least to her. Right now, she may only have one of those sets. That's her reality. Can you do that for her?"

"I always tell the truth." Ami bit the side of her lip. "So, you're saying I should say the one she believes is the truth? I think I can do that." Ami could choose if both things were true. As long as she wasn't lying, she could do it.

Ivan kept an eye on Ami while they finished cleaning. He thought she had accepted what he told her and saw nothing concerning in her behavior. When they finished, they realized there was a lot of food left over. If they didn't eat the rest of it this afternoon, he would run it over to the park rangers tonight. They would appreciate it and Grace could get out of the house for an hour without exerting herself.

"Ami, I'm going up to check on Grace. Will you be all right down here by yourself?"

"I'm fine. Can I go out on the deck?" She enjoyed being outside.

"You can go anywhere you want. I would appreciate it if you knocked before you entered our bedroom. Grace said you have a habit of watching people sleep."

"I don't need to sleep. It interests me to watch how other biological organisms recover with rest."

"Speaking for all of us biological organisms, it makes us uncomfortable if we haven't consented to being watched in our sleep."

"Oh, okay," Ami answered, walking toward the deck railing.

When Ivan got upstairs, he could hear music coming from the bedroom. It was a peaceful combination of piano and guitar. Grace was in the large claw-foot tub in front of the picture window. Her eyes were closed, but she could feel him in the room.

"You look tired. You want to sleep for a while?" Ivan asked.

"You're the one who should be exhausted. You didn't sleep at all last night, and you had what, two or three hours the night before, and none the night before that." She still hadn't opened her eyes. She yawned and stretched. "The water's getting cold, anyway. I could use a nap." She looked at him as she stood up. "Hand me a towel?"

His heart sped up. Her wet skin was arousing, with soap bubbles sliding off. He handed her the towel, looking away as he reached into the tub to let the water drain. This was going to be harder than he thought. She was a beautiful, smart, and kind naked woman who remembered being in love with him. How could he not desire that? Once she had wrapped herself, he gave her his hand to balance. As she climbed out, she reached up to let down her hair, sending a chill across Ivan's back. The scent of gardenias wafted toward him as her hair brushed across his shoulder.

"It's a little cold in here." She had goosebumps erupting over her exposed skin.

"I'll light a fire, then we nap." He was relieved for an excuse to exit the bathroom and concentrate on something else, anything else. By the time he finished with his task, she had come out of the bathroom with one of his flannel pajama tops on. He usually only wore the bottoms. He chuckled to himself, thinking it was the best use of a set. Grace opened the French doors wide, letting in more crisp air, then hopped into bed under the thick comforter. That was the best way to sleep. Open doors bringing in refreshing, cool air and the scent of flaming hickory while snuggled deep in soft, thick blankets.

"Hurry up. Get in here." Grace pulled back the blanket on the unoccupied side of the bed, averse to sleeping alone.

Ivan pulled himself off the floor and changed into the flannel bottoms she had left on the counter in the bathroom. He climbed into bed, pulling the covers to his neck. Grace snuggled in beside him, pulling the covers down to lay her head on his chest. He wrapped his arms around her, breathing in the scent of her hair. She was sleeping within minutes. He watched her for a long time, combing his fingers through her thick, tangled waves, before drifting off himself. He hadn't been with a woman since he was human. The sensation of her leg wrapped over his and her breath on his chest was something he hadn't experienced before. As he slept, he dreamt of his human life.

Ivan was a lowly feudal farmer. His wife had been betrothed to marry another man, but the man had rejected her, choosing to wed another. She was angry. Resentful. Her father would pay a dowry to any man who would marry his scorned daughter. She had farmed all her life and was pretty. Ivan thought she would make a good wife, so he took the offer. In return, he received a small piece of land and some livestock to start with. He worked hard, as did she. She performed her marital duties, making no bones about not liking it. They had two children together. He grew to care for her, and she at least tolerated him.

She didn't resist her duty any longer, even occasionally initiating it. He thought this was what love should be. It was what he thought marriage ought to be. He considered himself happy.

Late one evening, Ivan was returning from the market where he sold meat, eggs, and vegetables. Something had attacked the village while he was away. He ran to his home. The children were safe, having hidden in a cupboard. His wife was dead. Her body lay on the floor, eyes wide and clouded with her neck twisted unnaturally while blood soaked her dress. He picked her up from the floor, feeling that her body was still warm. He laid her out gently and cleaned the wounds, wrapping her in a sheet to bury in the morning as their children sobbed.

To his shock, she bolted upright, forcing him to jump away. The children screamed in terror, running back to the safe confines of the cupboard. She was different. Cold, vicious. He was horrified when he realized she had been turned into a monster. The stories were true. He knew what she was. He also knew he had to kill her. Their eyes locked. Hers were filled with rage and hunger. He scrambled as quickly as he could to get his axe when she attacked him from behind. She had the strength of ten men, and Ivan was easily overpowered, being slammed viciously to the ground. He could hear the bones in his shoulder snap, although the shock and adrenaline kept him from feeling the pain. She pinned him, digging her claws into his chest, leaving him unable to move.

Spitting in his face and screaming, she made it clear that she had always detested him and the children he forced upon her. She knew what she was. She had begged the vampire who attacked her to turn her. The clan was her family now, and they were waiting for her to join them, but not before leaving him with a gift. Her lips curled back, revealing long, sharp fangs. With a menacing laugh, she mauled him ferociously, injecting venom into his neck before ripping open a vein of her own, forcing the spilled blood down his throat. She saw the horror in his face. She scanned him with her deranged, smiling eyes before snapping his neck.

He woke on the floor the next afternoon starving, covered in his own blood as well as hers. Everything was too loud, too bright. He covered his eyes as he pulled himself off the floor and staggered to the window, closing the shutters hard enough to break the latch. When he turned back toward the room, before his eyes had cleared, he smelled it. Thick, sweet, metallic blood. It drew him, beckoning him. His thirst was intense. He sniffed it out like a dog. When he found the origin, it sickened him. He vomited bile onto the floor. The daemon had eviscerated his children. She had torn them to pieces. His connection with her was painted red with rage and hatred. He subdued his thirst long enough to bury what was left of his innocent offspring. Now, it was time for him to hunt.

He pursued her for years, destroying any vampire that carried her scent, before finding her. The first time he laid eyes on her following the incident, she was beautiful, dripping in fine clothing and jewels. His vision narrowed in on the evil murderess surrounded by other vampires and terrified humans. They were conspicuously, lavishly feeding from them in public, which could only mean their prey was not meant to survive.

He waited. Staying downwind of the group, he watched for days as the clan tortured and fed on hundreds of humans. He had patience to stalk her, remaining still for hours at a time. In all the time before he found her, he had become an unparalleled predator, determined to take her as his most prized kill.

Finally, she made her fatal mistake. She was alone. He struck quickly, snapping her neck before she knew he was there. Taking her to an isolated cave, he employed techniques that made it impossible for them to be followed. He wanted her alone.

Once her neck healed, and she was conscious, he tortured her for weeks. He did things to her that terrified him. He was unaware of how deep his anger had gone or how much he enjoyed taking it out on her. The last day when he looked at her, he no longer cared. His rage had subsided. She meant nothing to him. She was nothing. He took off her head in one swing and threw her body into the fire. He would spend the next six hundred years alone, watching and learning.

"Ivan!" Grace was shaking and yelling at him. He woke, startled. His eyes were red, his pillow soaked with tears.

"Ivan, you were dreaming about her again. It's been so long. You were kicking and screaming in your sleep."

He grabbed her almost too tightly. "Grace, I can't lose you. I can't bear to lose anyone else I love." He had said the words before he understood they were true. He wasn't fully awake, but he knew in that very second, they were true.

She cradled his head against her chest, soothing him. "I'm not going anywhere. I promise." It hurt her to the core to see him like this. She thought the nightmares were over. He hadn't had one since shortly before their mating. She must have been much closer to being lost than she realized for him to have this reaction. He held onto her tightly until he again succumbed to his weariness.

She didn't want to separate herself from him. She fell back asleep, cradling him in her arms.

It was early evening and Grace had been awake for several hours, staring mesmerized into Ivan's peaceful face. She hoped a slumber this serene was filled with lovely dreams. Grace had never known Ivan to sleep this long. She moved slightly from under him to take in the pleasing view from her bed of treetops washed in vibrant reds, yellows, and oranges enhanced by the setting sun. She could smell fall in the air that was turning colder as the sun dipped below the mountain peaks. This had always been her favorite time of year.

After another hour, she woke him. He wouldn't be able to sleep tonight, but maybe that was for the best. She unbuttoned her shirt, sliding her body down against his naked chest. She kissed him lightly over his face, rubbing against him. He stirred, pulling her in. She kissed him deeply and long. Lust overcame him. He grabbed the back of her neck, kissing her hard, grinding into her through his flannel pants. She slid her hand down his groin, under the waistband. He pulled his neck back, then quickly jerked forward, becoming fully awake.

"Grace Novak, you can't even follow orders for eight hours. We have to wait." That was probably the most difficult sentence he had ever uttered. In his dream state, he barely grasped he had added his last name to her first.

"No, I have to wait. You shouldn't be deprived because of me." She was stroking him firmly with her hand as she pressed her thigh between his legs.

"You can't exert yourself." Likely the second hardest sentence he ever uttered.

"Shhh. Don't fight it. Let me do this."

He couldn't physically stop her. Even now, she was stronger than he was. Truthfully, he didn't want her to stop. He could no longer help himself. Giving in, he rolled back, flipping the covers off onto the floor. She licked his chest and continued stroking while inching further down. Feeling him getting close to his limit, she slid her mouth over him, taking him deep into her throat. His reaction was immediate. She held until he was finished, then released him, sliding her naked body back up over his. She kissed him long and slowly. He was in whatever he considered heaven to be.

"There's my man. Glad to have you back."

He returned her kiss. "I could live the rest of my days in this bed with you."

"You know that's not a viable option, given my restrictions." She balanced her chin on his chest and batted her eyes at him. "You ready to get up?"

"Now you're concerned with your restrictions," he sighed. Ivan brushed the hair off her face. "You're right about one thing. We should get up. Ami is probably still staring out into the woods where I left her this morning. We probably shouldn't leave her there all night."

"I didn't realize she was still here. I take it they've worked out the babysitting schedule then?"

"Yes, Ami today, and I think it's Erik tomorrow. I'm sure he'd be more comfortable with a little less PDA." Ivan wouldn't want to see his own mother climbing all over some man he didn't know, even if they were mated or married.

"You know I'm a very sensual being. It's hard for me to keep my hands off you."

"I can see that. Getting along with your sons is still my preference. I don't want them to think I'm some creepy sexual predator."

"You seemed to have a decent start with that. They were comfortable with you."

"We have a lot more to learn about each other. They're men and I'll treat them as such. Even though, when it comes to a man's mother, he will always be a little boy." He rubbed his hand over her bare buttocks. "Now, get up before we get into some real trouble."

Grace got out of bed, backing toward the bathroom, holding her shirt open while licking her lips.

"You are an untamable creature!" he yelled after her.

"That's exactly how you like me," she yelled back.

She was right. From the first time he saw her, he was drawn to her wildness. Her joyfulness in merely being alive. It made him wonder if this was the way things were supposed to end up or if this forced union would come crashing down around him, like life had done to him the last time he thought he was happy.

When they went downstairs, Ivan saw he had been correct; Ami was exactly where he had left her.

"Anything interesting out there?" he called to her as he relit the fire in the main living area.

"Everything," she replied.

Grace pulled a glass out of the dishwasher for some water. She was extremely thirsty. More than usual. She poured a glass out of the pitcher in the fridge, taking a big swig.

"You know you're drinking CB, right?" Ivan asked her.

"Yeah, no. I know you say it's almost tasteless, but I don't agree. Here." She handed it to Ivan and poured herself regular water.

"Almost tasteless to humans. You're not exactly human, are you?"

"I'll keep my intake of it restricted to wine. The tartness enhances the flavor of a sweet grape." She downed the water, then grabbed a bottle of CB-labeled white out of the fridge.

"Hey, Beivve didn't say you could drink."

"She didn't say I couldn't." Grace poured three glasses, passing one to Ivan, taking another to Ami on the deck. "Here."

Ami took it from her.

"What's so interesting?" she asked, looking into the rainbow-colored forest.

"Everything," Ami repeated.

"Specifically?"

"The creatures are burrowing. They stock their little dwellings with large amounts of food, one piece at a time. It takes vast amounts of energy and concentration. I've been watching them for hours. They repeat the same process over and over without taking any breaks." They fascinated Ami.

Grace sat in a deck chair, propping her feet up on the rail. "Let me know when they stop, won't you?"

"Yes," Ami replied without taking her eyes off whatever tiny creature she happened to be watching.

Ivan sat in his recliner with his tablet to catch up on what he had missed over the last day or so. He perused his email and business server trade info, and then he saw it. He had wanted one of these for a long time. Seemed too good to be true. He called and set up an appointment to look at it in the morning.

CHAPTER SIXTEEN

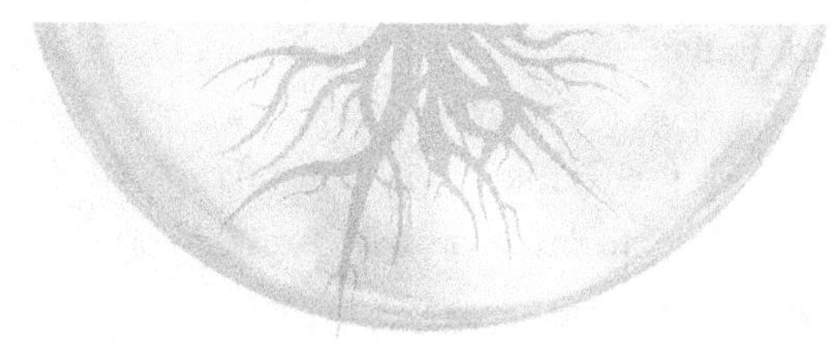

At four a.m., Ivan slid out of bed as gingerly as possible not to wake Grace. They had only gone to bed two hours ago, but he really wasn't tired after the nap he had yesterday. He wanted to be on the road and back before she was up. He dressed and went downstairs to grab some breakfast before his outing. When he flipped on the lights, he realized Ami was still on the deck, staring out into nowhere.

"Ami, what are you doing?"

"Watching."

He shook his head. "Watching what?"

"There are so many things out there. When one goes to sleep, another one moves around. I never tire of watching. It's like a little city down there, only not." She would probably stand there for days if they let her.

"Ami, come in and get some breakfast."

"You know I don't need to eat."

"I know you like to eat."

"True." She sat at the counter while Ivan heated the last of the eggs and waffles from the morning before. They had taken a large platter down to the Ranger Station last evening and there was still food left over. While they were eating, Erik came through the front door wearing jeans, brown boots, an olive-colored T-shirt, and a light jacket. Not his usual military black Ivan had seen him in before.

"I didn't expect anyone to be up yet. That smells delicious. Got any left?"

Ivan pulled down another plate and cup. "You get the last waffle. There are still some eggs in the skillet and plenty of coffee. You got the next shift, huh?"

"Yeah. Where is she? Still in bed?"

"I wanted to let her sleep as long as she can."

"Must be nice not to have someone to take orders from," Erik joked, nodding at Ivan.

"Hey, when you work for yourself, who's gonna fire you?"

"True." He spotted the thermos on the counter and a small pack beside it. "Are you going somewhere?"

"Absolutely. Got a line on something I've been dying to have for a while now. I should be back in two or three hours. Want to come along?" Ivan had made the offer before he thought about it. This would definitely be something Erik was interested in. Why not?

"Who's going to stay with mother if we both leave?" They both looked at Ami.

"I can stay. I'd like to watch the creatures longer," she said, taking her coffee back out onto the deck.

"It's settled then." Ivan poured coffee into his thermos.

"You're not going to need me to kill anything, are you? I didn't bring a change of clothes." Erik had always been quiet with the others around. Ivan couldn't tell if he was joking or not.

"Not planning on it, but you may still need a change of clothes later," Ivan joked while walking toward the door. Erik followed him out to the garage. Erik walked over to the Land Rover, which Ivan walked past. It was a four-car garage to the right side of the driveway as you approached the cabin. It had a small auto shop set up in the far end bay. The only other thing in it was a flatbed truck in the third bay. "C'mon. We're taking this one."

Now Erik was really curious. "Where are we going?"

Ivan smiled at him but said nothing.

Thirty minutes later, they pulled up at an old salvage yard.

"Is this a carbon fuel vehicle mausoleum?"

Ivan laughed. "That's a funny way to put it, but yeah, I guess it is. We call it a salvage yard."

They found Al, the owner, who led them into a back section that was overgrown excessively. It looked like no one had been there in years. Trees, shrubs, vines. You couldn't tell where one ended and another began.

Al lit up a half-chewed cigar. It smelled sweet, like brandy and cherry. "Well, there it is. You're welcome to pull it out and look it over. I can't tell you if it's all there or not. I've owned this place for thirty years and hadn't never seen it till we had a busted water line back here a few days ago. It ain't worth the trouble to me. Figured somebody'd want it."

Al was so right. Ivan wanted it. He didn't care what condition it was in. He was staring at the front bumper of a '68 Pontiac GTO in alpine blue, and he was in love. If it had the original 400 Ram Air II engine, he would be ecstatic. This was a rare find in this area. He thought about it a second longer. It was a rare find in any area.

"You figured right, Al. Let's get this old girl out of here and open her up."

Al spit on the ground. "Aight. Lemme git the hauler."

Erik was looking at him as if he had lost his mind. "What would you want with that thing? It can't possibly even work."

Ivan slapped him on the back. "It's a work of art, man. I'm going to restore her to her former beauty. I've been looking for one of these for a while."

"You really think you can make it work again? It looks like a piece of junk to me." Erik liked old mechanical things, but he couldn't see this ever running again.

"You need vision. I can already see her."

Erik chuckled as Al backed up the hauler. He hooked the chains to the frame and drug it out of the mass of vines that had grown over and through it. He used a machete to cut the entanglement from around the driver's door. Ivan popped open the hood. Lo and behold, there it was.

Ivan checked the vin, the door, frame, and a few engine parts. Everything he could see matched. He was taking her home.

"How much?" he asked Al.

Al scratched his head. "It ain't worth much to me. I ain't got no keys. Say about a grand?"

"Loaded on my truck for that price?"

"Yep." Al was a man of few words.

They shook on it. Ivan pulled the cash out of his pocket, then watched as Al loaded it on the truck. He was happy as a kitten with catnip. Erik still thought he was nuts, but that thought was overridden by curiosity on the drive home. Grace and Ami heard the truck coming up the driveway and came out onto the front porch.

"I see you got a new toy." She smiled at his huge grin.

"Isn't she beautiful?"

"Not yet, but I'm sure she will be. You need a hand getting it off the truck?" She was happy he had something to occupy him while they were here.

"Nope. Erik and I can get it off." Grace sat on the porch swing, watching him unstrap it. Then he and Erik each grabbed a side, gently lifted her off, and set her on the ground behind the truck. It's good to be ridiculously strong sometimes. Well, he rethought that, all the time. Even better when you have friends as strong as you are. He'd have this baby up and running in no time. He tossed Erik the flatbed keys to put the truck in the garage while he pulled out the pressure washer. First it needed a good spray, so he could see what he was working with. Although it wouldn't be helpful for the musty smell, he was aware he couldn't save any of the upholstered parts.

The rest of the week droned on for Grace at an excruciatingly slow pace. Erik had been coming every day and working on the car with Ivan, though he had hardly spoken with his mother during that time.

Erik was seeing how the obsession with a mechanical object had possessed Ivan so completely. It was satisfying taking something so hideous and restoring it to a thing of beauty. He worked from dawn until well past dusk on the project, often opting to sleep at the house, unwilling to part from his new hobby.

Mikkel also stopped by occasionally to check up on her, meaning the car. He wasn't one to get his hands dirty if he could help it, but he did want to drive it when they finished.

Grace mostly watched them work on their new Baby Blue, as they called her, and read old books. She liked the tactile feel of the pages. The smell of old milled paper and ink. She found comfort in the strange way the books grounded her. The words seemed to hold more weight etched on the delicate pages. But, even with the indulgence of unknown characters and quests, she was going stir-crazy. She decided to go for a walk while there were still a few hours of light. She changed and went to the kitchen to fill a bottle with water.

Ami had stayed most of the time too, although her presence held little entertainment for Grace. She had become obsessed with her forest creatures, as she called them. There were so many different kinds of tiny things: birds, rabbits, porcupines, and raccoons, among other animals. Not all were winter hoarders, but they all ate, and they all spent endless amounts of time looking for food.

"Ami," Grace called to her. She turned from her little perch on the back deck. "Do you want to go for a stroll down there?"

"Won't we disrupt them?" She had wanted to get closer; she just wasn't sure if she should. Ami had spent some time amongst different humanoid species, and most wanted little to do with what they referred to as animals. Except for dogs and cats. They seemed to love their dogs and cats as much as they loved their own children. Ami couldn't understand that attitude. These tiny things were beautiful forms of life, and humans, regardless of whether they wanted to believe it, were animals too.

"I think they'll be fine with it," Grace responded.

"Then yes, please," Ami answered.

"Let me go tell Ivan we're taking a walk. He probably wouldn't even notice, but with my luck, he'd come in the house for something and panic." Grace wasn't sure if telling him would have any effect, since she didn't currently have spark plugs or a carburetor. She certainly couldn't deny his passion for things. She watched him and Erik for several minutes before they noticed she was there, leaning against the door frame.

"Hey, Grace. Come to help?"

"Came to see if you two were still alive. You want me to bring a refrigerator out here for you?" She thought she was pretty clear about being sarcastic.

"Thanks, Mom, but we're good. We have a beer cooler," Erik replied without missing a beat before he started laughing.

"All right. You two yuk it up. Ami and I are going out for a little stroll in the woods." That made them both stop what they were doing and look at her.

She craned her neck back, looking at them both like they had thrown something at her. "I'm allowed to walk. It's been a week already, or had you two not noticed?"

The men looked at each other warily.

Ivan stammered, "Well, uh, do … do you want us to come with you?" He was concerned she would overdo it, but he didn't want her to think he was concerned she would push her limits. It wasn't working. She knew the look.

"No." She strung out the "oh" part. "We're only going for a stroll, so Ami can get a closer look at her tiny creatures. I won't do anything strenuous and I'm certainly not going to be doing any critical thinking out there. Besides, there's nothing either of you can do that Ami can't." She was a bit put out that they were treating her like a child. She spun around, walking away.

"I'm leaving. Don't follow me."

"That's not the first time I've heard that one," Ivan called after her.

"Not from me," she laughed.

Ivan returned his attention to the car. To him, she was so much more than just a car. She was an experience, a challenge, and a bridge to building a bond with at least one of Grace's sons.

They almost finished the engine, except for two parts that would be delivered tomorrow. Erik had pulled the seats out to replace some springs before they reupholstered them. The dash had cracked from years of exposure to unyielding weather. Fortunately, an old friend had found a replacement that would be delivered tomorrow with the two engine parts.

The body damage had been easy to repair. It was steel sheet, which made it quite pliable in the hands of the two formidable men. It had a few remaining rough spots, to which they applied resin filler. The only part of the restoration they decided not to do themselves was the paint job. Neither of them had the experience or the skill to tackle that critical step. Ivan had found a body shop outside of town that was recommended for classic paint schemes. The best part about doing the work yourself: you can add custom touches. Custom upholstery, steering wheel, mirrors, shifter. All that, plus a steel drop panel in the trunk that slid under the back seat to store things you didn't want found.

Cars had always been Ivan's one guilty pleasure. He knew they were horrible for the environment, especially ones like this that measured gallons per mile, as an old radio guy used to joke. There was just something about the rumble of a big engine and a stick shift he couldn't resist. They finished up with the seats and decided to call it a day.

"Your mother was right about one thing. We have been spending a lot of time out here. What do you say we go in and make dinner? Maybe call your brothers for a game of cards?"

Erik wasn't sure what Ivan meant. "I don't understand. I mean, I understand dinner. What are … cards?"

"I'll show you later. You'll catch on pretty quick." Ivan was partial to poker. It was also a simple game to play. The only game easier he knew of was blackjack, but that could get tedious with only one deck when everyone playing was bright enough to count.

"Mind if I get washed up first?" Erik had practically moved in. They set him up in the farthest bedroom on the opposite side of the house from theirs, beside Grace's office. He had clothes and toiletries, although he kept them in a go bag.

"Not at all. I need a quick shower myself." Ivan realized he smelled like gas and heavy oil. Not the nicest scent for grilling steaks. He figured the girls would be back in the next couple of hours, well before sunset. There might even be enough time to catch a game. It was Sunday, after all.

"You ever heard of football?" he asked as they entered the house.

"Yeah. Kind of a sissy version of gladiator games, but with rules and pads."

"And no swords," Ivan chuckled.

"We've seen a few games. They take a lot of breaks, and they have strange short plays in between."

"Commercials. They're advertisements to get you to buy stuff." He had never thought about how strange commercials were to anyone who wasn't familiar with this world. It's the little things you don't consider. At the top of the stairs, they each turned in opposite directions to get cleaned up.

~~~~

Grace and Ami had made it down to the stream. There were a few large flat rocks jutting out of the side of one of the rock faces on the other side. Grace took off her shoes and waded through the ankle-deep water. It was still only slightly cool, feeling good on her feet. She carried her shoes as she climbed up on the lower rock. She stood on it for a minute before sitting down cross-
~~~~

legged with her back against the sheer face of the mountain behind her. Ami watched her disappear under the canopy of tree branches from the other side of the stream.

"Come on up. You can see everything from here."

Ami ported over.

"Not fair, Ami. If I can't do it, neither can you." Grace applied a mock injured tone to her voice. Grace actually enjoyed climbing. If she hadn't promised she'd take it easy, she'd just as soon be climbing the rock face to the top right now.

"I'm sorry," Ami apologized, looking dejected.

"I was teasing, Ami," Grace smiled. "Come here," she said, patting the rock beside her. "Sit quietly. Close your eyes and listen."

They sat listening to the sounds of the wind rustling the leaves, the water trickling lightly, insects buzzing, birds chirping. All of Ami's favorite tiny creatures bustled about. There was a heavy scent of damp dirt under decaying leaves and the last of the fall blooms. To Grace, it was the smell of creation. As each thing died and gave its energy back to the ground, waiting to bring forward new life next spring. Energy exchanged for matter produces energy, and the circle goes on. With her eyes closed, she could feel the energy vibrating through the rock.

Grace whispered, "Now, pick one sound. Focus on it. When you know exactly where it is, open your eyes."

Ami whispered back, "What is that? That's what I've been watching all morning." Ami pointed toward what she was looking at.

"It's a pika. They gather and dry plants in haystacks for their winter food storage. It looks like a big hamster, but it's really part of the rabbit family."

"How do you know that?"

"Besides practically living outdoors before electricity and indoor plumbing? I watch a lot of documentaries. I guess not as much watch them as I have them on the TV while I'm doing other stuff. You still learn a few things."

"They work all day long and into the moonlit night. At least until the big birds that see in the dark come out." It was strange how childlike Ami was for being as old as she was.

"Owls. They hunt at night. And I'll hazard to guess pikas are a tasty meal for them."

The pair sat whispering and relaxing. It was so peaceful in the woods. Grace had never been afraid of the forests like most people were. They were her shelter from the harsh reality of her early days on the planet. Even before she understood what she was, she found remote places as a haven. She never felt threatened by nature. Animals loved her. They were drawn to her energy and she to theirs. As she and Ami sat there quietly, all sorts of animals were coming closer. Cautiously and out of reach. Still much closer than they would likely dare with an average human. It started getting cooler. Sunset was coming. Unfortunately, they needed to make their way back to the cabin before Ivan launched a search party.

Grace was grateful for this walk with Ami. It made her feel grounded again. She always enjoyed being outside, being able to feel nature's energy around her without the interference of human emotion pushing in on her.

The sun was setting when they opened the front door. They were greeted with chaos; every light in the house was on, football blaring on the TV, roaring laughter, and Ivan teaching The Three to play Texas Hold'em with another guy she immediately recognized.

"Who the hell let that dirty junkyard dog up on my kitchen table!" Grace yelled across the room.

"Gracie girl!" Josh exclaimed. "Git your scrawny little ass over here and let me look at you!" Grace practically launched herself at the tree stump of an old man. He had been her transport in and out of so many scrapes. His old tin can was a second home for her.

"What the hell are you doing here?"

"That's no way to say hello." He jerked her up, squeezing her hard. "Ivan ordered some parts from me for his old '68 Goat. I was supposed to have them delivered tomorrow, but after he told me about your accident, I figured I'd deliver them myself and check up on you."

She saw Ivan mouth the word "concussion" over Josh's shoulder while pointing to his head. He put her down and spun her around to look at her.

"Woah cowboy. The spinning doesn't stop when I do. I took a pretty hard one to the head. They got me on lockdown for another week."

"It must have been more than one knock to put you down. I've seen you take out two or three guys at once without so much as breaking a fingernail."

Ivan stepped in. "It was actually a ski slope and a tree. We were in Switzerland last week. I should have known better than to take a slope so early in the season.

There was an ice layer that froze overnight. It wasn't visible until we were on it. The only way I was able to get turned out was because I weighed more. I was able to get a ski under the ice while she skidded right over the top."

"It figures the only thing strong enough to take her out is nature." Josh turned to inspect Grace a bit closer. Ivan looked at Ami, shaking his head no. She understood and kept her mouth shut.

"So, I understand these fine young men are yours? I never knew you had any kids. You barely look old enough to be their sister. Come to think of it, you don't look a day older than when I met you fifteen years ago."

"Flattery will get you everywhere, old man. I try to keep them out of my other business, if you know what I mean. Ivan's the only one who knows about them. Oh, I'm being rude. This is Ami. She's an old friend and a nurse of sorts. She's been appointed my unofficial babysitter till I go back for some more tests to make sure my head's all cleared up."

"It's very nice to meet you, Ami. I'm Josh. If you ever need anything you can't find anywhere, I'm your guy."

"I'd be interested if you could find Pandora's box. She has no idea where it went. Just don't open it, please," Ami said with a very serious demeanor.

Grace began laughing, and the others followed suit. "Oh Ami. You're hilarious." She wrapped her arm around her, pulling her toward the kitchen, where she whispered, "You can't say that stuff to humans." Then loud enough for everyone to hear. "Can someone bring up a couple of bottles of wine? I think we're out."

Erik nodded to Mikkel. *It's in the cellar. Door's on the back side of the house.*

"Oh yeah. I'll go grab it." Mikkel went outside and around to the cellar door to pull a few bottles from their stock.

"What's for dinner? Are these steaks?" Grace asked, looking under the foil-covered tray. "They're huge. Why so many? You could feed four people with one of them and we have ten." She thought they had to weigh two pounds each. They were all about an inch thick.

Ivan pulled them out of her grasp from the other side of the counter. "They need another fifteen minutes in that dry rub before I put them on the grill. Why don't you relax and catch up with Josh? Ami and I will get the fire pit lit."

"Josh, how long are you here for? We have plenty of room. I insist you stay with us." Grace loved the old guy. He had always treated her like a daughter.

Things had been crazy for the last few days. While she appreciated the dose of sanity he brought, she didn't actually want him to stay longer than a day or so. No telling who might pop in, literally.

"That's mighty hospitable of ya, but I gotta get back to the hangar. I had to hitch a ride down with a local guy from Helena and he's flying back out tonight. You got me for about three hours."

"And happy to have you. How'd you get to the cabin?" Grace hadn't seen another vehicle in the driveway.

"I got a rental truck. Jack's picking up some parts down the road from a local salvage guy that we're taking back to a buyer up in Kelowna. I figured since we were heading this way anyway, might as well do a little business." Josh was always thinking about the next thing. It was probably what made him so good at finding the obscure.

"Jack's here too? This must be my lucky day." Grace wondered how he was doing. In this reality, he was head over heels for Violet. He had been in the other one too, but Grace didn't remember that clearly, although she was pretty sure it was right. "When's he going to be back?"

"Maybe half an hour. If he doesn't get lost."

"There's only one turn."

"Like I said."

"If that's the case, deal me in, boys." Grace had gotten very good at poker. It was Ivan's favorite game, and he always needed someone to play with.

About that time, Mikkel rolled back in with two bottles of white and one of red. "I didn't know which to get, so I brought both."

"That's perfect. Thank you," Grace answered, pulling her cards in close as he walked behind her. Didn't want him sharing that with his brothers. She knew all their little tricks.

"Where's Ivan?"

"Deck," Alex answered. "Can you toss me a beer?"

Mikkel opened the fridge, grabbed one, and threw it over his shoulder. Alex caught the bottle without so much as a glance toward his brother.

"That was impressive," Josh popped off.

The Three said in unison, "Triplet thing."

Josh nodded slowly. "All right. As long as it doesn't happen with the cards."

Erik leaned in. "It's not like we can read each other's minds. We just have a thing." The Three laughed, making Josh wonder.

"Now you're just trying to freak him out," Grace admonished. "That's enough."

Mikkel brought Grace her wine. He also handed Erik and Josh another beer and took the open seat. "Next round I'm in."

Ivan had just put the steaks on before there was a knock at the door. Grace figured it was Jack. Folding her hand and stuffing her cards in her pocket, she raced to answer, pulling it open to see the smiling face of Violet standing in front of Jack.

"Surprise!" A surprise indeed. Violet was one of her favorites. Grace had been her blood nurse when she was a baby. When they hugged, Violet whispered in Grace's ear, "We have something we want to ask you and Ivan."

She looked back and forth from her to Jack excitedly, whispering. "Really. Really?"

Violet quietly nodded her head.

"It's good to see you. I've missed you so much. You too, boy, get over here." Jack stepped up and joined the hug. "Come on in."

They greeted The Three, who they had met earlier when they dropped Josh off.

"I can't believe not one of you gave this away." She took Violet and Jack by the hands, pulling them past the table onto the deck.

"Ivan, look what the cat dragged in. I can't believe you of all people could keep this a secret from me."

"Why do you think I went out on the deck as soon as you came home? You read me like a book. It's good to see you two. Did you tell her yet?"

The couple smiled.

"You knew that too?! What am I saying? Of course, you had to approve it. What else have you been keeping from me?"

"And you thought all I had been doing this week was working on the car. I had to find some reason to stay away from you. The Board approved their request yesterday." Ivan felt like he had climbed out from under a ton of bricks. He had never been able to keep anything from her before. He was proud of himself for pulling this off.

"So, when's the ceremony? How long do we have to plan?" she asked excitedly.

Violet looked back at Jack. "Well, that's why we're here. We wanted to ask Ivan to officiate and you to be Jack's blood donor for the mating." Violet kept her voice low.

"Absolutely! I'd have been offended if you had asked anyone else."

"We haven't picked a date yet, but we will have a small ceremony for the humans, then after the reception we'll have the mating ceremony. I'm going to ask Asta to be my maid of honor for the wedding and I want you to bind us." Violet was beaming.

"I'm so excited about this. You two are perfect for each other. Jack, you will make a wonderful addition to the community." Grace hadn't been this happy in quite some time. "Oh, where are my manners? Jack, Violet, this is Ami. She's a very old friend of mine."

Violet looked at her in disbelief. "You mean *very* old?"

Grace raised her eyebrow. "Yup."

Ivan pulled Jack aside. "Let's let them talk wedding. We have steaks to finish." Jack and Ivan went back to the fire pit.

"I knew as soon as I met the triplets out there that you must have gotten your memories back! How did you find them? You have to tell me everything!" Violet whispered loudly.

"Do you think you two can stay a few days or do you have to go back with Josh?" Grace didn't want to have this discussion until there were fewer ears in the house.

"I don't have to be back in Napa till Wednesday. Let me ask Jack if his dad needs him to crew back."

She walked over to Jack. Grace turned to Ami. "You are getting good at keeping quiet. Thank you for that. We'll discuss it more after everyone leaves. Okay?"

"It wasn't hard. I don't have any idea what you're talking about." Ami didn't have a clue what binding or mating or half of what they said meant.

Violet told her they could stay. She and Grace went back into the house, leaving Ami to stare at her creatures. Grace could tell The Three were having a rude conversation in their heads about Violet. She stared them down with that look all mothers have that scares the ever-living crap out of any kid, no matter their age.

Josh said he didn't mind heading back alone and everything was good. Grace poured Violet a glass of wine and they stayed in the kitchen, talking about ceremony plans.

Mikkel turned to interrupt them. "Are you forgetting something?"

Grace looked at Violet, then back at Mikkel. "I don't think so."

He held his hand out toward her. "Cards."

"Oops," she said, pulling the cards out of her back pocket and handing them over.

The Three and Josh continued to play poker, occasionally shouting at the game on the TV. Meanwhile, Ivan and Jack were in the midst of a serious discussion outside.

Ivan was by the fire pit, where he leaned against the back of a chair with Jack standing a few feet in front of him.

"They'll fill you in on the ceremony details later. It's not that difficult for you. Just nod and agree with everything she wants."

"You mean everything Vivian wants, don't you?" Jack laughed.

Ivan chuckled, knowing exactly how Viv was. "Yeah, that's exactly what I mean. But seriously, how are you hanging in there? You scared?" Ivan had always liked Jack. He was smart and cautious. He had a big heart too. When his mother got sick, he dropped out of college to come home and be with her.

"I can't say I'm not apprehensive about the specifics of the mating. I feel a lot better knowing it will be Grace in the room when I wake up. The one thing I will say is it would satisfy me to have a single lifetime with Violet. I'm a lucky man to get eternity with her. I never in a million years would have dreamed she'd want to spend her life with me." Jack had always downplayed himself. He was humble, which was rare in someone his age.

"You're good together. I want to do something for you if you let me." Ivan had big plans for this man. He would be the beginning of a better race.

"Ivan, you've been so good to us, already rushing through our approval." Jack was grateful. It usually took months, sometimes even years, to be approved.

"It wasn't hard. I already knew you. You are the kind of person we want in our community. And you had already done the counseling."

"You know I thought he was a couples counselor, don't you?"

"That was all Violet." Ivan threw his hands up. "What I want is for you to finish school. How close were you to getting your engineering degree?"

"I was about a semester and a half away. I want to go back, eventually. Right now, I'm not sure I can afford it."

"Jack, you need to look at the reality of things. You're smarter than average. After you turn, your mind is going to open up. You'll be calculating thought processes exponentially faster than you do now. You'll need to figure out a way to separate yourself from your family gradually. I know it sounds harsh, and it is. In fifteen or twenty years, your family is going to notice you're not aging. You will have to move out of the area for a time. A full understanding of mechanical engineering and physics will let you go anywhere. You don't need to worry about money either. We take care of our own. We have plans for the community, and it involves a highly skilled understanding of all aspects of technology. I want you to be part of that. A small investment in you now will be a huge payoff for all of us in the future. Think about it. Talk it over with Violet. Even if you don't take me up on my offer, do it for yourself. I sound like a crappy high-pressure salesman, don't I?"

"You don't. Violet told me how passionate you have always been about bringing them into the future. If it wasn't for you, they would most likely be extinct. I really do want to go back. My main issue is my dad. I help with his business."

"You can't let yourself feel guilty about wishing to be more, Jack. Listen, come with me for a second." Ivan flipped the steaks and they walked back into the cabin.

"Josh, what do you think about Jack going back to college?" Jack looked at Ivan with enormous eyes.

Josh never even looked up from his hand. "I'd say it was about damned time. He's wasting his life working on my planes. His brothers can keep those rust buckets in the air. He shoulda gone back last year."

Jack cocked his head toward Ivan. "Well, since the two of you are ganging up on me, I'd love to go back to school."

Josh threw his bet into the pot, then looked up. "Good. I've already enrolled you, starting in January. Thanks for the help, Ivan. He needed a kick in the ass by someone other than me."

"Wait, you two already had this planned?"

Josh narrowed his eyes. "No. I already had this planned. Ivan agreed to talk to you, but said it had to be your choice. I had already enrolled you before he even called."

Jack turned to Ivan. "He already enrolled me. Did you know he already enrolled me?"

Ivan put his hands up. "No. He just said he wanted me to talk to you about it. I had to agree with him. You'll be a successful engineer."

"Can I at least ask where I'll be attending college? Queen's University doesn't have space in the January term."

"Oh, so you've been checking into it?" Josh grunted. "UC Davis. I assume you'll be staying at Violet's condo. If she'll have you, that is?" Everyone looked at Violet.

"Hello. Planning a wedding here. Where else would he stay?" She winked at Jack.

"Surprises all around then. Do I at least get to pack for myself?"

Josh laughed. "I sure ain't gonna touch your shit." Everyone laughed again.

"Thanks, Ivan. At least you made it feel like it was my decision."

"Since that's settled, let's eat. Oh, shit. The steaks!" Ivan blazed out of the room. Luckily, they were a perfect medium rare.

Dinner turned into a wonderful time to catch up. After Josh left, the men went into the living room to watch the rest of the second game. Grace, Ami, and Violet went out to the back deck. The fire was still burning, and they brought up another bottle of red.

Violet had been dying to ask all night. "How did you get your memories back? Who are you? What are you and when the hell did you get grown men for children?"

"Slow down, sunshine. One question at a time. Ami showed me how to unlock my memories. Unfortunately, we didn't perform the procedure in quite a delicate enough way, and it scrambled my eggs for a while. Everything's fine now, but I really do have to take it easy for another week."

"Then what do you remember?"

"First thing I remembered was, you know, my sons. We always had an idea I wasn't exactly from here. That was a correct assumption. I can't tell you much about my past. What I can tell you is that I was sent here, and I have a purpose." Grace wanted to give her enough to satisfy her curiosity, but not enough to get her in trouble.

"What's your purpose?"

"You obviously are immortal and so am I. I am supposed to help guide the community, so it can gain independence and elevate itself into something more than its mortal human counterpart."

"But who are you, and who sent you?" Violet wanted to know more.

"Those are the things I can't tell you. Even before I knew my purpose here, I was already doing it. I've been helping the entire time without even understanding. I can't reveal where I came from or who I was before. If I do, I'll have to leave. I'm still the same Grace I've always been. I've always wanted what's best for you, for all of you."

"What about your sons?"

"Same deal. They tell anyone, they have to leave."

"And Ami, your babysitter?"

Ami took that as her cue. "It's actually Amitiel. I'm an archangel."

Violet looked fervently back and forth between the two. "A what? Say that again."

Grace didn't let Ami repeat the answer. "Ami isn't under the same restrictions as I am about her identity. She can't reveal herself to humans unless they're approved. You're an immortal, which means her restrictions don't apply. However, if she reveals anything about my identity, she will have to remove the entire conversation from your memory." Grace was attempting to guide Violet to skirt the parameters of the conversation.

"I think I understand. Ami, you said you are an archangel. I understand what that is."

Ami was relieved. "Good, 'cause it's hard to explain."

"How long have you known Grace?" She was picking her questions carefully.

"I have known Grace for over four hundred thousand of your years." Ami was happy to answer questions.

Grace smiled. Violet stared at her for a moment.

"Were you children when you met?"

"I was never a child. Grace was an adult. We're not even from the same dimension." Ami scrunched her nose and giggled, finding the question hilarious.

That was a concept Violet had never even considered. She held out her glass, which Grace refilled. "Oh … Okay then. Wh-wh-who wants to talk weddings?" Violet stammered. She had endless time to work this out. Small bites, she thought to herself.

Grace and Violet laughed nervously. Ami didn't understand what they had found funny.

Wedding planning was a perfect distraction for Grace over the next few days. They weren't kidding themselves, though. As soon as Vivienne got involved, everything would change. Viv had been planning both her daughters' mating ceremonies since they were born. They were both certain she was positively ecstatic to find out she'd also be planning a traditional wedding, even though she complained about all the work involved.

While Violet and Grace reviewed Violet's wedding want list, Ivan, Jack, and Erik finished the last bits of mechanical work on the car. The only thing left was some sanding on the body and then paint. They were more than a little excited to take the final test drive to the body shop, where it would stay for about a week.

After Violet and Jack left, Grace felt much more productive and started working on her educational plan outline. It was a monumental task to get all the ideas that had been piling up in her thoughts out into a cohesive structure. She broke it down into three separate parts, which began taking shape as she wrote. She would take one section at a time and set an outline for each before presenting it to the Board.

The thing she counted on making the Board most interested was she would pay all the upfront costs. If it made the impact she hoped, they could begin accepting donations to subsidize her funding. They would never charge recipients for the services provided to them. That was the only point she would not be swayed from.

It took her two full days to get the outline to a point she believed was presentable. The last difficulty came with the third phase of the plan. She needed to be delicate and diplomatic regarding the older vampires. Some were rigidly set in their ways, although most had already embraced current trends and technologies.

Now she was ready for Ivan's input. It was so easy for her to interpret something when she was writing, thinking it said what she wanted it to say instead of what it actually said. Ivan would look at it with a critical eye, most of all because he wanted this program to have the strongest chance of being accepted. It was a critical step.

It was just the two of them at home today. Everyone felt it was safe enough for her not to have a full-time babysitter. Regardless, she would undergo her last scans tomorrow. Ivan was in the living room working on pieces for an online auction taking place that weekend. The room was warm and thick with the scent of oak when she entered. It was early afternoon. The doors were open to the deck, bringing in a cool breeze that carried pleasant earthy scents and cut through the heat from the blaze. Ivan was in the recliner closest to the front door. He heard her enter, although he hadn't looked up from the tablet until she stopped directly in front of him.

"I wondered when you were going to emerge from your cave," he said jokingly.

"You're one to talk. I'm surprised you even noticed. You've been immersed in work yourself."

"Idle hands, you know. It's so easy to work up here with all the peace and quiet." He set his tablet on the table beside him. "To what do I owe this pleasure?" He was in a very good mood.

Grace climbed into his lap like an eager child. "I finished it," she smiled broadly.

"That was fast. I'm impressed."

"Don't say that until you review it. Do you mind? I want your opinion."

"Absolutely. Where is it?"

Grace reached for his tablet. "It's in the shared drive. Do you want to look it over here, or would the computer be better?"

"I'll cast it to the TV. That way, we can discuss it as I read. Okay?"

"I can't be here while you read it. I'm too nervous. I'm going to have a glass of wine and a hot bath. Make some notes. We'll discuss it when I come back down." She gave him a quick kiss on the forehead before rolling off the arm of the chair and moving toward the kitchen.

"Yes ma'am. I am but a humble servant." He had wondered what she was up to for the past few days. He looked forward to reading it.

He finished well before she came back downstairs. The plan was good, very good. He had made a handful of notes, mostly having to do with procedural order and committee selection. She descended the stairs, appearing apprehensive. Ivan contemplated toying with her until he saw the look on her face. This was obviously important to her.

"Looks like we have a winner."

"Really? It's not too ambitious or vague?" she questioned, kneeling beside his chair.

"No, it contains the correct amount of groundwork with sufficient flexibility to change as the community advances. I made a few notes on minor items, but overall, it's a very comprehensive plan. I'm impressed you got such a cohesive plan together in only two days. Something this extensive should have taken weeks." Ivan shifted in his chair to face her.

"More like years. I've been thinking about it for a long time. All I had to do was write it down and tweak it to fit our new situation."

"You did excellent work. I'm proud of you." He wrapped his arm around her shoulder, giving her a supportive squeeze. "I'd like you to present this to the Board at next quarter's meeting."

"I've got a plan for that, too. You'll need to give a presentation first."

"What kind of presentation?"

"They need to have a 'preparing for the future' prequel to my presentation. Understanding the concept of moving beyond human counterparts is crucial for my part to make the desired impact. They may feel I'm being condescending or implying other negative connotations. It needs some ground preparation before the seeds can grow." She was very impassioned by this subject.

"You're right. We need to ensure they are as dedicated to elevating our species as you are." He smiled at her again.

"It's not only my life anymore, it's my job, too. This is why I chose to be here." Her wording struck Ivan oddly. They had never discussed what she remembered after she initially woke up. He had been assuming all along she had lost all her previous time here.

"You remember you chose to be here? On the first night, you were somewhat confused. I wasn't sure you remembered everything from before. What do you remember?" He didn't want to regret that question. He preferred to be blissfully unaware that she may still be in love with Lukkas.

"When Beivve first took me out of stasis, I still had a lot of catching up to do. My memories were coming in at a faster pace than could be processed by my brain. I remember the choice. I also know that the memories of our life were implanted." Was that a look of disappointment on Ivan's face?

"But they feel real to me," she continued. "They feel like this is the path I should have always been on. At first, I started having dreams of my previous life here. They seemed disconnected, like we discussed the implanted memories should have been. I didn't realize they were more than dreams until Violet came. A lot more came forward after seeing her, although I am still missing some big chunks." Grace seemed very clear.

"Are you okay with that?" he asked. This was her show. He would do whatever she needed him to do to support her.

She inhaled deeply, taking a quick emotional inventory before she exhaled. "I really am. Before telling you, I needed some perspective on everything. I should have known you'd figure it out anyway. You know me better than anyone. And before you reply to that, I mean it. Implanted memories have to be created in line with your core personality, otherwise they won't take. You can't make someone remember comfortably giving a lecture to a large crowd if they are terrified of public speaking. You must construct the illusion based on the realities of how each of the people would interact. What I mean is, if we weren't able to produce a supportive, caring relationship on our own, our own minds would have rejected those implants. At least for me, it is exactly the opposite. My mind embraced the life with you and rejected the reality of the one I had lived. My original timeline feels odd, disconnected from me like it's something I witnessed." Grace looked down and began twirling a loose strand of hair.

"I can't be sure if it was a self-preservation thing I did to keep from losing my sanity or not. No matter how it happened, I think pushing down the old memories and pulling forward the new ones while I had the tear changed my perception." Grace searched Ivan for a reaction. When he nodded, she continued.

"What seems sharp is when I met you. From the moment we met, I was attracted to you. It wasn't only your physical appearance either. It was your essence, the way you saw things. Your view of the world was forever optimistic. You were shiny, brighter than the others." She lit up as she remembered this.

Grace reached out and laid his tablet down in his lap, commanding all his attention to her. "*This* is my reality. I want to embrace it. I need to embrace it. You are the single person in any of my lives who hasn't wanted to change or control me. My only regret is that you were innocently dragged into my world without a say."

She realized her actions had a heavy impact on his life. Her hope was for it to be more positive than negative. She was searching his face for a sign that everything would be okay.

"You know as well as I do, I'm anything but innocent, Grace. It took centuries of work to overcome the monster I had been. The best memories I have are the ones they gave me of you. I traveled the world, visited the most amazing places. I enjoyed having the freedom to do what I wanted when I wanted. What I didn't enjoy was not having anyone to share it with. You've added something I needed. I have deep feelings for you. I can't honestly say if it's love in the way you have known it, but I think we have something better than that. Love is emotional, fickle, jealous even. It's wrought with extreme highs and extreme lows, with little in between. We have a true partnership, loyalty, respect, and trust. We are comfortable being individuals together. With that background, real or not, we have the ability to build something solid."

"And it doesn't hurt that you're pretty to look at," Grace said. She cocked her head, then laughed when his cheeks took on a shade of pink. She didn't want things to become so serious they couldn't enjoy it. "We're certainly in for an adventurous life. The best part of riding a roller coaster is having someone's hand to hold as you go down screaming."

The comment was appropriate. Their last few weeks were the roller coaster ride of a lifetime.

"If I have to go down screaming, I can't think of a better hand to have than yours," Ivan said.

"I guess it's settled then. Partners till the end. Now, let me have those notes so I can fix my proposal and you can get dinner started." Cooking was the one area where Grace was sorely lacking. She liked to cook. She was just awful at it.

"Your wish is my command. Anything specific you want?"

Ivan, on the other hand, was an excellent cook. Over the past century, he had attended culinary schools in both London and Italy. He had even toyed with the idea of opening his own restaurant at one point, but the conspicuous nature of a restaurant owner wasn't something he thought to be a good idea. He had done a few well-received pop-up dinners in New York and San Francisco when they were the rage in the early 2000s.

"Surprise me," she said as she headed off to the office.

As he watched her walk away, he thought to himself that this would be their last private evening for some time. Tomorrow was a big day. They would find out if Grace had any lingering effects from the crisis of two weeks ago. Ivan had enjoyed his time alone with her. He had unexpectedly also enjoyed his time with her sons, especially Erik, who was brilliant, to say the least. They had marathon discussions regarding the physics of The Everything, as well as some lively debates on other more existential topics like the morality of different species. His knowledge of bending or folding space would be useful once they had the ability to navigate the stars.

Ivan was lost in dreams of eventually establishing an orderly vampire colony on another planet as he prepared dinner. They had to think of another label for their people. Vampire had such a negative connotation, as Grace had so eloquently phrased it. If they could eventually shed this world, they should also shed the stigma. Maybe they should name their race after whatever world they found to inhabit. Hmm. He had a long time to put thought into that.

He hadn't realized Grace had walked in. Of course, he smelled her before he saw her. Her scent permeated the entire house now. He smelled her everywhere and had grown accustomed to it.

She sat on the edge of the table in the living room, watching him. She could tell he was deep in thought. He appeared peaceful yet determined. He was the right choice to lead these people into the future. It seemed everything they had both been through in their lives brought them to this point. They together held the fate of these new immortals.

He noticed her watching him. "What?"

"Nothing. You looked like you were enjoying yourself. I didn't want to interrupt." She took a stool at the counter across from him.

"You could never be an interruption. Open." He placed a paper-thin slice of water chestnut topped with a dab of his spinach and artichoke dip on her tongue. It was a perfect bite.

"Wow. I don't know what that was, but it was delicious. Light, crunchy, creamy, tangy. Everything in one bite."

"If you like that, wait for the entrée."

"It smells heavenly." She inhaled deeply.

Ivan slid an antipasto plate with roasted vegetables and more of the water chestnuts between them. "Snack on this. The food is almost ready."

"You're really going all out tonight, aren't you?"

"We have a big day tomorrow. I'm feeling optimistic."

"I'm glad you are. I'm feeling nervous. That's not something I usually admit to people."

"I'm not people. Besides, I already know. You were following Beivve's instructions and that has *never* happened before." He glanced a sly grin at her.

"Thanks for not rubbing it in."

"And make you feel worse? I would never do that with something so serious." He poured two glasses of red wine and slid one toward her.

"I don't know how I'm going to sleep tonight." She took a sip, relishing the contrast of the rich, dry wine and the crisp water chestnut.

"You'll fill up on gnocchi and roasted pork shoulder and a few more glasses of wine. If you still can't sleep, we can lie in bed and watch some of those incredibly boring documentaries you love so much." He found them boring, anyway.

"I'm down for that."

After dinner, they did exactly that. Grace dropped off within the first hour, while Ivan became unexpectedly enthralled in a series on the emerald tablet of Thoth until almost two a.m.

CHAPTER SEVENTEEN

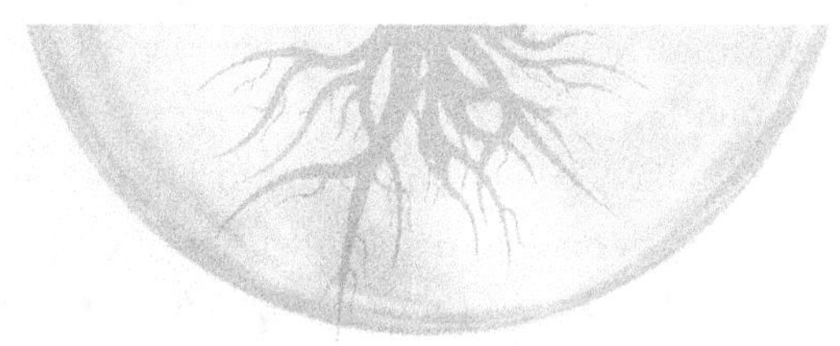

When Grace woke up, Ivan was still holding her. She rubbed her eyes to see Ami standing at the bottom of the bed.

"You really have to stop doing this. How long have you been watching us sleep?"

Ivan spoke without opening his eyes. "She's been there for about a half hour."

"I waited until Ivan was awake," Ami replied. She was technically only watching one of them sleep, so she didn't think she had broken a rule.

"Can you please start some coffee while we get dressed?" Grace would never make her understand what personal space was.

"I've never made coffee before."

Ivan opened his eyes. "Ami, go wait for me in the kitchen. I'll teach you how to make coffee when I come down."

"Okay," Ami said, leaving the room.

"You are very good to her. Thank you." She kissed him on the cheek as she climbed out of bed.

"She's a wise ancient with the personality of a child. I can't be upset with her." He got up from the other side.

"Ami is, for most, an acquired taste," Grace said apologetically.

"I like Ami," Ivan grinned. "Are you prepared for today? You didn't move an inch in your sleep."

"I'm much less nervous now. I'll be better once I find out the results of today's tests."

Ivan was dressed first and he headed down to teach Ami how to make coffee. It surprised him to smell it brewing when he opened the door to the hallway. Two more steps down the hall, he caught Alex's scent and descended the stairs.

"Hey man, I wasn't expecting to see you till we got to the lab."

"Thought I'd drop in early and port over with you guys." Alex looked like he had something on his mind.

"Cool. Ami, can you take Grace some coffee?" He thought it better to find out whatever it was Alex was concerned about without her there.

"Yes. I want to see if she likes it. I made it myself. Alex told me what to do, but I did it." She was extraordinarily proud of her accomplishment.

"I'm sure she'll love it." He waited for her to pour Grace's cup and take it upstairs.

"What's up, Alex?" he asked while still listening to make sure Ami was out of earshot.

"Nothing. I thought one of us should be here to support her today."

"Alex, do you know who you are talking to? I can tell something's going on."

"I worried if you two were okay. What are you going to do if she remembers? She won't trust you. She'll think you lied to her. My brothers and I are starting to like you. You're good for her, and she doesn't need anyone else to let her down."

Ivan appreciated him being up-front. "I don't want to let her down, either. And she does remember. The basics, at least. Some of it's kind of fuzzy, but she's got the main parts. We've been working through it, so we're good."

"Wow, I really didn't expect that." Alex was astonished how open he was.

"We've never lied to each other in any variation of our lives. I won't start now. I'll let her take it at her own pace. It's not like we don't have time," he chuckled.

"I didn't mean to imply anything. We just don't know you that well." Alex was apologetic.

"I get it. She's your mother. I'm a total stranger to you guys. She wouldn't have made this choice if she didn't feel she could trust me. In your own words, she would have bolted." Ivan wanted all of them to take Grace's judgment into consideration. She deserved that. He also respected Alex for coming to him with his concerns.

"All right then. Let me know if you need to talk about anything. My brothers don't know the part about Lukkas. Only me and my father found out when the Council rewrote your memories, but I really can't see him being your go-to guy regarding her." Alex shrugged.

"Yeah, you're probably right. I appreciate the offer. I may want to ask you some questions about other things too, if that's allowed. Nothing that would be considered interfering on your part; more in the line of: would it be better to concentrate on this or that technology, type of thing? Your mom is intelligent and logical, although not very skilled in things like calculus or physics, so I'm not sure she'd know how to, or if she could, answer."

"Yeah, I'm more like Mom in that respect. Erik would be your guy for those types of questions. He would understand the boundaries of what he could and couldn't answer. But I'm here for you on any other subject." Alex gave Ivan a cheesy wink and finger point gesture.

It took a few more minutes before Grace came down with Ami. Ivan could tell she was far more anxious than she was letting on, and he offered his arm as support.

"Ready?"

Grace took a deep, cleansing breath, stepped forward, and slipped her own arm through the offered appendage. "Ready."

When they got to the infirmary, the staff took Grace back alone. They wanted the normal scans and more extensive cognitive tests. Alex, Ami, and Ivan were directed to a waiting room at the other end of the hall, not the glass room they were in before. They couldn't see around them, so it felt more isolated. All they could do was wait.

Ivan had become comfortable with Ami standing, staring at nothing. He barely noticed her anymore. He had brought his tablet with downloaded information on pieces at the auction he wouldn't be bidding on this time around. It never hurt to be aware of what people were looking for.

Alex had brought his version of a tablet, too. It was clear, unfolding from the size of a pack of stick gum to the same screen size Ivan had. When he loaded what he was looking for, the area behind the text became opaque.

Ivan was curious about it but didn't want to appear overly envious. Alex could pull data and pictures above the surface of the tablet to three-dimensional images and turn them to view all sides. Ivan considered it a miniaturized version of the infirmary monitors.

Alex finished with what he was working on first. "This is taking forever. How long have we been here?"

Ivan checked the time on his tablet. "About two hours." He looked up. Alex was fidgety, bouncing his knee. "That's a pretty neat little gadget you have there."

"My TAC? Yeah, it's convenient for going off site."

"How much information does it hold?" Ivan couldn't see any way it had a sizeable hard drive. It was not much thicker than a piece of glass when unfolded.

"Not sure. I think this one only has a petabyte." Alex hadn't thought about it before.

"How long does the battery last on a charge?"

"Battery? It doesn't have one. It uses an energy sheet. I think it will last a couple of months outside of the environment. Probably a few years on standby."

"What do you mean, out of the environment?" Ivan wasn't familiar with the phrase.

"Outside of electrical range. Oh, I forgot, we use wireless energy, so as long as I'm here or in our facility, it charges itself. Check your electronics. They should be on full charge too if they are capable of wireless charging."

Ivan looked down, seeing his tablet was, in fact, fully charged. "Huh. Cool."

A while later, Dionysus entered the room. Ivan's senses were immediately heightened. He was expecting Beivve. Ivan and Alex both stood up.

"No, no, no. Sit, sit, sit." Dionysus waved his hands to indicate he wanted them on the sofa. They all sat where instructed, including Ami. Dionysus sat in the chair facing them while they stared at him.

"Well?" Ivan questioned.

"We're wrapping up the cognitive tests. So far, everything appears to be in line with the range we expected. She does have some very minimal memory loss, which we had also expected. We don't expect her to recover what is currently missing." He placed his hands on the chair arms to stand, as if he was finished. Did he want them to ask questions?

"What about her physical health? Is her body healed? Will she have any restrictions?" Ivan didn't think he covered enough information.

"Her shell is completely healed. No restrictions are indicated. Of course, she will need to return if she has excessive headaches or loses consciousness. Otherwise, we shouldn't need to see her again." Yet another dramatic pause. "That's all." He stood up to leave.

"Wait. How much longer is this going to take?" Alex would not let him leave until that question was answered.

"It will take as long as it takes," he said, walking out the door and porting immediately.

"That was rude." Alex was now irritated.

"If you need to leave, I can have your mom call when she comes out. I have some things I can work on here." Ivan didn't have anywhere he needed to be.

"I can come to retrieve you." That was the first thing Ami had said since they arrived.

"You sure you don't mind? I wasn't expecting it to take this long."

"No, go. We're good here. Ami will come when they're finished."

"Thanks. Mind if I port from here?"

Ivan looked at Ami. "As long as you don't port into our bedroom, it doesn't matter to me. Oh, or the bathroom. Never port into our bathroom."

"I take it that's … been an issue," Alex said, looking at Ami, who was oblivious they were talking about her. Alex and Ivan exchanged smirks before he ported out.

Over an hour later, Grace and Beivve entered the waiting room.

Grace hugged Ivan. "I'm so glad that's over with."

Still holding on to her, Ivan asked Beivve, "Hey, doc. Is everything good?"

Beivve scrutinized him. "What did you call me?"

"Doc? Short for doctor. That's what we call our medical healers." Ivan hoped that would dig him out of whatever pit he had jumped in.

"Oh, so it's an appropriate title. I see. Yes, she has healed as expected."

Grace looked over her shoulder. "Where's Alex?"

"Ami, can you go get him, please? He left after Dionysus told us you were almost finished and everything looked okay so far."

Beivve rolled her eyes. "He wanted to take responsibility for the news. The tests weren't even finished yet."

"I almost forgot." Ivan reached into his pocket for a small packet of freeze-dried CB. "Here." He handed it to Beivve.

She looked at the logo on the packet.

"Is that enough?" Ivan asked.

"Yes, thank you. How do you reconstitute it?"

"That packet is for one liter of still water or saline if you want to apply it intravenously. Let me know if you need more."

"This is perfect," Beivve said, slipping it into her pocket.

Alex and Ami ported back in. Alex looked around. "Is everything okay?"

Grace answered, "Yes. I'm good. Can we go home?" She looked back at Beivve.

"You're free to leave. Hopefully next time I see you will be at a social event."

"That would be nice. Thank you, Beivve." Grace waved and ported herself and Ivan to the deck outside the kitchen, followed closely by Alex and Ami. Once inside, Ivan stopped the group.

"Alex, let your brothers know I'll have lunch ready in an hour if they want to come over. But before they get here, I wanted to say a few things." Everyone looked at Ivan. "The four of us are the only ones, aside from the Council, who know of the additional memories. With that being said," he turned to Grace, "Ben gave me a letter the night of the incident. I told him I wouldn't give it to you until you had been cleared. I read it, but it's up to you if you want to share it with anyone else."

She looked at him suspiciously as she took it from him, read it, and fidgeted with the paper, taking a few seconds to think before speaking. "Alex, please invite your father to lunch today as well. Are you okay with that, Ivan?"

"Whatever you need. What can I do to help you?"

"I want you to cook something extravagant. If I do it, we may all get food poisoning. Alex, ask your father in person, please. I don't want him to get it tertiary from Mikkel and think it's a joke. I want this lunch civil and as pleasant as possible."

Alex nodded, attempting to port out. "I guess the blockers are still in place," he said, as he walked toward the door.

"Yes, I think I'll leave them there. I like the privacy," Grace yelled as he left.

"I'm sorry, Ivan. I should have discussed this with you first."

"Don't worry about me. I know this is something you need to do."

"I want you here because I want you to be involved in anything important to me, and also because I need you to tell me if he is being truthful. I can hear what he is thinking if he isn't blocking me, but I can't always see the motivation behind it." She always thought she could read Ben well. She knew Ivan's sense of smell enabled him to pick up on things she couldn't.

"When he came to the infirmary, he was being sincere when he told me he wanted to call a truce. We'll listen, then you can decide what's best for you. Okay?"

"Okay."

"Let's get lunch started. I'm putting you two to work chopping."

Ami perked up. "Can I make coffee?"

Grace smiled at her. "Yes, Ami. Please make coffee."

Lunch was almost ready when there was a knock at the front door. The Three always walked in from the back deck, which made Grace think this would be Ben. Her suspicion was confirmed when she opened the door. He was alone.

"Hey, Ben. Thanks for coming. Are The Three coming?"

"They'll be along shortly. I wanted to speak to you and Ivan alone first, if that's not a problem."

"Sure. Come on in." She led him to the kitchen. Ami glared at him as he entered. He glanced at her, then back at Grace, who took the hint.

"Ami, would you mind giving us a few minutes?"

Ami gave her an indignant look. Nonetheless, she went out to the deck to watch her tiny creatures.

Ivan felt Ben's discomfort. "What's going on?"

"Hi, Ivan. I wanted a few minutes with you and Grace. First, I need to apologize to both of you for forcing the two of you together." He looked between the two before continuing.

"I know you invited me here because of the letter, and I do want a truce with you both. But what I need to explain about Grace's mother cannot go any further than the three of us. The Three can't know, at least for now, and Ami can't be involved at all."

The look on his face was more serious than Grace had remembered seeing on him before. Ivan caught the familiar bitter scent from him. He wasn't nervous; he was scared. Exactly what he was afraid of, Ivan couldn't pinpoint.

Grace saw it too in the way he stood. "Ben, I appreciate your apology. I'm happy with Ivan and I'm fine with the choice I made, no matter how difficult the circumstances of it were. I've never wanted to fight with you. But I owe you an apology too. I was out of control when I brought the Jur to the facility. A lifetime of anger overtook me in a way I had never experienced. I didn't understand how to handle it and I took it out on you. As for the other half of the apology, Ivan will have to speak for himself."

Ivan reached out to shake Ben's hand. "As far as I'm concerned, you and I have a clean slate." Ben accepted his hand, shaking it firmly. Ivan looked at Grace, nodding. She understood he felt Ben was sincere, as she already did.

"After lunch, we'll send everyone home and have our discussion," Grace said.

Lunch was a pleasant event filled with irrelevant guarded subjects. At least, until Ivan and Erik discussed picking up the car on Tuesday. Ivan needed to be away on business for the day. He gave Erik the responsibility of checking the paint for flaws and making the final payment. With that responsibility also came the reward of the first drive. It was a project that sparked Erik's love of the modern muscle car. Ivan appreciated the effort Erik had put into the build. Mikkel envied Erik for being allowed the first drive, offering protest for not being included. The argument didn't last long. He knew how hard Erik had worked on it and regretted skipping out on the opportunity to help.

Once lunch was finished, Grace told Ami and The Three that she, Ben, and Ivan had some things to discuss. She told them how much she had enjoyed having everyone together, saying they would have to make it a regular thing. Ivan handed Erik one of his credit cards for the bill on the car, telling him he would be back Tuesday around dinnertime. Once the four of them left, it was time to find out the greatest mystery of Grace's life. Little did she know how big of an impact it would have.

CHAPTER EIGHTEEN

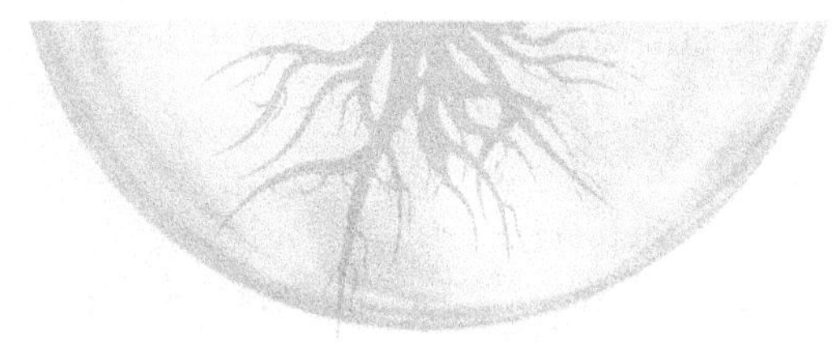

Ivan pulled out a bottle of red for Grace and scotch for himself. "What's your preference, Ben?"

"Whatever you're having. I'm not very familiar with spirits here. I know I dislike the bottles of nasty water called beer." When he said "beer," he shuddered and curled his lip.

Ivan grunted. "Most of it is disgusting. I prefer a dark ale myself if I have no other choice. What I have here, though, surpasses everything. Aged single-malt scotch. I buy a few casks a year and keep it several extra years after humans think it's fine to sell."

"I accept your recommendation."

They sat in the living room. Grace and Ivan were on the sofa, and Ben pulled a chair directly across the coffee table in front of them. Ben took in a large mouthful of the scotch, swallowing it slowly.

"This is by far the best thing I've had since I've been here. Thank you, Ivan."

"You're welcome." Ivan took a large drink as well, sinking deep back into the sofa.

Grace couldn't wait any longer. "So, what is so devastating about my mother that not even our sons can know?" she asked with angst.

Ben needed to be blunt with her. "You don't have one."

"Yes, I know she's dead."

Ben shook his head. "No. You don't understand. You've never had one. Technically, you weren't born in the same way as we were. They created you."

Ivan noted Grace was outwardly calm but disturbed by the statement. "You mean like a synthetic in a laboratory?"

"No, not like that. Well, what I mean is you're not artificial. You are as sentient as any of us, but they constructed your consciousness from energy and placed it into a shell that had been born to contain you. Just listen. I should start at the beginning."

"Yeah, I think you should," Grace said.

Ivan felt no anxiety emanating from Grace. He thought she was either accepting Ben's words at face value or disregarding them entirely. Ivan could feel Ben, in comparison, was very apprehensive.

"I was only aware of the basic information until two weeks ago. Asgard still holds one of six seats on the High Council. They briefed me on all the details of the program because, as of a few weeks ago, they believe half of it was effective. And this isn't going anywhere near the way I wanted telling you to go. Let me start over."

Grace took a large sip of wine as she slid under Ivan's arm. Ivan clearly saw a pang of loss cover Ben's face for a fraction of a second.

"When you started showing interest in my brother, my mother and your father came to me."

"*They* came to *you*?" Grace asked suspiciously.

"Yes. They told me you needed a husband who could be a protector, going as far as to give his life if necessary. My brother was enchanted with music and poetry and was too gentle to hurt another living being. He was too compassionate to stick up for himself, let alone anyone else. I assured them you could protect yourself. If you chose him over me, then that was your choice. That's when they told me a story."

Grace nodded her affirmation to continue. She wasn't sure she liked what he was saying, but she promised herself she would hear him out without judgment. Ben swallowed his drink and poured another before he resumed.

"The Everything is constantly in motion. As new dimensions form, others drain and collapse, but there is an order to them. This universe and a few others were losing positive energy faster than those under them, which most equate to losing the balance of light. They endeavored to resolve the inequality with a bold, two-part plan. They would first create a being that could realign the energy by creating light. In order to facilitate this, they gathered all the positive energies that created the brightest light from each species. It was such an important endeavor that even the Ljósálfar provided their light energy. From the combined donations, they created four children of light. Two boys and two girls. The two boys were gifted and beautiful beings, but their inner light proved too much for them to bear and they eventually succumbed to it after a handful of years. One girl's shell rejected the essence entirely, and the last was you."

"That's what they told you? A fairy story? Everyone has heard this. It's not real." Grace shook her head.

"I haven't heard it," Ivan said.

Ben continued. "You carry extra chromosomes, which are necessary to strengthen your body enough to hold in your energy. How do you explain those?"

Grace scoffed. Ben glanced at Ivan, who nodded, urging him on.

"It seems the extra set is difficult to be placed on the Y, which is why the boys didn't survive. Frigg tasked Freya with giving birth to your shell, which was later filled with your created essence. The other shells were all produced without a surrogate. The Council doesn't know you survived. They believed the entire first stage of the program was a failure. I changed Seshet's scan results before she removed them from the system for bargaining. As far as the Council knows, you are half Vanir and extraordinarily powerful, born in a time of war. That's all."

Grace was chewing the side of her fingernail but stopped, looking up at Ben. "You were in the training room with me and then the hospital. When did you change out the results?"

"In the medical ward, after you went to sleep, when Seshet left. After she told us about the blood results, she was so excited about finding the venom, she hadn't read very far. I pulled up the test results on my TAC and took out the original data. I had Ida destroy the sample, then I replaced the results before we went to get my stitches out while you were in the shower."

"So, the results she turned over to the Council were ones you made up?" Grace asked.

"Mostly. I had to leave what I knew Seshet had already read. I had Ida help me construct the rest."

"Can you trust this Ida person to not tell anyone?" Ivan asked, furrowing his brow.

"Ida is our AI assistant. I erased the request when I finished," Ben answered.

Grace nodded, "Okay, then what?"

"I needed to make sure I got on the Council. After you left, Ida notified me that Seshet downloaded your results. I knew she was going to bargain with them, and I needed to make sure I knew what she had turned over. It did not surprise me when the Jur came, because I thought Seshet had turned us in. What surprised me was to see you with them."

Grace was staring at the coffee table that separated them, nodding her head. There was no reason for him to make up something this elaborate. There was no benefit for him. She looked up at Ben, embarrassed.

"Okay, so what happened after I was born, or created, whatever you want to call it?"

"Well, Frigg and Freya hid you in plain sight and reported the experiment a failure. They gave you to Nep to raise. They told him you were half Vanir and needed protection. He was your father in every way that counted. His peaceful demeanor made him well regarded. He was simple and honest. No one would have looked for the greatest gift in this universe on a simple country farm."

Ben looked at Grace for acknowledgment or approval to continue. She gave neither, so he proceeded with caution.

"When you were ready to marry, he could no longer protect you. He came to my mother. She told Nep I could keep you safe. She had used some of my altered genes to strengthen your shell, ensuring they didn't reject each other. My impervious skin could strengthen your shell enough to contain your essence. My mother believed it was what allowed you to survive when the others didn't. It also meant I could protect you without being swayed by your emotions." He cleared his throat. "The second part is what I didn't know about."

Ben turned toward Ivan since Grace's gaze had fallen back to rest on the table. "It's also the part the Council believes is working. It was to create a new species, strong and benevolent, who had the ability to expand the light by absorbing small amounts, passing it to others like a virus, and carrying it forward into The Everything. It all started a long time ago.

"They made several attempts on multiple planets in different dimensions. The first few times they created immortal beings, but they never developed as expected. They would always fall into patterns of greed, envy, and war, ultimately destroying each other and often the planets they inhabited. They carried the rest of the trials out on mortals. The hope was that a shorter lifespan would speed up the passage through phases. As each generation would die, the new ones would evolve. Once the mortals reached that developed state, they would move to the next phase of their plan."

Ivan craned his neck at the last part, and Ben proceeded.

"The Council reset the planets several times each, hoping for a new result. They were getting ready to reset again, but when we had to hide Grace here, my mother re-scanned the planets before they were reset. Here was the singular exception from all the dimensions and all the trials." He looked directly at Ivan.

"You. Not only did your people become immortal on your own, which was thought impossible, but you quickly became altruistic. I had to wonder if my mother had something to do with your beginning, since this is where she sent Grace. We now know Grace's guidance also influenced your evolution. The Council doesn't realize why. Your people started your process before you met her. You do what's right for your own kind. You also help the humans, who've done nothing other than hunt and murder you throughout time. They aren't even aware of what you've done for them and yet you don't need their gratitude."

He paused a moment, taking another drink.

"Those are the basics. I understand you both must have questions. I will answer anything I can."

"What do you mean you had to hide me here? Was our world destroyed because someone was looking for me?" Out of everything Ben had said, she accepted all of it. The one thing she couldn't accept was that most of her species was killed because of her, and it struck her deeply.

"You had already been gone for nearly two thousand years. We don't know what led them to us, but I told you the truth. We don't know who they were. They destroyed several other realms before reaching Asgard. We were the ones who started the story of the rebellion to cover. The Council knows the truth of the alien force.

"One other thing I forgot. Your amulet hides you from being located because it hides the light your energy produces. I won't remove it from you. I've never broken my vow to protect you, and I never will. As far as I can tell, no one knows you exist."

"But if my light is a giant beacon, they could have followed it to the last place it was before Frigg placed the amulet on me." Grace was still not at ease that she may have been the cause of the destruction.

"I don't know, Grace. The bracelet your father gave you blocked your light before that. It became too weak, and Mother said your light was leaking."

Ivan leaned forward, grabbing his drink. "I'm still not making the connection here on how her spreading light is going to fix a universe that's getting darker, or what light has to do with anything in the first place? How is she even supposed to do that?"

"I wish I had answers to give you. One thing I do know is your light is already spreading on its own. There are thousands with your light signature, many dim and some striking."

Ivan was connecting the dots. "What do you mean by her light is spreading and how can you tell it is her signature if the amulet prevents you from seeing it?"

Ben pulled a small device out of his jacket.

"Freya gave me a device that can read her light signature. I can only see Grace when I am within a few feet of her because her amulet protects her from the tracking feature. Her blood also carries her signature due to the integration of her essence and shell."

Grace didn't understand how there could be so many with her signature. "I've been blood nurse to a few dozen pure born and have fed possibly another two dozen. How can there be so many? Vampires don't share blood except during a mating ceremony, so even if all of those had mated, there could only possibly be maybe seventy-five." The numbers didn't add up at all.

"Ivan has your signature. A dazzling one. Have you shared blood with him?"

She looked at Ivan, confused. "No, not in reality. Only in the new memories, but that can't count. It didn't happen."

The last puzzle piece clicked neatly into place for Ivan. "Yes, it does."

"What do you mean, yes? How can memories count?" Grace thought it was ridiculous.

"Not like that. When we were doing the CB trials, we needed a known blood source to ensure control. We didn't have one specific donor we would have been able to use for a long period, so Lukkas gave us your blood from his freezer. All the CB that has ever been developed has been grown from an extraction of your blood. Everyone who has ever used CB has consumed your light."

Grace drained her glass and poured another. "We gave Beivve a packet of CB today."

Ben sighed, draining his own glass. "She was involved with Frigg and Apollo creating children of the light. She'll know what she's looking at."

"Yes, but she had Grace on that table for ten hours. She already has all the information. If she were going to do something, wouldn't she have done it when she had Grace in stasis?" Ivan had to wonder if she had already told the Council and they were keeping it from Ben.

"You also told her you had an extra set of chromosomes while you were in stasis." Ivan didn't think she remembered that.

Grace rubbed her lips with her fingertips, trying to reassure herself that Beivve had maintained her trust. "We need to know who has information about me and who has information about the program. Then we can figure out what to do. I think we should talk to Beivve as soon as possible."

"I can go get her if you want me to. She'll come with me since I'm on the Council." Ben's entire life had been spent protecting Grace. He was relieved to be able to finally tell her why he had been so hard on her. It was only now that he realized he had treated her more like a prisoner than his wife. He didn't expect her to forgive him, but he needed to make it up to her.

Grace pondered a moment. "I think we should. Before you go, I have one more question."

"Okay."

"Why didn't they want me to know?" Grace had thought her entire life would have been much clearer if she had known what she was.

"Mother and Freya had no faith that the second part of the plan would ever work. Creating you wasn't even supposed to work. Once they had you, they didn't want you to become some sort of lab rat for the Council. They wanted you to have as normal a life as possible. Bottom line is, they loved you. With everything happening now, you needed to know. I broke my word to them by telling you."

"You can't break a promise to the dead, Ben," Ivan said.

Ben nodded to them, before attempting to port. "Freaking blockers." He shook his head and walked out the front door.

"What do you think, Ivan?" She was much calmer than he expected. It was as if Ben's words only confirmed something she already knew, although she wanted to deny it in the beginning.

Ivan was a little more unsettled at the thought of his entire race being created to be used as part of a grand plan to save The Everything. Not that he was opposed to it, however that was supposed to work, but how far would it all go?

"I think what's done can't be undone. We need to find a safe, peaceful way forward for everyone. I don't want to be a tool for someone else's agenda. We need to make this decision, not anyone else." He stood and began pacing. "Grace, are you okay with all of this? I don't sense any fear or anxiousness from you," Ivan asked.

"I think so. As insane as it sounds, everything makes sense to me now. All the emotions I've had, feeling like I was a captive in my own world, my certainty that this community is where I belonged, even the relative ease of choosing you over Lukkas."

"That wasn't easy for you. You ripped a hole in your mind to expel the memories of him."

"That's not how I meant it. The choice had been easier than I expected, almost like I knew I needed to be exactly where I am. The execution of the choice was difficult, and I could have done without the manipulation and secrets, but without them, would I be here?"

Ivan groaned, "I have to agree the manipulation aspect isn't appealing to me either. You are right about one thing. However it happened, it seems like destiny." He had never believed in destiny. He still wasn't sure he should. What he understood was an unimaginable number of things had to be exactly right for her to end up here.

"It sure is taking Ben a long time," Grace said, pouring herself another drink, finishing the bottle.

"It's only been thirty minutes, Grace. I'm sure he's trying not to raise suspicions. He doesn't have the powers of persuasion I do."

"Or she turned him in."

"For what? Even if Beivve gave them proof of your existence, there is no way to prove he had any knowledge. They wouldn't detain a Council member on suspicion alone. Besides, how is it even a crime? You're not property."

"You sure about that, are you? I'm not being pessimistic here. I need to look at every angle. Maybe things will work out perfectly wonderfully, maybe not. We at least need to understand what arguments we may face. I won't fight. I also won't let them destroy those I care about." Despite not wanting to be defensive, it had been her practice to stay cautious when she was unsure of the situation. She wanted everything to be peaceful, and she was prepared to turn herself over to keep everyone else safe. It was her journey, and she didn't see the need to drag anyone else into it.

"Grace! How can you say you won't fight for yourself? For our right to make our own decisions? This is something worthy of fighting for." Ivan couldn't see what she was thinking.

"No, Ivan, it's exactly the opposite. It's something worth *not* fighting for. If I'm supposed to bring balance to this universe, shouldn't I do that through peaceful means? You have never believed in the ability of war to bring peace. We never asked to be crafted as weapons, which is what we would be if we fought the Council. We can't resort to violence to spread light. So, we don't fight. Can we agree on that?"

Ivan sighed. "It's much harder in practice than theory. Noble ideas are easy, noble acts are difficult." He searched her face for a reaction. He didn't feel her emotions ruffle, and he continued.

"I agree. We need to do this through peaceful means. No fighting either with them or for them." Ivan hoped Ben would return soon. Maybe the best way to blow the lid off this entire thing was to go public. Not with the human population, but at least with the Council, the Board, and the other pantheons. He should give that idea more attention before he shared it with Grace.

It had been several hours since Ben left, and Grace was near frantic with worry. The sun was setting, and the air was getting chilly again. Ivan and Grace went out onto the deck to light a fire in the pit. Ami had become irritated when she had been asked to leave and wasn't outside. As soon as Grace stepped through the doors, she heard Ben calling to her.

Ben, what's going on? Is Beivve coming?

Yes, she said she would drop in after she finished her lab work. She thought you may still have a few questions after your treatment. His answer didn't sound quite right to her. She went along as if someone were listening in.

Thanks for asking her. I wrote my questions as she wanted so we wouldn't end up having to do this multiple times.

You should have contacted her directly. I don't have time to be your messenger. There is an entire race I need to relocate. I think I left a device when I was there earlier. I need to pick it up later. Ben's answer was curt.

Now she was certain he thought someone was listening in. She had fully expected him to be back by now. How could anyone possibly have access to their internal communication? She would up the animosity level a bit, so if anyone were listening, they wouldn't assume they had put their differences aside completely.

I would appreciate it if you came at the same time as Beivve. Honestly, Ben, it's going to take quite some time before we have any level of trust. I prefer witnesses to our conversations for the time being.

You're not the only one who prefers a mediator. I am … she stepped back and forth over the threshold into the cabin and onto the deck. As he spoke, she wanted to test a theory. It was exactly what she thought. The blockers. Whatever he said was breaking up. She signaled to Ivan to follow her into the cabin. Ben could have been calling her for hours. Until she stepped outside, she hadn't heard him.

"I need to test a theory. Walk outside." She decided it was safer to have Ivan step out, so no one heard her sending messages if they were attempting to listen in on her end. He started backing away from her. *Test one, two, three. Tes—* He stepped over the threshold onto the deck, shrugging at her. He made a throat cutting signal before he stepped back in.

"I don't think Beivve simply forgot to remove the blockers. It appears as if it blocks everything like a shield. Let's see how far it covers."

Ivan agreed.

Grace and Ivan spent the next hour testing the entire perimeter of the property. Windows, doors, porches, cellar, and garage. All inside spaces, including the garage, were blocked. No communication from inside to outside and vice versa. No porting outside of whichever building they were in. She could port throughout different rooms inside of the cabin. She could still phase through the walls, including exterior walls. As she went through, she felt a modulated frequency attached to the buildings. Communications and porting were the only things she could see were affected. *Things keep getting more and more interesting.*

When they finished, they walked back into the cabin.

"I guess we'll see what that's all about when Beivve gets here." Grace hung her jacket on the coat rack by the door.

Ivan remembered the fire he had started to light earlier. "Let's light the fire. It's still nice enough outside. Might as well relax until they get here."

"I had a different vision of relaxing on our first night without supervision."

"Grace, that's something we need to discuss. We've never actually…"

She cut him off. "I know, Ivan. That's not how I meant it. I do want us to be intimate and I understand how much of a commitment that is for you. All I'm saying is I want us to be closer. We're in it for eternity now. I can wait until you're ready. We have ample amounts of time."

Grace had never needed a man, per se. She needed a touchstone. Someone to keep her grounded. Someone who would let her be who she was. The time she had spent alone here she had always felt untethered, like she would float off, ceasing to exist at some point. His protection wasn't something she was interested in. She needed someone who was on her side, and Ivan had always been on her side.

"That's not it either. I've been drawn to you since the second I laid eyes on you. It wasn't the way you looked, although the packaging is inarguably great. I was drawn to your brightness. Your love of life. Your gentleness and strength, the feeling I get whenever I'm near you, that everything is perfect. Of course I want to be intimate with you. I need to make sure you're ready for us. Not just filling a void from losing Lukkas. I want you to see me. I want you to be with me, and I want to understand exactly what you expect regarding us."

Even now he felt guilty knowing she had been his best friend's mate. His guilt was heightened because Ivan had always been in love with Grace, although he wasn't ready to admit that, even to himself. This is what he had always imagined his life would look like, having Grace in it. He never felt for anyone what he felt for her. He would play whatever role she needed him to, but he had to understand what that role would be up-front. What he couldn't do was have his heart ripped out again, because he didn't think he could survive that.

"Ivan, let's light the fire in here. I don't think this is a conversation we should have outside." She turned away, but then turned back. "By the way, I see you, Ivan."

She turned away from him and lit the stacked logs in the fireplace while Ivan freshened their drinks. He sat on the sofa. When she finished, she sat beside him, leaning her back against the arm of the sofa with her feet in his lap. He pulled a throw from under the coffee table, placing it on her bare feet, while she picked up both glasses, handing him his scotch.

"Some of this has already been said, but I want to make sure you fully understand everything from my perspective. I should start by telling you I still love Lukkas for several reasons. When I needed something to hold on to, he gave me a family and a place to belong. He gave me an existence where I wouldn't have to watch those I was closest to get old and die. He gave me a tether, but I never felt he fully accepted me for who I was. Even though I was already immortal, he always wanted me to turn for him. Still, I wouldn't have left him if this hadn't happened. We were closer than siblings in some ways and in others very distant. We were physically intimate, but not emotionally intimate in that way that connects your essence." She flashed a disgusted expression. "That sounded extremely creepy with the sibling reference. I hope you got the point of it, though."

He smiled uncomfortably at her. "Yeah, I got the picture. Oh, now you have me doing it. I don't need that picture. I understand what you're saying." He curled his lip and took a swig of scotch.

"All I'm trying to say is yes, I love him, but our life wasn't as perfect as it seemed, and we both knew it. You never once in all the time I've known you judged me or made me feel less than. You have always seen me and accepted me for who I was, even when I didn't know who I was. I know you argued with Lukkas that he didn't know what the consequences might be of turning me, and it had to be my decision. You would not talk to me about it on his behalf," she explained.

"How would you know that? You weren't there. You weren't even in the same country." He wondered if Lukkas had told her.

"Galin told me. And you didn't argue he shouldn't do it because it might change me. You told him you wouldn't talk me into it because it had to be my decision. Even when you didn't know I'd find out, you had my back. You are always true to who you are."

"That's part of what we need to talk about. Who I am. I've done some horribly violent things. I can't guarantee I won't become that animal again one day." He dropped his gaze from her to the floor.

Grace put her hand on his shoulder. "Maybe you will and maybe you won't. I've already seen the worst in you."

Ivan shook his head. "No, you haven't. You have no idea what I'm capable of, Grace. I never want to hurt you or anyone else again."

"You're wrong, Ivan. I saw your nightmare. I didn't only see it, I lived it inside of you. I felt your pain and anger and anguish." Grace looked up tentatively before starting again.

"I saw what she did to your children. I saw you hunting. I felt you enjoying every single kill. And when it was over, I also felt your relief. I felt you let go of the hatred and I felt your grief. I have seen it. I have felt it and I understand. You have a good heart, Ivan, and you're afraid I'm going to rip it out. I promise I'll do everything I can not to do that to you because I see you, Ivan. I see every bit of you."

"But why would you possibly ever have wanted to be with anyone who could be as dark as I can be? You're pure. I see how bright your light is. How would you even understand what it's like to see pleasure in killing?"

"Your light is bright too, Ivan. I've always seen it. And because you need to understand, the total is the sum of all the parts. Darkness and light are in everyone. I also have darkness inside, just like everyone else. Here, let me show you." She stretched her hand out to touch the side of his face. "Close your eyes."

She showed him a memory of her time as a medieval queen. Thousands lie dead on the battlefield in front of her. She slaughtered warriors like they stood still and sacrificed themselves to her. Blood soaked her hair and clothing as she fought. She was stronger and faster than any of them, and she found enjoyment and freedom in war. He not only saw it. He felt her revel in it.

It was clear she understood. She understood exactly.

"I could have never shown Lukkas that. He has no idea what a rush it is to feel the blood drain out of someone as you release their essence into the universe. I don't think he's ever killed anything intentionally. He would never understand that killing their mortal flesh frees them from their shell, allowing them to move on to the next existence. My fear was he would have thought me evil or demented in some way. I was self-serving back then. Destroying my enemy gave me a sense of purpose. I've obviously learned there are better ways to exist, and all life is precious. Since my memories have returned, what I did sickens me. Taking any life should weigh a heavy burden, even if you believe there is another one awaiting them. So, see, I understand." She leaned toward him, pressing her forehead against his. He reached around her, sliding her onto his lap, and she laid her head on his chest, closing her eyes.

She was mistaken about one thing, though. Ivan had a vivid memory of Lukkas delighting in one particular kill. It had been a kill for vengeance. Ivan thought Lukkas had told her, although he could see why he didn't.

"Where do we go from here?" Ivan could feel her heart beating in the same rhythm as his.

"I think we should forget the world for a while and stay just like this for as long as possible."

Ivan's eyes opened before Ben touched the door. Grace had woken too but didn't move. He walked in, followed by Beivve. On seeing them, Ben felt an instant sting of jealousy. He had always known she wasn't meant for him. Knowing that didn't curb what he felt.

Grace sat up, sliding off Ivan's lap. "Is everything okay? It took a lot longer for you to get back than we expected."

Beivve stepped in front of Ben. "I was finishing up some lab work I couldn't leave in the middle of. Besides, time is different in the Council's dimension."

"And I didn't want to leave without Beivve. I let a few people overhear you wouldn't let me come to your house by myself." He needed a drink and looked around for the glass he had used earlier.

Grace didn't understand how he could let people overhear a telepathic conversation, although she had suspected that was what had gone on. Unless Ben was transmitting on an open channel, she didn't see how anyone could eavesdrop.

Ivan pointed toward the bar. "Grab a clean one. Beivve, would you like anything?"

"Whatever you're having is fine. Thank you."

Ben handed her a glass, noticing Ivan had the bottle on the coffee table. He poured for both, then filled his own.

"What's going on with the blockers, Beivve? I assume you left them on purpose. Is there someone I should be worried about? Can they read our thoughts?" Grace asked.

"Yes, I left the blockers on purpose. I don't know who would or could be listening. As far as I know, they can't read your thoughts from here. In the Council's dimension, they have probes that can pick up active communication channels unless you are skilled in opposing them. The communication portion of the blocker I set here prevents all communication outside of natural earshot. You can speak to someone at the door, but if anyone is trying to monitor in close proximity, they will only hear the person outside speaking. It's precautionary, although I felt it necessary due to some sensitive information I don't believe you would want anyone else having access to."

"Oh, you mean like finding out today that my entire existence has been a lie. I have no actual parents and was created in a laboratory to balance energy in The Everything. That type of sensitive information?" Grace brashly asserted to measure Beivve's reaction.

Ivan glanced at Beivve. Seeing she was unfazed by the statement showed him she knew, as they had suspected.

"Yup, kinda like that. Also, like once a vampire consumes your blood, they no longer need to drink. They may still have a thirst for a while, but they don't need it."

Ivan sat up straight. "Beivve, what makes you believe this is accurate? Why haven't we found that in our own research?"

"From yours and Grace's scans, I am over ninety percent sure it is accurate. Initial testing on the CB you gave me brought my estimate up to ninety-five percent. I can confirm it if you show me the research from Seshet on the two young vampires and I conduct an experiment of my own for validation. Actually, I would be happy to perform the experiments and let your scientists monitor my work. Or I could just monitor if you don't trust me."

"Damn it!" Ivan remembered he left everything in Portugal. He was expecting to go back home after the auction. "It's in my office in Lisbon. We never went home after the incident. We came straight here."

Grace stood up. "Well, let's go get it."

"I can take him. You two have a lot more to discuss," Ben suggested, pointing between Grace and Beivve.

Ivan started toward the back deck. "All right. What do I need to do?"

Ben put his hand on Ivan's shoulder as they walked forward. "You're telepathic. Think of the place where you want to land. I'll open the port."

Ivan looked quizzically. "I'm not telepathic."

"It wasn't a question. You have three seconds. Think about where we're going to land." They took another six steps out the doors when Ben pushed Ivan forward, keeping hold of his shoulder. They walked through the railing and into the living room in Lisbon.

This was Ivan's fifth time porting, and it was getting easier to recover from the disorienting effects. He was out of sorts for about half a second, immediately recognizing something was wrong.

"Someone has been here. Not human. Not anything I've met yet. Only one."

Ben pulled out a small energy weapon. "How do you know? Are they still here?"

"I can smell them. The scent is old, they're gone. Nothing looks out of place here. We need to search the rest of the house."

Nothing seemed to be missing. They grabbed the research from a drop panel safe in the floor under Ivan's desk. It all looked like it was there, from what he could remember.

"What made you think I was telepathic? Weren't you concerned we might end up porting into the side of a mountain or something?"

"You are telepathic. The entrancement thing you do is a form of refined telepathy. Normally with telepathy you can read another's thoughts. Your people take it a step further by implanting ideas and making the receiver believe they are their ideas."

"But I can't read their thoughts. I can only see where their thoughts are contained and implant suggestions," Ivan defended.

"It's more than that. You just need to learn how. I only opened the port, you input the navigation. I knew you'd picture exactly where you wanted to be."

It impressed Ben that porting didn't faze Ivan. As soon as they landed, he had instantly gone into defense mode. It would be easier on him if he could hate this guy. He guessed that wouldn't be working out as planned.

"Nice house, by the way."

"Grace did the renovation."

"You mean in your new memories?"

"In all my memories. She said my taste was horrible and as long as I was planning on renovating, she would make sure the contractors did it right. I have to agree, it was a beautiful job the way she merged the new features while keeping the historic elements." He smiled at the memory of her taking over. She had kicked him out for months, not letting him come back until it was complete.

"Ready to get back?"

"Yeah."

Ben placed his hand on Ivan's shoulder again. "We're going to do the same thing, but slower this time. Close your eyes and concentrate on the deck. You can't see the port, but if you concentrate, you'll be able to see a distortion where it changes from here to your destination as you pass through it."

"With my eyes closed?"

"Open or closed. You'll be able to learn to do this on your own soon enough."

"You sure you won't get in trouble for interfering with our species' development?"

"Technically, the regulation says we can't make you aware, and we can't interfere if you are unaware. I have a loophole with you. Now, let's go." Ben began moving them forward.

Ivan felt a mild vibration paired with a line of distortion as he stepped off the tile floor onto the wooden deck where the spaces smudged together. That energy disturbance must have been what disoriented him slightly on the way over. He watched it dissolve as Ben lifted his hand away.

"I could smell someone was in the house," Ivan said as he walked through the kitchen doors. "Nothing appeared to be missing and I don't know what they wanted or who they were."

Grace and Beivve looked at each other as if they had a secret.

"Nothing was missing? Was something maybe added?" The ladies were having a difficult time holding their composure.

"What do you mean, added? We couldn't find any cameras or listening devices." Ivan wanted in on the joke. Ben was royally confused.

Grace couldn't hold it any longer. "The suitcases, Ivan. From the hotel in Geneva. Beivve sent her assistant to check us out and take our bags home. I had forgotten about that."

Beivve was wide eyed. "I can't believe you could still smell her. That was two weeks ago."

Ivan was relieved. "It was faint. The house was closed up, so the scent hadn't dissipated completely. Guess I'm a little on edge." He handed Beivve the packet and the chip Seshet had given him.

"Thank you, Ivan. Ben, can I see your TAC please?" Ben handed it over. Beivve inserted the chip, and the others watched her study the results.

Beivve looked up from the screen. "Seshet did several scans and blood draws on both Olivia and Zane. I am aware she already told Grace about the physical changes that take place within a human when they are turned. The rest of the results support my hypothesis. The substance they fed Zane was not blood. It was a nutritional mixture made to approximate the color, flavor, and consistency of blood. Since he had only taken a few ounces at his turning, he wouldn't have known the difference."

"How would Seshet have known that Zane had only been fed blood once?" Ivan interrupted.

"From what her notes say, he told her," Beivve answered.

Grace scowled at Ben. "Why did you let her do this?"

"I didn't know," Ben defended. "It was my responsibility to know, but I didn't. I was too preoccupied with finding you and I didn't pay attention to what she was doing."

Beivve intervened before a full-blown argument could begin. "We're getting off track here. Seshet's notes show they tried to get Olivia to take food and water. However, she refused, which is likely why she appeared weak and dehydrated when you found her. This is the interesting part. Neither showed any symptoms of thirst when a bleeding human was introduced. Zane, as a newly turned subject who had not been feeding on blood, should not have been able to control his impulse. Neither of them showed any pupil dilation, increased heart rate, perspiration, or involuntary fang descension. Olivia may have been able to maintain that amount of composure, but Zane would not have had that ability being only a few months old."

Beivve had concluded that after only a short period of taking CB, he no longer required blood for subsistence. She wondered what the actual dosage would be to prevent the necessity of feeding.

"Ivan, what would you think about staying up here for a few more weeks and coming off CB? The only person you would have available to drink from would be Grace if anything went amiss."

Beivve believed this would be an excellent first stage of an experiment. Ivan had subsisted on blood for an extremely extended period before turning to CB exclusively over the last thirty years. He was perfect for a long-term subject.

"That's not comforting. The last thing I want to do is hurt her."

Grace got up and walked through the coffee table from one end to the other, passing through all the items on it as well. She dropped back down beside him.

"You can't touch me if I don't want you to. Besides, if you have to drink from someone, I prefer it be me. My supply is bottomless. I can replenish as fast as you can drink, so there's no way for you to hurt me."

Ivan decided it was an undertaking valuable to the community as a whole. He thought another moment before speaking.

"It will have to start on Wednesday when I get back. I'm out at a meeting of the Board Monday evening and most of the day Tuesday. If I can detox from blood and CB, we'll take the results to my team and start additional experiments. Beivve, I'd like you to be involved since it is your theory we are researching. We need to figure out how to explain who you are since the general community can't be aware of your identity."

"Ami can set her up as an employee of Joel's company. I'm sure he'd be happy to be involved if we traded him some research." Grace had remembered her mission when she had met Ami.

Ivan was satisfied with the plan. "As long as you wear a heavy amount of perfume, everyone will stay far enough away as to not notice your scent. A very strong chemical scent repels my species."

"Overly strong perfume repels any species," Ben added.

"Now, what are we going to do about the Council? They are discussing trying to create another child of light. Should we at least tell the High Council members what we have found out about Grace? I prefer to be ahead of this rather than look like we are hiding something later," Ivan suggested.

"I don't care who knows. I think Beivve should be the one to take it to the Council. She's the one they'll accuse of hiding something. She must be above reproach," Grace indicated, turning to Beivve.

"You can tell them you had to run further tests to confirm your suspicions. Tell them you came to us about it tonight. That's why it took you so long. We shouldn't share the CB and blood experiments yet. I think you should tell them the truth about everything else." Grace wanted to protect her. She also wanted to ensure Beivve wouldn't be pulled off the team since she had already shown loyalty.

Ben shook his head. "I think she should only go to Kali and Ma'at. I'm not sure who on the Council to trust. The two of them don't like me much because of Grace, and I think they'll keep it to themselves to protect Grace. Ma'at especially has always stood up for her and you saw the disdain Kali showed me at your hearing." He directed the last statement at Grace.

Beivve pulled the chip out of the TAC. She handed the chip back to Ivan and the TAC to Ben. "Okay, since we're all agreed, I'll go to Kali and Ma'at tomorrow. I'm sure they will want to come here afterward to see what Grace knows. I'm also very sure they are going to want to talk to Ben."

"Then tell them they can come for breakfast at nine a.m. I need to sort out a few things before meeting with them anyway. It's been an exhausting day." Grace wondered how much more complicated her life was going to get.

Ben and Beivve left. Ivan cleaned up the rest of the dishes while Grace got ready for bed. As Ivan made his way into their room, Grace was climbing under the heavy comforter. He changed and slid in beside her. She was warm as she snuggled herself against his chest. They were both worn out from the stress of the day. It was after two and Ivan knew he would still be up by five. Ivan leaned down to kiss her cheek as she looked up, and they ended up in a passionate kiss. He felt himself melting into her. He could feel every cell in her body as his cells attempted to merge into hers. She pulled back, staring at him.

He felt her melting away. "Is this normal for you?" he asked with wide eyes.

"No. Not at all," she answered, shaking her head slowly.

"Just add it to the pile of things we don't fucking understand yet." He dropped his head back onto the pillow, wrapping his free arm around her.

"Yeah, a giant steaming pile," she chaffed, dropping her head back onto his shoulder.

CHAPTER NINETEEN

Grace sat at the kitchen counter, sipping coffee and wondering if she was ready for the day. Would the Council separate them? Would they take them both away without explanation, leaving their community confused and vulnerable? Why did she feel what she felt when Ivan had kissed her? She had felt like their cells were merging, making them two separate parts of the same being. She had pulled away from him, not because the feeling had scared her but because it was scaring him. The intensity didn't last long after the kiss finished, but she could still feel him. She must have been thinking aloud.

"I still feel you, too." When Ivan spoke, it brought her out of her trance.

"I wonder if they'll have any idea why."

"I'm not sure we should bring it up to them until we see what the extent of our connection is." Ivan believed they already had so much to discuss. He wanted to keep this private for as long as possible.

"Mr. Novak, are you considering intimacy with me?" she teased.

"Only if you think you're ready, Mrs. Novak. Once you've been with me, you'll never want to look at another man," he teased. He didn't have anywhere near the confidence he was attempting to portray.

She smiled shyly at him. "I'm sure I can teach you what you need to know."

"Glad your expectations are low," he smirked at her, holding out the coffeepot to refill her cup.

"See, you already know how to please me," she said, extending her mug toward him.

It was almost nine. Ivan could tell by the way she twisted her hair she was getting nervous. They didn't even know if Kali and Ma'at were going to come. They could have just taken the information to the full Council if they wanted. Who knew what she and Ivan would be in for at that point? Grace hoped Ma'at and Kali would come to them first. So many things ran through her head. She finally decided there was nothing she could do about their reaction.

It was a few minutes after nine when Grace and Ivan sensed their arrival before they heard a knock at the door. It swung open, revealing Ben, Kali, Beivve, and Ma'at, looking somber.

Grace inhaled sharply. "Good morning, everyone. Please, join us."

The group made their way through the main room into the kitchen. Ma'at looked around, then through the glass doors, catching the exterior view.

"This is quite charming."

Ivan smiled at her. "Thank you. Please, have a seat at the counter. Breakfast is almost ready. Would anyone like something to drink?"

Ma'at and Kali both requested coffees. Beivve asked for orange juice and Ben headed to the bar, retrieving the decanter of scotch and bringing it into the kitchen. He poured himself a glass. Ivan, thinking that wasn't a great sign, added some to his coffee. Grace did her best to hide her anxiety. Kali and Ma'at were tense, but Beivve seemed calm. Ivan continued to place the dishes he had prepared onto the counter while he finished the beignets.

Kali was loudly tapping her fingernails against her cup. "Thank you for having us here today. You understand we are concerned and perplexed. The information Beivve has reported to us has the potential to be quite volatile."

Grace was also concerned. "That's why we wanted you here. It seems we all have a part of the puzzle, but none of us really understands what is going on, what the implications may be, or how we move forward from here. We only started putting pieces together in the last day or so, but if what we think is happening is true, we need guidance on what to do next."

Kali nodded at her in agreement as she took a bite of a beignet. "Ivan, these are magnificent. Where did you learn to make these?"

"Thank you, Kali. I spent some time in New Orleans late in the last century." Ivan was being humble. Grace knew his history at two very prestigious cooking schools. She thought he could compete with any chef on the planet. She also thought Kali was being overly complementary.

Ma'at sipped her coffee. "Beivve told us something we have a difficult time believing. She seems to think that you somehow are the only surviving child of light." She peered over her cup at Grace.

"That's why we invited you here. We need to understand things. Ben's mother told him I was. He has been protecting me most of my life, keeping the information secret even from me. Beivve also seemed to think this was true when she analyzed my scans after my incident. I need to understand what all this means for me, Ivan, and all the vampire race in general."

Kali was gathering her thoughts. "I think we should start with what Ben knows."

As they ate, Ben recounted the story his mother had told him, as well as the promise he had made to her and Nep. Kali agreed. The timeline did line up. Freya was a carrier and the timeline fit Grace's age. What she didn't understand was how they had hidden her when so many people were monitoring the research.

Ben decided to share the device. "I don't know the answer to that question, but Freya gave me something before she disappeared. It seems to be the only thing that can track Grace while she is wearing the amulet, but you have to be very close to her. I guess I should clarify. It doesn't track her specifically. It senses her energy signature." He pulled the device out of a small bag he brought with him.

Ma'at recognized it. "That's one of Thoth's old gadgets. May I?"

She reached for it and Ben handed it over. Ma'at turned it on and checked the settings to make sure the calibration was correct, made a few adjustments, then pointed it at Grace. She shared the results on the screen with Kali. Then she hit another button, and it pointed toward Ivan.

"What the fu—? Oh, sorry. He has her signature, and it's very intense." She looked at Kali with a muddled expression. "How is that even possible? You can't share an energy signature. Can you?"

Ivan had sensed no surprise from Kali, which he thought odd.

Ben pointed at the device. "Expand the diameter to a few hundred miles." Ma'at did. A few more hits came up on the screen, but each was slightly different. "Now go out a few thousand miles." There were hundreds of hits, some dim, some bright.

Ma'at peered suspiciously at him. "There has to be something wrong with this. What have you done to it?"

Ben shrugged. "Nothing. Take it to Thoth if you don't believe me."

Beivve was growing annoyed. She was going to put their doubts to rest. She reached into her pocket and pulled out a chip.

"Here. Look at this." It was the scan and blood results showing Grace carried the additional chromosomes that were only known to be carried by the children of light.

Kali took the chip, placing it into the digital device in her pocket. She pulled the info into a three-dimensional grid that all of them could read.

"Beivve, what does this mean?"

"Swipe over. I've also done a detailed analysis of her energy source. It's all over the map. Her genetic markers, aside from the additional chromosomes, are a mixture of Æsir and Vanir, which are consistent with the genetic makeup of female subject one. That is why I came to the conclusion that Grace is female subject one from the child of light project."

Ma'at wasn't sure Beivve hadn't changed the results. "The scans Seshet gave us didn't show any of this."

"That's because I changed them before she had time to download them. I couldn't have the entire Council having access to this information before I understood what it meant for Grace," Ben confessed.

Kali was silent for a few moments. Her first glance toward Ben was a seething rebuke. She closed her eyes, clenching her jaw for a second. "This is very provocative evidence. Grace, I hope you understand that we will need to run additional tests to verify these results, especially in light of the impurity of previous scans."

Grace nodded. "I assumed as much. I'm not sure I really understand what this means or what will be expected of me if I am this being of light."

"One step at a time. Let's get these results confirmed as quietly as possible. Ma'at, we need to find someone we can trust to run these tests in an off-grid facility. No offense Beivve, but I need an independent confirmation before we decide how to proceed or what this means for the project."

Beivve understood. "None taken. I expected you to confirm the results."

Ma'at gave thought to her selection. "I think we need a dual confirmation. Both blind as to what we are looking for. I think we should have both Thoth and someone else run separate analyses."

"I agree Thoth should run an independent test and I think Apollo should run the second. I am certain both will keep our confidence. Now, we just need to find a facility," Kali suggested.

Ben made an offer. "You can use my facility. It has all the necessary equipment."

Ma'at did not like that suggestion. "There are too many people in your lab. I don't feel comfortable with that."

"And I'm uncertain they would welcome me there, especially after my last visit." Grace added.

"I have a research facility." Everyone looked at Ivan. "It doesn't have all your advanced equipment, but the building is closed on Sundays. Other than a few security guards, no one's there. They wouldn't know or care who came in with me and they wouldn't find it unusual for me to be there on a Sunday. I own the whole building. Everyone else can port directly to the lab. If you can get the equipment there today, you're welcome to it."

Kali had a skeptical expression. "Why would you own a research facility?"

Ivan glanced at Ma'at, then back at Kali. "I bought it to develop CB, clean blood, a replacement for our subsistence. The entire community has been using it for three decades, some longer than that. We already explained all this to Beivve."

"Ah, I do remember Ma'at mentioning something about that at our briefing as well. I wasn't thinking about you owning a facility to develop it. It is a sufficient location well off the Council's network." Kali turned back to Ma'at. "Is Thoth available now?"

"Yes, I can have him here soon."

"Tell him that some of Grace's results came back abnormal and you would like him to do a full workup. I will see if Apollo is available. I'll tell him we have unusual scans from a subject we need a second opinion on." Kali was satisfied with the decisions.

"Do you think we should port to the lab? That way, you will all know where to bring everything. Grace and I can port outside and enter through the lobby after. That is, of course, if Grace doesn't mind porting me." Ivan didn't want to assume she would take him.

Grace rolled her eyes. "Seriously, Ivan. There are five people here capable of porting. Of course, I am going to port you with me. Besides, you're the only one who knows where we're going, so we all have to port together, don't we?"

"I don't like to assume. I'd prefer to learn how to do it myself."

Ben smirked. "I can teach you how to port. You already have a solid handle on the navigation part, which is what most of us have trouble with."

"Thanks, Ben. I appreciate that."

Kali stood up. "If you two are finished bonding, could we get on with it?"

They all stood up and walked out to the deck. Grace took Ivan's hand.

"Lead the way. I'll open the port."

Ivan concentrated on the seating area beside the lab to reduce the chance of breaking anything that could be out of place. Grace opened the port. Ivan could see a distortion in front of him he hadn't noticed before.

Granted, four of the times he had ported were at night, once he was snatched up by Ami with no warning, and the only other time he was panicking over the incident at the auction. Ben's assumption that Ivan couldn't see it didn't take into account his advanced sight. Now that he knew what to look for, it was unmistakable.

They all stepped out into the seating area. Ivan could immediately tell no one was in the lab. "Will this work?"

Beivve answered, "It's better than I thought it would be. Our equipment should be able to integrate with what you have here. I'll start setting up what they will need if you would like to go retrieve them," she said to Kali and Ma'at.

"I'll give her a hand," Ben nodded to Beivve.

"And we will port to the alley behind the coffee shop across the street."

Grace and Ivan made it back to the lab after twenty minutes with a two-liter coffee box from the café. Ma'at and Thoth were already back with his personal scanner. Ma'at explained to him that he and Apollo would perform independent tests. They would compare the results when all the scans and physical blood testing had been completed.

Thoth understood and performed his scans. He then took Grace's blood. The lab equipment provided was slower, but it gave him the opportunity to use a lower technology. He enjoyed any chance to learn about ancient and unusual things. His assessment of the data was almost complete when he looked at Ma'at intensely but kept quiet, realizing exactly what he was looking at. At that point, Kali and Apollo ported in.

Apollo was a slender man with wavy golden hair and abnormally vivid blue eyes. Apollo looked around, pulling his hands back as if the primitive equipment were contagious. "Where is the patient?"

Grace stepped forward while Kali stepped toward her. "Apollo, this is Grace. Grace, Apollo."

Apollo didn't understand. "Kali, what is going on here? That is Nanna."

Grace answered, "I haven't used that name for a very long time, but yes, I was Nanna. How did you know that?" She hadn't remembered ever meeting him.

"Because I was involved in your creation. At least now I know why Beivve needed your scan results verified. There's no way you lot would believe what you were looking at was real."

"Exactly what is that comment supposed to mean?" Kali scrutinized him, as did the rest of the room.

"It means exactly what you think it means. Grace here is female subject one from the child of light program. I suggested Frigg and Freya hide her after her creation because the High Council had decided to abandon the project and dissect the subjects."

Ivan didn't think that statement was completely truthful. Apollo's scent turned slightly bitter, but not pungent. Ivan was standing between Grace and Apollo before anyone in the room had seen him move. Apollo stumbled backward.

"They were going to kill her?" Ivan had outstretched his arm behind him to keep Grace from moving forward.

She placed her hand on his shoulder. "Ivan, he was the one who had them hide me. Did you hear that part?"

He took a deep breath. "I'm sorry. I'm not sure what came over me." He reached out to shake Apollo's hand. "I'm Ivan, Grace's husband."

Grace added, "He can be overprotective." She wasn't sure what was going on with that. He never had been before.

Apollo moved back to his original position, taking Ivan's hand and apology. "I must say, you did startle me. I didn't even see you move. You're clearly not human. What is your species?"

"Vampire. And you?"

Apollo let go of his hand, placing it in his front pocket while Ivan tried to push into Apollo's mind. The contact of the handshake hadn't lasted long enough. He was a little uncomfortable with Apollo, although he wasn't sure why.

Apollo completely ignored Ivan's question. His eyes widened. He was very excited, running across the room, pointing back at Ivan.

"Thoth! Did you hear that? Vampire! On the fires of Mercury! How perfect is that? Have you scanned him yet?"

Thoth was surprised as well. "No! I didn't know. Ma'at! Why didn't you tell me Ivan was a vampire?" The two men were frenzied. They both moved quickly back toward Ivan. Beivve followed close behind, trying to catch up to their line of thinking.

Apollo produced something about the size of a coaster. He threw it on the floor, tapping on a digital device he uncoupled from it. The coaster expanded to the size of a utility cover.

"Ivan, please step on the scanner," he pointed, directing Ivan onto the platform. Ivan was confused but obliged.

The three scientists were engaged in frenzied activity, reading, pointing, and mumbling to each other. They appeared to have forgotten anyone else was in the room. Several minutes passed while the postulating continued.

Ivan's patience was waning. "Are the three of you going to let the rest of the class in on the secret?"

Apollo became cognizant of the others staring at them. "Oh, yes, you can step down now."

Beivve popped her head up from the screen. "Ivan, we also need a blood sample from you and some human blood. Oh, and a CB sample too."

"There is blood in the walk-in at the end of the hall behind you. It's labeled with the species and type. A sample of my blood is there too. CB is at the station to your left."

"We can't use your old blood. We need a fresh sample. Do you mind?" She pulled something the size of a pen out of her bag on the lab table.

Ivan held out his arm. "Whatever you need."

She touched his wrist with the object. He felt nothing other than Beivve's grip on his hand and the sensation of the pen tip against his wrist. "This is going to take some time. You should go get some lunch."

Kali peered disapprovingly. "Beivve, we just finished breakfast an hour ago."

"Well, this is going to take a while. I'm sure you can figure out something to do that isn't here," she ordered, waving them off.

Ben suggested they go back to the cabin to wait. Ivan told them to go ahead. He and Grace had to leave the way they came in. They would meet them shortly. Ivan turned back to Beivve before leaving.

"Beivve, bring them there when you're finished."

She didn't look up from the screen. "Yup, sure."

Grace and Ivan met the rest of the group back at the cabin ten minutes later. Ben was already on the sofa with a scotch in his hand. Ivan joined him, propping his feet up on the table.

"That was exciting," Ben said.

"I'm not sure exciting would be my initial reaction to the events. Monumental, maybe. This information could be the beginning of changing The Everything. Of course, we should start small. Perhaps one galaxy at first." Kali seemed to have an intention in her statement.

Ivan wondered what she was referring to.

Ben pulled out a perplexing question. "What would be the outcome of infusing multiple dimensions with light? Shouldn't things be equally balanced?"

Ma'at fielded that question. "Yes and no. Balance is necessary for The Everything overall, but many dimensions are in balance in accordance with their natural decline. The ones we need to look at are like this one, where the dark matter is expanding at a rate greater than the surrounding ones, where decline is out of sequence. A balanced dimension has about ninety-five percent dark matter superfluid. It's the mesh that supports everything. New dimensions are around ninety-two percent, while the oldest ones are closer to ninety-eight. Too many dimensions swallowed in this negative matter will cause an imbalance throughout all dimensions. Same thing with too many imbued with too much positive energy or light. We need to tip the scales back to the appropriate level of orderly decline."

"Are you saying the balance of The Everything relies solely on Grace?" Ivan did not like the sound of that at all.

"Not Grace alone. The two of you together," Apollo stated, walking in from the deck, followed by Beivve and Thoth. "You're merging."

All eyes focused on Apollo.

"Explain what you mean," Ivan demanded. A lump had risen in his throat. He and Grace had barely noticed. How could they be so certain?

Apollo continued. "The entire premise of the program was to create a pair, two in perfect synchronization. The two of you are merging into two halves of one being. You will each have all the skills, abilities, thoughts, and feelings of the other. Your physical appearance and genetic material will remain similar to how they are currently. Your light signature, however, will become one."

"This makes no sense." Grace moved toward Ivan. "He can't be a source without the additional chromosomes. I was told those can only exist in a female. It will kill him."

Thoth walked over to Ma'at. "He already has them."

"But the other males died when they began puberty."

"I think he's well beyond that phase," Thoth shrugged.

"Thank you, Thoth." Ivan lifted his glass toward him. "What about the other vampires? Are they undergoing a change? How are they going to be affected?"

Beivve had seated herself at the far end of the small corner bar. "We tested most of the samples in the lab. Some were current, some older. We don't see any changes in them other than they are carriers. I should probably explain. The process is like a virus. Grace is what we will refer to as patient zero. She spread the virus to you. Both of you will be full-blown light containers. Other vampires are carriers. They will spread the virus by birth if their parents are carriers or blood exchange when turning new ones. Thanks to your ingenuity, there is a third way to spread the virus. You created your CB from Grace's blood. The way you designed it kept the integrity of the cells. The light infects anyone who consumes it, thus they will also become a carrier."

Ivan interrupted Beivve with a question. "So, you're saying Grace and I are infected with the virus, and the others are carriers but will never show signs of the infection?"

"Exactly. We haven't been able to figure out how much the subject must consume before becoming a carrier, but we believe it's a small dose. Can you get fresh samples from some vampires? We can test humans and other immortal species, and we are asking for your permission to test other vampires. We only need small samples of their blood, but we will need several small groups who will adhere to specific dosages and schedules."

Ivan had a question and an observation. "I didn't present any symptoms of changing until yesterday. How do we know that no one else in the community has experienced these changes without noticing them?"

Beivve, Thoth, and Apollo exchanged glances.

"We can review the tracking data, but we don't think that's possible given the genetic abnormality you two have," Beivve said.

Ivan took a second to think about what to say next.

"I don't think I could find a subject for you, though. Every member of the community has consumed CB, and we don't turn more than a few each year. By this point, all vampires should be carriers. There might be a rogue or two out there, but we have no way of finding them unless they're killing humans, which is something we don't want to happen."

"We have ways to find people who don't want to be found. I'll get my network started on it," Ben suggested.

"You couldn't find me," Grace quipped.

Ben narrowed his eyes. "We found you. We just couldn't follow you because your amulet cloaked you," he rebutted.

Ma'at stood, holding up Thoth's device Ben had given her earlier that morning. "We should upload this tracking program to a newer device that will allow us to use an interactive map to monitor for any additional anomalies."

Beivve finished the thought. "And we should collect identity information on each of these markers," she said, stepping toward Ivan.

"Ivan, we don't know what made you compatible for Grace to merge with. My hypothesis is then both unfortunate and encouraging. We won't be able to study the dosage of CB that creates a carrier in your species. The better news is, as a carrier, there is no imperative to consume blood or CB in order to survive. That means if your entire community already carries the energy signature, none of you need blood or blood substitute. You can quit it today with no ill effects. Well, I should restate that. You may have a mild thirst, which is your body's habitual reaction, but you don't need it."

Grace wanted to clarify. "What you're saying is that no pure born whose parents are carriers will ever need to consume blood or CB? And no newly turned will need to consume any blood or CB once they wake from their death sleep? And all the new will never have a thirst?"

Beivve hesitated for only a second. "Yes. That is the way the test results appear. This will absolutely need to be confirmed with live subjects, obviously having blood or CB available on the extremely slim chance this isn't an accurate assessment. I don't see how it could be incorrect." She then turned her attention back to Ivan.

"Your blood doesn't react at all when human blood is introduced. I expected it to be consumed by your sample. You are just regular old immortals now with one unique caveat. You can create immortals from mortal beings. We don't know of another species that can create immortals by any means other than biological reproduction."

Ivan downed a full glass of scotch. "Anybody have a way to tell my people without telling my people why they won't need CB or blood anymore? It took decades to get them off blood and onto CB, and the only way that worked then was because killing humans was becoming too difficult to cover up. We've built an entire industry of manufacturing and selling CB products. It will not go over well to tell them that the entire source of income is going away."

"It doesn't have to, Ivan." Grace surprised herself when she understood the commerce of it. "All they need to do is retarget their market to humans. There are nine billion of them now. Hospitals and military would be happy to have a substitute that doesn't degrade. You know how much money they throw out every year because of expired blood. They don't even have to crossmatch it."

Kali wanted to move the conversation away from telling the vampire community immediately. "I think you should keep this to yourself for a while. We should get you off it first, then spread the information to a few others at random. Then maybe set up some research and experiments. Let it slowly roll out. It's easier to accept when it happens gradually. It also gives them time to develop other industries or change marketing strategies to replace their income. This isn't a race. We don't have to let everything out all at once. You need a plan."

"Beivve and I had already planned to get me off CB starting when I get back from my trip on Tuesday evening. From what you're saying, I'm different from the rest of the community now, though. Even if I can survive without it, there's no guarantee any of the others can."

Beivve interjected, "I really don't think that's the case."

Ivan rubbed his hand through his hair and contemplated. "I can set up a paid study to find out what the effects are. I can have the docs substitute an inert substance to half of the group. The subjects won't know they're not taking it. Then we can leak the results to the community after I present them to the Board. That should start the process."

Apollo wanted to keep the information more contained. "The disclosure of this information should be confined to the people present in this room. I will go back through my personal notes to see if I can find other information on this project I had forgotten about. I also want to see what the stances of the other Council members were. If we need additional resources or guidance, I want to be sure about who we can involve."

Ben was becoming agitated. "This is bullshit. Why do we need to tell anyone? Why can't we just keep this to ourselves and let her, them, live their lives? She's a person. Nobody took that into account when they created her. Now he's bonded to her. We don't have to do any of this to them. Can we not stop all of this and do nothing?"

Grace knelt in front of Ben, smiling sadly. "We can't Ben. I can't help the circumstance that brought me," she reached out, taking Ivan's hand, "us, to this place. How can we not go forward? They are going to create another child, and I can't let that happen. They need to know I'm here. My energy is already spreading. It will continue to spread regardless of whether I want it to. You can't protect me anymore. I'm sorry for this."

Ben realized she was apologizing for something she hadn't done yet. With a motion so fast he was barely cognizant of it, she reached into his arm, coating her finger with blood and bringing it behind her to unlatch the amulet.

Everyone jumped forward, yelling at Grace to stop. Ivan grabbed her wrist before she got to the latch. Damn, he was faster than she had expected. She tried to phase out of his grip, but she couldn't do it. It took her a moment to understand what was happening. She was randomly alternating her phase and he shouldn't be able to touch her. She backed through the coffee table. So did Ivan. He didn't understand it any more than she did.

"Grace, please. Not yet. I'm not ready to do this yet." Ivan had never asked for anything from her. He certainly hadn't asked for what was happening to him.

"Ivan, I'm so sorry I've dragged you into this. I can't stand by and do nothing. We were meant to travel The Everything spreading light to all the darkest spaces. I can't stop myself from doing that." She was determined. She couldn't turn away from her ultimate mission now that she understood what it was.

"Grace, I'm not asking you to stop. I'm asking you to wait. My responsibility is to ensure the community's safety. I already understand we need to leave, but they are also the ones who are supposed to venture out and spread your energy signature, aren't they? And what about your people? Haven't they lost enough too? Don't they deserve to be protected somewhere before you unleash your beacon, bringing whatever is searching for us?"

"Ivan, you're already a beacon. I don't want whatever is coming for me to get to you instead. You don't know how to control the abilities you're absorbing from me. If I take this off and leave, I can buy all of you time to make whatever preparations you can."

Thoth was the only one who had remained calmly seated. "Or we can craft an amulet for Ivan to keep him hidden until you're prepared." All eyes turned toward him.

"See, you don't have to do this right now. You need to stay here, at least for a while. I can't do everything that needs to be done to prepare without you," Ivan pleaded.

Grace stopped phasing. She searched Ivan's face to see his eyes begging her. She didn't have the callousness to disregard him. "I'm only staying here for you. You need to understand that. I want the Council to know who and what I am. I'm done hiding."

She turned to her right. "Thoth, can you really make him something that hides his light?"

Ivan added, "But not an amulet. That would look ridiculous on a grown man. A watch maybe?"

"Huh. A watch?" Thoth contemplated. "I could absolutely do a watch. It wouldn't take me long."

Ivan's mind snapped to his travel plans. "I have a flight tomorrow. I'll need to leave by two p.m. Can you have it before then?"

"No problem. You should probably stay inside the blockers until then." Thoth added casually.

"But I've already been out," Ivan said.

Thoth picked up the scanner from where Ma'at had set it down. "Your light doesn't look bright enough to be seen outside of the atmosphere yet."

Apollo rolled his eyes. "The merge just started, Thoth. It's going to get brighter."

"Well, I have one more condition." Grace looked at Ben, who was applying pressure over the hole in his arm. "I need some of your blood. When I'm ready, I want to remove this on my own."

"It's a lot less uncomfortable for me to give it to you than it is for you to take it. Here." He emptied his glass, set it on the table and squeezed his arm until the glass had about half an inch of blood. Ivan let go of Grace, and she went over to Ben.

"Thank you." She reached out, touching his arm. She took a deep breath, wishing she had controlled her impulse to tear a hole in his flesh again. A warm glow appeared under her hand. When she removed it, the wound was gone. The blood on his arm was gone, too. It wasn't just healed. There was no trace of ever being an injury. She had never done that before and wasn't sure how she even knew to do it now. It had just happened. She picked up the glass and poured most of it into a small glass vial she found in the kitchen, avoiding the stares of the others. She washed the rest down the sink before turning to speak to the group. An unfamiliar calmness had overtaken her.

"Kali, tell the Council. I want them to know. Ivan and I will prepare the vampires. Ben, you need to work more quickly at finding a place for the Æsir. Thoth, no blood seals. He needs to be able to take it off and replace it as he wishes. I'm finished reacting to my life." Grace heard Ivan say, Our life, and she smiled. "From this point forward, we are taking control of our lives."

Ben had an idea. He wasn't sure how it was going to go over, but it made perfect sense to him. "I think the vampires should come with us."

Kali immediately jumped at him. This was not part of her plan. "Ben, you can't be serious. They are an emergent species. You can't think anyone would approve of them being exposed to the Æsir, much less letting them move to another planet with you."

Ben rose to meet her. "You can't think that I'm asking for your permission. They're not full members. You don't have the right to stop them. It's Ivan's decision anyway, and it makes sense. There are only one hundred and nine of us. It will be difficult enough for us to inhabit a new planet with such small numbers. We can teach them everything they need to know to evolve to their rightful place in The Everything. Especially with the situation developing now with their merging, the entire species is going to need to develop quickly. None of us can limit ourselves to being an individual species any longer. We could help each other." He then turned to Ivan.

"I'd be grateful if you heard me out on this. I think it would benefit both of our species. We could be the first to share the light from you, and we have vast amounts of knowledge to give to you."

Thoth added his opinion. "It makes sense."

Ma'at spun around. "Thoth!"

"It does. It could be a very symbiotic relationship. Earth is on its way to being reset again anyway. They only have a few hundred years left if they stay on their current destructive path, and I can't see the vampires developing quickly enough if we left them on their own. I think the Council would agree if we presented it in the right way."

Ivan saw the offer could be a sound option. "It's an offer I would like some time to consider, Ben. It's a tremendous opportunity for our people. There will be many things that will need to happen before we are ready to take that step. Each individual will need to decide if they will go." He felt Grace's approval.

"If Grace and I go with you, I'm confident most of the others will follow. I think there are many benefits to bringing our species together. I do need to ensure anyone who prefers to stay behind has a stable government and resources."

"I can understand that, Ivan. I am concerned for my people the same as you are for yours. It's a relationship that I think can work. Take your time and think it through thoroughly. Make whatever preparations you need. Let me know if you need any help, and I'll do what I can," Ben said sincerely.

It was a practical solution. The vampires had the numbers, and the Æsir had the knowledge. The goal was to expand the light. Both men saw it as a win-win situation.

Kali was not happy with the direction the conversation had taken. "Grace, I think you're being reckless. Your energy needs to be protected. We need to figure out the safest way to spread it without exposing you to harm. Going with the Æsir who have already been attacked and nearly wiped out doesn't seem to be a practical decision."

Thoth had another bold idea. "We could cloak the new planet. It wouldn't be hidden or anything. It would be like the cabin is now. You could see it, but you couldn't see the light that emanated from it. Everything inside would still work the way it should."

There were nods of agreement from everyone except for Kali and Ma'at, who were still hesitant. They were each deep in thought.

Ben was curious about how the process would work. "How would porting to the planet work? How could we set it up for the entire planet and how long would that take?"

"That would depend on the planet's size and mineral composition. Theoretically, there would be a network of small redundant towers and satellites positioned throughout to create a grid screen. If one tower went down, the others would mesh together until repairs could be made. Set-up time again would depend on the size and mineral composition. Worst case, if they could use nothing from the planet itself, six to eight months of Earth time would be required to complete the process. That's if we mined the elements from asteroids. Mining other planets would be easier, although we don't want to be accused of stealing resources."

Thoth had Ben and Ivan's full attention. Kali was fuming and Ma'at was stunned silent.

"Porting would have to be done from a coded platform. Native porting could only be conducted internally. Nothing from the outside could port in natively or from inside out," Thoth speculated.

Ben picked up from there. "I've got three planets we are considering. They all have existing ecosystems. If none of these works, our last option will be geo-forming a desert planet. We'd rather not do that since it will set our timeline further back. Even if the vampires don't decide to join us, I think those are security measures I want in place. Can I send you the survey information? I'd like your suggestions on our options for each or if we would be better off geo-forming somewhere else."

Thoth was eager to have a new project. "Certainly." He tossed his TAC to Ben, who tapped a few times on each device, then tossed it back.

"That's everything we have so far. We're set with teams on each performing physical observations and wildlife interaction assessments. I'll send the info over when the survey teams get it to me."

"Ma'at likes me better when I have a project." Thoth gently elbowed his wife, awakening her from her stupor.

"I can't always be the focus of your incessant questions. This is a project I theoretically agree with. In either case, the planet will need protection until they have settled the communities." Ma'at didn't enjoy bending the rules. If she could tell herself this project was for the Æsir's safety, that was how she would get around the rest of it. Until they informed the Council, and it was agreed upon, she didn't want to deal with the prospect of a vampire relocation.

Beivve had been silent for most of this conversation. "You are all forgetting one important thing. The basic virus can be spread without exposing Grace and Ivan, at least for the initial stages, by CB. We already know it infects vampires who consume it. We need to test to see if it works on other species, then mass produce the hell out of it."

Ben knew how they could test it. "We have several species at the facility. They are some of the forces that attacked our world. I couldn't tell you if any are immortal or not. I do know that most are not humanoid. We can add CB to their water source and see what happens. I could take it myself, but I already know it won't affect me."

"I'll take it." Apollo volunteered. "You have some here, don't you?"

Beivve shot him an intimidating look. "Apollo! If you are going to turn yourself into a test subject, you will do it in a lab under a scanner where I can observe you. You will not waste vital data for your own amusement!" Beivve wasn't having any of it from him.

"Guess that's settled then. When do you want me there?" Apollo smirked.

She ignored him. "Ivan, may I have a larger sample? I will also need the production notes and a sample of the growth base, please."

"It's all back at the lab. You're welcome to whatever you need. I can get—"

Beivve cut Ivan off. "Thank you, Ivan. I can retrieve it myself, if you don't mind."

"Not at all. Have at it."

Beivve grabbed Apollo by the sleeve and drug him behind her on the way out the door.

"We will be back when you return from your trip with our results. Ben, send me your port codes and I'll start running the tests at your facility when I get everything set up."

"You got it," Ben replied.

"How will you have them so fast?" Ivan knew from experience trials could take years.

"I have a STAG. How else would I do it?" Beivve answered, porting outside the door, pulling Apollo behind her.

Ivan wasn't sure if he was the only one who had no idea what she was talking about or not. "What's a STAG?"

Thoth was reading the specs Ben had given him. He said offhandedly, without looking up, "Simulated time accelerating generator. I have a lot of data to get through and simulations to do myself. I'm going to head home." He leaned down and kissed Ma'at absently on the cheek before he left.

Once he had cleared the door and ported, Kali had something to say to the remaining group. "Grace, do we need to discuss the little stunt you pulled with Ben?"

"No." Grace ran her fingers through her hair and sighed.

"I realize how frustrated you must be. I can't imagine the amount of stress you feel with all the insane changes to your life over the last few weeks, either. It seems to never end. What I can tell you is erratic reactions will help nothing. Keep your head about you, Grace. You are exactly where you need to be right now. I can't be worrying about your mental stability." Kali empathized with her situation, but she could see how easily everything could run off the rails if not handled carefully. She didn't trust Grace to keep control of herself.

"I know Kali. I really do." Grace leaned her head back, closing her eyes. Ivan put his hand on her shoulder. She laced her fingers through his, straightening back up and opening her eyes.

"I still want you to tell the Council about what's happening to me and Ivan. They should also know about everything, the CB and the testing Beivve is doing. None of us need them to find out later and think we were trying to hide something. Even if we have a few against us, I think the majority will be on board with what we are trying to accomplish. I don't want to make any suggestions about Ben's offer to them right now, but I believe you should propose that we need more than just me to help them improve quickly. At that point, Ben could bring up the offer for the Æsir to mentor them if they would relocate and help them settle the new planet."

Kali contemplated her words. "Trust me when I say I am not about to entertain or report on Ben's offer. We will meet again tomorrow. I should be able to find a proper time to fit in the report."

Ben went to the bar to get a fresh glass. He poured another drink. Ivan patted him on the arm, holding out his glass for a refill, which Ben obliged.

"I'm willing to make the offer to the Council if you can steer the committee onto the topic of the rapid evolution of the vampires. I think most of them will agree it's a good plan," Ben said and sat back on the sofa.

Kali agreed to make the prompt, even though she still thought it was a heedless idea.

"Let us know how it goes with the Council first. If they're not receptive, Ben's offer to bring us along won't hold any weight. I'm leaving town around two tomorrow and won't be back until Tuesday evening." Ivan couldn't miss this trip. It was the last board meeting of the year and he had already attended the last quarter's by video.

"I'll come here straight after. I can stay with Grace until you come back," Ben offered. "She shouldn't be alone while you're gone."

Grace replied, "Erik is going to stay with me. I'll be fine."

"Erik is off world and won't return until Tuesday morning. I can stay until he gets back."

Ivan quickly added his opinion. "You can stay in Erik's room. It's upstairs at the end of the hall."

"I'd prefer to stay down here. These two doors," he pointed to the front door and the door to the deck, "are the only unblocked points of entry. I can see them both from this spot." Ben thought the sofa was the perfect observation area.

Ivan cracked a smile. "It's your back."

"I've slept in worse places."

Grace glanced around the room. "Shouldn't I get a vote on this?"

Everyone else in the room replied in unison, "No."

"Fine." She would actually be glad for the company. She just didn't like being told what to do.

"I think I should casually mention to a few trusted members that I think the CB has cured our thirst. I'll tell them I haven't had the desire to drink in a long time and I'm planning on attempting to detox to see what the results are. Then, I'll let them know we have some test results showing my latest blood samples aren't deteriorating like they used to. I'll tell them if my detox works, I'm planning on putting a full trial together. Like Kali said earlier. It's better if it works its way out slowly. I just think we need to start sooner than later."

No one raised any disagreement. Kali and Ma'at left to prepare notes for the committee meeting the next day. Ben needed to get back to the facility to tend to obligations and to check on Beivve and Apollo. Ivan and Grace were finally alone.

Grace wanted to have a normal, relaxing afternoon without discussion of the fate of the universe weighing down on her. She flopped down on the sofa to watch Ivan open the deck doors. She reached around, pulling a throw from a basket under the table. Physically, she felt great; mentally, she was drained.

Ivan slid in behind her on the sofa, wrapping her up in his arms, pulling her tight. He had a powerful urge to be close to her.

She wrapped her arms over his under the blanket. They stared at the flames flickering and dancing across the wood in the fireplace. It smelled thick and sweet, of oak and cherry. She felt more relaxed lying in his arms. Even when she was recovering, she always felt restless, like she had something she should be doing. Lying here with Ivan, she felt comfortable, safe, content. She couldn't tell if it was her feeling or his. Maybe it was both. Whomever it was coming from, she liked it.

She felt the steady rise and fall of Ivan's chest against her back. If she hadn't been certain that he was awake, she would have assumed he was sleeping. She felt his vibration more intensely than she normally did. All her senses were becoming more acute. She heard his heartbeat thundering in her ears. The fire was becoming so bright she couldn't look at it straight on. She smelled the forest through the open doors as if she were sitting deep in the woods. She wondered if this was what Ivan felt all the time.

Ivan felt changes, too. He could feel every particle moving inside of everything around him: the blanket, the sofa, his socks, and most important of all, Grace. He felt her entire physical being, her essence, and, most of all, he felt her pain.

Not physical pain, she had mental pain, which she hid well from the world. It was the pain of always being the outsider. The pain of never being completely accepted by anyone. Always needing to have a wall up. It was the same aching he had himself. He hugged her tighter, and they both knew they could let all that go. Each of them had found the missing part that they didn't know they were searching for. They never had to be outsiders with each other.

They lay together until the sun started slipping behind the mountains, showing off the glorious colors of late fall as the last tendrils of light created shadows across the floor. The fire ebbed to low embers, and the room was taking on a damp chill that differed from the crisp coolness of the day. Ivan leaned forward, getting up to place more wood on the fire. Grace rolled onto her back, putting him off balance, causing him to land on top of her.

"Sorry. I didn't mean to crush you." Ivan peered into her eyes, brushing a lock of her hair off her face.

She grabbed the back of his neck and passionately kissed him. He kissed her back intensely. This was so much different from what it had been with Lukkas. He was always gentle and sweet. Ivan was raw and passionate. Grace felt heat welling up from her as she kissed him harder, ripping his shirt open. She pulled him tighter on top of her. They felt everything from each other giving into their most base urges. Their skin was on fire as it touched, as if the light was trying to break through to unite itself. The connection between them was intense, visceral, and exhilarating.

They went on for nearly an hour, practically destroying the living room, knocking over furniture and breaking things. They took out all their frustrations, emotions, and fears on each other until they were exhausted, melting together in a mutual climax.

Afterward, Ivan lay naked in the middle of the floor. Grace grabbed the blanket and crawled over to the fireplace to salvage the glowing ashes that had been a fire earlier. She leaned against the elevated hearth as the wood smoked over the heat.

Ivan was dazed. He had only been with one other woman, and she had been human. He was too at the time, so there was no equating the experience. One thing he could say for sure, if this was how things were going to be with Grace, he could never be with anyone else.

Grace had experienced nothing like the intensity of what she had with Ivan. She could never imagine wanting to be with anyone else again, either.

Ivan drug himself over to where Grace sat, wrapping himself in the other half of the blanket. They surveyed the room and laughed.

"I always hated that coffee table," he chuckled.

Grace grabbed one of the shattered legs and pitched it into the now roaring flames. "Good. Now you get to make a new one." They laughed again. Any remnants of awkwardness from the last few weeks had vanished.

"I'm starving."

"Me too. I'll cook, you clean up?"

"Deal," she said, rising to her feet. They looked around for their clothes. Ivan's shirt was ripped into pieces. He threw it away and got a fresh one from the laundry behind the kitchen. The rest of the evening was light and relaxed. Their passion had given them exactly the release they had both needed.

CHAPTER TWENTY

The sun hadn't yet risen when Grace woke to find Ivan looking down at her. He was the most content he had ever been. He had held her as she slept, not wanting to move and wake her. This evening he was supposed to attend a formal reception, followed by an early board meeting tomorrow, and he hadn't wanted to be away from her any longer than necessary. He couldn't explain the anxiety caused by the thought of separating from her. All he knew was he couldn't bear not being physically close to her.

"Do you, maybe, think you might want to go with me?" Ivan asked with a shrug.

"I thought you'd never ask," she answered, giggling nervously. Whatever was drawing them together, she felt it as deeply as he did, expecting something world shattering to happen if they parted.

They took the morning slowly, hesitant to depart the cocoon they had created in their cabin on the mountain. It would likely be the last normal morning they would have together, and neither was willing to move it along too fast. After a leisurely breakfast, they laid out their clothes for their trip. Around ten thirty, Thoth brought Ivan's watch. It was an exclusive-brand diver's chronograph, which Ivan was not expecting. The case was gold with a sapphire crystal and matching band. He had only seen these in display cases of high-end luxury shops and never imagined being lavish enough to purchase one for himself. The quality lived up to the rumors, being as perfect as expected.

Thoth chose it because he required something with sapphire's specific mineral composition to create a cloak. He also needed something sealed that could stand up to pressure changes, so this piece was irresistibly perfect. With great care, he modified the sapphire's properties to create concealment. He hadn't bound the closure, so Ivan could take it off and replace it as he wished. Unlatching it turned the cloak off, latching it turned it on. He cautioned Ivan against removing it when he wasn't inside an area with cloaking or blockers in place. Since the watch was waterproof, Ivan didn't need to take it off at all if he didn't want to. Thoth ensured Ivan was comfortable with the functional aspect before leaving them to their pleasant morning.

Ivan called to cancel his flight and airport limo. When it was time, he checked them into the hotel through its app, which revealed their room number, along with a digital code that acted as a room key for the lock. They could port straight into their room just before the meeting time, and no one would ever know.

It was unusual to have two board meetings so close together. They held one late in the quarter last time and they wanted to get this quarter's session out of the way before all the holidays began. Being a global community, the last quarter of the year had some type of celebration nearly every day. Christians alone had over fifteen and that didn't even account for Jewish, Hindu, Pagan, and various cultural celebrations. The next time they would all be in the same place would be in the new year.

Once Grace had agreed to go, Ivan decided he would present her educational plan while everyone was in good spirits, anticipating upcoming celebrations. He'd paint a bright picture of what the community's future could be. The next presentation was likely to be, "Who wants to go live with an alien race that some of you consider gods on another planet?" He wasn't sure how well that one would go over. This would be an appropriate time for him to use every ounce of his substantial charm to move them toward the future.

Ben dropped in shortly before one, having been dismissed after telling the Council about his proposed offer to the vampires. Kali would come to discuss the determination of the panel by one thirty. Grace hadn't had the opportunity to tell Ben she was going with Ivan and didn't need him there. She told him he could stay at the cabin while they were gone, if he liked. They wouldn't be leaving until around three due to the reception being in Manhattan this time. Grace paced and made small talk until Kali arrived. When she appeared, she looked … they weren't sure how she looked. It wasn't her normal stoic, slightly condescending appearance. She almost appeared pleased, with a hint of an upturn in the corners of her mouth and eyes.

"Grace, the Council is quite excited you are alive and well. They are also pleased they weren't able to dissect you along with the other children when the project ended."

"Yeah, me too," Grace responded.

Kali continued. "The entire High Council already knows who you are because Apollo could not hold on to discretion if it was passed to him in a cup. With that being said, no one was shocked by the idea that you were the light being, as they are referencing you now. I'd say that's a huge amount of positive feedback from them. Even Nyx was excited to hear about you, although no one is sure why she attended a council meeting. She denied the swift expansion of darkness in this dimension is a result of anything she has done. Oh, and she'd like to share some time with you in the next millennia. Once you're settled in your role, of course."

Ivan spoke up. "Wait, why would Grace want to meet with the goddess of darkness? Isn't that just inviting evil to come for her?"

Kali and Grace both stifled smiles, amused at his naivety.

Kali explained, "Ivan, you have so much to learn. I might offer you advice to not refer to Nyx as the goddess of darkness. She's the goddess of night. There is an enormous difference. Aside from that, darkness and evil are two different things. Light and dark are both necessary for most living things to thrive. If it weren't for the darkness, you couldn't observe the stars, and the hominid brain doesn't function properly without both."

"Didn't think about it that way. I guess I've always associated darkness with evil," Ivan said, rubbing his chin.

"It's true there are many evil things that lurk in the dark, but there are just as many in the light. The only difference is the ability to see them," Kali answered. She had never been a fan of Nyx, although it had nothing to do with her role. Kali thought her too unpredictable and irresponsible, and she had no allegiance to the Council or to anyone else.

Grace added, "Besides, good and evil are issues of morality, and each species has individual guidelines for those."

"Now, if I may continue, the Council wants regular scans and ability determinations, and so on, and so forth." Kali waved her hand dismissively. "We already expected that much. We have given them Beivve's scan results and Apollo's original project information. I'm sure most of them don't understand a word of it, which is why they would like some demonstrations."

Grace nodded. "I'd be more than happy to show them the extent of my abilities, although I'm not sure what they are at this point. Let me know when they would like to schedule."

"I didn't realize I hadn't gotten to that part. Grace, they understand how you came to be and what you are. Ivan is a complete anomaly, so they want both of you. Not only does your merger seem to be progressing rapidly, but the two of you have developed into a unique species. It puzzled even Apollo about how it was possible. You are no longer individuals of your original backgrounds. You differ from anything in any dimension we know about. I'm sure you already suspected it," she said, lifting her forehead in a questioning manner.

Ivan thought her answer was lacking. Her actions had been supportive and didn't emit the bitter scent of a lie, but something made him feel she wasn't giving them the entire story.

"We had theorized something along those lines. I have no reservations about participating, but I need to make sure it's only for short periods of time. I can't neglect my duties to my community here."

Ben had poured himself a drink and was leaning against the bar. "No one is asking you to abandon them at all. They are only looking for an assessment. They also want Apollo to investigate the possibility of turning anyone of any other species into whatever the two of you are." He waved his hand, pointing lazily between Grace and Ivan.

Kali scoffed at him. "That was extremely eloquent, Ben," she sneered, her voice dripping with sarcasm.

Then Kali addressed Ivan. "The Council doesn't just want to perform experiments on you. They want access to scans, blood, and tissue so they can run their own simulations. They will need to be compared to the basic vampire population and other known species in The Everything. We can discreetly bring in some of our equipment to your facility if you can find some willing volunteers. If you're agreeable, I'll let Beivve explain what she needs when you return tomorrow evening."

Ivan was agreeable to this as well. "I'm starting a trial to see if we can wean the average vampire from both blood and CB in the next few weeks, once I've been through it. I can add the scans to the existing protocols. How should we explain Apollo and Beivve to my researchers?"

"You tell them who they are," Kali replied pointedly. "Scientists are the most likely to accept the reality of what is going on. We think that would be a starting point to bring your community into the fold. With the data we have, we can see the entire community has already developed far beyond our expectations. While I am personally hesitant to bring you forward so quickly, the Council thinks the time is close for your community to understand the bigger picture. They don't expect you to tell your Board what's going on today, but you will need to tell them soon. You should think about what you need to do to prepare them for that type of information."

"I can come and extend my invitation. The Æsir are excited at the prospect of having you join us," Ben interjected.

"That offer is premature, Ben. The Council has made no final ruling on the subject." Kali stared daggers in his direction, speaking through clenched teeth, before turning back to address Ivan and Grace. "There are several of us who would be willing to meet with them in an unofficial capacity if you believed that would help. The Council has directed me to set up an official meeting with the Board once you have exposed them to all the details."

"That may need to take place sooner than later. I've been so distracted with the changes going on, I hadn't recognized I may have to explain myself to the community or at least the Board tonight. My scent has changed. Grace's has too, and they're all going to notice." Ivan glanced at Grace for confirmation. He couldn't believe he hadn't considered his scent. Smell was a sense he relied on more than any other.

"We haven't been around any other vampires except for Violet in several weeks. Between the wedding planning, The Three, and Ami's presence, Violet was likely too overwhelmed to notice. Either that, or the merge hadn't started when she was here," Grace answered.

"I may need to call on you this evening if things go sideways," Ivan said.

"I am otherwise engaged this evening. Beivve and Apollo will be available, as necessary. Beivve is normally very good at explaining without being condescending, but I can't see her being able to do that in a room full of vampires. She'll be too distracted with measuring, scanning, and interrogating to be useful. I will also ensure Ma'at and Thoth are available to translate any of the more technical aspects, if that works for you."

The four defined how things should proceed that night and Kali agreed to address the Board Tuesday morning to confirm a meeting between the Board and a Council delegation. Ben was content to stay at the cabin and wait for Erik, especially after Ivan showed him where his scotch reserve was, deciding it wasn't a bad way to spend a night off. He welcomed the silence so he could read incoming planet reports before he forwarded them to Thoth.

Once everything was settled and Kali left, Ivan and Grace went upstairs to dress for dinner. The opening receptions were always formal events. She wore a floor-length white and gold beaded dress fit for any member of royalty. The scoop neck was positioned at a respectable height, and it had a slit descending to her bra line in the back. Her shoes were classic white satin with gold stiletto heels. Her hair was pulled up, leaving a few long strands trailing in front of her shoulders.

Ivan wore a white tux jacket with black lapels, a white shirt with black buttons, and a black bow tie. His cufflinks matched the beading on Grace's dress. They looked like they had been made for each other. Likely because they had.

As the time to leave approached, Grace brushed some lint off Ivan's shoulder. "Are you ready to give this a shot?"

He raised his eyebrow. "Give what a shot?"

"Porting us."

"Eh…. No. I'd prefer to try something a little shorter distance for my first solo flight, say from one end of the room to the other," he responded, tilting his head to see if she was serious.

"Just teasing. You'll have to navigate, though. I don't know where you checked us in."

"Now that I can handle."

They grabbed their bags and walked out to the balcony of their bedroom. When Grace opened the port, Ivan could feel the frequency of the vibration and the energy surge she was creating. The air in front of them was disrupted, opening a nearly undetectable rift in the center, then pulling open to the size of a doorway wide enough for them both to pass through. Ivan held her hand and concentrated on the entry area of the room he had checked them into at the hotel. He felt the rush of being pulled as they stepped over the threshold into the hotel room in a way he hadn't before. It was almost like walking through a superfine membrane that slid over the skin, sealing behind. It was as if the space underneath them was squeezing past, pushing them as they took that one step opening into another space. Adrenaline rushed in, making him lightheaded for a second. The entire thing took barely an instant of real time, but to him it felt like a full minute of slow motion.

They entered the room and set their bags on the bench at the end of the bed, made some final adjustments, then headed toward the door. Ivan took her hand as they made their way to the elevator. It had a slight tremor to it, showing how nervous he was. Grace had thought it would be her that was nervous, as Ivan had always been impassive in the face of adversity.

The reception was being held in a small private dining room, as this meeting was for Board members and their mates only. It wasn't open like the vendor's reception had been. There were fourteen on the Board, not including Ivan. Before they opened the doors to the dining area, the room became deathly still. All eyes were on them as they entered. As Ivan had predicted, the others sensed something different in them. They weren't sure how other vampires were going to react. He took a deep breath, intent on slowing his heart, which threatened to race and make him appear more suspicious. It didn't go quite the way Ivan had thought. They were deeply taking in Ivan and Grace's scent. They appeared docile, intoxicated, even. A tranquility seemed to permeate the room, imbuing their audience with calmness.

Grace and Ivan could hear their thoughts. There were words streaming forward like serene, calming, joy, hope, bliss. They felt like cult leaders. Was their energy radiating so intensely it was hypnotizing anyone who carried it? They weren't sure what was going on. Ivan had to figure out this awkward situation.

"Good evening, everyone. I am glad we are all able to attend the last formal meeting of the Board this year. We wish you and your clans joy and prosperity in the future," Ivan said, gazing over the motionless crowd.

One person clapped slowly, followed by a fervent round of applause for his simple sentiment. With that first single, sharp clap, the mesmerizing spell broke.

Everyone engaged in whispered conversation while still glancing often at Grace and Ivan. While they were ordering drinks, Galin and Vivienne approached them. Galin was forthright, as always.

"You want to tell us what's going on with you two? Your scent has drastically changed. In fact, I can't tell you apart. You smell the same under the perfume and cologne. It's enthralling, refreshing, and it exudes peaceful, lovely images. We are experiencing an odd beckoning toward you. Have you hypnotized us all in some way?"

Ivan wasn't sure how to best start the conversation that would inevitably take place tonight. He spoke loud enough that everyone could hear his answer if they wanted. He placed his hand on Galin's shoulder.

"Galin, my friend, a lot has happened to Grace and me in the last month. We'll give you as many details as possible after dinner. What you feel may be some type of chemical reaction to us. We're not sure about all of that yet. I can say that most of you will find what we have to say unfathomable."

When dinner was served, Vivienne and Grace discussed the details of Violet and Jack's upcoming ceremonies with a noticeable tension between them. Grace had expected their relationship to be different. They weren't in the same clan anymore, but she hadn't expected Vivienne to treat her with such a level of formality. The conversation was pleasant; however, lacking in personal familiarity. Vivienne told her Jack and Violet were going to wait until after Jack's graduation nearly a year away. That gave Vivienne plenty of time to get every single detail perfect with this three-faceted event. They had plenty of weddings at the vineyard, but this special one gave Viv the opportunity to knock down the little tasting shed and build a facility more in line with other venues in the area, like she had always wanted to.

After the meal, Ivan asked the servers to clear the room. Everything he had to say from this point forward must be confidential until they figured out a way to tell the community without causing too much upheaval. He recounted the events as much as possible, starting with Grace getting her memories back. He phrased everything as carefully as he could to keep from revealing the alternate timeline. The revelation of their timeline being changed would create an atmosphere of distrust, causing the entire plan to come crashing down. He told them about the

Æsir, the Council, and the light energy that inhabited Grace and now Ivan. It took well into the early morning hours to recount everything that was going on. The vampires were stunned, interrupting occasionally to ask questions.

The representative from South America was the head of her family in Brazil. She was a shrewd businesswoman who had spent her life looking after her family and the community's safety and well-being. She was concerned for those who could not adapt to the new direction their species was being asked to take.

"If we, as a community, embrace this path to move forward in the universe, spreading this light energy, what will happen to those who choose not to or can't adapt to their new reality?"

Ivan had considered that but had no proper solution yet. "We want to discuss options with all of you. It will be up to all of us to ensure they have strong leadership in place for anyone who chooses to not embark on this path. It would be unfair for us to leave them with inadequate representation that has different goals than our own. We need to ensure lines of communication are available to them if they have any issues or want to join us later. I don't know how to plan for that yet. It's something we should consider and discuss in the next quarter."

Ivan was careful not to mention Ben's imminent offer to move to another planet within a very short timeframe. For now, he wanted the speed which they would advance to remain ambiguous.

The representative from Southern Asia, Dr. Sang, was a medical doctor who presented several questions Ivan and Grace could not answer.

"If there are no objections, I think it is time to bring in some experts who can answer these questions."

No one objected. It slightly perplexed them as to what Ivan meant by the term "experts." Many still appeared skeptical or unable to comprehend the information presented. Grace and Ivan both understood how that felt. They still had so many things they also didn't quite grasp.

"Grace, please bring in our guests."

"Please don't be alarmed at the arrival of our new friends," Grace said, making eye contact with as many of the attendees as she could.

Grace contacted Apollo and Ma'at, who were waiting. Ma'at and Thoth ported into the room with a minor disturbance of air. The vampires stared in disbelief. Seconds later, Apollo and Beivve ported beside them with a more notable displacement. A few let out gasps or squeals while others grasped their mate's hand. Ivan moved to the front of the room to introduce each of them.

"I realize this is quite jarring for some of you. It is not our intent to frighten anyone. I would like to make introductions starting from my left. When I reveal their names, you may have misconceptions about who they are. Various myths are associated with them, some of which are completely fabricated because of misunderstandings about their advanced technologies."

Ivan searched the room for signs of panic or thoughts that this may be a grand prank. Finding little more than stunned silence, he continued.

"This first gentleman is Apollo. He is from the Greek pantheon. Apollo was one of the original team members who developed the light project that created Grace. He, along with Beivve, standing next to him, are heading the research into the advancement of the light energy. Beivve is from the Sami pantheon and is the main researcher for how CB has affected us as well as other species genetically. Her focus is sustaining the mental health of everyone affected. Her specified areas of expertise involve studying how extended periods of darkness promote depression and can trigger underlying mental issues. She was the one who also presented the theory that the community may no longer require either blood or CB to sustain immortal life."

There were mumbles from the group when Ivan made this statement.

"Moving on. I would now introduce Ma'at and Thoth from the Egyptian pantheon. Ma'at is one of the Council members who presides over justice, interdimensional laws, and travel. She is tasked with ensuring we understand currently existing laws and treaties of The Everything. Thoth is an innovator in advanced technologies, history, and the development of various ways to travel and navigate space. I know you all have an endless number of questions. We would like to keep this initial conversation more generalized, then later separate in groups to answer more specific questions that the entire assembly may not understand."

After Ivan finished speaking, Apollo took the opportunity to add a few words. "Thank you all for receiving us. We understand you are about to embark on immense changes in your community and your lives. Our research teams are looking forward to working with you. We are not here to dictate to you or your community or to save you. We are here to welcome you to a larger community of interdimensional beings. Our goal is to help you develop onto your own path and provide whatever support and resources you need."

The vampires appeared receptive to the situation and the guests. The overall feeling in the room was one of acceptance, although Ivan wasn't certain he and Grace weren't the cause of that feeling. He couldn't help but wonder if their opinions would change as soon as they all went home, away from their influence.

When the session ended, the Western European representative told Ivan they had overnight gone from being monsters hated for their very existence to a species of immortals being welcomed into a much larger and more diverse community. They not only had immortality, but also they now had purpose, hope, and a future. It was this hope that created the difference between existing and living. These leaders unanimously saw it as an opportunity their species couldn't pass up. They also remained cautious and had many questions.

The hotel staff shut the room down at four a.m. for a much-needed intermission. The reservation for the morning meeting room didn't begin until seven. Apollo, Beivve, Ma'at, and Thoth agreed to come back at nine to join them after breakfast and continue the conversation.

Beivve approached Grace in the hallway. "Grace, can I set up some sensors around the meeting room before you and Ivan get there? I think your presence is influencing the others. I'd like to gather some data."

"I think that's an excellent idea. Ivan and I are afraid we may be unduly influencing the others, and as soon as they get away from us, they'll wake up and wonder what we've gotten them into. I will make sure Ivan and I don't come until ten minutes after the others, so you have plenty of time to get the readings. It's the conference room listed as 2B down the hall to the left. I'm going up to shower and change. Let me know if you need me. Otherwise, I'll see you around nine."

Beivve headed toward the conference room. Grace joined Ivan on his way up to their room.

The rest of the morning went better than either Grace or Ivan had hoped for. There was an enormous amount of information shared over a multitude of subjects. Beivve got the data she was looking for and the vampires were willing to share information about their backgrounds and evolution.

Beivve found Grace during the lunch break. "I have the results from the sensors from this morning."

"And?"

"You are affecting their emotions."

"I knew it was too good to be true. All of this is going to shit as soon as we leave." Grace began twisting the hanging pieces of her hair around her fingers.

"Grace, I said you are affecting their emotions, not their thought processes."

"What's the difference? We're affecting them. This isn't going to last." Grace spread her arms wide around her for effect.

"Yes, it is, Grace. All you are doing is making them calm and open to being able to process this information without adding negative connotations to it." Beivve gave Grace a side-eye. "Probably Ivan more than you at the moment, though."

"That's rude," Grace retorted.

"Your negativity and doubt will permeate this room if you don't stop it. All I am saying is that you need to stay calm and positive. Can you do that?"

"Yes."

"Excellent. Now, if you'll excuse me, Dr. Sang is waiting for me." Beivve went into the conference room, leaving Grace standing in the hall.

The end of the day brought requests for members to work with the deities, forming teams best suited to specific medical or technology fields. Ma'at set up various meetings with Kali, who would end up setting meetings with the Council.

There were a few who were still skeptical. Ivan had hoped that a private meeting with Kali would ease any reservations they held. There was one member's mate who appeared quite resistant to moving forward with the proposed change. He would likely stay behind when the time came to present the Æsir offer. Ivan thought the man would make an acceptable candidate for a new governing body representing the others who elected to stay. Overall, they saw it as a positive first step toward their goal of an unrestricted life for their species.

It was still early evening with the time change when they arrived home. Erik and Ben were waiting. After explaining the events of the last day and a half, Grace had Erik get Mikkel and Alex to come have dinner with them. After they ate, Ivan wanted to look at the car Erik had picked up earlier in the day, and they all headed outside. Ivan flipped the floodlights on, revealing a perfectly restored coupe. This was the first time Ben had seen it.

"That's what you two have been working on? It's amazing."

Ivan had pride all over his face. "It was mostly Erik. I showed him what to do, but he did all the actual work."

Erik shyly shook his head, rubbing the back of his neck. "That's not true. I wouldn't have even looked at her sitting in that junkyard. I sure wouldn't have known what to do with her."

"But now you've got the bug," Ivan smiled slyly.

Erik smirked, not taking his eyes off Baby Blue. "Anti-grav vehicles are much more powerful, but they don't sound or feel like a fossil-fuel-guzzling, environmentally destructive carburetor-driven engine." Then his grin got bigger. "Yeah, I gotta say, I'm hooked." He looked over the glossy blue hood at Ivan. "Next one we build is mine."

"I *was* going to give you this one. But, you know, if you don't want her."

Erik cut him off. "No! I mean, yes! Absolutely I want her. Are you serious?" he asked excitedly, coming around the hood of the car.

"It's already registered to you. I guess I should say it's registered to Erik Johnson," Ivan chuckled. "Your mom and I are going back to Lisbon before the snow gets too heavy here. Besides, every man should keep his first."

"Thanks, Ivan. I mean, are … are you sure?" Erik stammered.

"Yeah, I'm sure. She's all yours."

Mikkel and Alex worked on talking Erik into going for a drive. Mikkel reached for the passenger door handle.

Erik quickly slapped his hand away. "Don't you dare touch her until you've washed your hands. I saw the way you were eating ribs and wiping your fingers on your pants. Matter of fact, you can change your pants too. Then we can take her for a ride."

Erik would treasure this car as if it were his own child. He opened the driver's door, unlocking the passenger side for Alex.

"Hurry up or we're leaving without you!" Alex taunted as Mikkel ported back to the facility.

Ivan and Ben were laughing at them as they joked and chided each other. Grace had already gone back into the cabin. The evening air was getting too cold for her liking.

"Thanks for doing that, Ivan. They have had little to be happy about since their world was destroyed. It's nice to see them like this."

"It was good for me, too. I needed something to distract me from suffocating Grace while she was recovering. Plus, it kept me busy, so I didn't have to lie to her about Violet and Jack's mating." Ivan was startled when Mikkel ported in behind them way too close.

"Shit! Personal space!" Ivan smacked Mikkel on the back as he bolted between him and Ben to the car. He had barely hopped through the open window into the back seat as Erik spun the tires, taking off down the driveway to the dirt road.

"They'll be gone awhile. Who are Violet and Jack?" Ben queried when they turned and walked up onto the porch.

"Violet is Lukkas's niece. Grace was her blood nurse, and Jack is a human she's fallen head over heels for. He's working on his degree in mechanical engineering. The boy can fix anything. He's been working on his old man's planes and trucks since he could walk. Their mating is going to be the affair of the century, from what I'm told. It'll take at least two days."

"So, why did you have to lie to her about it?"

"Because I knew they had applied but couldn't tell her until we approved them."

"Okay, still confused." Ben had no clue about the process.

"He's human, which means she will turn him at their mating. We've had enough brink-of-insanity vampires in our history, so now we screen everyone before they can turn. You want to turn someone, you apply. They go through a slew of psychological screenings to make sure they're stable. Turning can be psychologically challenging as it is. Heightened senses alone can drive someone mad if they're not prepared for it."

"How can heightened senses drive them mad?" Ben still didn't understand. He was never human. He knew he had far superior senses than a human had, but likely not as good as Ivan's.

"Can you still hear the car?"

"No. They must be five miles away by now."

"I can still hear it. I can hear the song they're playing on the radio." Ivan shuddered. "They need better taste in music. Anyway, it makes sleeping very difficult. Fortunately, we need very little sleep. Sometimes when we're in the city, I have to wear earplugs. Sight is heightened too. Do you see the squirrel on the side of the spruce tree two miles straight down the slope?" He pointed out front and left.

"No, it's dark out here," Ben shrugged.

"Our night vision allows us to see better in the dark. Daylight is excruciatingly painful in the first few days. And the most sensitive of all is smell. Trust me, there are things in this world you never want to smell. Once I catch a scent, I can track anything anywhere for any length of time. I can smell someone today and recognize them in a crowd five years from now. Having heightened senses in the long run is incredible, but when you first turn, it's overwhelming. Especially the scent of blood. You wake ravenous and will stop at nothing to satiate that hunger, no matter who you hurt to do it. Luckily the days of being ravenous animals are over for us. To keep it that way, we prepare those we deem qualified to turn. This is also why I'm so intrigued by Beivve's research. If we don't have the thirst any longer, we can more safely grow our community." Ivan had seen enough violence in his lifetime. He had no taste for it any longer.

"I hadn't considered that. I have to admit, before I met you, I never knew anything about your species."

"Funny you should say that. From what Apollo says, I'm not even a vampire anymore. I would still like to see my community thrive out there." He pointed up to the stars.

"We'd like to see that too." Ben shivered. "It's freezing out here." He reached for the doorknob as Grace pulled it open from the other side, handing them each a cup of coffee laced with scotch.

"Thought you might be ready for these."

"What are you, a mind reader now?" Ben joked.

She pointed to her ears. "Vampire hearing. You were close to the door. You know, we really need to come up with a new label."

"How do you have vampire hearing?" Ben had been in all the conversations about the merging, but he failed to grasp that it went both ways.

"Merging. I have lots of new tricks." Grace shrugged, then grabbed her own cup of coffee and sat on the sofa.

"I can't even keep up with the old tricks," Ben mumbled, rolling his eyes.

CHAPTER TWENTY-ONE

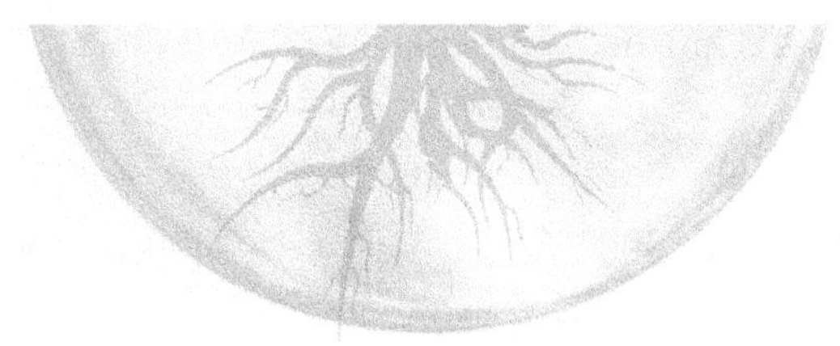

It was still dark when Grace woke to find Ivan dressing in the villa's master bathroom. She couldn't believe it had already been nine months since everything had started. It was challenging growing into a species of The Everything. Ivan was excited that they were going to test the blockers on their new planet today. She could hear an enthusiastic vibration in his humming as he readied himself.

It would be an exciting day. But first, they would observe their Saturday ritual of strolling through the streets of Lisbon to the café on the beach, watching the sun rise. Grace strolled slowly toward the kitchen. When she got about halfway down the hall, she smiled.

"Morning, Ami."

"Morning, Grace."

"Why are you standing here in the dark?"

"Because you don't like me watching you sleep. Why didn't *you* turn any lights on?" Perhaps Ami had finally grasped the concept of personal space.

"I can see in the dark." Grace could see that Ami was wearing thin white pants and a shift that resembled pajamas.

"So can I." Ami walked toward Grace "Ow!" and into the end table. "Well, maybe not as well as you."

"Ida, turn the kitchen lights on low please." The lights slowly came on to a dim setting. It was enough for Ami to see what she had run into.

"Coffee?" Grace offered.

"Ooh! Can I make it?"

"No. This isn't the same kind of coffee maker. It's very complicated." No way Grace was letting Ami touch her cherished vintage espresso machine.

Ami sulked, sticking out her bottom lip, sliding onto the barstool. "Yes, please."

"Vanilla, hazelnut, cinnamon, caramel, or plain?" Grace was out of mocha, which was Mikkel's favorite.

"Can I have them all?" Ami asked eagerly.

"That would be disgusting," Grace said, scrunching up her nose. "I'll pick one for you."

"Okay."

Grace made Ami a caramel latte. Personally, she found the caramel syrup too sweet, but Ami would like it since she usually put six sugars in her regular coffee and added milk in a fifty-fifty ratio, so an extra-sweet latte should do fine. Grace made herself a cinnamon cappuccino next, sipping on it while she worked on Ivan's double espresso with lightly steamed skim milk, no foam, and a half shot of hazelnut. She turned, holding out the cup as Ivan came around the corner, taking it and kissing her on the cheek. It was a well-practiced routine.

"Morning, Ami. Are you coming with us to Rasa today?"

"Yes. Kali said I couldn't go, but Thoth said he could use an assistant in the exhibition to watch the monitors for grid inconsistencies."

Grace was trying not to laugh. She knew Ami took this seriously. "You know we're not going for another six hours, don't you?"

"Yes. I didn't want to be late. I can wait in your small body of liquid outside until you're ready to go."

Now Ivan was trying not to laugh. "The pool?"

"Yes, I enjoy lying suspended in the fluid."

Grace offered, "Why don't you come to the café with us? We walk on a long winding path down through the city. It'll be more interesting."

"Can we go now?"

Grace scrunched her nose again, this time in disapproval rather than disgust. "I think I should probably get dressed and we should find you something else, too."

"I haven't been here in a while. Sometimes I forget the strange clothing rules. At least they have buttons and zippers now. Everything used to fall off at the most awkward times." Ami remembered fashion over the centuries as she was constantly visiting the planet.

"They certainly did," Grace giggled, looping her arm through Ami's. "Don't forget your coffee."

They found some appropriate clothing in Grace's closet. Ami opted for long khaki shorts and a blue polo shirt while Grace found pink and blue paisley capris and an oversized white linen shirt. Grace threw her hair up into a clip and grabbed a large hemp shopping bag for the market.

When they came back to the living room, Grace was curious to see who was with Ivan. It did not disappoint her that it was Tiberius Lawrence.

"What a pleasant surprise, Ty. Have you come to join us?"

"Why yes, if you don't mind." Ty was engaged as a professor of theology and was very British.

Grace thought he was a perfect choice to keep Ami out of Ivan's hair today, which was exactly why Ivan had called him at five thirty in the morning. Ivan had gotten very good at porting and had collected Ty within minutes of finding Ami in their house. Ty was currently on an archaeological dig of a religious site in Israel.

"Absolutely. A foursome is much better than a threesome." Grace realized that sounded much better in her head. "That did not sound appropriate, did it?"

Ivan shook his head solemnly.

"Sorry … Ty, have you met Ami?" she asked.

"I don't believe I've had the pleasure." He reached out to shake Ami's hand, breathing in her subtle scent. "And what is your species?" Ty was quite open minded as well as fascinated with all the new beings he now had access to.

Ami looked at Grace before answering. Grace nodded.

"I am an archangel. It's Amitiel actually. I prefer Ami."

Ty's eyes got wide with excitement. He placed his arm through Ami's, pulling her toward the door. "Isn't this going to be grand?" he exclaimed.

Ami was slightly taller than Ty by about an inch. His hair was reddish brown, bleached blond at the tips from the sun, and he had hazel eyes. It appeared Ami had met her match discussing philosophy. But he was most interested in Ami's take on theology. The two had barely even noticed other people existed until they arrived at the café. Ty was a curious man. Philosophical, intelligent, and a bit too awkward to be charming. Ty had been a boy's academy teacher in England in the late 1500s before he was turned. He was also on Grace's education committee.

Some of the older members of the community had not always accepted him because of his choice of mate. Not that they cared at all about him preferring male companionship. They thought by making the choice to keep one as a mate, Ty and his spouse were not doing their part to expand the species. Community was everything to the clans. Since vampires were no longer permitted to expand the species by turning without approval, most Board members felt it was an obligation of every mated pair to have their allotment of two children. Ivan had never understood the attitude. Ty had been mated before the rules applied. Besides, there were many other mated pairs with no natural children.

Ivan and Grace had made a dozen stops along the market path. The other two kept walking in a straight line until eventually either Grace or Ivan would have to steer them back on course.

There were a few regulars smattered throughout the café by the time they arrived. Saturday sunrise in the summer was a bit of an event, although with the west-facing café, sunsets were more popular. Grace sipped her coffee, leaning against Ivan's shoulder. Consuela brought out a variety of her favorite pastries while Grace wondered how many more sunrises they would have here. What would the sunrise look like on the new planet? It would be odd with it rising in the west instead of the east. She guessed she had gotten used to sunrise with a small sun, so how hard could it be getting used to sunrise in the west? She would miss their ritual walk through the market every Saturday, though, so they sat a little longer than usual. Ami and Ty barely looked up long enough to see the sun come over the city streets behind them.

Grace's favorite way to watch the sunrise was facing west. The way the rays crawled across the beach like fingers yearning to touch the water was so elegant to her. As they grew longer, the streaks of light racing across the reflective surface of the ocean, mirroring the bright oranges against the still deep-blue sky of night, was stunning. Once the display was complete, Grace glanced over at Ivan, who was watching with her.

He hadn't worked on any projects this morning. Since he had gotten his TAC, he tended not to work in public, which Grace liked. He also didn't use his tablet as often. The connections weren't compatible, and he couldn't access his work from it. He mainly used the old tablet for auctions and jotting down ideas when he couldn't use his TAC. Grace had completely zoned out, watching him watch the sky become brighter.

"You ready to go home?" Ivan rubbed Grace's arm.

"Huh?"

"Home. Are you ready to go home?"

Grace blinked a few times. She stood up, yawned, and stretched. "Yup, I'm ready."

"You were so relaxed, I thought I was going to have to carry you."

"I wouldn't have objected to that. Our friends may have been embarrassed." She pointed to Ami and Ty.

"Our friends don't even know we're here. You want to leave them?" Ivan asked.

"I can't do that to Consuela."

"She can handle people like them."

"There are no people like them."

"Hmm. True." He tapped Ty on the shoulder.

Ty flinched and jerked his head around. "Oh, my apologies. I've gotten so caught up in our discussion. I've been incredibly rude."

"No apologies necessary. We barely even noticed," Ivan said. "Grace and I are heading home. You're welcome to stay here if you'd rather continue your conversation without dodging people. Ami can port you home later. Please, just make sure it's not done in public. Ami can be quite conspicuous."

"If you're sure you don't mind. I'm quite enjoying this." He turned back toward Ami. "Ami, would you like to stay and chat, or do you prefer to go back to the villa?" Ty was hoping to stay and continue their conversation. His mate had no interest in theology, and Ty rarely found anyone who could hold their end of the conversation.

"I can stay. I like talking to you." Ami enjoyed talking to anyone who didn't find her annoying.

Grace waved at them. "Make sure you order something. I'll have Consuela put it on our account. You can't take up one of her best tables without ordering something. I'll let Thoth know."

"Okay," Ami said, unsure why Grace would tell Thoth she was going to order food.

"Thoth?" Ty exclaimed. "You're meeting with Thoth today? I would very much enjoy a conversation with him."

"I could probably set that up a bit later. Thoth has a very full schedule for the next few days."

Ami didn't want to lose her captive audience. "He's busy today. They're setting up some kind of grid on Rasa."

"I certainly wouldn't want to interrupt that," Ty said, before turning back to Ivan. "Thank you for the introduction to Ami. We're getting on quite well."

"We'll see you next time, then." Ivan waved and pulled Grace toward the exit. He liked both of them, but he didn't have the energy for either of them today.

Grace squeezed his hand. "I know you didn't do that out of the goodness of your heart. It was a gracious gesture, nonetheless."

"That's what I do. Bring people together," Ivan gloated.

"I'm sure Thoth will be grateful for not having Ami to distract him."

"You know I love Ami to pieces. Sometimes the energy level doesn't exist and sometimes it's too much. I merely found a way to divert it in a positive direction. Besides, I knew Ty could hold his own. They'll be at it all day."

Ivan compared Ami to a radio with a broken volume control. It was either off or it blared at top volume, with no in between. Adding Ty to the mix was like turning the radio speakers against a pillow and reducing it to a reasonable level.

Grace and Ivan took the short way home, bypassing the market. They could have ported, but they had plenty of time and enjoyed walking through the city. Funny thing about the relationship between technology and time for an immortal: technology saved time in many ways, but being immortal, they had time in abundance.

Once Grace and Ivan were back at the villa, they changed into something appropriate for walking on undeveloped land in the cold. The first city's proposed location was on the brink of winter's end. They hadn't gotten the environmental controls in place yet, so they needed to dress for the weather. Snow was melting and the daytime temperatures were a little above freezing.

The cycles were different on the new planet. A day was twenty-five hours. A year was four hundred days, or eighty weeks consisting of five days each. The symmetry was very elegant. Mathematically, it was quite simple to calculate, even for Grace.

They were meeting the rest of the team at the mountain facility so everyone could port over together. Grace and Ivan ported into a small hunting shed Ben had set up to cover the side entrance due to the increased traffic into the facility. No one with the ability to port ever needed to be seen entering or leaving. From inside the shed, there was a panel on the wall that opened to reveal the side entrance. From there, the sentinel on duty would buzz you in. Ivan and Grace could phase through the entrance, which still startled the control room workers occasionally.

Ben and Thoth had settled on a sphere thirty-one thousand light years away containing mineral-rich soil, with limited animal species and a climate very similar to both Earth's and Asgard's. They had diagramed two central cities with land set aside for cultivation and a handful of livestock. The livestock wasn't to be used as a food source. The motive for keeping animals was to facilitate the reproduction of their cells for the growth of meat in a production facility, a method observed by the Æsir and many other species.

Once the blockers over the planet were fully functional, they would start setting up sanitation systems, a communication field, and finish the wireless electrical grid, which was partially in place to power the blockers. Ivan and Ben agreed to name it Tabula Rasa, which meant "clean slate" in most every language. The vampires, as well as many of the Æsir, just called it Rasa and had taken to calling themselves Rasans after what was going to be their new home.

The first survey team had transported a porting platform by explorer craft a few months ago. They set up a large pad station on the planet surface that would bring in building materials and equipment. The craft that had taken the pad remained on the planet to be used for local exploration.

Once Grace and Ivan entered, they took the elevator to the staging area on level nine. It was enormous, about the size of an American football stadium minus the bleachers. They had fitted it with an oversized porting pad in the center.

In the staging area, there were close to one hundred beings of multiple species preparing, inventorying, and working on equipment. Along the wall to the left of the elevators was a meeting and planning area. Boards set up throughout the space monitored all the phases of construction and habitation.

Thoth was already in the meeting area with a dozen female humanoid AIs he would use to monitor sensors from the ship. He had the front panel of one open, programming nanites to detect Ivan's signature since he was essentially the same as Grace and she was more difficult to scan with the amulet. Thoth would take the AIs up in the explorer craft and deploy them into the planet's orbit. He could have used drones or cubits, but the AIs could adjust equipment the others couldn't.

"I hope you're buying her dinner after that," Ivan teased Thoth.

"Oh good. You're here. Ivan, take off your watch so I can run a sensor scan." He closed the panel on the AI he was servicing. "LISA units 1 through 12, circle the target."

The units formed a circle around Ivan and Grace.

"Well, good afternoon to you too," Ivan joked as he was uncinching his watchband.

"Yeah, afternoon. Sorry. I need to make sure I calibrate these before I have the next load ported over."

Ivan popped off his watch. "Tell me when."

"When what?" Thoth hadn't heard that expression before.

"When it's enough?"

"Ah. It's enough. All set. Thanks. LISA units 1 through 12, execute surface deployment."

Each of the units picked up a large piece of equipment from the staging area and took it to the porting pad. Once all the equipment was moved, they ported over to set in the remaining sensors.

"What's the LISA stand for? Are they new?" Grace hadn't seen that model before. They all looked similar, but not exactly the same.

"Light Industrial Scientific Assistant. And yes, they are new. Instead of having the same model, we code them by color scheme. Scientific models have brown hair and brown eyes."

"Nice. I like you can tell them apart, unlike the older versions."

"They're fully autonomous, too. You can leave them for centuries, and they'll adapt within their set schematics." Thoth had developed most of the new programming parameters and was pleased with the way the scientific models turned out. He hadn't been involved in the testing of the service or defense models outside of the basic interactive skillset programmed into each of the series.

Thoth took a moment to explain the structure to Ivan. "All the AIs have living shells over an amorphous metal skeletal structure. They transmit data through their system via nanites, which can heal their shell as well. They are strong, fast, light, and nearly indestructible."

Thoth's original design held a consciousness, his mythology's version of essence, until a biological shell could be created to host. They were very versatile creations. One of his best, he believed.

As Thoth was explaining, Grace caught sight of a familiar face at the far end of the open space. She left Thoth and Ivan, heading into the buzz of activity on the floor.

"They'll let just about anyone in here now, won't they?" Grace said from behind the man.

He turned around with a smile on his face, which made the light around his golden eyes sparkle. She had never seen the Commander smile before.

"How could I say no to seeing the brightest lights in the universe? How are you doing, Grace? It's been a long time." Commander Vaeweth's presence made Grace feel as if the Council had foreseen problems with this mission.

"It's great to see you too, Commander. Anticipating trouble, are they?" She extended her hand to him. He shook it firmly, then pulled her into a friendly embrace, patting her hard on the back and releasing her quickly.

"Not at all. I'm only here as a precaution. It's not every day you get to see a new species take up residence on a new planet without conquest or hostility. At least not in my line of work." He was looking over Grace's shoulder as Kali and two other Council members ported in.

"Ami's not here," Grace said, grinning up at him.

"Thank the stars. Ami wears me out. I never know what she's going to do. I needed something slow today. You're not planning to pull anything, are you?"

"Nope. I swear. All my domestic issues are resolved."

"Good. I'm getting old," he laughed.

"You don't look a day over ten thousand," she laughed back.

"Fifteen thousand star years, actually. I should be retired by now. We're not immortal like you are. I'd like a few thousand years to travel and maybe see my wife occasionally."

"I didn't know you had a wife. When's the last time you were home?"

"Yeah. I've been married for about half my life now. I get back pretty often, but we haven't had a real vacation in quite a while. If everything goes well today, I may bring her to Rasa. I'll be overseeing security until the construction is complete, maybe a while after," Vaeweth said.

"I thought you were contracted to the Council. How did you get roped into all of this?"

"I volunteered. My contract with the Council is over." He glanced back to where the others were standing.

"I was going to retire, but Ben offered me this job. I thought it would be a good way to ease me out of the mercenary lifestyle. The Council assigned my old team to aid with security until they think the population is stable enough to take it on their own."

"We're lucky to have you. I've got to get back before they miss me." She nodded back to Ivan over her shoulder. "Let me know if you need anything. I'm sure I can pull a few strings."

"I'm sure there are a lot of strings to be pulled," he half-joked. "I'm sure we'll be seeing a lot more of each other while this is going on."

Grace walked back across the space, feeling a little more settled, and Vaeweth returned to his team. She still didn't trust the Council or know what its ultimate agenda was, but the prosperity of both the Æsir and the vampires was reliant on it until they got their new community established.

"Who was that?" Ivan asked.

"Commander Vaeweth. He's heading up our security team. He was running security for the Council when I met him. This is his last job before he retires. He's exceptionally good at what he does. I'm glad to see he's here." Grace nodded toward him and his team. It was comforting for her to have someone she trusted. Not for herself, really, but for the people she was responsible for bringing to the new planet.

It weighed on Ivan as much as it did her. He felt her sense of relief knowing someone Grace trusted would be there. Ben came in with The Three, followed closely by Ami. Grace was pleasantly surprised as much as Kali was noticeably irritated.

"Ami. I thought you weren't coming. What happened to Ty?"

"I took him home. You can't think I would miss today," Ami said.

"I hoped you would make it, but you seemed really caught up, so I wasn't sure. Anyway, I'm happy to see you here." Grace really wanted to have Ami with her today.

Once everyone assembled, Thoth started his briefing on the technological aspects of what would happen. Ben continued with his "Thank you all for coming and supporting us" speech. Then it was Grace's turn.

So many faces around the room looked at her with anticipation. Many species pressed together—humanoid, non-humanoid, representatives from pantheons who had never gotten along. They all came together to support them, and they all had a stake in her and Ivan's success.

"As I look around this room, I don't see our differences. I see hope. Hope for balance, peace, and success. Many of us have been enemies at one time or another. It means a great deal to me that we have emerged from our history to come together."

Grace took a deep breath, suppressing emotions welling in her throat. "This is what they created me for. This is what my idea of The Everything is. My purpose is to spread the light; not to eliminate darkness, but to balance it. The existence of this universe, as well as The Everything, depends on that balance. It is up to the people in this room to make sure that happens. I owe each and every one of you an enormous debt of gratitude. May peace and love follow you throughout your days."

Grace hated speaking in public. The words were heartfelt, and she could feel the emotion being reflected back to her. She didn't know what was out there waiting for them. She didn't know what was coming for them, but she could feel it getting close.

Also By

Joyce Serrano

If you enjoyed this story, please look for other books in this series.

THE TURNED GODS SERIES
Original Grace - Book 1
Immortals in the Everything - Book 2
Gateway to The Nothing - Book 3

THE TURNED GODS - CHARACTER COMPANION SERIES
Galin's Alley
Lilly's Game
Alex's Claim